After the second time the Anson bounced back into the air, Doris swore loudly and gritted her teeth. Wishing she could wipe the sweat from her brow, she concentrated and set the taxi firmly down at the third time of asking and then focused on braking before she ran into the ditch at the end of the runway. She'd managed to avoid that ignoble honor so far and didn't intend to spoil her record today. Applying left rudder to counteract the lack of her right engine, she brought the Anson juddering to a halt a mere ten yards from the ditch. Now she had the chance, she wiped her forearm across her forehead and began to taxi toward the flight line hut.

"Everyone all right back there?" she hollered, jerking her head around to see her five passengers give her a nervous thumbs up.

Before the plane had come to a full stop, Penny was jerking the access door open, narrowly avoiding being dragged along the ground five yards for her trouble. Coming to a final stop, she held the door open as everyone hurried past her, all except Doris, who was performing the shut-down checks, and Mary and Betty.

"You okay?" Penny asked the two, and when they both nodded, asked, "What happened?"

Praise for M. W. Arnold

"A skill of writing portrays the bravery of the women…"

~Nicki's Book Blog

~*~

"M. W. Arnold certainly knows how to grab the reader's attention and draw them into what proves to be one hell of a read."

~GingerBookGeek

~*~

"Overall, it was amazing to go back to this series and see where the story would go next."

~Jess, Bookish Life

~*~

"The friendships and the turmoils faced also pulls you in and it's easy to care about the characters and doesn't overtake the mystery, but enriches it."

~Bookmarks and Stages

~*~

"A perfect series for readers who enjoy historically accurate War time drama, with strong female characters at their heart."

~TheTwoFingeredGardener Blog

~*~

"*I'LL BE HOME FOR CHRISTMAS* is another fabulous story in this saga which made me feel as though I know the characters through and through. I can't wait to read the next one."

~Jera's Jamboree

In the Mood

by

M. W. Arnold

Broken Wings, Book 4

In the Mood

Cover Art by *The Wild Rose Press, Inc.*

The Wild Rose Press, Inc.
PO Box 708
Adams Basin, NY 14410-0708
Visit us at www.thewildrosepress.com

Publishing History
First Edition, 2022
Trade Paperback ISBN 978-1-5092-4373-0
Digital ISBN 978-1-5092-4374-7

Broken Wings, Book 4
Published in the United States of America

Acknowledgments

Here we are with book 4 of the Broken Wings series, and sorry, I haven't run out of story ideas, or wartime song-related titles yet!

I'd like to start out by thanking you, the reader, for purchasing these books—I guess I must be doing something right.

You are closely followed by all those wonderful Book Bloggers who've both joined my book tours and have been so gracious and kind as to allow me to guest on their sites through the past year—long may this continue.

To my ever patient and understanding editor, Nan. Where would I be without you? You put together what I send you and by the time it makes it out into the world, it's buffed and polished to as near perfection as I'd dare to hope for.

Isn't this a wonderfully striking cover from RJ! I love how what she does stands out from the norm.

Finally, to my Lady Wife, what else can I say?

By the way, to my non-American readers, American English is used as my publisher is based in the USA.

Take care all, be safe!

Chapter One

"I've lost count of how many times I've asked you this, Doris, but do you have any control over that bloody duck at all?"

Doris Winter, Air Transport Auxiliary pilot by day and fish 'n' chips addict by night, stared up at her friend. "You know," she mused, stroking the foul-minded fowl she was cradling in her arms, "I'm very impressed. I had no idea you could climb a tree so quickly!"

Scrambling a little, Penny gained a better handhold before treating her American friend to a glare which would freeze water, but which seemed to have little effect upon Doris. The ground was sodden with rain, as was Penny's hair, and the water was beginning to run down the back of her neck, causing her to shiver. "Look, I need to get down from this tree before I fall down. Plus, we all need to get to work before Jane has our guts for garters."

From the next tree along, Mary Whitworth-Baines made a grab for and failed to catch her ATA cap as it slid off her head, landing at Doris's feet. "Damnation! Pick that up for me, Doris?"

"Can't," she replied, holding up the duck. "Got my hands full with Duck!"

Leaning over the front gate of her beloved The Old Lockkeepers Cottage, First Officer Betty Palmer reached over as far as she could before straightening back up and looking again at her two friends.

"It's not funny!" Penny said, adding a scowl to her previous glare.

"Can you reach it?" Mary asked.

Betty shook her head, trying and failing to keep a laugh in. "It is, oh, it really is funny."

"Maybe from where you are," Mary allowed before turning her ire upon Doris. "Look, if you can't at least pick up my hat—and I really wish you'd put that damn duck down—at least make sure a gust of wind doesn't blow it into the river."

"Will do," Doris said, planting a foot upon the hat and earning herself a glare from Mary and another laugh from Betty, this time being joined by Doris.

Losing her patience, Penny snapped, "Doris! Either do something with Duck or, I swear, I'm looking at this Sunday's dinner!"

"But he never means any harm," Doris pleaded. "He was only playing."

"Do I look like I'm having fun?" Penny snapped.

"Or me?" Mary added.

Betty raised a hand. "I am."

"Not helping," both Penny and Mary yelled at the same time.

The two unexpectedly raised voices so startled Duck that he let out a loud, "Quack!" and leapt from Doris's arms in a flurry of wings and a few stray feathers. Before Doris could do anything about it, the slightly demented duck had landed in the river and was swimming off, issuing a long series of loud protests as it did.

"Situation resolved," Betty announced, opening the gate and bending down to retrieve her friend's hat. She looked up at the pair still up their respective trees.

"Either of you need a hand getting down?"

After much scrambling, both pilots made it back to the ground with a minimum of scratches, though both confronted Doris once they were down. Only after Doris turned to face her friends, once Duck had disappeared from sight, did she take a step back, the expressions upon Penny's and Mary's faces being thunderous. Sensing quite rightly she needed to placate her friends, Doris put her best smile on her face. "Okay, look, um…" She stumbled over her words before trying again. "I'm sorry, really I am."

"And your duck?" Penny demanded, shooting a look in the direction of her disappearing feathery nemesis.

Knowing when something had gone way past being funny, Doris nodded and bowed her head as she told them, "I promise. I mean, I'll do my best to make sure Duck behaves. I can't promise he'll take any notice, but I'll do my best."

Penny, Mary, and Betty exchanged looks before facing their now nervous friend. Seeing this, the three pulled the American into a group hug.

"Good enough," Penny told her, before taking a step back. "What do you say, Betty?"

Betty took a glance at her watch. "What do I say? I say, we get in to work before Jane sets a squadron of Spitfires upon us."

****

When the group finally hurried into the canteen, they were met by the sight of a foot-tapping Flight Captain Jane Howell. Turning to her friend and second in command, First Officer Thelma Aston, she asked, "Correct me if I'm wrong, Thelma, but is that a feather in Penny's hair?"

Leaning against the wall, Thelma glanced up from her cup of tea and couldn't stop a grin from stretching her face. "Sure looks like it. What do you think happened?"

"With this bunch?" Jane shook her head. "Pretty much anything. Care to take a bet?"

Thelma also shook her head. "If I didn't know them as well as I do, maybe. However, as I do, not a chance, boss."

"Don't blame you," Jane told her. "Come on." She took her friend under the elbow and made toward where the errant pilots were queueing for some breakfast. "Let's go and see what the story is."

Whilst they were speaking, the four had taken their trays and were settling at a table, though this only made it obvious they were doing their best not to catch either Jane or Thelma's attention. This was confirmed by Betty doing her best to shush her friends into silence as the pair pulled up seats, though the effort was a waste of time, as both Jane and Thelma noticed.

"So, girls, what's today's reason for nearly being late?"

Doris shot Jane what she obviously thought was a winning smile. "We're only *nearly* late, then. Do we need to have an excuse?"

"Perhaps not," Jane agreed. "Maybe I should ask about the feather in Penny's hair, then?"

Penny's hand immediately shot up.

"A little more to your left," Thelma supplied helpfully. "That's it," she told her as Penny's fingers came away.

"I think it's one of Duck's," she mused, holding it up toward the early morning light coming in through the window.

"A duck's?" Thelma asked.

Doris shook her head, reaching out to take the feather from her friend. "No, I think she means it belongs to Duck."

"Who's Duck?" Jane enquired, just as confused as Thelma.

"You're on your own," Betty piped up between sips of hot and tasteless tea. "I wash my hands of the whole affair."

"Only because you weren't chased up a tree this morning," Mary put in, confusing matters further.

Jane and Thelma looked at each other, but neither could make head or tail of what was said. "Do you ever wish you'd never asked a question?" Jane asked Thelma, sighing, and Thelma nodded in agreement. "Never mind the jest about not being late. Please can someone explain what on earth this *duck* is?" Jane pleaded, holding out her hands for and receiving Mary's cup of tea in sympathy.

"This is all yours," Penny told Doris.

Doris shrugged before turning her attention to an expectant Jane and Thelma. "You know there's this duck down by the cottages, which follows me and doesn't mind being held?" Somewhat dubiously, they nodded. "Well, as he seems to like me, I decided to name him— or her, I'm not totally sure," she added.

"And 'Duck' is the best you could come up with?" Jane asked in disbelief.

Nodding enthusiastically, Doris tried to make them understand. "It's not like it comes when I call, so what's the use of giving a normal name to something, in that case?"

After a few moments' silence, Jane turned to her friend and said, "Of everything you could have told me—and I can't quite believe I'm saying this—that makes a strange kind of sense."

Betty's slice of bread and butter flopped to the table as its owner stared at Jane in disbelief before shaking her head. "It does?"

Jane nodded, then clarified, "As much as anything which comes out of this one's mouth ever makes sense."

Everyone at the table dissolved into laughter at the expression of affront which their American friend tried to pull.

"Oh, very funny! Keep that up, Jane, and I'll take you off my bridesmaid list."

Jane recovered enough to shake her head. "It's what, the second of February, and the wedding is on the fourteenth. That gives you less than two weeks to find a replacement. I don't think you'd find someone else to put up with your shenanigans as much as I do, in that time."

Doris looked around the canteen. Barring themselves, the room was empty. "There's always Mavis?"

Betty shook her head. "I wouldn't, if I were you. By all means invite her, but if you give her a bigger role, I can see her wanting to take over the catering, and…well, if her cooking's anything like her tea…"

Remembering what she was drinking now, Jane pushed the cup away. "I must be getting old," she grumbled.

"Or losing your taste buds?" Penny suggested.

"Or losing my taste buds," Jane agreed.

"How are the wedding plans going?" Thelma asked.

Doris planted her chin on her hands and sighed. "As

dreamily as wartime allows," she told them. "The banns have been read, the padre's got over the shock of a Yank marrying a Brit—I think he thought the law banned it—Betty's made me a lovely dress to wear to the ceremony."

"Hey, if I'm going to be on the right side of the law now, I may as well make use of some old skills," Betty told them with a warm smile.

"And Walter and I very, very much appreciate it," Doris said, patting Betty on the arm. "Now, all we need to do is find somewhere to have a small honeymoon," she added.

"You've still not found anywhere?" Mary asked.

Doris shook her head. "Walter's being a little…awkward."

"Let me guess," Jane ventured. "He doesn't want you to spend a load of money."

"Spot on." Doris nodded. "It's not like I ever spend anything…"

"…apart from for fish 'n' chips," Betty interrupted.

"…apart from that," Doris agreed, "and that's a given. I've offered to buy a little cottage up in the north of Scotland, so we can all make use of that later. Only he thinks that's a bit much at the moment."

"Tell me. Is he ever going to be happy with how much you're worth?" Mary asked.

"Oh, he's getting better. He seems to have accepted I'm a millionaire. It's just the getting used to spending any of it over a few pounds here and there that he's not used to yet."

"Have you come up with any other ideas?" Jane wanted to know.

"I've an idea," Mary piped up, but was interrupted

by Thelma holding up a hand.

"I think we'll have to wait to hear that, Mary, sorry. Jane, it's past time when this lot need to make steps, or they're going to be late for the taxi."

Jane looked at her watch, got to her feet, clapped her hands together, and leant her hands upon the table. "Thelma's right. Mary, sorry, tell us your thoughts later. In the meantime, get to work, you lot. The war won't wait for your convenience."

Chapter Two

The rain outside threatened to force its way inside. Thelma was about to make a dash for the operations hut's door as it flew open again, only Jane beat her to it.

"Good one, boss," she said, covering the telephone's handset.

"Do you think we should nail it shut?" Jane asked, wiping her brow as she made her way back to her office.

Thelma pretended to give the matter some serious thought before flashing her friend a quick smile and going back to her call. "You'll have to speak up!" she shouted down the handset. "It's blowing a gale here, and I can't hear a word you're saying!"

Jane stopped where she was and tapped the table in front of Thelma to get her attention. "Is that Leeming?"

Thelma nodded before pressing the handset so hard against her ear Jane wondered if it would permanently affect its shape. "Yes! Yes, I think I got that! The train tracks are being bombed and there's nothing running. Okay, fine! Well, can't they put them up in the mess overnight?"

Jane made a gesture for Thelma to place her hand over the mouthpiece.

"Hang on a second, please. Jane?"

Putting down the piece of paper in her hand, Jane glanced out at the windows for a few moments before appearing to come to a decision. The face she turned toward her friend was full of determination. "Tell them we'll have a taxi with them as soon as possible."

Though she raised her eyebrows, Thelma did so, before hanging up. She too looked out the windows before asking, "Reason?"

Jane passed her the document she'd been looking at. "You've seen tomorrow's schedule?" Thelma nodded, but took a minute to quickly read it through once more before whistling and putting the paper down. "We're going to need everyone, aren't we," she stated.

"I can't see how we'll do it without all the crew," Jane agreed.

A crash of thunder interrupted their thoughts, and they both made a bit of a scramble for the door. Wrenching it open, it took them both to prevent the door from being torn from their grasps. Once they'd closed the door again, Thelma looked at Jane again. "You're sure?"

Jane was on her way back to her office. "I'm sure," she answered, as the sounds of rummaging came from behind the office door she'd half shut. When she came out, she had her flying helmet in her hands.

Somewhat to her surprise, Thelma planted herself in her friend's path and shook her head. "No, boss, it's not your job."

"Who else, then?" Jane asked, somewhat puzzled. "Everyone's out on a delivery, and the first taxi isn't due back until," she paused to look at her watch, "five. It'll take me a good couple of hours in this weather to get there, and by the time the taxi gets in," she paused to do some mental working out, "is turned around, the flight up there and back, we wouldn't get back until…"

"…silly o'clock," Thelma stated.

"So what's your suggestion?" Jane asked, turning her helmet around and around in her hands.

"I'll take the trip."

Unable to prevent herself, Jane frowned.

"I'm a pilot too, in case you've forgotten." Thelma couldn't help but defend herself. She didn't fly very often, but she'd always made certain she kept current, in case she was needed. Now, she felt, was that time, and she felt no compunction in telling Jane so. "Your job is here, boss. Trust me," she added, reaching out and clutching her friend's hands, stopping her fiddling with the helmet. "I can do this." With a wave, she went out, and Jane firmly closed the door after her.

****

The door of the operations hut crashed open, though this time it wasn't the weather but a boot-clad foot which was the cause.

"Blimey, but I wouldn't wish that kind of weather on my worst enemy!" Penny stated as the rest of her followed her foot into the hut.

"You're telling me," Mary agreed, shaking her hair as she trotted in close behind.

They were brought up short, as Jane had planted herself before them. "Firstly, you lot, why are you dripping water all over my floor?"

"Someone's locked the flight line hut," Betty answered, trying to stamp some life into her feet.

Frowning, Jane turned around and walked toward the key cabinet. Opening it, she reached in, took a key down, and turned to press it into Betty's waiting hand. "Sorry, the cleaner must have locked it by accident."

Betty passed the key to Doris. "Do me a favor. Go and open up and, er, stop dripping on Jane's floor." Once her friends had disappeared, Betty turned back to Jane. "You can't hide it from me—you're worried. What's wrong?"

Going and looking out the window as best she could, Jane rubbed her hand over the pane of glass, trying to clear it so she could see out. "Suppose I shouldn't be surprised I can't hide anything from you."

Staying where she was, so as to minimize her puddle, Betty asked, "Where's Thelma?"

"That's what's got me worried. I should have heard something from her by now."

Betty followed her friend's stare and put two and two together. "She's up in this soup?"

Jane nodded.

"Doing what? I mean, we barely got in and down in one piece!"

Jane showed her friend the same document. "We've a big day on tomorrow, for which we need every pilot we've got, and some of the girls are stuck at Leeming." Taking the document back, Jane threw it onto a desk. Opening the door, she ignored the rain hitting her face until Betty grabbed her, dragged her back into the office, and slammed the door shut.

"Hey! You're not going to help anyone if you catch a cold."

"She wouldn't let me go." Jane shook her head. "Insisted I should stay here, being in command and all. She took an Anson to go and get them."

"Thelma took a taxi?"

"Kept reminding me she was a pilot too."

"I suppose she is right," Betty decided, after thinking it through. A crash of thunder accompanied by a lightning strike on the far side of the airfield startled them both. "Er, how long ago did she take off?"

Jane looked at her watch. "About forty-five minutes ago."

"That's not too long ago," Betty replied, brightening a little.

"Except for the fact that we'd agreed she was going to check in about every thirty minutes, and she's a quarter of an hour late," Jane told her, her face grim.

Betty took this news in, shivered involuntarily with another bolt of lightning, and said the only thing which came to mind. "Bugger."

****

"Next time you have a dumb idea, submit it in writing and keep your damn mouth shut," Thelma grumbled to herself for the umpteenth time in the last twenty minutes, resisting the urge to bang the radio with her fist.

If anything, the weather had taken a turn for the worse almost as soon as she'd taken off, with visibility barely more than a hundred yards or so even after she'd got above what was the first layer of clouds. She thanked small mercies for the wonders of blind-flying training.

She didn't like the sound of the port engine, now she came to think about it, as a sudden gust of wind forced that wing sharply up. Regaining control, Thelma fixed her gaze upon the artificial horizon instrument and tried the radio once more, hoping she wouldn't get into too much trouble. What with this being the first time she'd flown in a long while, the conditions weren't conducive to helping her memory. Virtually as soon as she'd taken off, she'd forgotten the radio codes, not only for RAF Leeming but also for Hamble. This latter was especially embarrassing, and she expected her friends to not let her forget it when she got back home.

She tried not to give out too much information as she flicked the send switch. "Calling Hamble, calling Hamble. This is Aston." She felt very silly. However, it was the best she could come up with on the spur of the moment. Waiting a few seconds, she repeated four more times, but received no reply.

"Come on, come on, think, Aston, think!"

Squinting, Thelma looked around, hoping for a break in the clouds. The idea of turning back onto a heading which would direct her back toward RAF Hamble was tempting, so very, very tempting, but she discounted it for one sound reason. If she turned back and the bad weather stayed with her all the way, it would be all too easy to find herself flying over her station and indeed, over the Channel. Worst case scenario, she'd come down in the Channel. Only slightly less, she'd come down in enemy-occupied territory, be it France or one of the Channel Islands. Neither development held much appeal to her.

Tapping the fuel gauge, Thelma estimated she still had a little over two hours of flying time left to her, surely plenty of time in which to find somewhere to land. She frowned, tried the radio a few times more and, again, heard nothing. Damn this pea-souper, she swore, checking she was still flying level before renewing her search for a break in the clouds and resisting the urge to take drastic action and take to her parachute. It wasn't unknown for Air Transport Auxiliary pilots, low on fuel and caught in cloud, to point the nose of their aircraft to the stars, gain height and then bail out.

Shuddering, Thelma again put the thought from her mind. She'd never had to use her parachute and would do her best to avoid it, if at all possible. Deciding upon a course of action, since it was obvious she wasn't going to make it to RAF Leeming, she pushed the throttles forward a little and began a gentle climb. Maybe she could get above this new cloud layer. When she'd broken through the first and then came upon this one, she'd also been quite a bit above the height the ATA normally operated at, so had stayed where she was, trusting upon the artificial horizon. Now was as good a time as any to make a go at getting above this new layer. Perhaps she'd then be able to find a clear patch of sky and find out exactly where she was.

****

"Do you think it could be a problem at her end?" Betty asked Jane, reaching out to grab her fist barely in time. "I've already thought of hitting it," she said with a shake of her head. "I don't think it'll do any good."

Jane slumped back into her seat, tore the headset off, and threw it onto the desk next to the radio she'd been about to attack. "I suppose you're right. It only makes sense if she can't receive what we're sending. If I didn't know her voice so well, I'd think someone was playing a trick on me."

"Plus," Betty added, "it's on our frequency."

Jane nodded in agreement. "Still, remind me to tear her off a stripe when she gets back…calling Hamble. This is Aston." She ended with a nervous chuckle.

Betty joined in, saying, "Still, you'll have to give her points for originality, if nothing else."

"I'll give her something, all right," Jane replied. "I'll give her…"

"Mayday! Mayday! This is First Officer Aston. Am under attack by two Me109s!"

15

Jane and Betty stared at each other with open mouths, as the shocking statement blared out of the radio's tiny speaker in Thelma's unmistakable voice. When she'd simply been trying to get through earlier it had been in her normal, albeit frustrated, tone. Now unmistakable panic coursed through it.

The radio came to life again, only the first thing they heard this time was the chilling staccato chatter of gunfire! "I repeat, this is First Officer Aston of the ATA! I'm under attack. Rudder control is gone! My port engine's on fire! Am going down, roughly northeast of Oxford…"

White as a ghost, Jane automatically made a grab for the microphone, "Thelma! This is Jane Howell. Do you receive? Over."

After a few seconds, a voice came out of the speaker, barely audible, yet clearly that of their desperate friend. "Jane? Is that…"

And then, deathly silence…

Chapter Three

Ruth Stone, owner and editor of the local newspaper, the *Hamble Gazette*, was having a trying day. They'd run out of ink that morning, and she'd spent till noon telephoning around to get more. FinallyOnly she had pinned some down, though she wasn't happy about how much the price had gone up since the last time she'd stocked up. Biting the bullet, she'd bought enough to last six months this time, instead of her usual three.

Ruth decided a cup of tea would be well in order, but when she tried to get to her feet, she found she couldn't. Massaging her thighs, she muttered, "Didn't think I'd been sitting down that long." When she looked down, she found the real reason she couldn't get up. Fast asleep upon both her feet was Bobby, her black-and-white cocker spaniel. "You know," she told him, shifting one foot and then the other in an effort to move her beloved dog, "if those people at the station could see you now, they'd have a hard time reconciling you with your image as the station's hero."

Bobby half opened one eye in response to this criticism, though in deference to this person being his major source of food, he did deign to roll off her feet, falling promptly back asleep. His legs began twitching as he chased who-knew-what in his dreams. To look at him, you'd hardly credit that back in mid-nineteen-forty-two he'd raised the alarm—undoubtedly saving many lives—just before two tip-and-run raiders bombed RAF Hamble. Ever since, Jane had given him the run of the station and, in spite of wartime rations, he'd put on quite a bit of weight. Whenever anyone there ran into him and had anything edible on them, treats were willingly given in homage to their hero.

"Care for a cuppa, podge?" Ruth asked her dog, who merely let out a whimper and then a loud snore. "I'll take that as a no, then," she told him, smiling.

She'd managed to coax her legs, pins and needles and all, to life and was trying to steady her gait when she was nearly run over by her reporter—her friend and now her lodger, Walter Johnson—as he barreled up from the archives in the basement, his forward view obscured by a pile of old newspapers. She managed to stop just in time.

"Walter, you under there?" she asked.

"Ruth? Sorry, I didn't see you."

"Well, obviously," Ruth replied, taking a step back to allow Walter to come fully up the stairs and then shut the door behind him. "What's all this?" she tapped the top paper he'd dumped onto his desk.

Unconsciously swiping a hand across his wayward hair, Walter collapsed into his seat, nearly tipping over backward before grabbing the edge of his desk and saving his dignity. "Hoping for ideas."

"Ideas. For what?"

"Some place Doris and I can go on honeymoon," he replied.

"Really?" Ruth said, giving the pile a quick flick. She perched on the edge of her desk and looked at him over the top of her glasses. "Can you see the hole in your logic?"

Walter frowned, his gaze flicking between the pile of newspapers and Ruth while he tried to work out what she meant. He shook his head, "Nope. You're going to have to help me," he finally admitted.

Ruth picked up the top newspaper and held it, front toward Walter. "It's a very good idea, but these are all the ones *we've* printed. Everything's local. So, unless you plan on having your honeymoon within about a twenty-mile radius, you may need to think again."

Walter's face dropped. "Oh, bug…"

"Why not go and make a cuppa?" she suggested. "Then, we'll put our heads together and have another think, eh?"

Ten minutes later, Walter had fruitlessly flicked through a dozen or so copies of past newspapers, coming to the same conclusion as the one that had immediately hit Ruth. Letting his head fall onto the pile before him, he muttered, "I'm a dead man."

Ruth was puzzled. "I thought Doris was going to choose where to go."

"She was," he replied, peeling a page from his forehead, "but I wanted to surprise her."

"Well, you'd be sure of that if you managed to find a suitable place from going through that lot." Ruth laughed.

Walter managed a weak smile and picked up his cup, taking a quick sip. "She's taken on everything, you see, and what with all the time her flying takes up, I want to take some of the work off her shoulders if I can."

"Aww, that's so sweet of you," Ruth told him. "Does she know?"

"Of course." He nodded vigorously. "You know what she's like. I wouldn't dare to do something for the wedding without running it by her first."

"Quite wise," Ruth told him approvingly. "Do you have any other ideas?"

Walter shook his head. "Not a one. I suppose you heard about her idea about buying a cottage up in Scotland?"

"I did. From a purely selfish stance, I fully approve!"

Walter looked out the front door, as if he expected to see Doris appear and begin to quiz him. "Between the two of us, I do too."

Ruth leant forward, puzzled. "Then please explain to me, why don't you let her? I thought you'd come to terms with her having money."

"I have," he hurried to assure her. "Honest. And if she did, I'd probably love it and wouldn't have any problems with any of our friends using the place."

"So why not let her?" Ruth repeated.

"Let me see if I can explain," Walter said, before sitting back and taking a longer sip from his drink. "The best reason I can give is that, during these times, it seems a bit ostentatious. Does that make sense?"

Ruth didn't need time to think about what he'd told her. "Complete sense. And you've told her?"

"Certainly."

"And she's accepted your reason?"

"After a little bit of an argument, yes."

"And was that when you told her you'd find somewhere to honeymoon?" Ruth asked.

Walter nodded.

"And are you regretting that offer now?" Ruth guessed.

Walter now let his head drop a little before replying,

"You could put it that way."

Chuckling a little, Ruth shook her head. "You know you're going to have to talk to her about this, don't you?"

Letting his head drop lower, Walter nodded again. "I know. It's just that I really wanted to do this for her!"

Ruth picked up her cup and finished it off before trying a different tack. "Think of it this way. I think she'll love and appreciate you all the more for trying and admitting you need her help. You know how she loves to put on this independent front?" Walter, listening closely, nodded, and Ruth went on. "Well, you and I both know it's not entirely a front or, at least, it's not quite so since you came along. By admitting you need her help, you'll be allowing her to maintain that part of her whilst also placating that part which is devoted to you two as a couple."

Walter whistled. "Ever thought about writing a...what do the Americans call them? Agony aunt column?"

"Not on your life!" she answered just as the door opened, admitting a postman.

"Hey, Patrick," Walter said. "What've you got today?"

"Good afternoon, Ruth, Walter," he said, touching his cap in salute. "Only a letter for the lady today," he went on to say, handing the letter in question to Ruth before touching his cap once more and going on his way.

"He's running a little late today," Walter said, looking at his watch. "It's nearly five. I hope he doesn't trip in the dark. He's not getting any younger."

"It was good of him to come out of retirement to do the round again," Ruth observed, turning the letter over, as she didn't recognize the handwriting.

21

Walter noticed her puzzled expression. "Problem?"

Ruth held up the letter before reaching for her letter opener. "I've no idea who this Captain R. Derwent is. That's the name on the back. You ever heard of him?"

"Definitely not," Walter answered. "Is there a return address on the back?"

"That's the curious thing," Ruth admitted. "It's from the same POW camp my Joe's at."

"Um, do you mind if I ask if Joe's all right?" Walter asked, a little hesitantly.

Pleased that she could answer truthfully, Ruth said, "Yes. I heard from him a couple of days ago, and he seemed in fine form, all things considered."

"In that case, the only thing to do is to open that letter," Walter decided.

With a quick swipe, Ruth slit the letter open. "Very true."

Sitting back, Ruth read through the letter which, being a typical one from a German POW camp, wasn't that long. As she got to the end, she slumped back into her seat, gripping the letter tightly in one hand.

Walter leant forward, alarmed at the sudden change in his friend. "Ruth. Ruth! What's wrong?"

Ignoring his pleas, Ruth read through the letter once more before, her color a little more normal, she looked up into Walter's still-concerned face. "Sorry Walter. I had to read this again to make sure I'd read it correctly."

"If you can," Walter said carefully, "can you tell me what it says?"

Ruth took a deep breath. "Of course. This Captain Derwent, he says he's a friend of Joe's. He wrote to tell me Joe's back in hospital. He needs another operation on his stump, it seems."

"Why didn't Joe tell you that?" Walter ventured.

Some fire had returned to Ruth's eyes. "Believe me, I'll be asking him that myself in the letter I'm going to write tonight."

"And did this chap give any details on what kind of operation?"

Shaking her head, Ruth said, "He didn't, only that he thought I had a right to know."

"Touching wood," Walter said, knocking his fist upon the wooden desk top, "I'd say if things were serious, he'd have told you. Maybe he simply wants you not to worry about something you can't affect?"

After giving this statement some thought, Ruth slowly nodded her head. "I think I'd have to agree with you there. I'll have to write back to this Derwent chap to thank him." Looking at her watch again, Ruth heaved herself to her feet. "Come on, let's pack up for the night and go home. Are you on patrol tonight?" she asked.

Walter was a member of the Hamble Home Guard unit, not being passed fit to join the regular British fighting forces, and took his duties very seriously. "Only between seven and ten tonight," he told her. "Which reminds me, Matt asked if it'd be okay to pop in after patrol for a nightcap?"

"You can stop wiggling your eyebrows at me, young man." She tried and failed to keep a smirk from her face.

"Not possible!" Walter told her, disappearing out back to make sure everything was shut down and to let their staff know they could knock off.

Ten minutes later, having managed to shake Bobby awake enough to get his legs moving, the two were walking back toward Ruth's beloved and recently repaired—after sustaining some bomb damage the previous year—Riverview Cottage. As they passed their friend Betty's place, the lights were off, not unusual but strange enough for Walter to comment upon it.

"Maybe they're all waiting for everyone to land before coming home together?"

Narrowly avoiding one of a multitude of puddles left by the downpour which had fortuitously stopped a few minutes before they'd left work, Ruth paused to look the place up and down. "Hold on to Bobby a second," she said, before going through the gate and knocking on the front door. She peered through the letterbox, shouted out Betty's and her lodger's names, though when she got no answer, she made her way back to Walter and her rather impatient dog, who was lifting each foot, one after another, in a vain effort to keep his paws dry.

Walter was about to carry on toward home when Ruth gripped him firmly by the elbow. "Hold on. I've a very bad feeling about this." She looked over her shoulder at the cottage once more and came to a decision. "Don't ask me how or why, but I think we need to be at the station. Now!"

Chapter Four

"That's the guardroom," Betty said, her voice sounding hollow, even to her ears. "They want to know if it's all right to let Ruth and Walter on station?" When Jane didn't reply straight away, Betty went and stood by her friend, who stood staring into space in the open door. "Jane? Did you hear me?"

Slowly, as if her feet were stuck in treacle, Jane turned and nodded. Betty told the person at the other end, then simply went and sat down, letting her face fall into her hands until Ruth, Walter, and an obviously unhappy Bobby turned up a few minutes later, joining them through the still-open door, Jane having taken a seat next to Betty.

Seeing the distressed state of the pair, Ruth quickly shut the door behind them so Bobby wouldn't be tempted to run off. The dog, however, gave them nothing to worry about by mooching into Jane's office and flopping down on the small rug under her desk. Shortly after, the sound of contented snoring emanated from the room.

"What's wrong?" Ruth asked immediately. "That's the first time in a while I've had to get permission to come on station."

Walter opened his mouth, but before he could get any words out, they heard a cacophony outside, and the door burst open, admitting Penny, Mary, and Doris.

"What the hell's happening?" Doris asked without

25

preamble. "Penny said the two of you were on the other side of the gate, but by the time we'd made up our minds to go there, you were through. We weren't expecting you to run here, though."

Leaving Ruth's side, Walter stepped over to Doris's side and, ignoring protocol, gave his fiancée a quick kiss on the cheek. "You looked like you needed that."

"Thanks, hun," she said, reaching up and briefly caressing his cheek.

Meanwhile, Ruth had made her way to kneel down beside Jane. Laying a hand on her friend's shoulder, she gave her a gentle shake. "Jane? You're starting to worry me."

When Jane looked up, Ruth was so shocked at her appearance, she lost her balance. Regaining her feet, Ruth cupped Jane's tear-strewn face between her hands. "My God! I knew something was wrong! Talk to me, please!"

Pulling back from Ruth's well-meant ministrations, Jane pulled out a handkerchief and wiped at her eyes, a fruitless gesture, as fresh tears instantly replaced those shed and mopped up.

Equally alarmed as Ruth now, Penny and Mary hurried to where Betty was still face down on the desk. Only when their heads were at her level could they tell she was silently sobbing as well.

"For Christ's sake!" Mary surprised everyone by nearly yelling. "Will someone please tell us what's happened?"

"Where's Thelma?" Penny now asked, having become aware of the one member of their normal entourage who wasn't present.

"Dead!"

The single word had the same effect as if someone had fired a gun. Indeed, the only sound to be heard was the not-so-gentle snoring coming from Bobby in Jane's office.

"Would...would someone mind explaining that?" Ruth asked, her face now white as a ghost.

Getting to her feet, Jane ignored the request and went to Betty's side, where she pulled her distraught friend to her feet and drew her into a hug. The two stood like that for a good couple of minutes whilst everyone else in the room could only stand around in confusion. It seemed that the tension in the room had got through to Bobby, as the cocker spaniel trotted in from Jane's office, as wide awake as he ever could be. Going up to Jane, he stood up onto his rear legs and nudged his way, with a little whine, between the pair.

Jane reached down and picked him up, cuddling him to her breast before planting a kiss upon the top of his furry little head and putting him back onto the floor. Contrary to his normal behavior after being fussed over—finding a nice comfy place to go to sleep—he sat back on his haunches and, with eyes wide open, stared up at the two humans.

"Jane..." Ruth asked once more.

Whether it was the unconditional love of the dog, or the need to finally tell her friends what had happened, Jane made a supreme effort and, her voice barely audible, told them, "Thelma's dead."

****

At Jane's announcement, the room dissolved into chaos, everyone talking at once and nobody listening to anything anyone was saying. Even Bobby added a few howls. Then the questions started. "Are you sure?"

"What happened?" "Why was she flying?" "Are you sure she's dead?" Only when Betty stood up and banged both palms down on a desk, making everyone jump, did order prevail.

"Shut up! Shut up! Shut up!"

"Betty…" Penny began to talk, reaching out with a hand, but Betty shrugged her friend's good intentions aside. Instead, and despite the tears which still streaked her face, fire danced from her eyes. "Enough! All of you! You want to know what happened? I'll tell you what happened. Thelma's plane was shot down. We heard it over the radio. Satisfied?"

You could have cut the silence with a butter knife. Nearly everyone's mouth had fallen open in shock, and there didn't appear to be a drop of blood left in anyone's face. For her part, Betty strode over to Jane's office and slammed the door shut behind her, nearly catching Bobby on the nose as he made to follow her.

Finally, Ruth found her voice and asked, never taking her eyes from the closed office door, "Is that true, Jane? You heard everything over the radio?"

Slowly, as if each movement cost her immense pain, Jane nodded her head, her eyes too on her office. "Yes, it's true."

Taking her by the arm, Ruth led Jane to a seat and gently, yet forcefully, sat her down. She perched on the edge of the desk. "I…we're sorry to ask, but we need to know what happened. If you can tell us?"

Looking up, all Jane could see was the concern and support in the eyes of her friends. It gave her the strength to get through what she knew they needed to hear, her voice a monotone edged in pain. "We needed to get our pilots back from Leeming," she began as her eyes glazed

28

over. Whether she felt or was aware of Ruth's hand in hers was debatable. "I said I'd take an Anson up, to go and get them, but Thelma convinced me my job was here, and she'd take the flight."

"I wasn't aware she was current," Penny muttered, though Jane didn't give any indications she heard.

"So I let her talk me into her taking the job. At first, she was only late checking in on the r/t...I insisted she break radio silence. No one else was going to be up in that weather, let alone any enemy."

"But..." Mary gently prompted.

"I was wrong," Jane stated. "When we did hear from her, we couldn't talk back. There must have been something wrong with the radio in her plane. Then, it got worse, much worse. She put out a mayday call, and we had to sit there and listen. That's all we could do, bloody well listen. When she broadcast again, we heard what can only have been machine-gun fire. She said she was going down, northeast of Oxford, I think she said." Jane paused to wipe her sleeve roughly across her face. "And then came the worst moment."

"What could be worse..." Doris began to say before Walter shushed her, knowing Jane wasn't really telling them what happened—she was reliving each moment again, and if she didn't finish talking, the episode would haunt her for the rest of her life.

"Somehow, her radio must have started receiving again, as she then said my name. I barely heard it, and then...nothing."

Nobody said anything for a few minutes until Doris had to ask, "But that doesn't prove she's...dead." She had to swallow twice to force the word out. "Does it?"

Betty's voice made them all jump, as no one had

heard the door open, or her footsteps as she came into the room. "I don't think there's much doubt. She'd told us one of the engines was on fire, and that she'd pretty much lost control, and that she was going down."

Doris was unwilling to let go of her hope just yet. "I'll take a Magister. I'll go and see if I can find her. I'll…" She ran out of words before anyone had to tell her not to grasp at straws, allowing Walter to gather her into his arms.

Perhaps Doris's forlorn hope prompted Jane to recover her wits, as many as she could. Either way, she took out her handkerchief and did her best to clean up her face. Looking around, she focused upon Betty and held out a hand. Betty strode over, took it, and standing next to her friend, they fed upon each other's strength, each helping the other hold things together.

"Now will you lot go home? Please!" Jane urged.

Doris looked up from where she sat, placing a hand over the telephone mouthpiece she was holding, "No," was all she said before she turned her back on the room and began talking, though so quietly no one could hear what she was saying.

Despite the tragic situation, Jane had to smile. At least Doris was still Doris. "In that case, will someone please take Betty home? I need to make some…telephone calls."

As she'd expected, Betty immediately protested. "I'm not going anywhere. You need me here!" she pleaded.

Jane turned to face her friend, taking and squeezing her hands. "Yes you are. I know you want to stay. I would say yes, but this is something only one person can do, and it has to be me. I'm in charge, though heaven knows, at this moment, I wish I wasn't. Now, before you protest again, hear me out. You know what has to be done, who has to be called, and yes, Doris, that does include getting search teams out to look in the area Thelma reported before…uh, Thelma reported. Believe me, I'm praying with all I have that a miracle will occur, but I have to act now, so we'll know the truth." Jane tore her attention away from Doris and back to Betty. "So I'm going to need you as well rested as you can be tomorrow. I'm going to need at least one of us who'll be a little rested and able to think a little clearer than the other. Do you understand me?"

Sighing, Betty looked up and held Jane's concerned and earnest gaze as best she could. "I do. I don't like it, but I do."

Jane pursed her lips. "Thank you. Now…" She turned to face her other friends. "Who's going to take Betty home and stay with her?"

To her surprise, no one immediately volunteered, and though she was pretty certain she knew why, she was also annoyed. "Look, you lot, I know how you feel. But honestly, there's nothing you can do to help. I need one of you at least to go home with Betty and stay with her. Believe me, as soon as I know anything, I'll telephone."

"Does that mean you're going to stay here all night?" Penny asked.

"Because, if you are, then I'm staying too," Mary declared.

She was rapidly followed by Penny, Doris, and Walter. Betty too opened her mouth, but the door to the operations hut opened at that moment.

"You called, and I came as you asked." Nurse Grace Baxter entered the room and shook her cape. "Now, what's so urgent, Doris?" Grace wasn't a nurse only by profession. She proved she was also a student of human physiology as she took in the tension in the room in an instant. The tear-strewn faces of everyone present were also a big clue. "Okay, something's happened…"

To give both Jane and Betty some time to gather themselves as much as they could, Penny gave their friend a brief outline of what had happened. To her credit, she only had to pause twice, and though Grace's face lost some color, she merely nodded before going over to Betty, taking her by the arm, and gently but firmly saying, "Show me where your coat is, and let's get you home."

It may have been the nurse voice Grace used, but Betty allowed herself to be led over to the coat hooks by the door and then out and, presumably, back home.

"I'll go with them!" Ruth announced and took off before anyone could say anything.

Once the door had closed, Jane turned to survey the room full of her friends. Hands on hips, she surveyed them. "I'm not getting rid of you lot, am I."

Doris let go her hold on Walter and retrieved her flight bag. A moment later, she held up a small bottle of whiskey. "Of course not. Now, you start making what telephone calls you need to, Jane. Walter and I will make some tea. It's not coffee," she said, causing her friends to smile, as Doris had a long-standing and well-vocalized distaste for the British staple drink, "but with its help, we'll keep warm better."

Chapter Five

Detective Inspector Herbert Lawrence wasn't a happy man. The long night he'd had hadn't helped things. Despite having settled into his new post at Portsmouth, he'd lately begun to wonder if he'd done the right thing by accepting the promotion and the new post it came with. Yes, he felt he did deserve the promotion, and yes, it meant he was now based very near to his girlfriend, Third Officer Mary Whitworth-Baines, of the Air Transport Auxiliary, only a short drive down the road at RAF Hamble.

But he couldn't remember the last he'd been able to see her more than one night a week. Sometimes, he felt he'd spent more time with her when he'd been under cover as a pilot in the ATA, and though the circumstances were quite different, he couldn't help but reflect upon those times. Mind you, he mused, lifting his cup to his mouth and taking a sip, the way those girls seemed to attract trouble, it had hardly been the most relaxing of environments. At least now, on the few occasions they managed to snatch together, the biggest danger was being caught getting overly amorous on Betty's sofa.

Picking up one of the multiple reports that layered his desk, he flicked through it before throwing it back on the pile. Yet another black marketer! He was sick to the back teeth of this type of crime, especially as, and he'd never admit this out loud, a good percentage were simply ordinary, good folk trying to get that little bit extra to supplement the ration. Given his way, he'd merely tell them to be more careful and to be on their way. Those who were determined to make a profit off the back of the war were the ones he'd like to get his hands on. Give them a gun and throw them into the front line. That'd make them change their tune!

He selected another set of papers and raised an eyebrow. Now this was one the Air Transport Mystery Club, as Mary and her friends semi-jokingly called themselves, would love to get their teeth into, though he had to read the summary twice before he believed what was written down. A farmer had been tied to a stake in the middle of his pigsty, smeared with feed, and eaten by his own pigs! It sounded exactly like something you'd find in one of their favorite Miss Marple stories. Reading on, he was a little disappointed to find the wife had confessed. Apparently, her husband had been a little too generous with his extra-marital favors, the report said before he had to turn the page. Lawrence was relieved to find this had been with the wife of the next farm over, as the alternative which had briefly flitted across his mind had been too sickening to contemplate.

Returning the report to the stack, he leaned back in his chair and finished off his tea, trying and failing to stifle a yawn, something which his assistant, Sergeant Terry Banks, one of the lankiest bags of bones you'd ever come across, didn't fail to notice.

"Keeping you awake, are we, boss?"

With his eyes closed, Lawrence raised an eyebrow and told him, "Another remark like that, and I'll have you busted down to traffic."

Terry looked over the top of his bottle-bottom glasses and laughed. He'd grown to not only trust his Inspector, but to like him as a person. Apart from his attempts at humor, he simply wasn't very good at making or telling jokes.

"Whatever you say."

Lawrence grinned back. "Sorry, Terry. Feeling a little grumpy. Guess I'm tired of rubbish like this." He prodded the report on the poor woman who'd been fined for buying some black market butter. "Poor woman was only after some extra butter, and now—now she's got a criminal record. It's all rather pathetic."

"If I agree with you, promise you won't follow through on your promise from just now?" After Lawrence had nodded, Terry went and sat down behind his own desk, took a long drink from his own tea, and leant back. "Mind if I throw something at you, Lawrence?" Herbert may have been his first name, but he preferred to go by his surname.

"Go right ahead." Lawrence shrugged.

"Firstly, I couldn't agree more. If I had my way, I'd turn the other cheek on that kind of thing. I'm pretty sure most of us think the same. Now, would I be right in stating you're feeling a little...bored, with the pace of life down here compared to London? Plus, you're not seeing—Mary, I think her name is—as much as you'd like?"

Lawrence shook his head. "Uncanny. You don't have some gypsy in you, do you?"

Terry almost snorted his tea out his nose. "Sorry to disappoint you. I'm merely a student of human observance."

"A student of human observance. I'm not sure if

that's a thing," Lawrence stated.

Terry shrugged. "Well, I may have made that up, but I'm pretty sure you know what I mean."

Lawrence nodded. "It's what makes you a damn good copper."

"Most appreciated, boss," Terry answered, raising his cup.

A short silence followed before Lawrence added, "Well, I'll admit you're spot on about Mary. She's easily the best thing ever to happen to me, and I would like to be able to see her more, but you know what things are like. If one of us is off work, then the other's busy, and vice versa. I guess I'll just have to get used to it."

"I know how you feel." Terry nodded. "The missus and me seem to communicate by notes left on the kitchen table half the time now. She's busy with her war work a lot of the time."

"I've never asked. What does she do?" Lawrence asked.

"She's a conductor on the trains. Says she loves it, which is a little strange, as she hated travelling by them before this lot kicked off," he said.

"Well, good for her." Lawrence toasted with his empty cup for want of anything better. "As for being bored down here, I wouldn't put it quite like that." He knocked his fist on his desk. "But I think we'll leave that one there. Best not to tempt fate, eh?"

"Quite right," Terry said, picking up his telephone as it began to ring. After a moment, he put his hand over the mouthpiece. "We'll have to put breakfast on hold. It's Mary for you, boss."

****

The sound of a police car's siren cut through the

silence in the operations hut, and Doris opened the door. Blinking against the early dawn's glow, she shaded her eyes until she spotted what was indeed a police car, breaking station speed limits by quite a way, until it screeched to a halt, splattering mud everywhere. Despite not expecting a visit, Doris was pleased to see who jumped out, right into a deep puddle.

"Hey, Mary!" she shouted. "Looks like you've a visitor."

Within a few seconds, Mary had pushed past Doris and flung herself into Lawrence's arms, not an easy task, as he was doing his best to shake his trouser legs dry.

Doris was joined at the door by both Jane and Penny, while the sounds of Bobby's doggy snores could be heard emanating from somewhere in the hut. "I didn't know Lawrence was joining us," she said.

"Mary called him whilst you were snatching a nap," Penny told her friend. "Felt he should know."

Totally oblivious to their audience, Mary held onto Lawrence as tightly as she could. It had been a spur-of-the-minute thing to call her boyfriend. Though he wasn't a relation, he too had become a good friend to Thelma.

"Are you sure?" Lawrence asked, quietly into Mary's ear, very reluctant to let her go.

She'd been sparse with details when she called, and it'd only been luck he and Terry had been at work so early, having to oversee a few overnight raids which had been a waste of time. War or not, paperwork still needed to be done, and it had dragged on longer than either he or Terry had expected. As soon as he'd heard Mary's voice at such a time in the morning, he'd known something had gone terribly amiss, even without having to hear the tears behind her voice. Asking Terry to finish up, he'd barely taken time to say he needed to get to RAF Hamble before he'd torn down the stairs and jumped into his car.

Mary sniffed, and he held her at arm's length, looking carefully into her face. There were a few lines he hadn't seen before, her eyes were red raw, and he wasn't sure if he'd ever see her smile again.

"Jane took the telephone call about thirty minutes ago," Mary began. "Whoever was in charge of the search parties, she reckons they actually took notice of where she advised they should look." She paused to take a deep breath, and Lawrence handed her his handkerchief. "Thanks," she said, blowing her nose. "Jane says they've found her Anson…" she began, before shaking her head, unable to carry on.

"Come on," Lawrence told her, taking her by the elbow and leading her toward the hut where their three friends were still waiting. "Hello," he said as he reached them. It seemed quite inadequate, considering why he was there.

Doris stepped forward, took Mary by the hand, and together the pair sat down upon the steps, paying no heed to the dew which coated the wooden decking. Lawrence looked at Jane, then back to where Penny had taken a seat the other side of Mary, and, satisfied the two were taking care of his girlfriend, turned his attention back to Jane. Quite clearly, this was someone who was just about holding herself together.

Ignoring any glances, he took her by a hand. "Come on. Let's take a walk around the airfield."

As they set off, a "Woof!" came from inside, and they were instantly joined by a now wide-awake Bobby.

"Must be the magic of the word 'walk,' " Jane said,

shaking her head and then allowing her companion to lead the way.

At this hour, there weren't too many people around. A few fitters and engineers strolled past, on their way to the hangar and flight line to give the taxis their pre-flight checks. Jane waved automatically toward them, and they waved back, though Lawrence doubted she was aware of her actions. As they approached the flight line hut, Bobby rubbed against both of their trouser legs and bounded off toward the hedges behind the hut.

Lawrence made to call him back, but Jane told him, "Don't worry. He's only after rabbits."

"And has he ever caught any?" Lawrence couldn't help but ask.

Jane shook her head. "Not yet. I think the best he's done is scare a few mice. I think the chef keeps hoping, though," she added.

"Does Ruth know what her dog gets up to?"

"No," Jane said, with another shake of her head. "I think so long as he doesn't stow away in one of my planes, she's happy."

Hoping he'd read things right, now that he'd got Jane chatting first about the mundane, Lawrence probed, "Care to tell me a little more?"

Jane watched Bobby tear in and out of one bush, then another, before she turned to face him. Heavily, she leant her head upon his shoulder, the simple action confirming his thoughts on the state of her mind. Jane Howell was one of the strongest people he knew. Last year, her boyfriend of not very long standing, an American pilot, had been killed, yet he knew through his friends that she'd never missed a day of work and seemed as cheerful as ever. Glancing out of the corner of his eye, what he was witness to now hinted to him that she was far from as good as she tried to display to the world. True, losing anyone under your command, let alone a friend, would have a big effect upon anyone, but this was someone who needed to let out her emotions. He knew from personal experience that holding in strong feelings didn't do anyone any good. A while back, when he'd been working in London, he'd been forced to kill a criminal before they were able to do the same to him. He still woke up in the night, covered in cold sweat. The thought wasn't pleasant, but by being reminded of it, he resolved to tell Mary about it. He knew she'd understand, and perhaps talking about it would help him finally come to terms with his action.

Maybe Jane would let him do the same for her. "Jane, forgive me for being blunt, but it's for the best. Is Thelma dead?"

"Yes, and it's all my fault!" she blurted out, perhaps prompted by the bluntness of the question.

"No, it's not," Lawrence answered immediately, not wanting to give her time to dwell. "It could have been anyone in that aircraft. It could have been you," he said and then, stopped, seeing her tense beside him. "That's it, isn't it? You wanted to take that flight, didn't you? But Thelma told you it wasn't your job and took it instead."

Jane stepped up and turned to face him. "Explain how you know that."

Lawrence shrugged. "I think I know you better than you think. I wasn't just flying when I was undercover here. People-watching is something of a hobby of mine. I like to work out what makes them tick. Plus, it's what a good second-in-command should do, and I'm not one bit surprised she told you so."

"Amazing, but true," Jane said.

Lawrence tipped his hat briefly before replacing it. "Elementary, my dear Jane."

Jane tapped him on the shoulder. "'Don't get ideas above your station, my friend, or I'll let your aunt know," she told him, waggling her eyebrows at him.

"Touché," Lawrence replied. "Seriously, you need to keep telling yourself that this isn't your fault. Yes, I'm perfectly aware that's easier said than done, but it doesn't make it any less true. I also don't believe for one minute that Thelma would want you to blame yourself. Now, would she?"

Jane didn't answer straight away, instead watching in amazement as Bobby trotted out of the bushes, a limp, bloodied rabbit between his teeth. Stopping at her feet, Bobby let out a muffled *woof* before dropping the corpse at her feet.

"Well, what do you know?" she said, shaking her head. Dropping to a knee, she ruffled the proud dog's head, picked up the rabbit unhesitatingly by the neck, and held it up. "Looks like it's the chef's lucky day," she told Bobby, who barked and jumped up, trying to get his catch back. Linking her free arm through Lawrence's, she steered them back in the direction of the operations hut. "As for you, thank you," she solemnly told him. "We both know you're right, but we also both know it'll take a long while for me to accept that. Thelma was a great friend to me, and she died on my watch."

"Well, you have my telephone number, if you ever want to talk."

"Thank you."

"What are friends for, eh?" he answered, leaning down and, somewhat awkwardly, pecking her on the cheek.

The girls still sat on the steps of the hut when the two returned, each nursing a cup of something hot and steaming.

"That looks good!" Jane shouted as they came within earshot. "Enough for two more?"

By way of replying, Penny shouted over her shoulder, "Mavis! Two more cups, please?"

A minute later, their elderly mess manager appeared carrying another couple of mugs, the steam beginning to play havoc with her blue rinse. "Well, bugger me," Mavis exclaimed, looking at the gathering outside the hut. "If I'd known we were having a party, I'd have brought a bottle!"

Accepting the cups, Jane handed the rabbit to Mavis, who held it up and examined it with interest. "Hmm, decent amount of meat on this one. I'll see what the cook can do with it."

"Thank you, Mavis," Jane brought herself to say, hoping Mavis would take the hint and trot back to the mess. Fortunately, she did, picking up her bag from one of the desks and nodding at the group before making her way toward the mess.

"Does she know?" Jane immediately wanted to know, once Mavis had disappeared from view.

Penny shook her head. "No one else does. She was passing, and I asked if she'd mind making something hot for us, as we'd run out of tea. It's amazing what she keeps in that bag of hers! Anyway, I think she's been around long enough to know when something's happened. She didn't ask any questions, just nodded, pulled out some tea, and quietly made our drinks."

Shaking her head, Jane sat down on the steps and

stared off into space.

"Penny for them?" Mary asked.

"It's going to be a long day," Jane finally replied.

Chapter Six

"Settle down! Settle down!" Jane yelled at the top of her voice, waving her hands in the air to quell the rumble of low voices before her.

A little before eight on the morning after Thelma had been killed, everyone on station was gathered before her in front of the operations hut. Having instructed the men at the guardroom to tell everyone to make their way to the hut before anything else, as they came in, Jane was about to make the hardest speech of her life.

Behind her, there came a piercing whistle. Looking around, she saw this had been Doris, who gave her a grim smile as Jane nodded her thanks. Doris was standing with linked arms, between Penny and Mary, Lawrence having had to go back to Portsmouth with a promise to at least telephone later. When she turned back, everyone was staring at her in mute silence, though a few were digging a finger into an ear.

"Right, I know you've all got work to do, so I won't keep you long. However, I have very sad news to impart, and I'd rather everyone knew at once instead of by hearsay." She took a couple of deep, steadying breaths before planting her hands upon her hips. Then, channeling all the supporting energy from her friends behind her, she told her personnel what had happened the previous night, hoping she'd be able to get through it with a single breath. "Last night, First Officer Thelma

Aston took off in a taxi. She was going to RAF Leeming to pick up some of our pilots. As you know, the weather was terrible, but she didn't hesitate. However, and I don't have all the details at present, her plane was attacked by two Nazi fighters and...shot down. Thelma did not...survive."

You could quite clearly hear an audible intake of breath at this statement, and Jane had to hold up her hands again to regain silence.

"As and when I know more, and I deem it fit, I'll let you know. In the meantime, I'm sure Thelma would want you all to keep doing your best to help Britain win this war. To that end, we'll now bow our heads for a minute's silence, and then let's get back to work. Everyone?" All those before her looked up to where Jane stood on the steps of the hut, and those wearing headgear took it off. "Bow...heads!"

A minute or so later, as the crowd dispersed to either the canteen or to make an early start on their jobs, Jane noticed one person standing with her back to the hut, staring in the direction Thelma had taken off. Recognizing her, Jane turned to the woman by her side and said, "Penny. Do me a favor, please. I need you to take over Thelma's duties today. Make sure everyone knows where they're going and what they're flying. I need to go and see someone." When Penny didn't immediately go into the hut, Jane took her by the elbow and, with their friends watching, pulled her to one side. "Look, I'm sorry to spring this upon you, but that's Betty over there." She pointed at the person she'd just noticed. "She shouldn't be here. I need someone I can trust to get everyone back to work, and this is something you've done before."

Penny glanced over Jane's shoulder, assumed a serious expression, and nodded, with a firm, "Leave it with me." She watched Jane hurry over to Betty before turning to face her friends and all the other pilots who stood watching her. "Right, you heard the boss. Everyone inside and let's get back to work."

Though she knew she could trust Penny, Jane didn't break into more than a fast dawdle until she heard Penny say what she hoped she'd say. Fortunate or not, Betty didn't move an inch, barely stirring a muscle when Jane came to a halt before her. In fact, she didn't appear to realize where she was until Jane reached out and touched her on the shoulder.

"Betty?"

The eyes her close friend turned upon her were haunted, empty of life. In her time, Betty had endured and come through many hardships, including losing her twin sister and actually being kidnapped by her parents. Perhaps this was one too many?

"Betty, what are you doing here?" she asked, taking a firm grip upon both her friend's hands.

"Hmm?"

"You're supposed to be tucked up at home. What happened to Ruth and Grace?"

"Ruth and Grace?" Betty looked around, then shook her head a little. "Jane, what are you doing here?"

Jane frowned and tightened her hold. "You're on base, Betty. Do you know where you are?"

Releasing one hand, she gradually turned her friend around, once, then again, until her eyes looked like they were focused once more. "I'm on base! Jane, what am I doing here?" she asked, appearing more than a little bewildered.

Jane allowed a small smile, hoping it wouldn't alarm her friend. "Do you know what's happened? Did you hear what I said?"

Betty frowned. "I think you said something about…Thelma." At speaking that name, something seemed to click in her brain, and she suddenly knew exactly where she was and what had happened. "Oh, hell. For a minute, I thought I was having a bad dream, but it all happened, didn't it?"

Jane could only nod. "I'm afraid so. Sorry, but I need to know—Ruth and Grace?"

Even in her distraught state, Betty managed to look embarrassed. "Well, Grace had to go to work, and Ruth nodded off."

Jane put two and two together. "So you snuck out."

Betty shrugged her shoulders. "Suppose a part of me must have known you'd make some kind of announcement."

"'You did hear what I said, then."

Betty glanced over Jane's shoulder to where the pilots were hurrying over to the flight line hut to prepare for the day's flights. "I remember some of it," she admitted.

"That'll do me," Jane allowed. "Now, I want you to get yourself off home. Take the day off and come in tomorrow."

"What about you?" Betty said. "You've been up all night as well. I seem to remember the other girls snatching a few hours' sleep, but I don't think you did."

Realizing Betty had recovered much of her senses, Jane knew there was no point in trying to pull the wool over her eyes. "You're right. Tell you what, I'll do you a deal. You do as I ask today, and I'll take tomorrow off."

Betty stuck out her hand. "Deal."

After shaking on it, Jane asked, "Now, off with you. Do I need to arrange another escort?"

Shaking her head, Betty drew Jane in for a quick, urgent hug. "No, I'll be a good girl."

****

Arriving back at The Old Lockkeepers Cottage, Betty closed the door behind her and was undoing the buttons on her uniform jacket when she glanced down and noticed a letter on the doormat.

"John's very early today," she muttered, bending down to pick it up. Only when she turned it over did she notice it had neither a stamp nor a postmark. "Strange," Betty said, going into the kitchen, throwing the letter onto the table, and nearly tripping over Bobby, who was coming from the opposite direction. "My apologies," she said, bowing her head slightly as the cocker spaniel huffed at her in reply. The next thing she heard was him clambering, rather heavy-footed, up the stairs. "There are times I regret letting Ruth talk me into having that dog flap put in," she muttered. "Still, at least Matt made a good job of it."

"Did I hear my name?"

Betty nearly dropped the kettle she'd just picked up, "Christ, Ruth! You'll put me in an early grave if you do that again!"

Ruth stretched before leaning against the back of a chair. "Mind if I just call the newspaper? I need to see if Walter's in the office,"

"Help yourself. You know where it is," Betty replied. "Tea?"

Pushing the door half-shut behind her friend as she left the kitchen, Betty got on with the task, and by the time she was stirring the teapot, Ruth had finished her call and was back in the kitchen.

Stifling a yawn, Ruth took a seat and laid her head upon her arms on the table, mumbling, "Walter's looking after work." She cracked an eye open as Betty placed a cup of tea before her. "Tell me. Was I dreaming, or did you sneak out when I was supposed to be keeping an eye on you?"

Cupping her hands around her tea, Betty looked decidedly sheepish. "You weren't dreaming. I got onto base in time to hear Jane make an announcement about Thelma."

Ruth slipped her arms away and deliberately let her forehead crash onto the kitchen table.

Betty winced. "Don't be silly," she admonished her friend.

Sitting back, Ruth gingerly touched her forehead and grimaced. "You're probably right." She looked up. "How did it go?"

Shrugging, Betty told her, "About as well as you'd expect. Jane ordered me back home."

"Good for her," Ruth said, adding, "I expect she'll tell me off for not stopping you, later."

"Probably."

"It'll be worth it," Ruth said. "Personally, I think you needed to hear the words."

Betty sat back, taking a long pull from her tea before replying, "And you're probably right, too. Aw, Christ! I still can't believe she's gone!"

"Me either," Ruth told her. "And we won't, for a long while. How're you holding up?"

Betty let out a long and loud yawn. "No idea's the honest answer. Jane told me to take the rest of the day off."

"What about her?" Ruth asked. "I don't suppose she got much sleep last night."

"She promised to stay away tomorrow. I'll take over then," Betty said.

Ruth raised an eyebrow. She knew Jane as well as anyone. "Do you think she'll keep her promise?"

A creak from above their heads was heard, followed by the sound of bedsprings. "I think Bobby's making himself comfortable."

"I wonder on whose bed?" Ruth asked.

"So long as it's not mine," Betty replied, "I don't mind. So far as Jane's concerned? I'll make damned sure she isn't in work tomorrow. I don't care if she says she's fine. I don't believe she's over Frank yet."

Ruth finished her tea before replying, "That was a right shame. I know she was getting her hopes up."

"Bloody war," Betty let out wearily.

Ruth gave a sigh in agreement before a cheeky gleam came to her eyes. "On to a happier subject. How are things between you and your Yank?"

"Jim?" Betty said, suddenly too tired to spot the playful trap she was walking into.

"Jim. Major Jim Fredericks from Polebrook? The same Jim Fredericks you snogged at Christmas?"

"Oh, that Jim," Betty said, her eyelids beginning to close.

Ruth sat back, glad her friend couldn't see the pout on her face. "I give in, it's no fun when the other person's dropping asleep."

"Ha, ha!"

"What's this?" Ruth asked, reaching for the forgotten letter. "No stamp, no address, just your name.

Aren't you going to open it?"

One of Betty's eyes cracked open, and she snaked a hand forward until Ruth pushed the letter into it. Opening the other eye, she muttered, "I'd forgotten about this."

"So, no idea who it's from?"

Betty, a little more awake now, shook her head. "May as well open it," she said, sliding a finger in and tearing it open. Under Ruth's watchful gaze, Betty pulled out a single piece of paper—and promptly turned deathly white.

Chapter Seven

"That's all there is?"

Lawrence turned the piece of paper over again, as if, by that simple act, more information would be forthcoming. He flipped the envelope upside down and shook it before he finally laid it down and instead picked up his cup of tea.

"You mean that's not enough to go on, Sherlock?" Ruth teased her nephew, though her attempt at humor didn't reach her eyes.

Likely this made the policeman bite back any retort. "Aunty, I'm here as a favor because you asked me, and because you have, please let me do my job."

Ruth picked up the paper and read it aloud.

"*Return the money you stole. You have one month to return £5000. No police or those around you will pay the price. You will receive instructions in due course.*"

"I still wish you'd asked me before calling in Lawrence," Betty stated. She was leaning against the sink, her arms folded, with a look of extreme annoyance upon her face. "They say *not* to involve the police."

Ruth waved the paper in the air. "I can read, but come on." She slapped it back down onto the table. "Letters cut out of a newspaper? It's hardly professional!"

Betty pulled the seat opposite Ruth out and slammed it down before seating herself upon it. "Or, in case it didn't occur to you, perhaps that's what they want you to think."

Ruth opened her mouth, then snapped it shut upon seeing Lawrence had raised an eyebrow at hearing Betty's words. "You think Betty's onto something?"

"I think," Lawrence began, answering Ruth's question, though his eyes were firmly focused upon Betty as he spoke, "there's a lot more going on here than what's in this letter."

At these words, Betty hissed at Ruth, "And that's why I didn't want anyone else involved!"

"And if you want my help with this, you're going to have to tell me, well, everything, Betty."

"Everything?" Betty asked.

"Everything," Lawrence stated, using the voice he normally reserved for interviewing suspects. He was a little disconcerted, let alone surprised, to see the voice had no effect upon Betty. This was more than enough to fully pique his interest.

Ever since he'd first met Ruth's friend and neighbor Betty the previous year, various things had occurred which made him believe there was a lot more to this person than merely a pilot—not that the word *merely* could be truthfully applied to the job they did in the Air Transport Auxiliary, delivering planes all over the country in all weathers. Deciding upon a test, Lawrence sat back, steepled his hands together, and studied Betty from over his fingers. This was a pose he'd perfected from his first days in the police, and it had served him very well over the years. After a couple of minutes, he was most disconcerted to find he was the one with sweat trickling down his forehead, not the subject of his attention feeling the heat instead. Giving it a little more thought, something occurred to him, and he allowed a smile to creep onto his face. "It's not the first time you've been before a copper, is it."

Betty matched his smile and indeed steepled her own hands in mimicry. "No point in denying that."

"Good! Let's sit somewhere more comfortable, then, and you can tell me all about it."

Though he got to his feet and made to walk toward the lounge, Betty stayed where she was. "Betty? I'd prefer to get this over before the girls get in from work."

Betty waved a nonchalant hand in the air and told him, "Oh, they know all about me, and my sister," but she remained seated.

"Ruth?" He arched a questioning look at his aunt. She gave him a noncommittal shrug. All Lawrence could do was shake his head in wonder before muttering, "Some bloody copper I am," as he left the room.

Ruth quickly sat down next to her friend before Betty could follow Lawrence. "I'm sorry," she quickly said. "Have I really dropped you in it?"

Letting out a short laugh, Betty shook her head. "I doubt it. Your nephew, despite what he just said, is a damn good copper. If Eleanor and I had run into more like him, I don't think we'd have done so well."

"You lot going to join me?" Lawrence unexpectedly popped his head back into the kitchen to ask, before disappearing just as quickly.

Ruth and Betty exchanged glances but waited until they could no longer see him. "How much of that do you think he heard?" Ruth asked.

"Pretty much all of it!" Lawrence shouted.

Shrugging her shoulders, Betty got up and went to the lounge, closely followed by Ruth. When they entered, Lawrence, true gentleman that he was, got up from his seat and waited while the two ladies took their seats.

"Good pair of ears you've got there," Betty remarked as she hooked a leg underneath her.

Lawrence flicked one of his ears with a finger. "Best on the force."

Betty fixed him with a glance before asking, "So what do you want to know?"

"Everything."

****

"At least Duck didn't attack us tonight," Mary remarked, putting her key into the lock.

"That would just about have been our luck," Penny agreed, not troubling to keep the weariness from her voice.

"Anyone else have some little oick of a junior engineering officer try to tell you off because he miscounted how many Spits we'd brought in?" Mary asked as she pushed the door open.

"He didn't question me twice after I'd taken him around each new plane and made him keep a tally!" Doris replied, with a laugh, closing the door behind her and hanging her hat on a peg.

"You're a one, and all," Penny said with a shake of her head.

Penny had her foot on the first step of the stairs when a male raised voice from the lounge stayed her.

"Diamond Lil! You're telling me your sister was Diamond Lil?"

"Sounds like my Lawrence!" Mary announced, hurrying toward the slightly open door and shoving it open.

What she found was indeed her boyfriend, only he was in a state of great agitation, striding back and forth, up and down the room, arms flailing around and muttering to himself. In complete contrast, the other occupants of the room, Betty and Ruth sat side by side on the sofa, their faces the picture of serenity, though Betty's, if anything, appeared to be amused by something.

Mary gripped Lawrence by the elbow as he began to make another pass. Turning his head down to see who'd stopped him, his face broke into a grin. "Mary!" he cried, picking her up and hugging her in delight.

"Darling!" Mary said, giving him a huge kiss, seemingly unaware of the audience they had.

They were interrupted by a loud cough. "I thought we were having a serious talk here?" Betty said.

Putting Mary down, though keeping hold of one of her hands, Lawrence led her to a seat and then pulled a chair so he could sit next to her.

"About what?" Doris asked from where she was leaning against the door frame.

"What do you lot know about someone called Diamond Lil?" Lawrence asked, looking around at the girls, all of whom promptly went red to the tips of their ears. With a loud, "Hmm," he turned his attention back to Betty and Ruth. "How long have this lot known, then?"

Betty only had to give this a little thought. "From around the second day I knew them."

If Lawrence's eyebrows could have disappeared under his hair, they would have. He stroked his chin in thought for a while before looking up. "I'm going to take a leap here. If Eleanor was the thief, were you her fence?"

The smile that stayed upon Betty's face was all the confirmation Lawrence needed.

"Would someone care to tell us what's going on?" Penny asked, coming into the room and squeezing down next to Ruth.

"Read this," Betty said, pushing the letter into Penny's hands as Doris crouched down beside her.

It took the two only a few moments to read it before Penny, now a little pale, pushed it back toward Betty. "There's no signature."

"When did it arrive?" Doris asked.

"It was waiting for me when I got back from the station…"

"Hold on," Doris interrupted. "I thought you were supposed to be back here resting?"

Betty waved away the protest. "Never mind that."

"It does say not to involve the police." Doris felt she had to point that detail out, whilst glancing over at where Lawrence sat observing.

"Blame Ruth for that," Betty declared, nudging her friend none too gently in the ribs.

"It's Lawrence," Ruth pointed out, with a shrug of her shoulders.

"And I promised this will go no further, unless…" he hastened to add, "unless one of you is put in harm's way."

Betty got to her feet and stared out the window before turning around. "I hope you'll all forgive me for putting this out there, but do any of you think…" She paused to gulp down some air and compose herself. "Do you think Thelma could have been killed by…whoever sent that note?"

After a few minutes' silence, Ruth finally said, "Well, you certainly know how to throw the cat amongst the pigeons, I'll say that. What do you think, Herbert?"

Lawrence didn't wait long before shaking his head and answering, "I think, firstly, that you're annoyed, or else you wouldn't call me Herbert, but I very much doubt that. From what I know, she was in the wrong place at the wrong time. Like a lot of people in this damned war," he added.

"Well, then, any ideas who it could be from?" Mary asked.

"Not a clue," Lawrence admitted. "I'm still trying to get my head around our Betty's past life here. I am right, aren't I? About your part in your sister's affairs?"

Betty nodded. "Yes, but that's all long past now."

Penny shot to her feet. "I've got it!"

"What? Ants in your pants?" Doris asked, earning herself a glowering look from Penny.

"I'm serious! Hear me out."

"I'm sorry," Doris said. "Please, go on."

"It's got to be someone Eleanor stole from and that you fenced the goods for, Betty," Penny announced, turning toward Lawrence. "It's the only thing which makes sense! Well?"

Getting to his feet, Lawrence pulled Mary into an embrace before looking around at the expectant faces of his friends. "What do I think? I think I must be crazy. Another case for the Air Transport Auxiliary Mystery Club—that's all we need!"

Chapter Eight

"Anyone seen my socks?" Mary shouted the next morning from her bedroom.

"While we're on the subject," Betty said, poking her head out of the bathroom, "if anyone sees my cream slip, please let me know."

"My lucky bra's still missing, if anyone's interested," Penny added.

"No one is," Doris shouted from the foot of the stairs. "Get a move on, you lot. Breakfast's getting cold!"

When Betty, Mary, and Penny joined Doris, on breakfast-making duty that morning in the kitchen, they were just in time to catch her feeding Bobby some toast.

Helping herself to a cup of tea and some fresh toast, Betty waved it at the cocker spaniel's retreating rear end as it disappeared through their dog-flap. "I wouldn't let Ruth catch you. She's quite serious about putting poor Bobby on a diet."

"Well," Doris said, popping the remainder of her breakfast into her mouth and washing it down with a sip of tea, though not without the usual grimace of distaste, "I'd better not let her catch me, then. Betty, can you ask Jim if he can get hold of some more coffee for me, please? I've run out."

"You're batting those eyelashes at the wrong person." Betty laughed. "But I'll see what I can do."

Doris danced over and planted a loud kiss on the top

of Betty's head. "Bless you."

With a small smile, Betty looked at her friend. "If you really want to put me in a good mood, go and check that Duck isn't lying in wait for us, okay?"

Five minutes later, Doris stood alone on the other side of the garden gate, carefully looking up and down the riverbank, making certain the coast was indeed clear of her fiendish feathery friend. She turned back to face her human friends, none of whom had yet made a move to open the gate. "You can come out now. I don't think he's going to attack you today," she teased them.

"You're sure?" Penny asked, unable to keep a catch from her voice as she gauged the distance to the trees in case she needed to climb one again.

"Oh, my God," Doris said, shaking her head. "Would you take a look at yourselves? Wouldn't Hitler shake in his boots if he could see you now!"

"Hey!" Mary exclaimed. "Give us that one-balled bastard any day. Your duck? That's quite something else. I'm sure if we could train the bugger to lead our army, we'd win the war in a thrice!"

Doris folded her arms, then changed her mind, marched forward, and flung the gate open. "One, he's not my duck, he's just attached himself to me, and two, you're probably not wrong. Now, come on."

Instead of going to the mess, as was their normal routine, the group went straight to the ops hut. Leading the way, Betty pushed the door open and was immediately greeted by a loud buzzing noise.

"What the hell's that?" she asked.

"I think it's coming from Jane's office," Mary said, peering around the hut.

She was right, as the four found when they crowded

around the open door of the office. Down near floor level was the lady in question, fully clothed and flat out on her back on a camp bed beside her desk. A sixth sense must have clicked in as her eyes snapped open and landed upon her friends staring down at her.

"Please don't tell me you've spent the night here," Betty remarked, in complete contradiction to the evidence before her eyes.

Jane wiped the drool from the side of her mouth before swinging her legs to the side and hauling herself into a sitting position. Looking up at the concerned expressions of her friends, Jane didn't bother to deny it. "I didn't have the energy to go back to my bunk."

"But you had the energy to go and get this camp bed," Betty commented, not troubling to hide the annoyance in her voice.

With a hand-up from Mary, Jane stretched out the kinks from her back. "Not really. I knew we had one somewhere in the flight line hut. Didn't take long to find it."

Allowing herself one more glare, Betty softened enough to grab her friend's hand and proceeded to tow her out of the office, absently noting Jane hadn't taken off her shoes.

"Where're we going?" she asked, making a grab and just barely managing to snatch her hat and bag.

"We need to get some tea down you," Betty told her, adding, "even if it is Mavis's."

As Betty half-dragged Jane toward the mess, Doris asked Penny and Mary, "I know a shock to the system sometimes helps, but isn't this taking things too far?"

Fortunately, Mavis wasn't a mind reader, so when they entered an unusually somber mess, they weren't met by an irate blue-rinsed elderly woman. Instead, as soon as she saw the group enter, she rushed out from behind the serving counter and enveloped Jane in a hug. This was quite possibly the first time any of the girls had physical contact with her other than the occasional clip around the ear.

"Jane! I mean, boss. Come sit down, and let me get you a cuppa. You look dead on your feet, my dear."

Before the bemused stares of her friends, Jane allowed herself to be led to a table next to the sheet hung on the rear wall which visitors were invited to sign. Whilst Mavis scurried away to get the promised beverage, Jane allowed her eyes to rove over the, by now, crowded sheet.

"Getting pretty full, eh?" Penny said, pulling up a seat.

Jane nodded, not trusting herself to speak, as her eyes had been drawn to a spot on the sheet where Thelma had signed. Leaning forward, she took the glasses she'd begun to use for close-up work and placed them upon her nose.

First Officer Thelma Aston.
Until the end…and beyond!

She jumped a little when she felt a hand lightly grip her shoulder. "She had a way with words, didn't she?"

Without taking her eyes off the words, Jane nodded and reached up to grip the hand, knowing it would be Betty's. "That she did. Come on, tea's up."

Nobody uttered a word until Jane had finished the cup before her. When she finally pushed it away, she quite rapidly wished she hadn't.

"Are you ready to leave now?" Betty asked without preamble.

Jane let out a sigh. "I really should be here."

Penny was first to speak. "Not a chance, boss. You did a deal with Betty, remember?"

"And I doubt very much if you got a good night's sleep on that cot," Doris added.

Jane looked around the table, and all she saw was a sea of concerned faces. She allowed a small smile to creep across her face. "I'm not going to win this one, am I?"

Betty retook her seat, nodding in agreement. "Not a chance."

Looking out the window, Jane gave an involuntary shudder. This didn't go unnoticed.

"What is it?" Doris asked.

After a moment, Jane admitted, "I'm not sure I want to go back to my room." At everyone's curious looks, she elaborated, "Thelma's room is next to mine."

Almost immediately, Betty clicked her fingers. "We can't have that." She fished in her pocket and handed Jane a key. "Here, take my key, and get yourself back to the cottage. My bed's got clean sheets on, so I expect you to use it."

As Jane went to open her mouth to politely decline, all her friends stood up and leaned over toward her.

"No arguments," Mary said. "It'll be quiet, and you need to rest."

"Understand?" Doris asked.

Slowly, Jane nodded her head. "I'm not going to win this one either, am I?"

Everyone shook their heads.

"In that case, let me just tell you what I've found out about..." She had to stop to quickly wipe her eyes and take a deep breath before continuing, "...about how

Thelma died."

This unexpected announcement caused everyone to collapse back onto their seats, though Doris had to recover her balance quickly as she nearly missed hers. "What about everyone else?" she asked, looking around at where they were being scrutinized, quite openly, by the rest of the personnel present.

Jane looked briefly around, causing everyone who'd been staring at them until that moment to suddenly find their fingernails to be of intense interest. "No, everyone else knew her, but she was our friend. Apart from…Mavis!" she suddenly shouted, and the whole mess jumped.

Mavis's head appeared around the corner of the kitchen. "You hollered, boss?"

Instead of speaking again, Jane waved her over. "Pull up a chair, please, Mavis." She waited until the elderly woman had done so before saying to her, "What I'm about to tell you goes no further than this group. Understood?"

By reply, Mavis gave her a salute, which seemed to satisfy everyone present, though Doris couldn't resist teasing her. "I wouldn't have had you down as a Girl Guide."

Mavis half-turned and treated her favorite Yank to a rather toothless grin. "I make a very good hangman's noose."

Doris returned the grin with interest. "I'll bet you do. Had much practice?"

Betty cleared her throat to get the pair's attention. "Much as I enjoy some good banter, now is not the time."

Both Doris and Mavis merely turned back to face Jane and proceeded to ignore each other.

"Thank you, Betty. Okay, I'll keep this short. After we'd finished last night, I did plenty of telephoning around, and this is what I've managed to put together about what happened to Thelma."

Mavis drew in a sharp breath, causing all eyes to turn to her. "Sorry. Should have guessed. Please carry on, boss."

Jane nodded, and they all saw her draw herself up before continuing. "I suppose you could call it lucky, but the police were able to find a ground witness, a farmer. He told them he saw her Anson coming out of some low cloud, and as it cleared, it was almost immediately attacked by two Nazi fighters. Each made only one firing pass at her before making off toward the coast at high speed. From his statement, her aircraft was on fire from the first pass, and already going in."

"So no need for the other to attack?" Penny asked from between trembling lips.

Jane shook her head. "No, not if what this man says is true, and the policeman I tracked down swore blind the man had never told a lie in his life."

"She never stood a chance, did she," Mary said, shaking her head.

"Bastards," Doris simply stated.

"If I could get hold of them..." Mavis began, leaving the statement hanging, as everyone else nodded in agreement.

Silence reigned around the table as everyone became lost in their thoughts.

Jane looked at her watch. "Time to get to work."

Betty placed a friendly hand upon Jane's on the tabletop. "And time for you to go back to my place and get some sleep."

"You weren't going to forget, were you?"

"Not a chance."

Mavis got to her feet and told Jane, "Thank you for trusting me, sharing this information with me. I appreciate it."

Fortunately, she didn't expect a reply as Jane was too choked up to speak, so Jane just gave her mess manager a quick nod of thanks.

"Hey, Mavis!" Doris surprised everyone by yelling. "Any chance of a cup of coffee, instead of this muck?" she held up her empty tea cup to illustrate her point.

"Doris!" everyone at the table reproached her.

However, Mavis didn't appear to need anyone to fight her fights for her, as she swiveled around, picking up a ladle from the counter as she went, and waved it at her antagonist. "Look here, you bloody Yank! How many times do I have to tell you, the whole blinking lot of you haven't got a decent taste bud in your whole flippin' country!"

Apparently satisfied with giving as good as she got, Mavis put the ladle back down with a clang and barged into the kitchen.

"What the hell?" Jane rounded upon her American pilot, her face scarlet with fury.

For her part, Doris didn't appear affected by either Jane's or anyone else's anger and confusion at her behavior. "Trust me," she merely said, getting to her feet and making her way toward the exit.

As she got level with the kitchen door, it opened a crack and, much to the surprise of all, Mavis's voice was heard saying, "Be safe up there, Doris!"

"See you later, Mavis!" Doris replied as she exited the mess, leaving her friends exchanging bemused glances before hurrying to catch her up.

It wasn't until the girls had nearly finished climbing into their Sidcot suits that Doris explained. Plonking herself down on the bench to pull on her boots, she looked up into the still half-mad, half-curious faces of her friends. "Look, I've not gone bananas," she began. "I know Mavis's type. The last thing she'd want when anything terrible happens is to be treated like some delicate thing. It's normality she craves, and that's what I gave her, someone to have a go at."

After a while, Penny finally broke the silence and said the only thing possible. "You, Third Officer Doris Winter, are a wonder and a force of nature!"

"Guilty as charged." Doris flipped her friends a salute.

Chapter Nine

"Did you see the chippy's changed owners?" Doris asked, settling back into her seat and warming her hands around her cup of tea.

"It never has!" Betty said, with a shake of her head.

"He's a strange chap," Doris carried on after taking a sip. "First time I went in, he simply leaned against the wall, watching someone who claimed to be his son, though he didn't looked anything like him—and he didn't seem old enough for a son—do all the serving. Never said a word to anyone. In fact, the only time I saw him raise so much as an eyebrow was when Maude from Woolies greeted me. Then, he didn't take his eyes off me. I swear they followed me as I left the shop!"

"Whose eyes followed you?"

Leaning forward, being careful not to tip over her cup, Doris kissed the top of her fiancé's head. "Never you mind, hun. I'm sure it's not important."

"What's not important?" Jane asked as she came into the lounge.

"Walter's jealous."

"I am not," Walter pouted, looking up at his American girl from where he sat on the floor between her outstretched legs.

Doris put her cup on the floor and, leaning forward, wrapped her arms around him, nuzzling her head against the rough material of his Home Guard uniform. "It's okay if you are. I don't mind," she assured him. "It's kind of romantic, if you're jealous. Not that you have anything to worry about," she quickly added.

Walter turned his head a little so he could kiss her cheek. "In that case, I'll allow myself to be a little jealous."

"Mmm, I could get to like that," Doris murmured as she leaned farther down so she could deepen the kiss.

"Are they always like this?" Jane asked the room in general, taking a seat between Betty and Mary on the sofa.

"I'm afraid so," Mary replied.

Jane glanced back toward the pair before asking, "How long before they marry, again?"

"A week now," Doris briefly came up for air to say.

"Only a week?" Betty said, moving a little so Jane could have more room. "Tell me, have you found somewhere for your honeymoon yet?"

This seemed to shake the pair from their tender ministrations. They both looked around the room, as everyone was paying attention to them for another reason now. "Not yet," Doris admitted.

"You could always stay at my parents," Mary offered from out of nowhere.

This simple statement got everyone's attention. Apart from briefly mentioning she'd grown up in a manor house, no one had managed to get anything else out of her about her life prior to joining the Air Transport Auxiliary. Well, that wasn't quite true. Mary had apparently told Celia, Penny's little sister, some things last Christmas, only she'd refused to divulge what she'd been entrusted with, and no one had pushed her. A promise was a promise, Celia had insisted. But now, from out of the blue, Mary had suddenly offered the use of her home for her friend's honeymoon.

"Say that again?" Doris said.

Not surprisingly, everyone in the room was leaning toward Mary, who was now trying to disappear into her seat. Nobody reacted to the rap at the front door, nor to the three follow-ups.

Penny popped her head around the door. "Is everyone deaf?" she asked and then, when she didn't get an answer, turned around and made for the front door where whoever was on the other side was still rapping away. She muttered to herself, "What does it come to when a girl can't wash her hair?" Rewrapping the towel she'd hastily spun around her head as she'd dashed down the stairs, she pulled the door open.

"I saw the light was on, but was beginning to wonder if anyone was at home," Ruth said as she stepped through the door, closely followed by Sergeant Matt Green of the Home Guard.

"Ruth, Matt," Penny greeted them before closing the door. "Everyone's in the lounge—but I don't know if there's anyone home," she added to the newcomers' quizzical faces, as she disappeared back upstairs to the bathroom.

Popping her head around the door, Ruth wasn't greeted by anyone. Everyone present seemed to be staring at Mary, who was squirming very uncomfortably in her seat.

Mary looked incredibly relieved as she invited them to "Come in! Please, come in and take a seat."

Taking a couple of seats by the table next to the front window, the pair exchanged glances before Matt asked, "Are we...interrupting something?"

"Me, putting my foot in my mouth, I think," Mary replied, somewhat enigmatically.

When she didn't elaborate, Ruth asked, "Would someone please tell me what that's supposed to mean?"

Walter was the first to speak. "We got around to talking about our marriage and where we were going to honeymoon..."

"Still?" Ruth said.

"Yes, still," Walter replied with a smile. "Anyway, next thing we know, Mary offers us the use of her parents' manor house."

"That's...nice," Ruth replied, her eyebrows joining practically everyone else's.

Not as up to date as everyone else in the room, Matt innocently commented, "It is, but why's everyone being so strange about it?"

When no one else replied, Mary let out a sigh and told him, "Because I generally don't talk about my family."

"Generally?" Doris said.

"All right, never," Mary replied with a shrug.

Unable to help himself, Matt asked, "Why ever not?" and then hastily let go of Ruth's hand as she dug her nails into his.

Mary began squirming again. "Can I just say I'm not close to my family. It's not that they're not nice people. It's more that we're typical upper class in that we can't stand being around each other more than we have to."

"Upper class?" Matt couldn't help but ask, his voice going up a couple of octaves.

Mary tried to wave away his surprise. "It's nothing, really. Don't read anything into it, please. This is who I am. Where I come from makes no difference."

Matt opened his mouth but quickly shut it when he noticed everyone else in the room shaking their heads at him. Whatever other questions he may have had, he took heed and changed his mind, getting a "Thank you," from Ruth for his consideration.

"So is that a yes, you two?" Mary asked, addressing Doris and Walter.

Both made the mistake of nodding eagerly and as they were so close together, they immediately banged their heads together. Once they'd finished rubbing them, Doris replied for both of them, "Yes, please! That'd be wonderful!"

"As the cat's a little out of the bag," Betty said, "whereabouts is this manor?"

"Aberdeenshire," Mary replied. "Best way to describe would be up near the northeast coast, roughly five or six miles from Fraserburgh."

"I haven't a clue where that is, yet," Doris replied, leaping over Walter's head, falling to her knees before her friends, and awkwardly hugging Mary, "but you can fill me in later. Funny, though, you don't sound like any Scot I've ever come across."

"That's what comes of being sent to live with an aunt in England before I went to school, and then to an English rather than a Scottish school. Now, if you heard my father, I doubt you'd understand a word!" she told them, managing to finally extricate herself from Doris's grip.

"Well, I look forward to meeting him," Doris said, with the first real smile she'd had since Thelma's death.

Mary shook her head. "You'll probably be disappointed. When the war broke out, the family handed it over to be used as a hospital. Well, most of it. My father arranged that the family could keep the use of a suite of rooms in the north wing. It's a couple of bedrooms, a bathroom, and a small lounge, but I'm sure you'll be comfortable there."

"You're sure it won't be a problem?" Walter asked. "I mean, they won't be using the rooms when we'll be on leave?"

"Good point," Mary muttered, heaving herself to her feet. "I'll go and telephone him now to check."

"Well," Doris said, once Mary had left the room, pointedly closing the door shut behind her, "that was unexpected."

"True," Jane agreed. "But very nice of her."

"So," Ruth asked, "how are you finding living with this crowd, Jane?"

Before replying, Jane shuffled along the sofa until she was next to Betty, taking her hand and squeezing it tightly. "It's a complete madhouse. I don't think anyone would disagree with my saying, however, right now, especially right now, it's the best place I could be. I mean, Mary doesn't snore, there's plenty of room for two in the attic bedroom, and we can barely hear Penny. I have no idea how either of you manage to get any sleep, with that racket going on."

"Ear plugs!" both Betty and Doris said at the same time.

"Are you going to stay long?" Ruth asked.

"As long as my friend will put up with me," Jane answered with a smile. "I don't think I could have got through the last few days without this bunch, especially Betty here."

Betty drew her friend in for a hug, saying, "Hey, what are friends for?"

"I thought Celia was coming here to live, once she finishes school," Ruth asked.

"We'll work something out," Betty simply said.

The door opened, interrupting further conversation, and Mary came back in, Penny close behind her. "Mary's just filled me in."

"And?" Doris said. "Did you manage to talk to your father?"

Mary nodded. "You're all sorted. How does the sixteenth to twentieth of February suit you pair?"

Doris and Walter both exchanged identical looks of amazement before Walter shot to his feet and wrapped his arms around Mary, swiftly joined by Doris.

"This is going to be perfect!" Doris squealed, beginning to jump up and down with joy before coming to a hasty stop and releasing her friend. Standing back, she asked the room, "Is it wrong I feel so happy? I mean, Thelma should be here, she should be sharing our happiness."

Walter quickly took Doris by the shoulders. "Don't go there! You, and everyone here, know she'd only want you…us, to be happy."

Slowly, Doris nodded, wiping an errant tear from her eye. "Well, getting married in the station chapel and then a honeymoon at the manor house of one of my best friends—it's as good as it gets."

"And," Walter said, "Doris and I have discussed it— Thelma's going to be with us, in more than just spirit."

"What's that supposed to mean?" Penny asked, sitting on the arm of the sofa next to where Mary retook her seat.

Doris coughed, all of a sudden, appearing a little nervous. "Look, I know it's normal these days for people to be buried where they...fell," she managed to say, "but I couldn't bear the thought of our poor Thelma lying in some anonymous graveyard miles and miles from us."

"What have you done?" Jane asked her voice serious.

"I've spoken to the padre, and for a...donation, shall we say, he's agreed to let us bury her in his graveyard."

"But...how..." Jane stuttered.

"I wanted to do for her what I couldn't do for my first husband," Doris blurted out. "He's buried in some field in Spain, and I've no idea where. I can't mourn for him, so I want to be able to mourn for Thelma. I want to be able to speak to her whenever I can."

"And the authorities are okay with this?" Betty asked, arching a skeptical eyebrow at her friend, who shuffled a foot awkwardly.

"Well..."

"Well?" Betty echoed.

"Can I put it this way? Money talks. Look, simply put, she should be back with us. We're her family."

"Is that why you asked me if she had any family, a few days back?" Jane asked.

Doris shrugged. "Sorry. I didn't want to tell you my plan, in case you talked me out of it, and as she hasn't got any, so far as I'm concerned that does make us her family."

"And when's the funeral?" Betty wanted to know.

"Day after tomorrow," Doris revealed. "She's coming in on the last train tomorrow night."

"Monday," Jane mused. "Morning, or afternoon?"

"The funeral's set for ten in the morning," Doris squeaked.

Jane shook her head at Doris. "And you were going

to tell us this…when? I'll have to rearrange some deliveries so as many of the personnel can attend as possible, if I can."

"Ah, sorry, I didn't think."

"No, you didn't," Jane agreed before saying, a little more softly, "but if you had, you wouldn't be our Doris, would you. I'll go in tomorrow morning and make some phone calls."

"I'll come and help," Doris offered.

Jane shook her head. "No. Penny, will you come in and help? There's something I need to talk to you about in private too."

Curious, Penny nodded in agreement.

Into the silence which followed, Matt gave Ruth a quick kiss before straightening his battledress jacket and addressing Walter. "Come on, Walter, time you earned that Lance-Jack stripe. If we don't get a move on, we'll miss our transport."

Matching his sergeant's gesture on his wife-to-be's cheek, Walter made for the door. "Sorry, got a night exercise. I'll see you tomorrow."

"On Saturday night?" Doris nearly shouted.

"Just another night," Matt half-explained.

Doris joined Ruth as they followed the men out into the hall to the front door. All were nearly bowled over by Bobby as he charged through from the kitchen and began to paw at the front door.

"I sometimes wish we didn't have that dog flap at the back," Doris said. "I mean…" She gestured down at where Bobby had begun to whine and paw at the door. "What's the point of this? He'd have been just as quick to run around the house!"

Ruth shrugged. "I gave up trying to figure out his

doggy brain a while ago. He's a completely new dog since you lot came on the scene."

"Sorry about that," Doris said, adjusting the blackout before turning off the hall light and opening the door, upon which Bobby darted out and came to an almost immediate dead stop, his nose sniffing wildly at something upon the ground.

Noticing this, Ruth strode over and bent down to pick up a piece of meat just before Bobby's jaws could clamp around it. Turning, she went back inside, the other three following her in curiosity. With the door closed and the blackout curtain once more in place, she turned the light back on, ignoring the howls of Bobby from the other side of the door.

"What's that white powder?" Doris asked, peering over Ruth's shoulder.

Ruth's face had gone the same color. "I think its rat poison."

Chapter Ten

Watching and listening to Jane make telephone call after telephone call for the best part of an hour wasn't what Penny expected to be doing that Sunday morning. She'd totally forgotten that Jane had said she'd be taking her in to work and so had been surprised when Mary stumbled in, barely half awake at seven in the morning to deliver a message from her bedroom buddy, asking to meet her in the kitchen in ten minutes. At least Jane hadn't insisted they should wear their uniforms.

So far, she'd made them each a cup of tea and was now flicking through the latest copy of Ruth and Walter's *Hamble Gazette*. Ruth had decided to lead with a story on the relief of Leningrad in the Soviet Union after being under siege for well over two years. She'd skip-read the edition a couple of times at home, but this was the first time she was able to really read what had been written. Details were understandably scarce, yet she was very impressed with the article and could only shake her head in wonder at what their ally's people had endured.

"All done," Jane declared, throwing a glare at the telephone before turning to face Penny who, because she was still slightly annoyed at being dragged out of her warm bed on a Sunday morning, finished the last paragraph of Ruth's article before looking up.

"Great!" Penny said, a little too obviously cheerful.

"Now, what did you want to talk to me about?"

However, Jane didn't say anything straight away, merely looking at Penny from across her desk. For her part, Penny tried to remain calm and not show her annoyance anymore, although she aimed an eyebrow at her boss.

"Right. First, sorry for the cloak-and-dagger, but I felt I needed to talk to you away from the rest of the Mystery Club." Penny's eyebrow went up a little farther. Rubbing her forehead, where she now had a small scar as a reminder of the crash the two had suffered before last Christmas—her broken arm had healed well—she said, "I'll get to the point. I know you didn't enjoy working in Ops when you were pregnant last year, but I now need a..." Jane had to stop and swallow at the real meaning of what she was about to say. "I need a new number two."

Before Jane could say anything more, Penny opened her mouth and protested, "You're right there, Jane. I much prefer flying."

Jane nodded in agreement. "I believe you, and in an ideal world, that's what you'd be doing, but it's not an ideal world. We both know that."

Penny didn't like the way this conversation was going, and tried again. "I really, really like flying. I don't like flying a desk."

This time, Jane shook her head and waved a hand absently around her office. "And you think I wouldn't rather be doing that? I so rarely get the chance to go up these days, I'm having trouble keeping current on the Anson."

Penny got up from her chair and hurried around to kneel beside Jane. She went to raise her right arm to place it around her friend's shoulders, but as it got level with her own shoulder, she let out a whimper of pain and let her arm slump to her side. Neither the sound nor the gesture were missed. Jane immediately pushed her chair back and carefully helped Penny into her chair.

Not bothering to ask, Jane took hold of her friend's right arm and raised it slowly, all the while watching Penny's face, until it neared the same height at which Penny had let out her cry of pain. As she did, Penny flinched and pulled her arm out of Jane's grasp.

"No!"

Leaving her friend in her chair, Jane perched on the edge of her desk and treated Penny to her best annoyed face. "How long has that caused you trouble?" she asked.

Penny shrugged and immediately regretted it, as her hand flew to and gripped her arm, right where she'd been shot. "A while."

Jane frowned. "How long a while?"

Knowing she'd been caught, Penny slumped back, rolling her wounded arm around and around, not troubling to keep her discomfort hidden. "About a month."

"And you've been flying all this time," Jane stated in exasperation. "Bloody hell, Penny!"

"I know, I know!" Penny shrugged, again with a wince.

After a minute of silence, Jane cranked one side of her mouth up in a wry expression. "Well, you've just made my decision easier."

Penny regarded her friend in open suspicion now. "What decision?"

Jane got to her feet and held out her hand. Penny got to her feet and, somewhat warily, took the handshake.

"First, you're seeing the doctor in the morning. I want a full report on your arm, and until I get that, you're grounded. Also, congratulations, Second Officer Alsop, you're now my second in command."

After a few seconds, Penny blurted out, "But what about Betty? She's a first officer, and she helped out before!"

Jane shook her head. "I'll admit, she was my first thought. However, she's only just got back into the swing of flying again, and I don't think it would be good for her if I took her off. That pretty much made up my mind, but when you let the cat out of the bag about your arm, you left me with no doubt in my mind."

Whilst Penny sat trying to find a hole in Jane's argument, Jane tidied up her desk, folded her glasses away, and tucked them into her bag. Getting to her feet, she treated her friend to her best smile. "Come on. We need to get back to Betty's. I want everyone looking their best at the funeral tomorrow."

This got through Penny's annoyance, and with a single nod of her head, she got to her feet and followed Jane out, waiting for her on the steps as she locked up the hut.

Linking arms, the two huddled a little closer against the blustery wind blowing that morning. Jane waited until they'd been waved through the barrier at the guardroom before bringing up the subject she'd been wishing to broach for a while. "Have you heard from Tom lately?" Penny's fingers tightened upon Jane's arm, and even through her coat, she felt the grip.

Jane wasn't surprised when her friend didn't reply straight away. Before Christmas, Penny had confirmed she was pregnant, and though her husband was over the moon, the mother-to-be herself wasn't as sure, something which did not go down well with Wing Commander Tom Alsop. Things came to a dramatic head at Southampton hospital the day after the two of them had been shot down when they'd blundered into the middle of a fight between a Spitfire and a German bomber. Tom had made it to Penny's bedside, but his concern for her had changed dramatically upon learning that as well as being shot in the arm, she'd also lost the baby. He'd stormed out, and that was the last anyone in their circle had seen or heard from him. The one time he'd telephoned, Penny had refused to talk to him.

It appeared the couple of months since Christmas hadn't healed the relationship between them at all. In the short time since Thelma's death, she'd found her thoughts going back to the troubled relationship more and more. Since she'd found out about the death of her own boyfriend, an American pilot named Colonel Frank Lowlan, she'd kept an eye out for any kind of dialogue, or better still, a breakthrough, between the pair, but with no luck. As her friend winced again in pain, Jane wished she'd also taken a more careful watch on her physical health too. At least there she knew she had a good excuse, not that she'd ever admit it, in that she'd also been recovering from her own injuries, though she considered what she'd suffered had been nothing compared to what Penny had been through.

By the time they turned left and began to follow the riverbank toward the Old Lockkeepers Cottage, Penny still hadn't said a word. Jane decided her friend needed some tough love and so dug her heels in, bringing the two to a stop within sight of Betty's cottage.

"Hey! What's the idea?" Penny said as she came to

a jarring halt.

Jane unhooked their arms and stepped in front of Penny so she couldn't step around. "Okay, I'm saying this as a friend. I think—no, I *want* you to telephone Tom. Am I right in thinking neither of you have spoken to each other this side of Christmas?"

As she'd expected, Penny immediately tried to sidestep her, but Jane was ready.

"Oh, no, you're not going anywhere until we've sorted something out. Do you hear me, young lady?"

Penny planted both hands upon her hips. "I don't need him," she said. "If he doesn't want to talk to me, then I don't want to talk to him."

Jane cocked her head to one side. "That's a rather childish point of view, isn't it? You married the man, so you must love him."

"I did!" Penny blurted out, before saying, "I do...I think."

The cold air made Jane shiver, which helped to keep away the smirk which nearly came to her face at her friend's words. "So what's stopping you? I don't think Betty would mind if you wanted to telephone him."

Penny let her head thump forward onto Jane's shoulder, who then had to strain to hear what Penny said. "What if he doesn't want to speak to me? He accused me of being glad I'd lost the baby!"

Jane placed a finger under her friend's chin and raised it so they were eye to eye. "I'm not defending him, but you must believe me when I say I'm sure that was said in a moment's anger and he regretted it almost immediately."

"But he walked out on me!" Penny felt she had to point out.

"Again, something I would bet he regrets."

"If that's the case, then why hasn't he contacted me?"

"Pride?" Jane ventured, before adding, "You're two sides of the same coin. Look, one of you has to make the first move. Don't you want to be a couple?"

Fortunately, Penny didn't have to give that question a moment's thought. "Yes! More than anything."

Jane turned her friend back around, took her by the hand, and started back off down the riverbank. "Good. Remember that. Now, let's go and make that telephone call."

"All right," Penny agreed with a weak smile, as she allowed herself to be led, "but watch out for Duck. He hasn't caused any trouble in a few days, so the little bugger's overdue."

Jane shook her head as she scanned their route ahead. "Duck. Honestly, only Doris could come up with that name!"

****

The mood was subdued in Betty's cottage that Monday morning, with no one talking to anyone else, and with Penny in particular being in a poor humor. As she'd promised yesterday, she'd tried to telephone her husband, but she'd failed to get a connection, finally giving up and going to bed around ten thirty at night.

It had just turned half eight, and Jane had just come back in having been at the station to make sure word was spread about Thelma's funeral. She'd made it clear that anyone who could be spared and wished to attend had her permission. As the funeral was set for ten, the first Anson wasn't due to take off until half past, and Jane was still surprised she'd obtained permission to set that day's deliveries back by two hours. It meant they would be working late that day, but all the pilots had no problem with that. Each was keen to pay their respects.

Finally, they all set off. It took them only a few minutes to walk down the riverbank and turn toward the village center, coming to a stop outside the lych gate of the church of St. Andrew the Apostle. They had to stop, as it seemed at least half the personnel from RAF Hamble were making their way through the gate, wending their way along the path toward the gravesite. Shaking their heads, the group from both Betty's and Ruth's cottages joined the end of the line just as a car pulled up to a stop outside FW Woolworth's. Mary was delighted to see Lawrence and his sergeant, Terry Banks, tumble out and jog toward them.

"Good," Lawrence said as he kissed Mary on the cheek. "I was worried we wouldn't make it in time."

Ruth leant in to give her nephew a quick hug. "Thanks for coming. It means a lot to us."

Lawrence looked around the crowd before straightening up and announcing, clearly so every one of his friends could be certain to hear, "By the look of things, Thelma meant a lot to everyone." He offered his arm to his girlfriend. "Take my arm, Mary, and let's say goodbye."

As they neared the freshly dug grave, the crowd parted as if a silent command had been given, and the group of friends took their place at the graveside. Before them, laid upon a couple of planks, was a highly polished wooden coffin, Thelma's final place of rest.

Betty tapped Doris on the shoulder. Taking her head from Walter's shoulder, she canted her head as Betty told her, "Nice. You didn't spare any expense, did you?"

Doris shook her head, whilst Walter squeezed his fiancée's hand in support. "It was the least I could do. She deserves the best, so that's what she got."

Penny gently dug her elbow into her friend's ribs. "And we shouldn't ask where you managed to find a classy coffin like that in the middle of a war, eh?"

"Not if you don't want me to lie to you," Doris replied, with a weak smile.

"Well done, love," Walter told her, kissing Doris quickly on the lips, ignoring a disapproving glance from the padre.

The padre raised his hands to the sky and the graveyard began to fall silent. Taking a last look around, Doris's gaze was drawn to a surprising presence. "Hey, Walter," she began before lowering her voice a little, "any idea why the new owner of the chip shop would be here? He can't have known Thelma."

"Where is he?" Walter leant in to ask, looking around.

"Over there, beside that angel statue." Doris pointed. She frowned. "He's staring at me again!"

A cough from the padre the other side of the grave forestalled any further conversation, and they bowed their heads to listen. As the elderly gentleman began to talk, the clouds covering the sky since they'd left their beds that morning parted, and beams of bright sunshine broke through, to be joined by the joyous song of a solitary bird high in a tree in the churchyard. Nature itself had decided to give Thelma as happy a send-off as it could.

Chapter Eleven

"Well? What are you waiting for?" Flight Sergeant Stan Atkins let his hands slump into his lap in exasperation.

"I don't know what you're pissed off about," Wing Commander Tom Alsop told his navigator from the other side of his desk. "You're not the one who finally plucked up the courage to telephone his wife…"

"After I've spent the better part of two months having a go at you to do so," Stan couldn't resist adding, with a grin a shark would be proud of.

To his credit, Tom canted his head in acknowledgement. "As you say. Anyway, you and Sharon will be very happy to know that I picked up the telephone last night."

"So." Stan sat back and stroked his chin in puzzlement. "Why'd you call me into your office, then?"

"Because," Tom said, wagging the handset at his friend, "all the damn lines must have been down last night, and I couldn't get through."

Stan rolled up his left sleeve and absently scratched his arm.

"How's that doing?" Tom asked, using the handset as a pointer. When he'd been wounded last year, his friend had also suffered burns, and he liked to make sure he didn't overdo the scratching and open up his still-tender scars.

As Stan glanced down, his eyebrows rose as they usually did when he realized what he was doing. "Not too bad, thanks, but wouldn't it be nice if I didn't always feel like scratching the skin off, though." He rolled his sleeve back down. "One of these days, eh?"

A wry smile passed between them, with thoughts and feelings shared only by two people who'd been through so much together that actual words weren't needed. "Suppose I'd better try again, eh?"

Stan coughed and ran a finger around his collar to loosen it. "I'll leave you to it," he said and heaved himself out of his seat.

"Oh, no, you don't!" Tom told him. "Get your ass back in that seat. I may need to borrow some of your courage. Now…" He began to dial. "Sit down and keep quiet."

First, Tom tried the cottage, but when he didn't get an answer, he swore and muttered, "Idiot. They'll be at work by now," as he looked at his wristwatch.

Though he was doing his best not to listen, Stan was realistic enough to know his boss and friend would know he could hear. Looking down at his own watch, he frowned. The time was coming up to nine thirty, and he'd bet any money he had that Penny and the rest of the girls would be out on deliveries by now. He opened his mouth to speak, but when he looked up, he heard Tom asking to be connected with RAF Hamble. With nothing else for it—his friend might be lucky—he shut his mouth and waited. He didn't have long before the call was answered.

"Hello. RAF Hamble? Yes, this is Wing Commander Alsop here. Can you put me through to Operations and Flight Captain Howell?" As whoever was at the other end of the phone spoke, Tom's brow furrowed until you could almost sow potatoes in his forehead. "She's where? At a funeral!" Not only did Tom's voice rise a few octaves in barely controlled panic, but he also flew to his feet, to be joined a moment later by Stan. They may not have been blood family, but the two men cared for each and every one of those young women.

Tom was speaking again now. His voice had lost some trace of his panic, but he'd gone that color he went whenever he lost one of his squadron. "Oh," he said, retaking his seat and running a hand through his hair, making a right mess of it. "I see. Please pass on my condolences to everyone, and can I leave a message for Third Officer Penny Alsop?" Stan pretended to be deeply engrossed in an edition of the *Flight* magazine he'd snatched up from the desk. Tom said, "This is her husband, and I'd like to speak to her…as soon as possible. Tell her…tell her…oh, heck! I'll tell her I love her myself." He may have not realized he'd said that before hanging up the telephone.

Stan waited a minute for his friend to fill him in. He'd distinctly heard the word "funeral," and about the only thing he could be sure of was that it wasn't for Tom's wife, Penny. When he didn't show many signs of speaking, Stan couldn't bear the wait any longer. He leant forward and gripped his friend's arm, giving it a quick shake. "Boss?" And then, a little louder when he didn't respond, "Boss! Who's dead?"

The last word seemed to pierce Tom's demeanor, and he looked up, clearing his throat to find his voice. "Sorry." He let out a sigh, reached down to open the bottom drawer of his desk, and pulled out a half bottle of whiskey and two glasses. Pouring a decent measure into each, he held out one for Stan to take. Coming around to stand beside his friend, he laid his free hand on Stan's shoulder, took a deep breath, and told him, "Thelma Aston's been killed."

"Bloody hell," Stan replied after a few seconds.

Tom raised his glass, and Stan matched the gesture. "To Thelma. We'll miss you."

They both knocked back their drinks, and Tom immediately refilled their glasses before putting the bottle away and settling into one of his easy chairs, gesturing for Stan to take the other.

"What happened?"

Tom shook his head, "No idea. That was the guardroom I spoke to. Penny, along with most everyone else, was at her funeral."

The two sat in thoughtful silence before Stan asked, "Did they tell you what happened?"

Again, Tom shook his head. "I didn't think it the right time to ask."

"So what are you going to do? Are you going to ring back later?" Stan asked.

This time, Tom nodded. "Hell, yes! I'll try Betty's around six. I should be able to get a quick chat in before our op."

"A *quick* chat?" Stan commented.

Tom wagged a finger in his friend's face. "Don't start. I've got to begin somewhere."

"Hmm. Well, so long as you make the most of it. You do, don't you? Want to make things right between you?"

Pre-war in the Royal Air Force, the sight of an officer and a non-commissioned officer sharing a drink together would have been a rarity, if not actually frowned upon. Perhaps stimulated by wartime experiences, though still not encouraged, it was far from unusual for the two to mix, especially amongst those who flew into danger together most days. Stan rarely noticed the differences between his and his friend's uniforms, and would willingly give up his life for Tom, secure in the knowledge that Tom would do the same for him, without hesitation.

"I want her back, Stan." Tom looked his friend in the eye, and Stan could see the worry in his friend's eyes. "If she'll have me."

****

Betty took Nurse Grace's hands between hers and waited for her friends to turn the corner toward the station. She'd catch them up shortly. "Have you got a minute?"

Sliding off the saddle of her bicycle before she fell, Grace managed to get both her feet down in the nick of time. What on earth could be so urgent? She observed her friend with interest. "What can I do for you?"

Betty released the nurse's hands and took a few deep breaths.

"I was, er, wanting…hoping, to ask if you've heard from Marcus?" Betty stumbled over her words, and though Grace believed she really did want to know about her brother—half-brother, she corrected herself—something else was going on. Her suspicion heightened when Jane spotted Ruth and called her over.

Deciding to play along, Grace answered, "He's well. I did ask if he could make it for the funeral"—she gulped as a catch caught in her voice—"but he couldn't."

"Yes, I was hoping to see him too," Betty said. "It's

been what? A month since he's been able to make it down. It's not quite the same thing, speaking on the telephone, is it?"

Grace shook her head with a sigh. She'd only met Pilot Officer Marcus Palmer over Christmas, and the two had become instantly besotted. Neither had used the expression "love at first sight," though all her friends had ribbed her endlessly over the few days of leave he'd been able to snatch. One of Britain's fighter pilots, he'd lost the little finger on his right hand when it was shot off. He'd let slip that he considered it to be such a trifling wound, he was back on operations the next day. However, what with her nursing duties and his operations, they'd been able to get together only rarely since, and then she'd felt guilty not sharing him with Betty, who had made plain she was desperate to get to know her brother. After all, it's not often you suddenly find you've a new relative, especially when, like Betty, you'd grown up in an orphanage.

"No," she said, summoning up a smile for her friend, "it's not. He is hoping to make it down this coming weekend, but we need to talk to confirm."

Betty's face also lit up with pleasure. "Oh, that's wonderful. I do hope the two of you will pop in to see us? We're not flying on Sunday. Is it Sunday he's hoping to be down?"

Grace nodded. "Why don't you call him tonight? I'm sure he'd love to hear your voice."

"I will! What a good idea!" Betty replied, and then asked, "If you're not on duty tonight, why don't you come over? You can use our telephone and then stay for some tea. It's only leftovers, but you'll be very welcome."

Grace nodded. "That would be lovely! I'll be around about eight. Is that too late?"

"You're welcome any time," Betty declared.

Ruth had been standing to one side whilst this conversation ran its course, but now said, "You called, Betty?"

Betty looked around, as if making certain the three couldn't be overheard, raising Grace's interest. Perhaps now she'd find out what had been the real reason Betty wanted to speak to her.

"Have you still got that meat?" Betty asked, not at all what Grace expected to hear and making no sense whatsoever.

"Not on me," Ruth replied, "but I haven't thrown it away. Why?"

Betty didn't reply straight away. Instead, she asked Grace, "Would you be able to confirm if something was poison?"

The conversation was turning a bit surreal. "I know someone who could," she answered.

"Are they trustworthy?" Ruth asked, catching on. Useful it undoubtedly was, having a nephew in the police force. However, sometimes things needed to be as unofficial as possible, even with discretion being assured. This was one of those times.

Grace knew her friends well by now and nodded. "If you can let me have a bottle of Ruth's elderflower wine, I think I can guarantee it." Ruth nodded in agreement. "Now, what's this all about?"

Quickly, as Betty could see in the distance that Jane had stopped at the guardroom and was waiting for her, she told her about the letter she'd received, with Ruth adding about what Bobby had nearly eaten.

Grace shook her head. "Bastards," she spat, causing her friends to raise their eyebrows in surprise as neither had heard the quiet nurse swear before. Kneeling down, she gave Bobby, who'd followed his mistress and was lying flopped down at her feet, a big fuss before getting back to her feet. "You're certain he didn't have any?"

Ruth nodded, her face grim. "I'm sure. I've kept a close eye on him since, and haven't noticed anything."

"That's good." Grace nodded, her head suddenly jerking up as she noticed something over Betty's shoulder. "I think we'd better go and get this whatever—piece of meat, I assume—and be off. I think Jane's about to send out the guard for you, Betty," she finished with a grin, pointing toward the station's gate where Jane stood watching the group, her hands upon her hips.

Betty glanced over her shoulder. "Aah."

Chapter Twelve

"Ssh," Betty urged, putting her fingers to her lips as she opened the door to Grace later that night, indicating Penny, who sat cross-legged on the floor, gripping the telephone between fingers turning white. "She's waiting for Tom."

Immediately catching on to the importance of the moment, Grace hurried after her host, carefully stepping around Penny, who didn't appear to notice the disturbance. They hurried into the kitchen, shutting the door behind them as they head Penny draw a breath.

"Tom? Oh, sorry, Stan. I thought Tom was coming on the other end. He'll be right along? Yes, I'll wait," she said, letting more of her annoyance than she'd intended into her voice. "Whilst I've got you, how are things with you? Have the burns healed?" This was something she honestly wanted to know, as she'd run into him when he was waiting outside her husband's hospital room, deliberately putting off getting treatment for his own injuries until he knew his friend would recover.

"I'm pleased to hear that," she told him, hoping he'd be able to hear she genuinely was. "He's here now? Great! Look, it's been lovely to speak to you again, Stan. I hope we'll all be able to get together again soon. Now, please pass me over." She took a couple of breaths to steady her nerves, which had started to jangle now she was about to speak to her husband for the first time in a couple of months.

"Hello, Tom," she said, praying her voice didn't break. "Yes, yes, I'm fine. My arm? Still got the two of them, so can't complain. And you? How are you feeling? The wounds healing, I hope?" She really did, though she knew they were both dancing around the subject of her pregnancy and the loss of their unborn child. Who would be the first to broach the subject?

After a couple of minutes more of nonsense talk, which veered dangerously close to touching on what they thought of the weather, Penny snapped, "Oh, for heaven's sake! Are we adults? Aren't we supposed to be married? Yes, that was a rhetorical question," Penny barked. She let out an exasperated breath. Men could be so annoying. "Look, cards on the table—do you want to remain married? That was quick! Good answer," she told him, unable to completely keep the surprise from her voice, as she'd steeled herself for him to say no. Now she was temporarily lost for words. "Well, that is good." She stumbled a little over her words before gathering her thoughts and telling him the idea she'd had last night.

"Let me run this by you, but don't interrupt until I've finished, agreed? Good. Now, I think you'll have to agree, we may be married, but we don't know each other all that well. I'm coming to it, patience! I do love you— good to hear. I love you, but I don't really know you, and I believe you know this to be true. I think what's happened between us goes to prove that. So I think we should start over, go out, get to know each other again. I think that would be a good start."

Penny gave Tom a few moments to mull over these words, hoping he'd think especially of when he'd accused her of not wanting children and then stalking out of her hospital room. By his reply, he'd got her point, and with no one else to bear witness, she slapped the floor in satisfaction. "Good. I'm glad you don't think it's a silly idea. One more thing before I go. I gather you've heard about Thelma? Yes, it's fair to say everyone's in shock. Thanks, Tom, that means a lot, and I'm sorry you couldn't get down for the funeral too. Now, I think we should both go and mull over what we've discussed, for a few days. Call me soon. Yes, love you too. Keep safe, Tom. Bye!"

Reaching up, Penny just about managed to hang the phone up without dropping it, letting out a loud, heartfelt, "Mmm..." She stretched out her legs and rocked from the waist side to side a few times to draw the kinks out of her back after a long and difficult day. Finding her way to her feet, she noticed the house was unnaturally quiet. The door to the lounge was open and the room itself empty. Turning her ear toward the kitchen, she listened closely and thought she could make out some hurried, whispered voices behind the closed door. Slowly, she slipped off her shoes and in her stockinged feet, tiptoed the few paces to the kitchen door. Pushing it open, hard, she watched in undisguised glee as both Mary and Doris tumbled backward.

Chuckling, she held out a hand to each and helped them to their feet. "If you want to know what we said, it would have been less painful if you'd have waited," she told each as they took seats at the table. "Surely you know I'd tell you."

Mary slapped Doris none too gently on the shoulder. "See? I told you!"

Betty shook her head and leant in toward where Grace was sitting, a look of quiet bemusement upon her face. Tapping her on the shoulder to get her attention, Betty waited while the nurse turned to face her, the better so she could read Betty's lips. "You know, I sometimes think I'm running a guest house for wayward children."

Before she could prevent it, a snort escaped Grace, and her hands flew to her mouth. "Sorry," she muttered, "but I do see what you mean."

"You don't have to nod so enthusiastically," Doris said to Penny, who looked like the proverbial Cheshire Cat.

"So what did he say?" Grace asked before anyone else, nearly bouncing up and down on her seat and not noticing Betty shake her head in silent despair.

"I need a cup of tea first," Penny said, holding out her hands for a nonexistent cup.

"That's bribery," Doris said, as she got to her feet.

"Could Mary make it?" Penny hastily asked.

Doris planted her hands upon both hips and leant over Penny. "I beg your pardon?"

Angling her head up until she was nearly nose to nose with her friend, Penny replied, quite clearly, "Doris, I love you dearly, but amongst your many talents, the ability to make a good cup of tea is not present."

"Well," Doris said after a few seconds, "why didn't you say so?" and promptly retook her seat.

With a shake of her head which could well mean she didn't know how she came to be filling up the kettle, Mary asked Doris, "Why are you looking so happy with yourself?"

Doris pasted a self-satisfied smile upon her face. "Because dear, sweet, beautiful, kind-hearted Penny here has just given me the perfect excuse never to make another cup of tea ever again!"

Mary's mouth opened and closed a few times before she settled upon merely shaking her head. "Winter, you've a lot to answer for."

"Perhaps, but not in this life."

"Whilst we're waiting for the superior cup of tea," Betty said, "tell us what happened. Are you and Tom going to be all right?"

Penny mulled things over for a minute before saying, "Perhaps."

"Perhaps?" Betty repeated, before Penny had the chance to elaborate.

"Give me a chance," Penny said. "We talked, or rather, I mostly talked and Tom mostly listened. I suggested we begin again, go out on dates, as if we're just getting to know each other."

"And what did he say to that?" Betty asked.

"Well, to his credit, he didn't argue," Penny told them before letting her head slump to her chest. She brought it back up and looked around the room. "I've given things a lot of thought these last few months. I love him…or…" she confided, "I believe I do. Or will…or do—oh, I'm so confused," she finished off, before pushing herself to her feet and taking a single spin around the kitchen before retaking her seat and looking around the room at her friends.

"Here," Mary said, hastily pushing a steaming cup into her hands. "It may be a little weak, but I need to know where this is going, and if I wait any longer, it'll be undrinkable."

"Where's mine?" Doris asked, pouting a little.

"In the pot," Mary replied. "Seeing as you love tea so much, I thought it best that you make your own."

"I really need some more coffee," Doris muttered as

she got to her feet. Placing a hand upon Betty's shoulder, she bent down and said as clearly as she could, "Please, please, ask Jim if he can get me some more?"

"I'll see what I can do, again," Betty replied, patting the hand before telling her, "Four more cups won't go amiss, whilst you're up. Now, get on with it, Penny."

Before getting on with it, Penny took a deep swallow, finally finishing, "I've told him to take a few days to think things through and then call me."

Grace shot to her feet, nearly knocking a cup out of Doris's hands. "Call me!"

"I beg your pardon?" Betty said.

"What the hell!" Doris uttered, successfully juggling the cup before setting it down.

"It completely slipped my mind! Betty, can I phone Marcus?"

"Be my guest," Betty said. "And I promise, no one will listen in at the door this time."

****

Tom had finally got clearance to fly again, his headaches all but gone. The medical officer at his last assessment had been honest with him. In an ideal world, he'd have stayed grounded until they had completely disappeared, only—and he'd made certain to fix Tom with his best stare as he'd said the words—they didn't live in an ideal world, not even close to one. So he'd been cleared to fly and had wasted no time in reclaiming Stan as his navigator.

Now, walking toward his Mosquito for his first operational mission in too long, Tom was quiet, too quiet, and Stan easily picked this up.

"You okay, boss?"

Tom nodded, and they walked the few steps more

which took them up to the nose of their deadly two-engine bomber. Fully fueled and bombed up, she was still nearly the fastest thing in the skies, and Tom laid a hand on the entry hatch hanging down from the fuselage.

"Happy to be back?"

With his back to his friend, Tom nodded, though he couldn't see the look of concern on Stan's face. "Me too. I'm sure Dashwood's got a death wish!"

This at least, got a small laugh from Tom. "Not sure about that, but I'm glad I've never had to fly with him."

Stan looked at his watch, noting they still had twenty minutes before they were due to take off. "As we've a few minutes, do you want to share what Penny said?"

"Her timing wasn't great," Tom first said, shaking his head.

"Don't try to dodge the question, boss."

If it had been anyone else, Tom would have told him to mind his own business, but it being the one man he'd trust his life to, he said, "She wants us to date."

Stan stopped midway through checking his map case. "She what?"

Tom turned back and nodded. "She does. Said we didn't really know each other, and essentially, that's what we should do."

When Tom didn't elaborate, Stan could only say, "And that's how she left it? Nothing more?"

"Only that we should think things through for the next few days." He shrugged.

"I'm not sure what to say," Stan managed to get out.

"Well, that makes two of us," Tom admitted. "I guess all I can do is what she said, take some time."

As the two began their pre-flight walk around the Mosquito, Stan said, "I hope you don't mind my asking, but do you want her back?"

Tom straightened up and slammed a hand against the port engine cowling. "Damn right I do!"

A cold, cloying mist was gathering that evening, and Stan straightened up, his eyes scanning the sky for what he wasn't quite certain. Tom stopped his checks as he noticed his friend's strange behavior. "What's up?"

"Can you hear something?" Stan asked, not looking over to him but instead now turning his head toward the sky.

As the squadron prepared for that evening's sortie, the airfield was far from quiet, but the background noise wasn't overbearing, and whilst all around him continued their pre-flight checks, Tom and Stan stood there, eyes and ears open. As the commander, Tom had the responsibility to get everyone off the ground on time, only in that moment keeping to schedule was pushed to the back of his mind. Not only was Stan Tom's navigator, he also kept the best lookout of anyone he'd ever flown with, his eyes being responsible for spotting more enemy fighters looking to attack them than he cared to count. So if Stan thought something was wrong, he trusted him implicitly.

Gradually, he became aware of a buzzing-type noise coming from the direction of the east perimeter of the station. Squinting toward where he believed the sound was coming, Tom's hand went subconsciously to clutch his breast. "I don't like this, Stan," he said.

No sooner had the words left his mouth than a hurricane of noise and white light erupted from the direction they were looking. By now, Tom and Stan were aware they weren't the only ones who'd stopped their pre-flight and had been trying to find the source of the strange noise. A flash of orange in the sky made him blink, followed a moment later by a tremendous crash as the initial orange ball died down in a moment and was replaced by the sight of a twin-engine aircraft trailing flame from one engine, licking its way down the fuselage. Before either man could comment, this plane hit the ground and somersaulted its way down the main runway, exploding and flinging burning metal out in all directions. Several whooshed between the pair and sliced the top of their Mosquito's fin clean off.

"Down!" both men yelled at the same time, each dropping to the ground and rolling behind what protection a main wheel could provide. Around them, nobody needed to be told twice, as men dived to the ground and scattered in all directions.

With his hands over his ears and his mouth wide open, Tom found his eyes drawn toward the shot-down aircraft's companions. Despite the risk of being hit, he couldn't help but glance up as three more Nazi aircraft, Ju88 medium bombers, he thought, roared over the airfield. One held its course and dropped its bomb-load down the runway, whilst the two following peeled off and made for his squadron's dispersals and his Mosquitos. All this, Tom took in and surmised in a few seconds. Realizing that if they stayed where they were, they were as likely to end up casualties as well as the aircraft, he scrambled to his feet and made a dash to Stan, who was still huddled under the other wing.

"Up! Move!" he shouted, grabbing his friend by the collar and, with the strength of desperation, hauling him to his feet.

The trust between the two came into play once more, and Stan didn't question his superior's behavior, simply following him and joining in Tom's shouts of, "Run! Get to the shelters!" as they ran as fast as they could toward the nearest shelter on the other side of the dispersal. A sixth sense told both of them to dive to one side, though they were still a good five yards from the shelter. They weren't a moment too soon, as zipping sounds like a thousand bees in their ears filled the air, and bullets loosed by the attacking bombers stitched the ground right where they would have been if they'd continued on course.

A scream from behind them told them someone hadn't been so lucky. Without hesitation, both rolled to their feet and dashed back the way they'd come, being passed by most of their squadron mates as they did. As they reached the wounded man, the first bombs hit, and though neither was wounded, they were both thrown back the way they'd come by the concussion.

"Christ almighty!" Tom muttered, dragging himself, with much difficulty, into a sitting position. Putting his hands to his head, he rubbed, trying to get rid of the ringing, and when his left hand came away smeared with blood, he tried not to be too worried. Tentatively, he quickly patted his head with his semi-clean other hand and discovered the blood was coming from his left ear. When he couldn't find anything else wrong, and with very little he could do anyway, he began to heave himself to his feet. A hand clamped him under the armpit, briefly causing him to jump, despite the continued explosions and bark of anti-aircraft gunfire. Looking up, he was relieved to see Stan. "You okay?" he shouted.

Stan didn't waste breath with replying, instead nodded and finished helping Tom to his feet. Together, the two dashed toward the man who'd been shot, as the two remaining raiders disappeared into the gloom, their bombs unloaded and the airfield an artwork of destruction and flame.

When they reached the man, he was face down, though it wasn't apparent if he was dead or alive. With no time to be gentle, they turned him over and had to stop themselves from reeling back. The man had a line of four bullet holes going diagonally from his left shoulder to the right of his groin. Flight Lieutenant Dashwood was clearly dead.

Chapter Thirteen

"And your friend's certain?" Ruth asked, her arms wrapped tightly around Bobby, who looked as if he thought his mistress had gone mad.

This was the third time in as many minutes she'd asked Grace this question, as if the mere act of asking could change the answer. Grace had hurried around, straight away she'd knocked off from work, to give them the results. Though what they'd all expected, it still came as a shock to hear it confirmed—someone had indeed tried to poison Bobby! They'd all been around long enough that they'd accepted Ruth's diagnosis on trust when she'd found the piece of meat, but it didn't make it any easier to hear when put into as near official words as they were likely to get.

"If I get hold of these bastards…" Ruth began to say, absently beginning to twist poor Bobby's ears between her fingers.

The cocker spaniel at the center of events let out a little squeal, and Betty reached out and firmly stopped Ruth's none-too-gentle ministrations. "You may want to stop that. Bobby's not too happy."

Ruth immediately glanced down and realized what she was doing, instead taking her dear companion between her hands and bringing him up to head level so she could kiss him on his furry forehead. "I'm sorry, Bobby." Then she hugged him to her chest before telling the room again, "Just leave them to me, promise?"

Everyone was quite happy to nod agreement—everyone except Lawrence, that is, who after a moment's thought told her, "In all honesty, Aunty, I would love to accommodate you as it'd save our overstretched justice system some work." He shook his head. "But no, I know I promised to keep this on the quiet, and I will, for as long as I can, but things are already getting out of hand. What so nearly happened to our Bobby"—who'd now fallen asleep with his head tucked into Ruth's neck—"could only have been done by someone close, someone who obviously knows where the two of you live."

Ruth and Betty both blanched at this statement, which didn't go unnoticed by the policeman.

"Good." He nodded. "I hope you both know I didn't mean to scare either of you, but you needed it spelled out. You all do!" he told everyone in the room, raising his voice a little to make certain he had their attention. "Look, you're all very smart, that goes without saying, but sometimes being smart isn't enough. I think it's fair to say this person—or persons, since it could be more than one—is dangerous. If they're desperate enough to send that note, and then try to poison Bobby…well, anything could happen. I want you all to promise me you'll be careful, more careful than you've ever been in your lives!" He leant forward, dug into the inside pocket of his jacket, and handed everyone a card. "My number's on it. Don't be heroes. If you need to use it, use it. If I'm not there, speak to Terry. You can all trust him. I hope you know that."

Somewhat timidly, Grace put up her hand. "I almost hate to ask, but," she said, when Lawrence smiled and nodded at her, "does this include me?"

Grace promptly went the same color as her friends as he nodded and replied, "I reckon so. Whoever this is has to be watching at least this and Betty's places. It's safe to surmise they'll have seen you coming and going as well."

Summoning a smile, which she flashed around the room, Grace said, "I knew you lot were trouble, the moment I made the mistake of letting Bobby onto the ward." She then quickly added, when at least Betty and Penny looked like protesting, "But I wouldn't have it any other way, so don't worry about me. I'll be careful, I promise, Lawrence."

"Sorry to veer off the subject," Penny said, leaning over and giving Bobby a huge fuss around his much-maligned ears, "but unless my ears were deceiving me just now, Grace, you told me and Betty off, even though I was behind you! How? Has your hearing come back?"

Grace had half-turned around to face Penny and now made a point of staying in that position. This time, genuine joy was behind her smile. "Not completely, but enough so I can hear most of what's been said behind me now."

Before she knew it, Doris had thrown herself at her nurse friend and gave her a huge kiss on the cheek. She was rapidly followed by Mary, Ruth, and Betty, with Bobby waking up in time to join in the celebrations. Lawrence waited until he had some space and then added his own congratulations before retaking his seat, this time with Mary plonking herself down upon his lap.

Finally, Penny was able to give her friend a big hug. "I'm so pleased for you! That must make things so much easier for you at work, too."

Grace nodded enthusiastically. "You have no idea!"

"How does Marcus feel about it? Come to think of it," Mary added, "when did it start to come back?"

It took a moment for Grace to reply. Obviously her friendship with Betty's half-brother was progressing nicely. "I first noticed a few weeks after Christmas, but I didn't want to say anything—to anyone," she hastened to add, "in case I was wrong, you know, imagining things."

"But you're not?" Betty asked.

Grace shook her head. "Definitely not. The same doctor who looked at the poison has been testing me since I first thought things were improving."

"And he's certain?" Doris wanted to know.

"A hundred percent," Grace said firmly. "He's a bit of a jack-of-all-trades, but he knows his stuff so far as ears are concerned. He doesn't think they'll get much better, but what I've got back is far better than I ever thought would happen. I'll take it. Oh, and before I forget, Marcus wants to know if he can kip down on your sofa on Thursday evening."

"He's coming over!" Betty exclaimed excitedly.

****

Leaving Mary to enjoy some quality time with Lawrence, everyone else said their good nights and made their slow way back along the dark track toward The Old Lockkeepers Cottage.

"You lot go ahead," Jane said to Doris and Betty. "I need a quiet word with Penny, here."

Doris and Betty exchanged looks before shrugging their shoulders and tucking their hands into pockets against the cold as they hurried ahead. "We'll put the kettle on!" Doris shouted over her shoulder at the pair.

"Make certain Betty makes the tea!" Penny shouted

back.

"Thanks a bunch! Useless Yankee clodhopper!" they heard Betty jokingly tell her friend.

"I don't think Doris is going to thank us, if things go on this way." Penny laughed, shaking her head.

Jane waited until Penny had stopped laughing before saying, "What excuse do you have for not seeing Doctor Barnes, then?"

Even in the dark, Jane would swear her friend had gone beetroot red.

"Ah, I suppose I'm being silly to think you'd let that drop, aren't I?"

"Very."

"And me trying to convince you my arm's feeling a lot better wouldn't help?"

"Not a chance," Jane declared straight away. "Why? Do you fancy an arm wrestle?"

Penny's hand immediately flew to cover her bad arm, answering Jane's question for her. "You. Me. Tomorrow. Doctor. First thing. No arguments!"

Penny hung her head in shame, partially because in slapping her arm she'd caused a pain to flash before her eyes. Looking up, she saw only sympathy in Jane's eyes together with concern. She gently reached out and tucked the hand Penny had placed upon her arm through the crook of hers. "Come on, let's get home and see if Betty's made a deliberate muck-up of the tea."

As they opened the cottage's gate, Penny stopped and said to Jane, "You don't need to come with me in the morning. I promise I'll go to the doctor."

Jane squeezed Penny's hand. "Humor me."

****

"Well, well," Doctor Raymond Barnes said in

surprise, looking up from his first cup of tea. "This is a surprise," he said, as Jane ushered an obviously reluctant Penny into his consulting room before her. "I've never known a station full of such healthy individuals, you know. Short of stitching up the odd cut, I seem to have very little to do."

"And you're complaining?" Jane asked, taking a seat by the door, just in case Penny tried to make a dart for freedom.

"Not at all," he replied with a smile before adding and letting slip, "especially after what's happened recently."

"At least she's still close," Penny said into the silence which followed.

The doctor turned his head to look out the window, in the direction of the church. "That she is," he added before putting down the nearly forgotten cup. "Now, what can we do for you, Penny?"

Jane got to her feet to intercept Penny and her move toward the door. Catching hold of her arm, she placed a finger directly over where her friend had been shot. "For the answer, Doc, press here!"

Penny snatched her arm away, shot Jane a most unsavory glare, and plonked herself down in the seat Jane had vacated. "Very bloody funny, I don't think."

Trying and nearly succeeding in keeping a grin under control, Doctor Barnes clapped his hands together. "Well, Penny, tell me what's wrong."

Knowing she'd get a flea in the ear from Jane if she didn't speak up quickly, Penny hurried to tell him. "My arm's been hurting me for a while now, and, well, Jane's grounded me until it doesn't."

"That's...helpful," Barnes replied with a shake of

his head. Obviously to give him some thinking time, he turned his head to Jane and asked her, "Whilst you're here, any problems with yours?"

Jane twirled and flexed the arm which had been broken in the crash landing, until the doctor gave a satisfied nod.

"And your head? No headaches, or any other problems?"

"None."

"Flipping show-off," Penny muttered, which was ignored by both the others.

"Right, Jane," Barnes said, "you can leave now. I'll send Trouble, here, on when I've finished, together with my recommendation."

Hauling herself to her feet, Jane clapped Penny on the shoulder, immediately causing her to yelp in pain. "Oops," she said, though the fact she couldn't keep a small laugh in earned her another glare. "Sorry, but at least you know why I've grounded her," she added to the doctor, scooting out the door before Penny could retaliate.

****

Being on taxi duty that week, Mary was lounging in the seat Thelma used to occupy in the ops hut when Jane came in. The mug of tea in her hands stayed its course toward her mouth when Jane came through the door, still laughing. "Care to share? I could do with a good laugh."

Noticing the serious tone in Mary's voice, Jane immediately asked, "Why? What happened?" and then hurried over and made a grab for her friend's arms. She was about to lift up one of her friend's legs when Mary stopped her by shoving her seat back until she was out of reach. "I'm okay, boss! There's nothing wrong with me."

"Don't do that to me!" Jane said, then made her way into her office, where she dumped her coat, hat, and bag before rejoining Mary, who was in the process of putting on the kettle. "Now, tell me what happened that you need a laugh."

Mary jerked a thumb toward the flight line. "Port engine packed up on me just as I lined up to land."

"Bugger," Jane swore, making a grab for the nearest phone.

"Don't worry, boss, I've already got engineering onto it."

"Is the other Anson serviceable?" Jane wanted to know.

Mary nodded. "All fueled up and ready." She glanced at the clock on the wall. "I take off in twenty minutes. Now, what's so funny?"

Reminded of what she'd been chuckling about, Jane sat herself down before saying, "You know I was making sure Penny saw the doctor about her arm?" Mary nodded. "Well, I only wanted to wish her the best before leaving, so I gave her a friendly slap on the…"

"You didn't!" Mary said, a hand flying to her mouth.

"I did." Jane nodded, letting out a chuckle again. "Right on the spot."

"Poor girl," Mary said with a shake of her head. "Ah, well, serves her right for hiding this from us."

"I don't think I'll repeat that last bit to her," Jane told her.

"Knowing Penny, I'd very much appreciate that."

A heavy rain began to fall as the kettle boiled. A minute later, Jane was nursing a nice hot cup of tea. She glanced outside before pulling the schedule toward her and running a finger down a column. She looked over at where Mary was slumped in her chair with her eyes closed. "If you're tired," she slowly said, "I can take this flight. I wouldn't want—"

Mary cracked open one eye as she interrupted, "…anyone to get hurt?"

Jane didn't say anything for a good minute. Finally, she met Mary's eyes and asked, "Am I that transparent?"

Mary treated her friend to a smile she hoped was an understanding one before she drank deeply from her cup and gave a deep sigh of satisfaction. "Ah…only to your friends. Look, you wouldn't be human if you weren't worried about sending us out, especially"—she twitched her head toward where the rain was lashing down against the hut's window—"when it's raining cats and dogs."

Jane followed her glance, and when she turned back, a single tear was running down her face. "It should have been me, you know," she said. "I shouldn't have let her overrule me."

Mary placed her cup down and hurried over to perch on the edge of the desk beside Jane. She took one of Jane's hands and lightly smacked the back. "Now, you stop that. You can't let yourself think that way. We won't let you. What's more, Thelma wouldn't want to hear you talk that way."

Jane squeezed her friend's hand, matching it with a small smile. "You may have to tell me that every now and then."

"Here whenever you need me, boss," Mary told her, taking out a semi-clean handkerchief and drying the tear on Jane's cheek.

"Thank you," Jane said. "If there's anything I can ever do for you, just ask."

"Funny you should say that, boss," Mary replied,

looking slightly embarrassed to say the words.

Chapter Fourteen

By Thursday evening, Betty had pushed the note to the back of her mind, almost as if it never existed. The reason? As Betty brought the Anson into land at Hamble's grass runway, her thoughts were almost totally engulfed with thoughts of seeing her half-brother Marcus again. Taxiing toward the flight line hut, she got ready to touch the brakes once more, gradually coming to rest where she was supposed to. Taking a deep breath, she went through the post-flight checks as the engines wound down.

"Not a bad landing there, Palmer," Doris told her friend, patting her on the shoulder. "Keep this up, and I may not need to take a tranquilizer when you fly!"

"Ignore her," Mary advised, kissing their taxi driver on the cheek. "We're both very tired."

"Who isn't?" Betty replied, throwing off her straps and getting to her feet. Following her friends out of the aircraft, she hopped down, bypassing the steps entirely, landing nicely and going straight into a stretch a cat would be proud of. Reaching back into the Anson, she picked up her flight bag and parachute, then set off at a mild trot to catch up with her friends, slapping a dawdling Doris on the behind as she went. "Come on! Get a move on there, Yank!" She sped past her and up the stairs into the hut, anxious to complete the paperwork and get back home.

"Why the hurry?" Doris yawned from behind her, as she slipped past.

Betty didn't answer until she was able to join the two in getting out of their flight gear. "In case you've forgot, Marcus is coming tonight."

"Isn't he coming to see Grace, though?" Mary asked from somewhere inside her jumper.

"And that too," Betty allowed. After she'd pulled off her boots, she added, "All right, I'll allow that, but I can't help it! I still don't know him very well, and now Eleanor's gone…well, I want to get to know him as quickly as possible. You…you never know what's going to happen, do you?"

Neither Mary nor Doris replied. There wasn't much either could say to that. Marcus was a fighter pilot, with all the danger that implied. The two had kept in quite regular correspondence since they'd been thrown together the previous December when her estranged parents had kidnapped her. In a last desperate effort to restore their fortune, they'd hoped to convince her to sell off her cottage so they could take the proceeds. Marcus had been instrumental in bringing them to justice, his natural sense of what was right winning over any lingering feelings he had for the pair. To cement a happy Christmas for everyone, Grace and Marcus had fallen in love at first sight right in Betty's cottage.

Mary and Doris peeked at each other from their half-removed jumpers, then over at where Betty sat, now slumped on the bench, one boot on, one off. They nodded at the same time, and in a flurry of activity, both were dressed in their ATA uniforms in record time and set to with helping Betty get out of the flying clothes and into hers, though from the loud protests coming from their friend, helping may have been the last thing they were doing. Nevertheless, in short time, the three were striding toward the ops hut where both Jane and Penny, the arm where she'd been shot in a sling, could be seen waiting for them on the steps.

"Betty, can you tell me why your jacket is on backward?" Jane asked, the edges of her mouth twitching.

Shrugging off the grips her two friends had upon her elbows, Betty heaved her jacket over her head and, with a glare at both Doris and Mary, hurriedly unbuttoned it and put it back on the right way before she replied, "Because I was flying with two of the maddest buggers ever to walk this earth!"

"Well, there you're not going to get any arguments," Penny agreed.

"Yes, yes." Betty waved her hands impatiently. She faced Jane. "Please don't tell me we've any last minute deliveries?"

"Penny?"

In response, Penny hurried over to her desk, shuffled a few bits of paper, and looked up. "Nope. That's it."

Betty clapped her hands together. "Great! Any objections if I shoot off home?"

Jane shook her head, and before anyone could say anything else, Betty waved a hand in their general direction and headed off toward the guardroom and home.

"What was that all about?" Jane asked as she watched her friend disappear from sight.

"Marcus is supposed to be coming over tonight," Doris supplied. "I think she wants to create a good impression."

Penny shook her head. "As if she needs to. From what she's told us from his letters, he wants to know as much about her as she does about him."

"You don't think Grace will prove too much for him?" Mary asked.

Penny shook her head. "I don't think so. I don't know about you girls, but I'm not sure Grace has family of her own, so I think she'll enjoy talking family with him as much as Betty."

"Speaking of family," Doris said, going over and wrapping a friendly arm about Penny's shoulders, "isn't it tonight Tom's coming over?"

For someone about to see her husband for the first time in months, Penny wasn't showing a great amount of enthusiasm, something which her friends didn't fail to notice.

"Seriously, if you want a chaperone..." Doris offered.

Penny eyed her best friend with a skeptical eye. "I'll keep that in mind, but," she hastened to add as a look of slightly malicious delight came to Doris's eyes, "only if I think there'll be a need to have him beaten to within an inch of his life."

"In that case," Doris said, not troubling to keep the glee from her voice, "I'll be hanging around out of sight with a cricket bat."

Penny quickly took both Doris's hands in hers and gripped them tightly. "I haven't forgotten either, Doris," she told her, remembering how her American friend had had to be held back from chasing after her husband after he'd walked out on Penny as she lay in her hospital bed. Doris had been furious, and no one had been in any doubt as to what would have happened if she'd caught him.

Doris fixed her gaze upon Penny. "I'm not kidding."

Penny gripped her friend's hands harder. Everyone should have a friend like Doris, even one occasionally in a slightly homicidal mood. "Perhaps just stay indoors and be ready? Deal?"

"Deal," she agreed, with a sigh.

"What time's he coming over?" Jane asked, looking at her watch.

"About six," Penny replied, after consulting her own.

Jane made shooing gestures with her arms. "Well, that leaves you about an hour to get ready. Off you shoot!"

"Me too, boss?" Doris asked.

Nodding, Jane began to make her way toward her office.

"You two go ahead," Mary said. "I'll catch you up." So saying, she followed Jane, shutting the office door behind her.

Jane looked up at the noise, unused to the door being shut by anyone but her. "Something on your mind, Mary?" she asked, leaning back in her seat and steepling her fingers.

"Well, firstly, is Penny all right? She seemed a little…annoyed…distant…I'm not sure what the right word is."

"You're not wrong," Jane replied, rubbing her eyes before continuing. "We heard from the doctor today. Basically, Penny needs to rest her arm for at least a month, or she could end up losing some use of it."

"Ah, so I assume that means she's grounded, for the meantime at least."

Jane nodded. "Which doesn't make her happy. The

promotion doesn't come close to easing her hurt at not being able to fly."

"I can understand that. I'd hate to be grounded too," Mary said. "Certainly explains the sling."

"That's Penny dealt with," Jane said. "What was it you really wanted to talk about?"

"I was wondering what the chances are of getting up to Scotland with Doris on Saturday," Mary said, without preamble, and at her friend's surprised face added, "I want to show her around the manor, make sure it'll be all right for her honeymoon."

Jane allowed a smile to creep over her face.

"Let's see what we can do. I've a feeling we may be needed to make sure Doris doesn't brain Tom before he has a chance to speak to Penny."

****

"You're not wearing civvies?" Betty asked, leaning against the kitchen door, cradling a cup of tea in her hands.

Penny looked down at herself. She'd followed her first instinct when she'd got home, and after a wash and brush up, she'd changed into her full Air Transport Auxiliary Transport uniform—even, damning the cold evening, including the skirt.

"Well, make sure you don't freeze to death out there," Betty was able to say before there came a knocking at the door.

Doris rocketed down the stairs, yelling, "I've got it! I've got it!" and jumped the last few steps so she reached the door a few steps ahead of Penny.

Quickly, Penny laid a hand on her friend's shoulder as she went to open the door. "Hand over the cricket bat, Doris."

Looking not one bit contrite, Doris passed over the bat she had hefted over a shoulder. "I only wanted to scare the hell out of him," she muttered.

"And I love you for it, I really do," Penny told her friend, kissing her on the cheek.

"Can I still open the door?"

"Penny took a couple of steps back. "Be my guest."

Jane and Mary, appearing from the lounge, joined arms with Betty in a show of unity for their friend. "Go ahead," Jane urged Doris. "We all want to be here for this."

"This is going to be so good," Doris uttered, jerking the door open.

Standing in the open doorway, Tom, at the sight before him, looked incredibly like a blue uniform-clad deer, his eyes out on stalks. Taking a step back, he whipped off his hat, ran a nervous hand through his hair, and took that faltering step forward, his gaze flitting from one openly hostile girl to the next. None of them said a word in welcome.

Penny took a step toward him, throwing a grateful smile to her friends as she closed the door. "Come on, let's go for a walk," she said, letting him peck her on the cheek before walking past him and down the path.

Behind her, she heard but didn't see the door reopen so all her friends could watch as the two of them walked down the riverbank, a distinct gap between them. As they passed out of sight, the door closed.

"Do you think she'd mind if I tailed them?" Doris immediately said, picking up the cricket bat once more and slapping it down onto her hand. "Damn!" she swore, swapping hands and blowing on the one she'd hit, now reddened from the smack.

Betty reached over and took the bat from her well-meaning friend. "Let them have some privacy," she said. "I'm sure if she needs someone to brain her husband, you'll be top of the queue."

"Good to know." Doris managed a smile as there came a knock on the door again. "Already?" Doris made a grab for the bat, which Betty hurriedly snatched out of her way.

Mary went forward and opened the door, whilst Doris proceeded to chase Betty around the kitchen table. "Hi, you two!" Mary said, stepping back to allow Grace and then Marcus to enter. "Hang up your coats," she added and then stuck her head around the kitchen door. "False alarm, Doris. It's Grace and Marcus, Betty," she announced.

"They're here?" Betty nearly shouted, dropping the bat, which only just missed the American's foot. Rushing past Mary and an amused Jane, she went up to the pair, clearly not sure whom she should hug first.

Marcus took the decision out of her hands. He stepped forward and opened his arms, smiling. "Hello, sister!"

Beaming from ear to ear at these simple words, Betty stepped into his arms and wrapped hers around him, resting her head upon his shoulder. To their side, Grace looked fit to drop with happiness.

"I'll go and heat up the stew," Jane announced.

"And I'll put on the kettle," Mary added, grabbing Doris by the hand and dragging her with them to give the three in the hall some privacy.

After a few minutes, Betty led Grace and Marcus into the kitchen, where they all sat around the table.

"I don't know if the two of you have eaten?" Betty

began. "We've more than enough, if you'd care to join us."

Beside her, Marcus placed a hand over his sister's. "Speaking for myself, I'm famished. Us pilot officers aren't paid all that much, so I'm delighted to scrounge as much off you as I can."

Doris and Mary burst out laughing, soon joined by Jane and Betty, whilst Grace treated her boyfriend to a big, wet kiss. "Well said," Grace told him.

Soon everyone was enjoying a good, hot, rabbit stew, and the only sounds to hear were happy and contented slurping and lapping. Before too long, everyone had finished. Getting to his feet, Marcus reached for Betty's bowl, only to have his fingers rapped by Doris, who in typical Doris fashion declared, "You and Grace are both guests. Only those who live here clean up, so go and take a seat in the lounge. Mary and I will clean up."

Betty was on her feet in a shot. "I'd not give her the chance to change her mind."

Once everyone was settled in the lounge, Mary poked her head around the door. "Everyone like a cup of tea?"

Jane frowned. "It depends. Are you making it?"

"I heard that!" Doris yelled from the kitchen.

"Well, learn to make a decent cuppa!" Jane shouted back.

"So noted, boss," Doris yelled back, after a few seconds.

Marcus, happily settled on the sofa with Grace snuggled in at his side, raised an eyebrow at the banter. "I take it Doris's tea isn't…good?"

"We're thinking of marketing it as paint-stripper,"

Betty informed him.

"Can still hear you lot!" Doris shouted, causing everyone to laugh.

Jane lowered her voice. "It doesn't mean it isn't true."

"Anyway," Betty said, "how are you keeping, Marcus?"

Marcus held up his hands. "Not bad. At least I haven't lost any more fingers."

His rather blasé statement made Betty decidedly uneasy. As she squirmed in her chair, she asked him, "Please, don't say things like that. Seriously, you are being careful, aren't you?"

Letting go of Grace's hand, he leant toward her. "Sorry. I didn't mean anything by it. It's the nature of the job."

"I don't like it either," Grace put in, "but you'd be unhappy with a ground job, wouldn't you?"

Marcus nodded. "That's the short way of putting it, but yes, I love flying." He smiled as he looked at Betty. "I'm sure you feel the same."

"Hmm, it's not quite the same, but I suppose I understand," Betty replied.

"How about we don't talk about work?" Marcus suggested.

"Good idea," Grace quickly agreed.

"What's a good idea?" Mary asked as she kicked open the door.

"Not talking about work," Grace informed her, getting to her feet to clear the table so Mary could put down the tray she was carrying.

"Thanks," Mary said. "Doris will be in shortly. She's still sulking."

"I am not sulking!" an American voice sang out.

"Nothing wrong with her hearing, though." Mary laughed, giving the teapot a swirl.

"After a hard day, that's always a good idea," Jane added as she turned to Grace. "Betty was telling me your hearing's got better?"

Grace treated Jane to a beaming smile. "It has! It's not perfect and never will be, but it makes work so much easier again."

"I couldn't believe it when I found out, either!" Marcus said, leaning back into Grace's side and giving the nurse a huge smile of his own. "Mind you, I only found out when she made me repeat myself three times, getting louder each time, before she turned around and told me she'd heard me the first time."

Accepting a cup, Grace nudged him in the ribs. "I couldn't resist it. He couldn't spot a joke at two feet!"

"Luckily," he told them, with a shake of his head, "Nazi planes are a little easier to spot."

"Are you saying I can't tell a joke?" Grace asked him with a pout.

Marcus hastily shook his head. "Never, darling. I'd love you even if you never told another again."

At this, Grace's mouth dropped open, and she sat there doing a fair imitation of a fish out of water. Fortunately, a loud knock at the door sounded, breaking the slightly awkward moment.

"I've got it!" Doris yelled, and before anyone else could move, a Doris-shaped blur moved past the open lounge door.

"Was she carrying the cricket bat?" Mary asked.

"I'm not sure," Betty answered slowly, putting down her cup and getting to her feet, "but I'll go and

126

check."

"You love me?" Grace suddenly said, as Betty left the room.

Surprisingly, for a man, Marcus didn't appear one bit embarrassed by the use of the L word. Instead, he took her hands in his, turned the full extent of his scrutiny upon her, and replied, "Yes. I'm only sorry I never told you before."

Not trusting words, Grace instead threw herself at Marcus and proceeded to kiss him soundly, until Mary felt she had to make them aware of where they were. She coughed a couple of times. "I'm very happy for the two of you," she said slowly and loudly enough to get the two's attention. It worked, for Grace hastily pulled back, but was unable to wipe the smile from her face.

"Sorry," she mumbled, though her full attention was on the man at her side.

Betty and Doris came back in from the hall, Betty with the cricket bat in one hand, a slightly annoyed-looking Doris just behind.

"Who was at the door?" Mary asked. "I'm assuming it wasn't Tom or Penny, going by how annoyed Doris looks."

Doris shook her head. "Sergeant Green," she answered.

"Matt? What did he want?"

"Apparently, Walter and Ruth arranged for the patrol to come by our cottages a few times each night. You know, to try and make sure we're as safe as we can be," Doris added.

Marcus looked across, curious as to what they were talking about. "The Home Guard? What kind of trouble is the Mystery Club in now?"

Chapter Fifteen

"Tell me again," Doris asked as they settled into the back seat of the RAF staff car that was to take them to Fraserburgh. "How did you persuade Jane to give us this time off?"

Extracting her coat tail from beneath Doris's bottom, Mary tried to make herself as comfortable as possible, though without much hope, for the long journey ahead of them. "A very good question to which, in all honesty, I wish I had a good answer. Strangely enough, right after she heard us talking about seeing if we'd be able to go up to my family home before your wedding, she found she needed us to drop off a Hudson at Turnhouse. Well, the rest, you know. It's now," she took a look at her watch, "half five. That gives us the evening to settle in, assuming they got my message and the room's ready, and until about midday tomorrow, to make sure it'll be what you and Walter are after."

Doris also wriggled around a little. Whoever had been in her seat last needed to lose a few pounds, in her opinion, as her bottom kept slipping into a deep dip. "I'm sure it'll be lovely," she said, patting one of Mary's hands. "It's a pity we have to catch a train back so early tomorrow. The scenery looks breathtaking," she added, staring out the window. "I mean, I've flown over plenty, but this!"

Mary took a minute to reply.

Indeed, Doris was on the point of nudging her in the ribs, thinking she'd perhaps nodded off. Not that she could blame her, as the flight up had been long and boring, and she could do with a nap herself.

"I'd forgotten how beautiful it is," Mary finally admitted.

Doris gripped her friend's hand hard. "I can't wait to see the manor! Oh, I can't thank you enough, Mary."

Mary turned her face back from the view outside. "I only hope it lives up to your expectations."

"It's going to be wonderful. I just know it!" Doris tried once again to get herself comfortable and, once again, gave up. "Whilst I think about it, how did Jane wrangle a staff car to pick us up and take us to your house?"

Perhaps their driver had been waiting for this opening, as he half-turned to address the pair. "Don't ask me. All I know is, I was told an hour ago to drop everything and get my ass down here to pick up two ATA pilots. Of course, if they'd told me they were two beautiful ladies, I'd have made an effort with my appearance."

"Bend!" Mary shouted, just in time for the driver to turn back and jerk the wheel so the car managed to swerve around the bend in the road without harm.

A minute later, he leant back around, only Doris never gave him the chance to say anything. "Don't bother with the flannel. I'm engaged, and Mary's boyfriend is a police inspector."

"Ah," was all he said after a few seconds, before turning back and, to the relief of the girls, putting all his attention back onto the business of driving.

Doris elbowed Mary gently in the side and indicated

she should bob down, where Doris joined her. "I think it'd take much more than an hour for our driver to become…presentable."

The pair shared a chuckle before they were interrupted by the driver again. "My boss wanted to make sure you both got this," he said, dangling a flask over his shoulder, this time keeping his eyes on the road.

Raising their eyebrows at each other, though he'd given no indication he'd heard what they'd said, Mary thanked him, and he then replied, kind of answering the last question, "If you ask me, I think this Jane person—presumably your boss—must have something on our Station Commander. No sooner had he come into the MT office than, two minutes later, I had my orders to take the cleanest car we had and pick up the two of you—Bugger! Watch out where you're going!" he then yelled at a pedestrian who was walking along the wrong side of the street without anything bright showing. "Honestly," he muttered, "some people have a bloody death wish."

Quickly glancing through the back window, the girls were in time to see a very bedraggled policeman haul himself out of the ditch beside the road and shake his fist at the rapidly departing car. "I wouldn't stop, if I were you," Doris tapped the driver on the shoulder.

"Or go drinking anywhere around here for a while, either," Mary added.

Half turning around again, which seemed to be a habit, he asked with, hopefully, one eye on the road, "Why?"

Unable to keep a smile from her face, Mary told him, as Doris unscrewed the top of the flask and began to pour a welcome brew into the cup. "Because unless I'm much mistaken, that was the local bobby you just ran into a ditch!"

"Good point," he replied, though both girls noticed his knuckles were white as they gripped the steering wheel. As his passengers shared the tea, which seemed to actually have sugar in it, the driver advised them, "You may as well sit back and enjoy the ride. It'll take us about an hour to get back to the hospital."

"Do you think he's right?" Mary asked. "Could Jane really have something on this Station Commander?"

"You know," Doris said, "based on everything that's happened since I've known Jane, I'd say there's a very good chance our Jane has something on Winston Churchill!"

****

Doris craned her neck as she stood outside the front entrance to Mary's home, now a busy army hospital. Swiping a hand through her hair, she let out a whistle and was so engrossed Mary had to pull her friend out of the way as a pair of stretcher bearers barreled past her and disappeared inside. She appeared not to notice, instead turning around on the spot before grabbing her friend by the hand. "If my father saw this place, he'd want to buy it off you!"

Mary raised her eyebrows in surprise. Doris rarely talked about her family. About all she knew was they'd had a huge falling out to do with Doris's first husband. She waited for her American friend to elaborate, but she was left disappointed. "Ha! In his dreams! Now, as for me and Walter, if your lot ever decides to sell, you have to give us first refusal."

Slightly flummoxed, Mary opened and closed her mouth. This time, Doris had to pull her friend out of the way as another stretcher was taken inside. "But you haven't seen the inside yet. And it won't look anything like it used to in its heyday. Hell, I don't know what the rooms will look like!"

"Hun," Doris began, squeezing Mary's hand, "they could be the size of box rooms and I wouldn't care a fig! It's beautiful. Come on!" she said, dragging Mary through the entrance. "Hey, will you show me your rooms?" she asked, as they waited at the reception desk.

A little thrown by the excess of exuberance Doris was showing, quite beyond her normal level, which itself was sometimes hard to take, Mary found herself nodding whilst wondering if those attic rooms had been put to use already. As the hospital would probably require all the space it could get its hands on, this was a pretty good bet. Mind you, being the old servant quarters, the ceilings were low and angled, not to mention unheated, apart from those she'd used, which had been specially plumbed into the house's central heating system for her. The thought put a smile on her face. It would be lovely if her rooms were undisturbed.

Unfortunately, the captain who greeted them at reception couldn't tell her. "I've only been here a week myself," he apologized. Looking down at his desk, he picked up a piece of paper, studied it carefully, and then looked up at the two ladies before him. One, standing calmly before him, took no notice of the prominent labels upon the walls indicating what had been hung there in its previous guise as a family home. The other caused his eyes to nearly pop out of his head. This one was bouncing up and down on her heels and doing her best to look everywhere at once. "Well, it seems I should be welcoming you home, Miss Whitworth-Baines," he said, getting to his feet and holding out his hand. "Captain

Mark Wood, at your service."

"Please," Mary replied, "it's Third Officer Whitworth-Baines, but call me Mary. Anything else is too much of a mouthful. My over-excited friend—she's American," Mary added, receiving a playful pinch in return, "is Doris Howell."

"Hi, y'all!" Doris played up in her very worst western American accent. "Call me Doris. Yee-ha!"

"You don't happen to have a psychiatric wing, do you?" Mary asked, leaning down to the now-seated officer, who chuckled and shook his head, obviously taking the joke in good heart.

****

"Anyone else notice how quiet things are when Doris isn't around?" Betty asked, as she speared a chip.

"Or how you can actually eat all your chips without fending her off?" Penny added.

"And enjoy a leisurely bottle of Guinness without wondering if she'll drink your second before you've finished your first?" Jane said. "Didn't take me long to spot that."

"Plus," Ruth said, "we can keep the bottle of vinegar in the room with us!"

"You do realize," Walter piped up, "that I'm under orders to report all seditious talk to my fiancée when she gets back?"

Ruth batted her eyes at her friend and lodger. "Now, you wouldn't turn in your landlady, not to mention your boss, would you?"

"Or your best friends?" Penny said, indicating everyone else with her fork.

Walter immediately laughed. "No, of course not. Though, in all seriousness, she did ask me to tell her any juicy gossip when she gets back."

Jane laughed. It was a nice sound, which perked everyone up and made them look over at the lady. "In that case, you're just going to have to tell her what a boring lot we are!"

"I think I can manage that." Walter smiled back and shoveled more hot battered fish into his mouth.

Silence reigned whilst everyone sat around enjoying the good food and the company.

"It really is quiet without Doris around!" Walter suddenly said, his face a mask of shock which caused everyone to burst out laughing.

"Okay, hands up, who wants to tell Doris he said that?" Penny asked.

Everyone's hand shot up.

"Perhaps it would be best if we kept quiet about this conversation," he mumbled, putting his head down and pretending to take great interest in the remains of his dinner before asking Ruth, "Any news on the application to the ARP?"

The way she speared her last chip was all the answer anyone in the room required.

"Still nothing?"

Ruth shook her head. "The only thing I can think is that it's been such a while since we had any air raids that they may not need any more staff. I think," she added slowly, "I may have missed my chance."

"But, and I hope you'll forgive me, surely that means the authorities are hopeful they've got enough people to last until we win this war," Jane said.

Having this pointed out to her only caused Ruth to let out a deep sigh. Betty reached out and took her friend's plate from her. She'd finished all her chips, the fish too was gone, and all she was spearing now was the pattern. "I'm quite fond of that plate, so…" Betty gently informed her friend as she took the plate off her friend's lap.

Ruth now appeared sheepish. "Sorry. It's only that I'm sure Jane's right and maybe I've missed my chance to do my *bit*."

No one knew how to answer or what to say to this, especially as she was very likely right. In fact, when they all heard something being put through the letterbox, everyone except Ruth scrambled to their feet to go and retrieve it. Penny got there first.

When she took longer than was expected to come back, Betty shouted, startling Bobby briefly awake from where he lay in front of the fireplace, "Penny, are you lost?"

As Penny entered the room, everyone looked up, and all movement stopped. Held between her hands as if it might explode was an eerily familiar-looking envelope. She stopped in the doorway and looked around before saying, "I think we've got another message."

Chapter Sixteen

You must think I'm stupid. Do you not think I don't know what a copper looks like? You have one warning. If I see him one more time…

Your dog was lucky. The next time, whoever I choose won't be!

You now have 3 weeks!

Lawrence turned the note over, though as before, there wasn't anything else. "Not exactly eloquent, is he," Lawrence stated.

"Here," Betty said, pushing a cup of hot cocoa into his free hand. "Again, we can't thank you enough for coming out so quickly, and at such a late hour, too."

"Ten thirty's not so late," he managed to get out before having to cover his mouth as he yawned.

Penny leaned in and kissed him on the cheek, nearly spilling her own cocoa into his lap in the process. "There's no need to be gallant. We really do appreciate it."

Ruth and Walter somewhat sleepily nodded in agreement.

"What do you think we should do?" Ruth asked.

"Well," Lawrence said, after scratching his head for a minute, "for a start, I'd keep a very close eye on Bobby. Whoever this swine is, he's now made a direct threat against him."

"Let them try," Ruth told them. "They'll not only

have me after their hide, but the whole station, too!"

The cocker spaniel in question merely raised his head from its position on Ruth's lap and treated everyone to a very wide yawn before settling back down, as if safe in the knowledge that what his owner had said was true. Last year, RAF Hamble had been the victim of a sneak raid by a lone fighter-bomber and, largely because of his turning up and barking his head off in warning, there had been no fatalities, though Betty had suffered a few cuts. Ever since then, he'd had free rein to go where he pleased on the station.

Lawrence turned to Betty and asked, "Forgive me, Betty, but I have to ask. Have you thought this through? Do you intend to give this…these people, the money?"

Betty firmly shook her head. "Even if I had it, I wouldn't. I've never given ground in my life, and I'll be damned if I'm going to start now."

"Good for you!" Penny declared, banging her mug on the kitchen table.

After a moment's thought, Lawrence nodded. "Good. Never give in to blackmailers. Now, I'm assuming you've been giving some more thought as to who could be behind this?"

"And I still can't think of anyone specific."

"Specific or otherwise?"

Betty shrugged. "When we were…*active*," she settled on with a wry smile, still trying to be careful even though Lawrence now knew about her role as her jewel thief sister's fence, "there were too many jobs to keep track of. It really could be anyone. I don't suppose it helps that a lot of them were decidedly on the dodgy side, so we undoubtedly made a lot of not-so-nice enemies."

Lawrence took a satisfying sip from his mug before

replying, "You're right, that doesn't help."

"We were very careful," Betty added, not bothering to keep a hint of pride from her voice.

"I'm sure you were," Lawrence agreed, looking at her over the top of his mug.

"All of which doesn't help us at all," Penny pointed out.

"Sorry about that," Betty answered. "Look, it's not like I'm trying to be unhelpful, Lawrence. It's just that I honestly have no idea who it could be."

"And you did give most of the money you inherited from Eleanor to charity," Penny felt inclined to add, "so you really can't give it back anyway."

Walter summed things up nicely. "All of which leaves us up a creek without a paddle."

"I'm not quite certain what a creek is," Ruth remarked, "but I get what you mean."

"Doris tells me it's something to do with water," Walter supplied.

"Never mind," Lawrence broke in. "I can't remember if I asked you before, but have you noticed anyone hanging around? Anyone who's just turned up, out of the blue?"

Betty's eyes flicked around the room, as if seeing if anyone else was going to say anything before she made up her mind. "I don't know if I've mentioned this to you, Lawrence, but there is someone new around the village, someone Doris insists she doesn't like the look of."

"Who's this, then?" he asked, leaning forward and setting his elbows on the table.

Penny nudged Betty's arm, then told Lawrence, "It's only the new owner of the fish 'n' chip shop. Doris thinks he looks…fishy!"

Betty lightly smacked her friend on the hand. "Oh, very funny! And how long have you been waiting to use that one?"

Penny wagged her head from one side to the other. "Oh, virtually since the first moment Doris mentioned him. Do you think I could get away with using it with Doris too?"

"Probably," Betty replied after a moment.

Lawrence ignored the two's banter. "Nothing's nothing," Lawrence muttered, before finishing off his cocoa. "What's so strange about this man, then?"

A little on the spot, Betty rubbed her forehead before saying, "Well, for a start, he seems to know very little about fish 'n' chips…"

"And Doris should know." Penny laughed.

Lawrence looked over at Penny. "Please, not now."

"Sorry," she mumbled.

"Go on," Lawrence urged Betty.

"Well," she began, throwing Penny a glare, "Doris told us he simply stands to one side whilst someone else serves. Plus, the first time she was in there and Doris's name was mentioned, he just stared at her."

Lawrence coughed. "If you'll pardon my mentioning one small fact, she's rather a stunning young lady. That would explain why he'd stare at her." Looking around the room, Lawrence added, "Just a thought, but where's Mary?"

"She's up in Scotland, with Doris, looking over her family manor," Jane told him. "They'll be back tomorrow for work on Monday."

"You're a hard taskmaster," Lawrence said, with a shake of his head and a quiet chuckle.

"Lots of planes to deliver, not enough pilots." Jane

shrugged.

"Well, I'll check what you said with her when she gets back," Lawrence told the room. "In the meantime, I'd really like to take a look at this chap for myself."

"Um, just a thought," Jane said. "If, on the off chance, this man has something to do with all this, wouldn't knocking on his door and asking to see him simply prove you're a policeman?"

"And working on this case, official or not, it wouldn't matter to them," Walter added.

As Lawrence got up to leave, Jane said, "How about, until this mess is over with, you meet up with us in my office on the station? I'm aware," she hastily added, upon seeing the expression which had come to Lawrence's face and correctly reading its meaning, "this means you can't see Mary around here for a while. I'm sorry, but I feel this is the best way forward."

Lawrence mustered a weak smile. "You're right. I'll be at the guardroom about six."

"I'll leave orders to the effect you're to be admitted with as little hassle as possible, until further notice," Jane told him.

"Ruth, should I assume you and Walter will be meeting up at the ops hut too?"

"Try and keep us away," Ruth replied.

"Right, fish 'n' chips for"—he paused to do a count—"six it is."

****

Lying in her bed that night, Doris flicked on her bedside light and turned to face the now illuminated face of her friend. "Are you awake, Mary?" When she got no response, she pulled out one of the pillows from beneath her head and threw it at Mary, whose eyes immediately flicked open. "Ah, good, you're awake."

"Well, I am now," Mary grumbled, sitting up and throwing the pillow to the floor. "What's wrong?"

Picking up the pillow, Doris hugged it to her chest and let out a squeal. "I can't believe I'm sleeping in a castle!"

Mary propped herself up on an elbow. "Firstly, it's not a castle, and secondly, you woke me up to tell me that?"

"Well, to your uncultured American cousins, it's a castle," Doris told her, still sporting a grin.

Mary peered at her watch. "Okay, at three thirty in the morning, it's a castle. Now, do you mind if we go back to sleep?"

"Go back to sleep?" Doris said. "I haven't *been* to sleep!"

Mary's flailing hand found the switch for the light between them and switched it off, plunging the room back into darkness. "Please try. I'm tired."

After a few minutes, Doris switched the light back on, and Mary groaned.

"Sorry, sorry," Doris told her, flinging her blankets and sheets back. "I'm going for a wander. I'm just too excited to sleep."

"Just be careful, and don't disturb the patients. At least they're asleep," she finished, grumbling and throwing her covers over her face as Doris pulled on her robe.

Five minutes later, Doris had managed to locate the torch she always carried in her bag. Opening the door to their rooms, she was greeted by the long, silent corridor which led toward the main staircase. Listening carefully, she could detect no noises apart from the odd low groan coming from downstairs. Switching on her torch, Doris padded her way along the wooden-floored corridor, thankful she'd remembered to pack her slippers. Shivering, she tightened the cord of her robe, which didn't help any. Mary hadn't been joking when she'd said the house got very cold in winter, let alone at night.

"Maybe just a quick scoot around," she mumbled to herself.

Coming to the top of the stairs, she paused and listened once more. The temptation to go down and have a mooch around was tremendous. However, Mary as well as Captain Wood had asked—nay, ordered—her to keep away from anywhere medical. In this house, that literally meant everywhere, except the rooms they occupied and the attic spaces. Doris remembered the relief on Mary's face when she'd asked about the attic, without specifying her childhood rooms, and been told that the officials had looked at those areas when they first moved in, but had decided it would be too awkward to use them for patients. Some of the medical staff had initially moved in to some of them—but not hers, he believed, though he wasn't a hundred percent sure—only to declare them too drafty. They had been much happier taking up residence in the Nissan huts erected for the personnel in the grounds. As Nissan huts were notoriously cold, this said something about how cold the attic rooms were. Once out of earshot of their new army friend, Mary had wiped her brow in relief.

A rapping noise startled her out of her reverie. Looking up, Doris shone the torch beam before her, trying to locate the source, and then turned around when she saw nothing and shone it back the way she'd come. Whilst her head was turned, it came again, this time from directly above her head and slightly behind her. With the torch beam fixed upon the ceiling, Doris took to her heels, the rapping noise insistent but low enough that she doubted it would reach the lower floors. Coming to a door, she pulled it open without even thinking it could be locked and was halfway up a narrow set of stairs before she turned around, briefly wondering why it wasn't locked. Then, not thinking of any reason it *should* be locked, dismissed the question as not worth dwelling on.

Nevertheless, when she came to a door at the top of the stairs, she stopped to push it rather than rush through. Closing it behind her, she found herself in a long, bare corridor. With no carpet upon the floor and only bare plaster walls, these had to be the attic rooms Mary had so fondly talked about when they first met. Flashing the beam of light down it, so far as she could see, nothing was around which could be making the rapping noise she could now hear more clearly than ever.

Suddenly, a flash of light came from the far end of the corridor. Taking to her heels, Doris hurried toward where she thought it had come from. Only when she found herself outside the last door on her left did she realize the noise had stopped. Holding her breath for as long as she could, she listened harder than she'd ever done in her whole life. Something told her this wasn't normal and could be important. By the time she had to take a breath, the rapping still hadn't come back.

"Well, this is going to be an interesting subject to talk to Mary about later," she told herself. Only then did she shine the beam of the torch around, searching again for what could have caused that flash of light. On the walls, she now noticed there were candle holders, but none had any candles in them…plus, she knew it hadn't been candlelight she'd seen. Apart from those, nothing else was of any interest in the corridor. Turning around, she noticed another door directly opposite the one she'd come through at the other end of the corridor. Surmising this could only lead back down stairs, she tugged on the handle and wasn't surprised to find this one was also unlocked.

Facing the door on her left, she placed her hand on this door handle and found it to be locked. Deciding upon a little test, she turned and walked back down the corridor the way she'd come, trying every door handle of each room. They were all on the same side as the locked one, and as she went, each opened, though all proved to be of no interest, containing not even a stick of furniture. She turned and made her way back toward the locked room. Bringing the torch beam up, she shone it around, quickly finding something to pique her curiosity. Taking a step closer, she read the sign on the door.

Mary's room. No admittance!

Chapter Seventeen

"Next!"

As he was the only one waiting to be served, Lawrence thought this was a bit foolish. Nevertheless, he took one more step to his left so he stood right opposite the man behind the counter. Taking off his hat, he nodded. "Hello, I'm Lawrence. I've not seen you before, what happened to Fred?"

Instead of replying straight away as he'd expected, the man, who had a very distinctive scar running from his temple to the left of his mouth, immediately brought a hand up to cover that side of his face and dashed around the back toward where Lawrence assumed the kitchen must be. As the woman they'd previously served exited the shop, this left as occupants only Lawrence and the chap who'd been leaning against the wall whilst the previous customer had been served.

Studying him, Lawrence had a strange sense of déjà vu. He couldn't place it, but though half in the shadows as he was with only his lower face visible, he had a chin, as weak as a baby kitten, which seemed to be all a quiver, even when he hadn't spoken a word the whole time Lawrence had been there. He coughed. However, the only response was another chin quiver, but this time, he brought up a hand to stroke that weakest of chins. Lawrence's eyes widened briefly. Now he knew Doris's instincts were spot on, as were his! That weak chin had started the bells ringing, but as soon as the man showed that hand, Lawrence was nigh on certain he knew who this person was—the hand was missing the two outer fingers. Nevertheless, he had to keep calm. It could still be a complete coincidence that he was here, if he was who he thought he was, though Lawrence didn't believe in coincidences, and it escaped him what this kind of person could be doing in Hamble for an innocent reason.

Despite being nearly sure, Lawrence decided it would be best to play the role he came to play and not to reveal or confirm what he was, unless it couldn't be helped. So he coughed again, and this time, the chap took a step, only a single one, toward him. Lawrence ramped up his role of disgruntled customer. "Look, I don't know what's wrong with your mate, but if I don't get six lots of fish 'n' chips to my friends in the next half hour, I'll be down six friends. I presume you're the new owner? Now, are you going to serve me, or not?"

What followed would have been funny as all hell, if Lawrence wasn't both concerned about getting some good food to his friends whilst also wishing he could go back to his Portsmouth headquarters and check his files. Obviously the man hadn't served a fish 'n' chip supper in his life!

Firstly, he was so nervous he dropped the chip scoop in the frying oil. When he reached forward as if intending to pluck it out, Lawrence had been on the point of yelling at him not to be so stupid, but in the nick of time the man pulled his fingers back from the boiling oil. Then the man made the mistake of placing the fish on the paper first, before shoveling a single scoop of chips over each and wrapping them up. Doris would have let him have it for being stingy with the chips!

During the whole farcical operation, he never said a word, though his being in unavoidably close contact with Lawrence did give the policeman several good opportunities to take a closer look at his face. The temptation to go into full copper mode was almost unbearable. However, he kept his cool and managed not to laugh when the man had to unwrap one package, as he'd included his chip scoop in that one.

"How much do I owe you?" Lawrence asked when the packages were finally ready and before him. Surely the man had to speak now?

Indeed he did, and Lawrence's instincts promptly went into over drive. He could almost hear a whistle going off in his head. The man had a voice like someone had kicked him in his gentleman's tackle—high, squeaky, and wheezing.

"Nothing. Take it as a present," he said in that strange, unmistakable voice. "I'm closing this shop down tonight."

Lawrence couldn't help himself. "Really? You've only been open a few weeks."

The man shrugged, came from behind the counter, and held open the door for him. "My business," he said. "Goodnight...*Officer*."

Trying to keep the surprise from his face, Lawrence picked up his packages and marched through the door, giving him a polite nod of his head as he went. This wasn't returned. As soon as the door banged shut behind him, Lawrence saw the man turn the sign to Closed and double-lock the door.

Despite the massive load of information and further possibilities going through his mind, the one which kept forcing its way to the forefront was, "If the fish 'n' chip shop is really closed, Doris is going to murder me!"

****

True to his promise, Lawrence pulled up outside the ops hut a few minutes after six. Waiting for him outside were the remaining members of the Air Transport Auxiliary Mystery Club together with, much to Jane's annoyance, a few guest members. Bobby yanked his leash out of Ruth's grasp immediately Lawrence had one foot out of his car, his nose buried in the bottom of the pile of newspaper packages he was juggling.

"Would someone mind grabbing hold of Bobby, please?" he asked, doing his best to fend off the hungry hound with the foot, whilst half in and half out of his seat.

Hurrying forward, it took both Ruth and Betty to drag Bobby off, so intent was he on claiming his share of the wonderful smell emanating from Lawrence's hands.

"Thank you," he said, once Bobby had been secured by his leash to a wooden post.

With Jane holding the outer door open for him, Lawrence entered, still acutely aware of a dog's nose too close to his behind for comfort. Turning his head, he said to Ruth, "Do me a favor and put some chips and fish on a plate for Bobby first? I don't think he'll leave us alone if we don't."

Laughing, Ruth veered toward the side of the hut opposite Jane's office and tied Bobby's leash to the foot of a desk. Kneeling down, she ruffled his ears and told him, "You be good, and I'll be right back."

As if he understood every word and what they implied, Bobby barked once and then sat down, his tail happily wagging away.

"You know," Betty said as she began to slide the fish 'n' chips onto plates spread across a cleared desk, "I swear he understands every word we say."

"Walter? Of course he does!" Penny answered, patting the startled newsman on his head and then darting away before he had a chance to retaliate.

"If I wasn't so hungry, Alsop," he told her, picking up a chip from the plate Betty pushed into his hands, "you'd be in a world of trouble."

After everyone had had a chance to have a few chips and a bit of fish, Betty asked, "So? What happened?"

Hurriedly swallowing some still-hot fish, Lawrence put down his fork to say, "Well, for a start, he's never served behind a fish bar in his life."

"It is rather untidy," Penny agreed in between mouthfuls.

Not really knowing how to answer that, Lawrence instead ignored it. "However, in all seriousness, I'd have to say Doris is spot on. The one who was serving when I went in made himself scarce as soon as I asked about Fred. By chance, that made it easier to get a look at the one Doris was suspicious of, as he had to serve up." He paused to take on board a few chips and some more fish before looking back up at his captive audience. "I've definitely seen his face before. Plus, what makes me even more certain, he's missing a couple of fingers, and his voice sounds a bit like Mickey Mouse."

"Who do you think he is?" Jane asked, between mouthfuls.

Lawrence shook his head. "I'd rather not say. At least, not until I've had a chance to get back to the office and check some things out."

"I can understand that." Betty then added, "But I need to ask you, how much danger do you think we're in?"

"Well, he definitely knows I'm a copper," Lawrence announced, causing everyone to pause in their dining. "He called me 'Officer' as I left."

"I suppose," Penny mused, "that doesn't really change much. All it does is confirm something we suspected."

"Yes," Lawrence agreed, "but don't let your guard down. Not," he hastened to add as everyone opened their mouths to protest at the same time, "that I expect any of you to do so."

"You do realize that when Doris finds out you've cut off her supply of fish 'n' chips, you're a dead man, Herbert!" Ruth told him, echoing his earlier thought.

****

Over a semi-warm breakfast of porridge the kitchens had sent up, Mary eyed her friend who, after being up half the night, still didn't appear tired. She wagged her spoon at Doris. "Are you trying to tell me you saw a ghost last night?"

Doris finished off her bowlful and washed it down with the remains of her cup of tea before replying, "I didn't say that…exactly. What I said was that I saw a strange light up in the attic last night."

"Which you couldn't find any reason for."

"Which I couldn't find any reason for," Doris agreed.

Mary let out a sigh. "I don't know what you saw, but we don't have a ghost."

"You're sure?"

"Positive." Mary nodded. "Believe me. My family's lived here for as long as I know, and I've never heard anyone mention a ghost."

Doris looked disappointed, but quickly rallied. "But

that doesn't mean to say there aren't any! Maybe they're..." She paused, thinking, as Mary watched her friend trying to come up with something plausible. "...shy!"

"Shy?" Mary repeated, sitting back in her seat and crossing her arms. "A shy ghost."

Doris mirrored Mary's stance. "Why not?" she said with a pout. "You don't have to be some dashing prince to be a ghost. It could be someone who always hides whenever someone living is around," she added, warming to her subject.

Mary sloshed her tea around in her cup, finishing it off at the same time there came a knock on the door. "Come in," she shouted, glad of the distraction.

The door opened and ushered in the receptionist from last evening. "Good morning, ladies," he said, closing the door behind him, whilst staying as close to the door as possible. "I trust you slept well?"

"After my friend there left me alone for a wander, I did," Mary answered and was rather surprised to see the captain's eyes widen in unmistakable panic before he recovered himself.

"You went for a wander?" he asked, unable to hide his curiosity.

"Uh-huh," Doris said after a few moments, during which she shared a quick look with Mary. "Only up to the attic, as you did ask us not to walk around downstairs. I didn't stay long. I'm sure you know there's not much to see up there, but—" she deliberately paused, hoping Mary would be following what she was saying, "—I did see something strange."

When she didn't elaborate, Wood had to ask, "Something strange?"

Resting her head on an upturned hand, coincidentally ensuring the officer could no longer see her left eye, Mary winked at Doris. "Doris thinks she saw a ghost!"

Wood was unable to stop his eyes opening wide at this statement. However, that could have been because of the word *ghost*. "Um, I'm not sure what to say about that."

Doris pounced. "Have you seen anything strange here? Do you know if anyone's seen a ghost? Mary here"—she pointed a thumb at where Mary was trying to keep a straight face—"swears there're no ghosts here."

Making a show of the action, Mary stood up and crossed her heart. "I've never heard of one, nor have any of my family ever mentioned any."

Standing a little straighter, Wood gestured at Mary's uniform. "I hope you don't think I'm being rude, but you're not Wrens, are you?"

"Don't hit him, Doris!" Mary burst out, causing the officer to back up until he collided with the door. Doris burst out laughing.

Doris got to her feet and pulled out a free seat at their breakfast table. "She's joking now. Come and take a seat, please." Once he'd done so, she added, "I never hit anyone before midday," and he did his best to shuffle his seat back.

"I'm joking!" Doris told him, giving him a smile which persuaded him to stop.

"I can see why you'd be confused," Mary began, running her hands down her trousers. "It's about the same color as their uniform, but we're both pilots in the Air Transport Auxiliary."

If the army officer had looked surprised when the

talk had been about ghosts just now, that was nothing to how he looked now. Even in 1944, there still appeared to be men who were surprised to hear of such a thing as female pilots. To his credit, he did recover his composure quickly. "You'll have to pardon me. I've spent most of the war out of the country since I joined up in thirty-nine. If you'll both indulge this ignorant idiot, would you tell me what that entails?"

"Go ahead," Mary told Doris. "I'll go and retrieve our hats."

As Mary got up to go back into the bedroom, Wood half got out of his chair, at least proving he had manners.

"In a nutshell, if an aircraft needs delivering anywhere, to any branch of the services in the country, then we deliver it," Doris informed him.

The man slumped back into his seat before asking, "Spitfires too?"

Doris laughed just as Mary came back into the room. "One of my favorites. Thanks," she said as Mary tossed her service hat to her.

Seeing Doris get to her feet, Wood did the same. "I just popped my head around as I wanted to see if you were comfortable and that the porridge didn't kill you. If there's a need, we use it to case broken limbs—works just as well as plaster!"

Both girls smiled at the weak joke, but enough that they hoped he'd see they appreciated his effort.

"Quite comfortable, thank you," Mary said.

"And if we feel like we're carrying around a rock in our stomachs later, we'll know to go and have a word with the cooks," Doris added, treating the man to her best evil grin.

"That, I don't doubt," he hastened to say. "So why

the uniforms?"

"Our boss made it a condition of allowing us to come up," Mary informed him. "We tend to get some respect when people find out we're doing our bit for the war effort, if they see a uniform."

"Even if they think we're navy," Doris cut in.

"Even if they think we're navy." Mary laughed.

"Plus, they help us get a seat on the trains," Doris added, seriously.

Wood placed his hand on the door handle. "If you'll forgive me one more question?" Both girls nodded. "You're here, doing what? I mean, my boss told me your parents own this place," he nodded to Mary, "which is why you're staying in his room for the night."

"That explains the pipe on the dresser," Doris said with a chuckle.

"If we don't see him, would you please pass on our thanks?" Mary asked.

"Certainly," he said, with a tilt of his head.

"And to answer your question, Doris here is getting married soon, and I've offered her the use of these rooms for her honeymoon. I wasn't aware your CO used this suite as his quarters," Mary then said. "I don't mean to be awkward, but I'm not sure that was the arrangement my father made with him, but we don't want to cause any trouble, so if Doris is okay with honeymooning here, we'll let you know."

Not giving the now obviously flustered officer a chance to respond, the girls made for the door, forcing him to back out ahead of her and Doris, until Mary was able to close the door behind them.

"Right. I'm going to show Doris around outside, and we'll be back in around an hour. I believe we're booked to take transport back to Aberdeen for midday?"

Now, thoroughly flustered, it took the poor man a minute to find his voice. "Er, um, right. Yes, that's right. I'll see to your bags, if you like," he offered. "I'll keep them in my office."

Mary shook her head. "That's all right. We're going to take a look around outside, but I want to show Doris my old room up in the attic before we go, so we'll pick them up on the way back down."

"The attic? Right, well, I'll leave you to it," he mumbled, before turning around and, somewhat to the girl's surprise, instead of heading downstairs as they expected, he shot off in the direction they both knew led toward the attic.

"What was that all about?" Doris asked.

Chapter Eighteen

After going around the manor house twice, Doris stood once more staring up at the front. Shaking her head, she asked the ever-patient Mary, "Explain to me again what 'neoclassical' means? It's nothing to do with classical music, is it?"

Mary waved her arms vaguely around, pointing, so far as Doris could tell, at random points of the front of the house, admitting, "To be honest, it's what my father always describes the place as. As far as I'm concerned, home is home, and I never really gave what it looked like any thought."

"So," Doris said, looking quite smug, "you don't know either."

Mary shrugged. "Not really. All I know is from what I've read. You see the columns either side of the main doors? They're meant to be in the Roman style, and the lack of embellishment on the walls is also supposed to be an indicator of that style."

"Hmm," Doris replied and turned back to stare around at the front. "Can I just say I love it?"

Mary drew her friend in for a hug before gripping her shoulder at arm's length. "You may."

"And I'm sure Walter will too. If the offer's still open, we'll take it!"

"Of course it's still open. You know you'll be under the same rules as we are today, I'd imagine."

Doris shooed away her friend's concerns. "Psh, I'm sure we won't be in the way. Certainly, we'll be eating down at the pub in the village, so I doubt if we'll see much of anyone here."

"Well, that's that," Mary said after a moment. She linked her arm through Doris's and led her back up the steps and into the entrance hall.

Stopping off at the tiny reception office, Mary recalled it had been the room where the family changed from their outside footwear. How the military had managed to shoehorn a desk in there, she had no idea. Either way, the perennial Captain Wood stood up, nearly banging his head on the ceiling in the process.

"Mary, Doris," he greeted them. "May I ask how things went?"

"You may," Doris imitated what sounded like a private school accent. "If you'd be so kind as to inform your CO, my future husband and I shall be staying for our honeymoon."

"And when, may I ask, are you getting married?" Wood asked.

"The fourteenth," Doris proudly informed him.

His eyebrows rose before he held out a hand. "Valentine's Day! How very romantic. My heartiest congratulations!"

Doris shook his hand, and then the two started to back out of the office, there being not really enough room to comfortably turn around, stopping as he said, "You've about thirty minutes until your transport's due. Would you like some tea? To pass the time."

"No, thank you," Mary replied. "I'm going to show Doris my old room, and then we'll grab our bags and be down in time."

He leant over his desk, shouting as they left the office, "I can give you an escort, if you like."

Before either girl could reply, a doctor came rushing toward them, his white coat flapping around his ankles and a very annoyed expression upon his face. Ignoring the two ATA girls, he put a finger to his lips. "Will you shut the hell up, Captain! The colonel's on his rounds, and you know he likes quiet!" As he turned back, he seemed to notice the girls for the first time, his demeanor changing to one of a fawning lackey, something both girls noticed. "And what can I do for the Wrens?"

That he misidentified what they were only further annoyed the two. Mary took the lead, mustering all her unused lady-of-the-manor mannerisms. "Firstly, old boy,"—both happily noted him bristle at being addressed thusly—"we are pilots in the Air Transport Auxiliary and not, I repeat, *not* Wrens. Secondly, I happen to be Mary Whitworth-Baines, the daughter of the owner of this place."

"And we do not require anything from you, thank you very much," Doris ended firmly. The two promptly re-linked arms and headed up the stairs.

As they took the stairs at a steady pace, they were met by a chap in scrubs coming down the other way. Before they passed, he leant in and said, "Nicely done. Pickering's only a major, but the way he behaves, you'd think *he* owns the place."

Doris stopped and glanced over her shoulder, just in time to see the major hurrying back the way he'd come. "Glad to be of service. Meet the lady who does own this place, Mary." She did the introductions. "I'm Doris."

"Pleased to meet you both. Lieutenant Oxford," he said, with a nod of his head, then saying, "What's up with

Wood? He seems to be watching what you're doing."

"It's my father who owns the manor," Mary supplied as she too glanced over her shoulder. "I've no idea," she said as the man in question noticed he was being watched in turn, and ducked back into his office. "He's a strange man. Or he acted very strangely when I told him I was going to show my friend where I used to live before we left."

Oxford shook his head. "Well, I agree he's a strange one. You'd think after six months he'd be used to the way things are."

Mary and Doris's heads immediately turned to face each other before Doris voiced what both were thinking. "Months? He told us he'd only been here a couple of weeks!"

"Well, can't help you with that," Oxford replied. "Got to be getting on. Nice to meet you both."

Left alone, the two shrugged their shoulders and carried on up the stairs, past their quarters, and to the same door Doris had gone through in the wee hours of that morning.

"Any idea what that was all about?" Doris asked, standing behind Mary as her friend opened the door.

"Not a clue," she replied, as she climbed the steps. Pushing open the door at the top of the steps, Mary waited so Doris could come through and then reached up to flick on a light switch, mostly hidden, toward the top of the door frame.

"Now that I could have done with knowing last night," Doris told her.

"Why, what did you use last night?"

"Flashlight," Doris answered.

"Come on," Mary told her friend. "My room's down

the other end."

"I know," Doris replied. "I found it last night, exactly where I saw the light."

Stopping before her door, Mary turned her head to ask, "You didn't go inside, did you?"

Doris laid a hand upon her friend's shoulder. "No. I'd never have gone inside without your permission."

With her friend's hand still upon her shoulder, Mary took a key out of her pocket. "You wouldn't have been able to get in anyway," she said, as with a decided creak, the wooden door swung open.

"You sneaky woman," Doris declared, slapping her friend lightly on the behind. "You knew it was locked, and you'd kept the key!"

"And I'd kept the key." Mary nodded over her shoulder and then stepped aside so Doris could step past and into the room. "Welcome to my little space."

"Wow!" Doris uttered as she stood beside Mary. "I guess, next to this whole castle…"

"Manor house," Mary corrected her with a smile.

"Castle," Doris insisted, "this is a little space, but for an attic, it's huge! I think my Central Park apartment would fit inside this whole room!" She stepped a little forward and looked to her left. "I could swear there are more doors in the hall, but there's none here."

"They're fakes," Mary told her. "Both sides of the house used to have staff quarters, but when I moved in up here, my father moved the remaining ones around to the back so they were all in one place."

"Weren't they a bit crowded?" Doris asked, going to the windows and flicking open the curtains, then coughing in the cloud of dust which enveloped her.

Laughing, Mary shook her head. "No, there weren't

that many. So then, he boarded up along the wall and left the doors where they were, though this room doesn't take up the whole side of the attic."

Brushing herself down, Doris nodded. "I saw. Nothing much left in any of them."

"We didn't see much point in leaving anything in them. This room," she swept an arm out, "isn't as big as it looks."

Doris raised an eyebrow. "You keep telling yourself that. Mind if I have a nose around?"

"Help yourself," Mary replied, making her way toward the far end of the room and a row of shelves, upon which were lined up soft toys, especially teddy bears, of all shapes and sizes.

Being a little more careful, Doris opened the curtains at the other three sets of windows, flinging open the last ones she came to and letting out a whistle. "Now that," she exclaimed, "is one hell of a view!"

Seeing where her friend was, Mary came and stood beside her. "It's one of my favorite views. Anyone who wants to come here has to come up that drive. Plus, if anyone came I didn't want to see, it gave me plenty of time to hide."

"Sneaky," Doris said, wrapping her arm around Mary's waist. Turning them both around, she let out another whistle. "Honey, I can see why you loved this place. You're alone, but if you want company, you've only got to go downstairs."

When Doris didn't add to these words, Mary turned her head and saw what could only be described as a melancholy expression upon her friend's face. "Penny for them?"

"Huh?" Doris grunted.

"Your thoughts. What are you thinking?"

Doris sniffed before saying, "I'm being silly."

Mary squeezed her friend encouragingly. "No such thing between friends." When Doris didn't reply straight away, Mary led her toward the single bed and sat her down, again in a puff of dust. "Now, come on, what's on your mind?"

Not answering right away, Doris stared around, taking in the room, flooded now with light. Green-patterned wallpaper that stopped three-quarters of the way from the ceiling helped, together with the white painted ceiling, to make the space appear larger than it was. A small writing desk was under the second window, the longest, so when she sat at the desk, Mary would have been able to look out down the drive. Two cupboards were either side of an expensive-looking chest of drawers.

Nodding toward the furniture, Doris asked, "Are those still full of your clothes?" Mary nodded. "Anything you'd like to bring back down?"

Getting up, Mary walked to the nearest wardrobe and opened the doors wide.

"Holy cow!" Doris uttered, stepping to her side. "There's enough gowns here to throw a party at the Ritz!"

Reaching out a hand, Mary idly flicked a few aside, running her fingers along the neckline of a red satin one. "You're probably not wrong."

"I guess I miss my family," Doris blurted out of nowhere.

Mary studied her friend closely. "I thought so. Is it this place? Does it remind you of home?"

"Oh, no." Doris shook her head. "Not at all. My

family may be rich, but they live in the heart of New York. My parents have a…I think you Brits would call it a six-bedroom town house. So it's big, but nowhere like this place. I don't know what made me say that," she then added after a minute. "Despite this being a hospital now, it's clear to see it will be a very fine family home again after the war. Ignore me. I can't wait for Walter to see it! He's going to love it."

Mary gripped her friend's hand. "I'm glad, and don't apologize. We're all missing people."

"Even you?"

Mary thought for a few moments before replying, "Yes, even me. I may not have got on that well with them, but now…now, yes, I think it would be good to see my parents."

"Then why don't you?" Doris asked the obvious question.

"Too busy," Mary replied.

"We all make time," Doris told her.

"Perhaps," was all that Mary answered.

As if she'd let out too much of her thoughts, Doris got to her feet and went to study her friend's soft toy collection. "This is quite a sight!"

Joining her, Mary seemed to relax as she looked at them with pride in her eyes. "My parents were never very imaginative when it came to presents," she said, looking up and down the shelves. A frown came to her face. "That's funny."

"What?" Doris asked, following her friend's gaze.

"Mr. Bunson's missing."

Doris arched an eyebrow. "Mr. Bunson?"

"My first bear," Mary said. "He's a Steiff."

"A Steiff?" Doris asked, not understanding what her

friend meant.

As she continued to search the shelves, Mary explained, "They're a German make, top quality, and Mr. Bunson…well, Mr. Bunson gave the best cuddles."

"You old softy," Doris told her. "And he's not here?"

Mary pointed at the center of the middle shelf. "When he wasn't in bed with me, that's where he stayed, pride of place."

"I hope you don't mind my asking, but why didn't you take him with you?"

Mary shrugged. "I don't know. Maybe a part of me always knew I'd be back."

"Was that why you wanted to come up here today? To collect him?"

"Now I think of it, probably."

A sharp, brief scraping noise made them both turn their heads, searching for its origin. Before either could begin a proper search, they heard a sharp rap on the door, which opened immediately, not giving either girl a chance to speak. Poking his head around the door was Captain Wood.

"Sorry to disturb you, ladies," he said, once he'd caught his breath. "Your transport's here."

Mary looked at her watch with a frown. "It's not due for another fifteen minutes."

Now with the door wide open, Wood tilted his head. "What can I say? The army's never on time. I'd take it, though, as there won't be anything else, I'm afraid."

The words may have been apologetic, but his demeanor wasn't, something which both girls noticed, yet didn't wish to comment on in his presence.

"Ah, well," Doris said. Only Mary was aware of the

false cheeriness in her voice. "Better get our bags, then."

"Has anyone been in here?" Mary couldn't prevent herself from asking, as she went to lock the door.

"I doubt it," Wood said. "No one's been able to find the key," he added, looking down at the one in Mary's hand.

"Bit of a pity, that," Mary told him, pocketing the key.

Chapter Nineteen

Detective Sergeant Terry Banks hurried along the corridors of Police Headquarters in Portsmouth that Monday morning. Firmly clutched in his hand was the information he'd spent nearly the whole day accumulating, alternately making numerous telephone calls, interspersed with searching through too many photo-fits and descriptions of known villains to think about, and reading documents in the archives. To begin with, he'd spent half the time muttering to himself about not knowing exactly why he was engaged in the exercise, Lawrence having provided him with a description of the person he was interested in, together with roughly where to begin. Only when he'd hit the bullseye within the second hour did he stop muttering and devote his full attention to the task. He may not have known exactly why he was doing what he was doing, but the photo-fit eventually led him to information which Terry was certain would be exactly what he'd been sent off to look for, and it made very intriguing reading.

Frustratingly, when he arrived back at his boss's office, Lawrence wasn't there. Deciding a celebratory cup of tea would be in order, he set to and was on the point of pouring when Lawrence appeared.

"Terry!" Lawrence said with a grin. "Any luck?" he asked without preamble, throwing himself down behind his desk and making a grab for the edge of his desk, when the action caused his wheeled chair to begin shooting him backward at a rate of knots.

Placing a steaming cup before him, Terry nudged the buff folder. "I think what you're looking for is in there, boss."

"Excellent! Take a seat, will you," he offered as he ignored the tea and picked up the folder instead. "And please don't mind me."

Taking the weight off his feet, Terry held his cup between cold fingers. Nobody ever thinks of heating basements, and naturally, that's where the archives were. His boss's expressions, as he read, alternated between frowns and nods and pursing of lips, until he placed the folder back down before him.

Lawrence looked up at his sergeant. "That's very good work, Terry, very good. I hope it wasn't too cold down there," he added, pointedly looking at the way Terry was still gripping the cup.

Terry grinned back. "Not too bad."

"If it makes you feel better, from what you've found, it was well worth it."

"Care to share why you're looking into one of Moseley's blackshirts?" Terry asked, not taking his gaze from his boss.

Lawrence didn't answer straight away. He leant back, clasped his hands behind his head, and without looking at him, said, "There's been an... *incident*, over at my Mary's place." Terry raised a very pointed eyebrow, and Lawrence raised one in response. "Yes, I know what you're going to say. When isn't there something going on around there."

"You've got to admit, boss," Terry said, sipping his tea, "they do have a knack for getting into trouble."

Shaking his head, Lawrence told him, "Not quite. I'd have to say that trouble has a habit of finding them. Of course, it doesn't help that one of them has a less than savory past."

"I've a feeling I know who," Terry replied, "but so long as you trust them, that's still good enough for me."

Lawrence gratefully nodded his head. "And I still very much appreciate that, Terry. Believe me, it's not misplaced."

Terry took another sip before asking, "So what've they got themselves into this time? Or shouldn't I ask?"

Lawrence had a good think before saying, "Perhaps I should have said this to you before I got you to do all that searching…"

"Buy me a beer, and we'll call it quits," Terry told him.

"Deal. Anyway, I'm investigating a piece of blackmail my aunt Ruth's best friend Betty's having trouble with."

"Blackmail!" Terry said in surprise, leaning forward, his interest well and truly piqued. "They don't do things in half measures, do they?"

Lawrence shook his head. "You don't know the half of it, and," he continued when Terry's eyebrows once more tried to disappear under his hairline, "believe me, you don't want to."

"Probably not," Terry agreed. "Carry on."

"Well, the first note was pushed through her door a few days ago, demanding five thousand pounds."

"Five thousand!" Terry couldn't help but interrupt. "How on earth would Betty have that much money?"

"I can only say," Lawrence informed him after mulling over his words for a minute, "she doesn't, at least not anymore." Terry looked skeptical, so Lawrence tried to elaborate. "This is the part where you have to trust me, Terry. I know exactly what she did, and...well, obviously, it wasn't legal. None of it, though, physically hurt anyone, and she's a very good person..." Terry still appeared a little unconvinced, "now."

Though he obviously still looked like he wanted to argue a point or three, Terry instead said, "Go on."

"She doesn't have the money, or I should say, she doesn't have the money any more. It's gone to charity, so even if she wanted to pay them, she couldn't. Things also took a more sinister turn a week last Sunday. Somebody tried to poison Bobby with some meat."

Terry looked confused for a short while before realization hit. "Bobby's your aunt Ruth's dog, yes?"

Lawrence nodded. "And to say she's furious is putting it mildly."

"I'd imagine." Terry nodded in turn. "I take it, from the way you phrased it, no harm came to him?"

"He's fine, and getting kept on a short leash at the moment, so he's not very happy. Then another note, accusing her of going to the police, and that's you up to date."

"And where does this chap you had me looking for come into this?"

"You remember Doris?"

"The Yank?" Terry nodded his head. "She's a bit hard to forget."

"Anyway, the chippie in Hamble has changed owners, and Doris didn't like the look of him, so I decided to go and take a look."

"Just because Doris thought he looked a bit iffy?" Terry asked.

"She's a bit of an acquired taste, especially at first," Lawrence admitted, "but her instincts are usually spot on. By the way, don't you dare tell her what I just said."

"Cross my heart," Terry told him, doing so.

"Well, this bloke, he doesn't know the first thing about serving a fish 'n' chip supper, for a start. More to the point, when I asked about the whereabouts of Fred, the previous owner, his mate buggered off without a word, and he never said a word about him. About all he said was to tell me the supper was on him and then called me 'Officer' when I left."

"Not much to go on, by itself," Terry muttered, before looking up. "I take it that's why we only have the description. Still, all things considered, he's rather conspicuous."

"Which is why I had full confidence you'd find him," Lawrence said, tapping the folder. "That's the chap, all right."

"From what I can see," Terry began, "I'd say he can't have been out of Holloway too long. I'm not surprised he's after money. From what we've got, his creditors took his house and everything else they could find whilst he was interned, so he's trying to get money any way he can. He must see Betty as an easy mark. I've a question—where'd he get the money to buy the chippie?"

Hastily pulling his forgotten cup of tea toward him before it went cold, Lawrence took a long draft before replying, "Good question. We'll have to look into that. He may have been born with a semi-silver spoon in his mouth, but if our suspicions are even partially correct, he didn't mind breaking a few jaws if he felt it needed to be done."

Terry turned the folder around and flicked it open before settling back. "Harold Verdon. Not someone I'd heard of before. Shall we go and have another word with him, boss?"

Lawrence shook his head, though his face showed his frustration. "Believe me, I'd like nothing better than to go and have a *word* with him, but apart from serving a terrible portion of fish 'n' chips, I've no reason to question him."

"Even taking into account his acquaintances?" Terry wanted to know.

"Unfortunately not."

"Should have left the bloody lot of them in prison to rot," Terry muttered, his eyes hooded and dark.

"Quite agree with you," Lawrence said.

Terry's head snapped up. "Any other suspects?"

"None come to mind," Lawrence admitted.

"Worth checking the blackmail note against a sample of his handwriting?"

Lawrence shook his head. "You can have my job, if he wrote it. He won't be that stupid."

They were both silent, contemplating for a while what they'd discussed. Then Terry asked, "I assume you've warned the girls to be on their guard?"

Lawrence nodded.

"I guess all we can do is sit and wait, then."

Lawrence leant forward, his face determined. "I'm not leaving the girls unprotected," he stated. "As we're off the clock on this one, I'm taking a few days' leave and going to camp out in Betty's attic. There's a window up there with a good view of the front. The girls are flying all the time, and I don't want them having anything on their minds but that, so we need to nip this in the bud as quickly as possible. I may need to be a little…unconventional."

****

"How did it go?" Stan asked, poking his head around Tom's door.

Tom looked up from the document he was reading. The shadows beneath his eyes seemed a little darker, but as they'd been such a part of him for so long, this was difficult to tell. "One funeral's much like another." He shrugged.

Coming all the way in, Stan shut the door behind him and took the seat in front of Tom's desk. Without needing to be asked, Tom opened the bottom drawer of his desk and took out the whiskey and a couple of tumblers. Pouring two measures, the two raised their glasses in a toast. "To Dashwood," Tom toasted, and they both knocked their drinks back.

"Cheers," Stan said, as they both retook their seats, "but I wasn't on about the funeral." At Tom's quizzical look, Stan cleared things up. "I meant with your missus last Thursday. I've been meaning to ask before, but, well, you know how busy we've been and how bad the last two sorties have been."

Tom ran a hand through his hair. "Tell me about it. That last one nearly gave me a new parting!"

"I'm going to start carrying you strapped to my hip, boss." Stan laughed.

Tom shook his head. "Don't get carried away, mate. You and I both know how close we're getting to the end of our tours."

Stan zipped his fingers across his lip. "Message received and understood. Now, your missus? Please? Sharon's dying to know!"

It took a short while for Tom to reply, and when he did, he started off by shaking his head. "In truth, I really don't know. Yes, it was lovely to see her again, but it felt as if we weren't married. I went to hold her hand and she hesitated." Stan waited patiently for his boss and friend to find his voice, which eventually he did. "I don't know if I can do this, Stan. We touched more on our first date, the real one, than we did on Thursday. Plus, her mystery club's involved in something else."

Stan regarded Tom for a few seconds before taking a deep breath and saying, "For the meantime, forget that. Do you mind if I'm brutally honest?"

Tom immediately shook his head. "Go right ahead, old son. You know there's nothing you can't say to me."

"In that case, and I don't know how this is going to come out, what you need to do is to treat this exactly as she said the other week—as if you don't know each other. You walked out on her whilst she was in hospital after being shot and losing a baby. You need to prove to her that she can trust you again, and if that means doing exactly what she wants, no matter what's happening down there with her friends, if you want to have a chance at a marriage, then that's what you have to do. You have to understand things from her perspective. Do you?"

By the time Stan finished, Tom was slumped back in his seat, his eyes wide open after listening to what his friend had said. "Wow! You weren't holding back!"

Stan waved the comment away. "Never mind that. Do you...*can* you see things like that? From what I know, that's exactly what happened."

"But..." Tom began, but Stan interrupted.

"And I know what you're going to say. A child meant everything to you, especially after you'd lost your brother. But—and I'm certain of this—you didn't mean what you said to Penny about her not caring she'd lost it. I know that, you know that, and that's probably the most important thing you need to come to terms with, and then find a way of making sure Penny believes you didn't mean it. There can't be any doubt in her mind on that point, or I can't see a way you two can get back together."

Tom didn't say a word. Instead, he took the whiskey back out of his drawer and poured two more generous measures. Pushing Stan's tumbler back toward his friend, he raised it in a toast to his friend. "Keep this up, you'll put the padre out of a job!"

Chapter Twenty

"I hate to bring the subject up, Doris," Betty said when they were all around the kitchen table, "but isn't someone supposed to be getting married tomorrow?"

Their favorite American was slumped over the table, her head buried in her arms. From somewhere amongst the mess of arms and disheveled hair, there came some mumbles. Mary reached over and smacked her friend around the top of the head. "Speak up!"

Doris raised her head enough to say, "I know!" before allowing it to slump back down.

The other four occupants of the cottage all looked at each other. "You ask," Jane said. "I officially know nothing."

"Wish I'd thought of saying that," Betty muttered, before turning back to say, "Well, unless you're going to tell us what's going on, we've an awful lot to do before tomorrow, don't we?"

There were more mumbles, swiftly followed by Penny taking her turn at swatting her.

Doris lifted her head again to speak, though now everyone could see that her eyes were red from crying. "We've had to put it back."

"Does the padre know?" Jane asked.

"He does. I spoke to him about this on Saturday."

"It would have been nice to know these things," Jane declared.

Doris wiped a hand across her eyes and sniffed. "I'm sorry, and you're right, I should have told you, only…"

She never finished what she'd been about to say. Instead, she dissolved into tears. This was all very un-Doris-like, and momentarily, everyone was too shocked to move or say anything. Penny was the first to come to her senses and, in one swift movement, was out of her chair and kneeling at Doris's feet, awkwardly wrapping her arms around her friend's waist.

"What's happened? Is it Walter?" she demanded, ducking her head under Doris's arm in case the man himself was present.

In between sobs, Doris blurted out, "There simply wasn't time! We ran out! I lost track of the date! I'm upset because my chip shop's closed! One day blurred into another, and before… And Hitler refused my invitation!"

Right up until this last declaration, all her friends, including Jane, had been making various cooing noises, trying to placate her. However, when this latter found its way into the world, they all looked at each other, Mary going so far as to rub her ears before, as one, they all burst out laughing.

"If that's not the strangest excuse not to get married I've ever heard, then my name's not Jane Howell!"

"What I'd like to know is how did you get an invitation to Hitler?" Betty asked.

Sniffing into a handkerchief she'd retrieved from her sleeve, Doris looked up, her face a visage of confusion. "I…beg your pardon? I invited…who?"

Mary wiped her eyes before telling her, "You told us you couldn't get married because Hitler refused to accept an invitation!"

Somewhat confusedly, Doris gazed around the sea of faces. "I did?"

"You did," everyone said at once.

Doris slumped back in her seat, her handkerchief falling to the floor. "Well, bloody hell!"

Before anyone else could say a thing, Jane had jumped to her feet and was clapping her hands for attention. "Right, you lot. I know there's a lot that needs talking about, but let's do it on the way to work. If we don't get a move on, we'll be late. I have it on good word that your boss is a tyrant!"

Ten minutes later, they'd turned the corner toward the station and were all striding along, arm in arm, whilst Doris relayed a slightly more coherent version of why the marriage had fallen by the wayside.

"Walter and I were talking before he went out on patrol on Saturday night, and we both came to the same conclusion at the same time. Though we'd decided upon Valentine's Day as a great time to get married, that was about all we'd done, made a date. Okay, we'd checked with the padre that he could marry us, but that really was it. Stupidly, we'd let the days turn into weeks, then into months, and we hadn't done anything else. I suppose I got a little cold feet, what with the way my first marriage turned out."

"Oh, Doris, from what we know about you, that's being very silly," Penny told her, leaning around Jane, who was between her and Doris.

"What about Walter?" Betty asked. "How does he feel about this?"

"Oh, you know Walter," Doris said. "He couldn't even arrange a honeymoon. He's one of life's reactors. He'd been quite happy to go along with everything I told him was happening for the wedding and thought everything was rattling along nicely." Doris stopped and scuffed the toe of her shoe in the dirt before looking around. "He feels guilty about not doing anything to help, though in fairness, I had told him I'd fix everything barring the honeymoon."

"What happens now? Do you still want the manor?" Mary asked.

Doris stopped the group once again and scooped Mary up in her arms in a huge hug, before setting her back down on the ground. "Oh, do I ever!"

"In that case, I suggest a house meeting tonight," Betty said.

They were approaching the gate guarding the station as Jane told them, "Don't worry, Doris, we'll sort everything out tonight. Go and bring Walter and Ruth over when we get back. In the meantime, business heads on, girls, and let's go deliver some planes."

****

"Where the hell have you been?"

In spite of being much larger in stature than his boss, Percy Croft quailed under those piercing blue eyes. Bringing a hand up, he rubbed a cracked, dirty finger along the scar marring his face, sorely wishing he'd not changed his mind and come back. Among a multitude of bad decisions, this was right in the top ten. Dumping his rucksack at his feet, Croft shoved his hands in his pockets before pulling them out and assuming a stance which could be mistaken for respect. Hopefully, he thought but didn't say out loud, the time would come when he wouldn't feel the age-old pull of servitude his family had with the Verdons. He'd had nothing but trouble all his life since becoming part of the household staff, and this latest was becoming the straw to break the camel's back. Hell, he was a deserter from the army now.

"Snap out of it, man!"

And all because he was still obeying his father's instructions to serve the Verdon family! "Bloody politics," he mumbled as he made a conscious effort not to look down his nose at the man.

Verdon took a step closer, "What was that you said?"

"Nothing…sir," he added, as was expected.

"In that case, answer the damn question!"

Thinking quicker than he'd done for a while, Croft made his face a blank. "I thought he was going to arrest me."

"Arrest you? Why?" Verdon asked.

Croft resisted the temptation to roll his eyes, wondering, not for the first time, how some people were supposedly the cream of society yet rarely deserved it and had the gift to bring everyone down with them. "Because I'm a deserter from the army. Like a bloody fool, I answered your letter to come and be by your side, again."

Verdon waved the protest aside, turning his back and walking back upstairs as if this explanation didn't affect him at all. "Stop bothering me with trifles." He turned and stood at the top of the stairs, using the extra height to his advantage. "It's no more than what you should have done. Everyone should know their place, you more than most."

Resisting the urge to pick up his rucksack and march out again, the thought of simply turning himself in being very tempting, Croft instead marched up the stairs and into the small flat's lounge.

"You do realize, by your running out as soon as that copper asked you one question, you've put my whole scheme in peril?" Verdon ranted, as he strode up and down in front of the pulled curtains.

Croft took a seat on the sofa, knowing from experience that his boss was going to be raving away for a few minutes and no input from himself was needed. Using a technique he'd found useful in basic training, he slowed his breathing, willed his limbs to relax, and began to hum a favorite song, Vera Lynn's version of "We'll Meet Again," inside his head.

Meanwhile, Verdon stalked up and down, occasionally waving his arms around. "Because you ran out, I had to serve him. Me! Serving fish and chips! I've never eaten the wretched stuff, and after being forced to live in this stinking flat, above a bloody fish and chip shop, I never will. Now I've had to close the shop, cutting off what little income I had, and pretending I've left by putting up a Gone on Holidays sign. I'm sure that copper recognized me, too. He didn't appear to be the normal type of country bumpkin you get outside the city, either, so I'll have to be careful, but also move up my plans. That bloody Betty woman still doesn't appear to have done anything about getting my money together, either. I've been watching—which should be your job, Croft—and all she's doing is going onto the wretched station and flying bloody aeroplanes!"

Croft had also been watching her and her friends, and so far as he was concerned, they were doing a fine job. Maybe he was becoming more and more delusional. He knew he hadn't been a good soldier—he suspected his old sergeant was quite pleased to be rid of him—and together with the dastardly deeds he'd done for Verdon and the other blackshirts, he'd quickly become quite ashamed of what he was. If he had his way again, he'd thought during his time away, he hoped he'd be a better person. Looking up, the weasel of a man before him was standing with his hands upon his hips and a look of complete disdain on his face. Sighing, he squared his shoulders and resigned himself to doing what his father would expect him to do.

Chapter Twenty-One

The cushion hit Doris square on the forehead, jolting the American awake.

"Hey!" she yelled, jerking her head from Walter's shoulder, where she'd been asleep since supper.

"Do try and stay awake," Jane asked, licking the tip of her pencil. "If we're going to sort out your wedding, it's a great help if the bride herself is *compos mentis*."

"Compos whatsit?" the lady in question asked as she ruffled her hair, stretched and yawned.

"It means, awake," Mary explained. "Generally."

Doris narrowed her eyes at where Mary sat on the edge of her seat. "Answer me this, Mary Whitworth-Baines. Just how are you so compost mentis? I don't remember you getting much sleep on the train last night."

Mary raised an eyebrow at her friend's slip of the tongue, yet shrugged and took a sip of her perennial cup of tea. "What can I say? I don't need much beauty sleep."

Doris began to bristle. Indeed, she opened her mouth—before Walter placed his hand upon hers and simply shook his head. Immediately, she nodded and leant her head against his shoulder again, but doing her best to appear wide awake and attentive.

"You're going to have to teach us that trick," Betty said with a small laugh.

"Teach you what?" Walter asked, earning himself an affectionate squeeze of his arm from his fiancée.

Betty rapped her knuckles against the table beside her. "That's enough," she said. "The sooner we get this sorted, the sooner you can go back to sleep, Doris."

"Good...plan!" Doris managed to say.

Mary held up a hand, exactly at the same time a knock on the door sounded. Putting her hand down, she got to her feet. "I'll get it!"

A few moments later, she came back into the room, towing Lawrence by the hand, closely followed by Ruth, who complained, "Don't worry about me. I'll take my own coat off. Plus," she added, grumbling, "you nearly took Bobby's nose off when you shut the door."

Obviously far from traumatized, the cocker spaniel trotted in behind her and wagged his tail at one and all before flopping down in front of the roaring fire in the grate. Ten seconds later, he was asleep.

"I've said it before and I'll say it again, that's a helluva trick," Doris stated.

Ruth lowered herself so she could sit beside her now comatose dog. Ruffling a fluffy ear fondly, she looked back up at her friends. "True. If I could bottle whatever he's got, I'd make a fortune!"

"I would have brought around some food, only the chip shop's closed," Lawrence announced.

With this statement, Doris's eyes snapped back open, and she was alert as anything. "Thanks for the reminder, Herbert!" she said, using his hated first name, which instantly got everyone's attention. "I knew something was on my mind. What did you do? Now, where am I going to get my fish 'n' chips from?"

Ignoring the jibe, Lawrence allowed a small smile to grace his lips before replying, "I'm sorry this is the result, Doris, but from the reaction I caused, the men I saw have to be the ones behind Betty's problem."

"You're sure?" Walter asked. "I'm not a believer in coincidences, and for the ones causing all this trouble to be so close to home is, well…a coincidence."

"And don't forget who put Lawrence onto them," Mary pointed out, directing her comment toward Doris.

Doris flopped back once more, pouting. "I suppose that's fair enough. Me and my big mouth."

"Look at it this way," Lawrence told her. "From what Terry and I have found out about the man you got suspicious about, your instincts are spot on."

"So who is this person?" Jane asked, leaning forward.

Lawrence consulted his notebook before addressing his friends. "It goes without saying that anything we discuss tonight goes no further. Are we clear?" He waited until everyone had either said yes or nodded at him. "Good. Any other answers, and I'd have made this official straight away. Now, there were two chaps in the shop. The one Doris has dealt with is called Harold Verdon. Bit of a nob—that's short for nobility, Doris—but don't let that fool you. He's quite a big supporter of Moseley, back in the day, one of his blackshirts. From what we've found out, he lost everything when he went inside. We figure he's trying to claw back some of what he once had."

"But why me?" Betty asked, voicing the question on everyone's mind.

Lawrence half-shrugged. "So far, Terry and I haven't found out the answer to that."

Betty replied, after a few moments, "Be sure that you do tell us, as soon as you find out."

"And this other chap you mentioned?" Penny asked.

Lawrence shook his head. "That one's a bit of a puzzle. So far, we've not found out anything, though we both figure he has to be a known companion of Verdon. Terry's working on it." From talking to the room, Lawrence now turned to Betty. "I need a favor."

"Go on," Betty told him, perusing him with a shrewd eye.

"I want to take up residence in your loft for the next few days, just in case something happens."

"Do you think something's likely to happen?" Jane asked, reaching for and squeezing Betty's hand in support.

To be fair to him, Lawrence didn't try to pull the wool over Betty's eyes. "Quite possibly. By himself, Verdon's not especially dangerous, but this other fellow? Well, he's this huge scar down one side of his face, and you don't get those by playing nicely."

"So why don't you pull him in for questioning?" Jane quite reasonably asked.

Shaking his head, Lawrence said, "Unfortunately, I have to play by the rules. So far, I've no proof he's done anything, so I can't do that, and—" Here he stopped and pointedly looked around the room. All the girls were in a dangerous line of work, but that didn't mean he wanted to see them get hurt. Already, in the time he'd known them, Betty had been stabbed, Jane and Penny had been shot down, breaking Jane's arm and leaving Penny with a gunshot wound to hers. Being brave was one thing, but erring on the side of caution was the sensible line. "By being here, I hope to lessen the risk of anyone else getting hurt."

"I guess," Betty said, getting to her feet, "we'd better see what the state of the loft space is. Mary's room takes up half, but I forget what the other half looks like."

As the two went to the door, Jane said, "If you two don't mind, we'll stay here. We got a little off the subject just now." As soon as Betty and Lawrence, closely followed by Ruth, left the room, Jane turned her attention upon the engaged couple. "Right, you two, it's been a long day, I'm hungry, and you need to make some solid decisions…now."

Both Doris and Walter raised their eyebrows at Jane's tone but then nodded, knowing she was right. "Well," Doris began, managing to string out the last letter for a few more seconds than necessary and subconsciously taking the ring from her first marriage out from around her neck and rubbing it between two fingers.

The motion didn't go unnoticed.

"You're still," Mary said whilst pointing out to Doris what she was doing, "wearing that, then?"

It took a while before Doris glanced down at her fingers. She let the ring drop, and it hung on its chain before she tucked it back down her blouse, noticing that Walter's eyes were still fixed upon the chain.

"You know," Penny mused, "there aren't many fiancés who'd be okay with their girl still wearing their dead husband's ring, albeit on a chain."

Doris's head snapped up, and she turned her full attention to Walter. "You know, I've never thought twice about taking it off," she mumbled, once again fiddling with the chain, though looking at Walter this time.

Walter shrugged before saying, "And I wouldn't ask her to."

Doris took one of Walter's hands in hers and, looking deep into the eyes of the one she wanted to spend her life with, told him, "And that's one of the many reasons I love you." After kissing Walter on the cheek, she sat back, reached behind her neck and unclasped the chain. "But it's only right that I should take it off."

Sitting with the ring nestled in her hand, Doris felt Walter clasp his hand over hers. "Keep it safe," he told her, returning the kiss.

"Oh, hell! Pack it in, you two, or I'm going to burst out crying. I've never seen anything so beautiful in my life!" Mary declared, launching herself at the pair, being rapidly joined by Penny.

"Nor me. Don't let this one go, you hear me?"

Doris's muffled voice said, "I won't."

****

Tom kicked the hatch open. Bitingly cold air spilled into the Mosquito, replacing the stale air which had built up over the long sortie. Dumping his parachute down the hole, he wearily exited the aircraft and immediately placed his hands on his hips and leant backward and to the sides, trying to work the kinks from his back. A groan above and behind caused him to shuffle a little away from the hatch, allowing Stan to follow him down to the safe surface of the hard standing.

"Tough one," his navigator commented as he mirrored his friend.

"Uh-huh," Tom said when he found his voice. "Good call," he added, bending down to pick up his chute pack, "spotting that One-Ten. Cheeky bugger, trying to sneak up on us out of the cloud like that."

Stan shook his head. "Only chance he had, trying to bounce us. Pity we don't have guns. Would be nice to get some payback for once, instead of just showing a clean pair of heels."

On half-dead feet, the two made their way to a waiting truck which had already picked up the other crews from that night's operation. The six men exchanged weary nods, more than a little relief showing on each face as they all recognized that everyone had made it back alive and unharmed from the sortie. Everyone's head either slumped back against the canvas of the truck's body or down onto folded arms on their knees, and not a word was said as they were driven back to the squadron offices to file their post-operation reports and talk with the intelligence officer. Though the operation to mine the waters around Heligoland, a small archipelago in the North Sea, had been routine, the fog and cloud had come down earlier than expected, giving Stan some trouble with his navigation and nearly allowing the German night fighter the chance to catch them unawares.

Tom nudged Stan with his boot.

"Boss?" he answered, not troubling to open his eyes.

"Remind me to buy you a packet of carrots later."

Stan cracked open one eye. "Leave that bumf for the newspapers. Make it a brandy, and you're on."

"It'll be my pleasure," Tom replied, shaking hands with his friend.

With a squeal of worn brakes, the truck deposited them outside their hangar, and the pilots and their navigators trudged inside, shading their eyes against the glare of the harsh lights. About an hour later, Stan followed Tom as he entered his office, shutting the door behind them and flopping into one of his old, comfy seats, his arms draping either side of the arms.

Leaning over his desk, Tom pulled a drawer open, extracted a half empty bottle of whiskey and two tumblers. Dangling it beneath his armpit, he said, "Sorry, no brandy."

Stan leant forward and pushed one of the tumblers back toward Tom. "Fill her up."

Neither knocked the drink back, knowing from long experience that their stomachs wouldn't react too well to alcohol so soon after a flight. Some got lucky, but neither Tom nor Stan fell into that lucky category, so both sat in the quiet of the office, savoring the company and the warmth the whiskey sent through their tired bones.

"That hits the spot," Stan stated, and when Tom didn't reply, he looked up to find his pilot staring at the framed photo of his wife he kept on his desk. Taking a quick sip, Stan cradled his tumbler. "Mind my asking...have you heard from Penny since?"

It took a moment before Tom seemed ready to reply. When he did, he appeared more fatigued than what normally resulted from the stress of flying an operational sortie over enemy territory. His eyes were hooded, dark, and seemed—though Stan would never think of himself as remotely poetic—empty. Stan knew Penny well and hated the estrangement the couple were going through and the effect upon his friend. So far, it hadn't affected his flying abilities, but allowing for that possibility, anything he could do to bring the two back together would also benefit and improve his chances of surviving the war.

"No," Tom replied, pushing the frame to one side, causing it to topple, picture first, onto the desk.

"Look, I'm no Casanova, but don't give up on her."

Tom mustered a weak smile and swept a hand through his hair. "I won't."

Chapter Twenty-Two

Matt held the door of the Victory pub open for Ruth, who ducked beneath his arm and then took it as they strode quickly back through the rain toward Riverview Cottage.

"Thank you for a lovely evening, Matt," Ruth said, snuggling farther into her boyfriend's overcoat.

Matt squeezed her waist and planted a kiss upon her head as they walked. "My pleasure."

"And more than I deserve," Ruth half mumbled.

Despite the rain, which was getting heavier, Matt pulled Ruth under an overhanging tree's branches and turned her to face him. "What do you mean?" he asked.

"For any number of things," Ruth told him, banging her head against his chest.

Laughing a little, Matt placed a finger beneath Ruth's chin and gently lifted it until he could see her eyes. "I know we've not been able to see much of each other lately, but you're not making much sense, love."

"I've not been much of a girlfriend," she mumbled again.

Matt lowered his head and, this time, kissed Ruth on the lips, both ignoring the rain now coursing down their faces, before Ruth buried her face under his chin.

"I'll try again," she said as Matt pushed her hair out of her eyes. "For standing you up..."

"When did you stand me up?" he interrupted. When

Ruth didn't reply straight away, Matt prompted her, "Ruth…"

It took her a few moments, but then Ruth answered, "When Thelma…died."

They'd stopped at the turn which led one way to Ruth's cottage and the other to the village and the church where Thelma was laid. Both lifted and turned their heads, and Ruth, for one, was glad the rain masked the tears she could now feel flowing.

Matt found his voice. "Now that's the end of that. You've nothing to apologize for, and I won't hear any more nonsense."

"Is it strange," Ruth asked, "that I miss her? Even though we didn't spend much time together? I mean, I don't have any idea if she had any family. I never asked. Isn't that terrible?"

Instead of replying, Matt took her hand and, to Ruth's surprise, towed her off in the direction of the village until they came to a stop before the lychgate of St. Andrew's. Stepping under the dubious cover it provided, Ruth asked, "What're we doing here?"

"Going to say hello to Thelma," he replied as the heavens did their best to drown them.

"But it's tipping it down."

"Do you think she'll mind?" Matt asked.

Ruth frowned. "You're not making much sense, Matthew Green."

"Aren't I?" he replied. "We'll see. Come on!"

After some time getting their bearings in the dark and searching through a surprisingly spooky dark-clad graveyard, they came to Thelma's grave. The grass hadn't had time to grow yet, so they both stood to one side of a slightly raised mound of earth, the simple headstone, clean and pristine, bearing the simple engraving:

Here lies First Officer Thelma Aston
She died for your freedom—3rd February 1944
Remember her!

Both stood still, the silence broken only by the wind whistling through the trees and the rain splashing upon the numerous graves and headstones. Eventually, Ruth managed to say, pointing at the words they'd both read, "If Doris didn't choose those words, I'll eat my hat."

A crash of thunder half-deafened them, causing them both to automatically duck. The rain began to pour down harder. "A hat wouldn't be a bad idea right now," Matt commented.

Ruth reached up a finger and flicked Matt's chip bag Home Guard hat, laughing. "Not that yours is doing you much good." She looked down at the grave and winked. "Eh, Thelma?"

****

"What the heck?"

"Sorry about the mess, Betty," Ruth uttered, shaking her hair.

Ruth looked down at her dripping wet coat, shoes, and stockings, inadvertently sending more water flying every which way as she shook her head in disbelief. "We didn't realize we'd stood there so long."

Betty briefly glanced past her friend before shutting the door. "Who's the 'we'?" she asked.

Surprise showing on her face, Ruth turned around on the spot. "Well, I'll be…I swear Matt was behind me. He did say he had to rush off for parade," she finished, allowing Betty to help her off with her coat.

"That'd make sense," Betty agreed. "Walter rushed

off not five minutes ago too. Come on." She took her friend by the hand. "Let's get you in front of the fire before you catch your death."

"Gracious!" Jane exclaimed, springing to her feet as the two entered the lounge. "You look like a twice-drowned rat! What happened?"

Ruth took a few minutes to warm her hands at Betty's fire before replying, "We stopped off for greetings to Thelma and lost track of the time."

It took everyone a short while to catch their meaning, but soon, typically, Doris made an attempt to make light of things. "And neither of you, I'm assuming this is Matt we're talking about, noticed the rain?"

Ruth turned around so the fire could dry the backs of her legs. "We may have noticed a little bit of precipitation in the air, yes."

"Cup of tea's what you need," Mary declared, getting to her feet and leaving the room for the kitchen.

"I take it you left Bobby at home?" Penny asked.

"He looked so cozy on the foot of my bed, it seemed a shame to disturb him," Ruth answered.

A burst of thunder timed itself perfectly. "And I bet he hasn't moved an inch since," Jane added with a laugh.

Feeling she was dry enough, Ruth took a seat upon the sofa. "In hindsight, he's a most wise spaniel. Still," she said, "I'm very glad I went. Doris, I love the inscription," she told the American.

Doris raised an eyebrow, with a sad smile. "I think she'd approve. What do you say?"

Mary opened the door. "Hey! Some of us want to hear what's being said. What did I miss?"

Doris told everyone what she'd chosen as the inscription upon Thelma's headstone, and shortly, very shortly, there wasn't a dry eye in the house. Betty had to remind Mary to go and take the kettle off before it boiled dry, though no one else was able to find their voice for a good while.

When Jane managed to drag herself upright, she went to sit next to Doris. Drawing her into an embrace, Jane told her, making sure everyone in the room—and Mary—could hear, "Doris Winter, you never cease to surprise me. Promise me one thing?"

"What's that?" Doris asked, once she'd loosened her friend's arms so she could speak.

"Don't stop trying to surprise me."

****

The sight which met Lawrence as he entered the room made him stop and stare. A pot of tea, cups, and saucers sat upon the table, but no one in the room seemed to be interested in the beverage. Standing in the doorway, hands upon his hips, all he saw was every occupant seemingly trying to hug every other occupant.

"Well, I can't see that anyone's died…" he began, but got no further, as they all burst into tears. Not knowing what he could have done to cause such a reaction, Lawrence did the only thing he could think of. Stepping into the room, he poured himself a cup of tea and waited.

Ruth recovered herself enough to clamber to her feet and, with a quick wipe of her eyes and nose, went over to her nephew. "You must think we're all mad."

Lawrence made the mistake of agreeing. "The thought had passed through my mind," he said, earning himself a playful whack upon his arm. "So what did I miss? And what did I say to cause…that!"

Ruth turned toward where everyone else was also in

the process of blowing their noses and wiping their eyes dry. "We...myself and Matt, that is...have paid Thelma a visit."

His cup was halfway to his mouth when his aunt said this, and it stayed there. "Talk about putting my foot in my mouth," he uttered, staggering back until he collapsed into a fortunately vacant seat.

He looked so distraught that Penny hurried to take the cup from his shaking hand before he dropped it.

Ruth leant over him and pressed her forehead against his. "Don't be upset. It was...good."

Surreptitiously wiping a stray tear from his eye, which the girls all pretended not to notice, Lawrence stood up. "If you'll all excuse me, I have to go back to the station. There are some preparations I have to make. Jane," he said after retrieving his hat and coat, "do you mind if I come and see you tomorrow afternoon? I'm going to need your help in smuggling myself back here without our little friends noticing."

Jane nodded. "The guardroom already has its instructions. Come along to the ops hut. Penny and I will be there."

Chapter Twenty-Three

"When you lot have quite finished laughing…"

Lawrence left the sentence unfinished as none of his friends, let alone his girlfriend, was taking a bit of notice. Dumping the duffel bag he had upon his back onto the floor of Betty's hall, he tramped past the five girls, all of whom were still gripping each other in fits of laughter and slumped down on the stairs.

Pulling off his shoes, he massaged his stockinged feet, rubbing their soles and glaring up at Mary, who upon seeing the sight of bare white thigh where his skirt had ridden up, had dissolved into more hysterical laughter. "Honestly, Jane, was it really necessary to wear the whole uniform? Couldn't I have worn trousers instead?"

Wiping her eyes, Jane went over and laid a hand upon his shoulder, and though her shoulders were shaking as much as anyone's, she told him, "I told you I had an idea to smuggle you in so no one would be able to tell it was you, didn't I?"

For whatever reason, Lawrence let out a "Harrumph," got to his feet, and without any regard for who was present, hitched up his skirt and unclipped his stockings before rolling them off and holding them up for Mary to take. "I don't know why I had to wear stockings, though. Bloody things took an age to get on!"

Mary stretched out her stockings before rolling them

up and tucking them away in her pocket, telling him, "If you had shaved legs, they wouldn't have been a problem."

No one noticed Ruth and Walter in the open doorway.

"Oh, I wish I had my camera on me!" Ruth wailed, her eyes wide at the sight before her, as Lawrence had hefted his duffel and was halfway up the stairs. Only problem was, his skirt was stuck on his thighs and the view everyone was getting was one only Mary seemed to not find amusing.

"You might want to tug your skirt down," she shouted, but he ignored her and continued up the stairs. They heard the bathroom door open and close.

"Would..." Walter began, before he had to take a breath to compose himself, "would someone like to tell me exactly what I've just seen? I don't know whether to hope I'm asleep because, if I am, this is some kind of weird nightmare, or to just tear my eyes out."

"Shut the door and come into the kitchen," Betty replied.

Once everyone had hung up their bags and hats, they all traipsed into the kitchen, where Betty was already filling up the kettle. From somewhere above them came the sounds of stomping feet and muttered curses.

Mary cast her eyes around at her gathered friends, most of whom looked like it wouldn't take much for them to fall about laughing once more. "Please," she asked, looking around, "when he comes back down, don't make fun of him."

Walter looked like all his birthdays had come at once. "Are you joking? I've never seen anything like it in my life! Plus," he added as Mary opened her mouth to protest, "if I know you lot right, then you spent every moment, since you first saw him in that get up until Ruth and I came in, ribbing him nonstop. Am I right?"

At least nobody had the nerve to deny this, with no one able to meet his eye. Walter sat back in his seat, a self-satisfied expression upon his face. Doris noticed this and punched him on the arm.

"Hey! Normally, I'd agree with you. However, I think we've already done enough damage, so please, please be kind. Remember, you still need to ask him a question."

Walter opened and closed his mouth a couple of times. "Bugger, I'd forgot!"

"Forgot what?" the subject of the conversation asked from behind them. Now changed into a pair of gray trousers and green pullover with the collar of a white shirt sticking up, Lawrence pulled out the chair next to Mary and, planting a kiss upon her head, sat down.

Ruth and Mary both nudged Walter at the same time.

"All right!" he grumbled, rubbing each side of his ribs. "Mate," Walter said, "the sweet Doris…"

"Sweet?" Betty interrupted, nearly missing the teapot when she began to pour the water out of the kettle. "You're certain you're talking about Doris?"

Doris shot Betty a venomous look. "Careful! I'm sure I can dig up another bridesmaid, if it comes down to it."

"Drink your tea," Betty told her friend, placing a cup before everyone and then adding the large teapot in the center of the table.

"As I was saying," Walter tried once more, "Doris

and I…"

"Hey!" his fiancée interrupted him. "Aren't I sweet anymore?"

Showing infinite patience, Walter told her, "Of course you are, always. Anyway, if I can continue…Doris and I are going to get married on her birthday."

Ruth reached up and ruffled Walter's hair. "Which I still say is a very clever way of never forgetting either one."

"And I haven't decided if it's the sweetest or cheekiest thing I've ever heard of," Doris added, batting her eyelashes at Walter.

"So that gives us two weeks before the twenty-seventh to work with," Walter valiantly ploughed on.

"Well, that's very good to know," Lawrence said, but what do you want to ask?"

"For cripes' sake!" Walter muttered. "All I wanted to ask is, will you be my best man?"

Without hesitation, Lawrence got to his feet and held out a hand. "I'd be delighted. You look so excited you're liable to go off on honeymoon without your bride."

Walter got to his feet and accepted the handshake. "Obviously, you can wear a suit or a skirt. The choice is up to you."

"Ha, bloody ha!" Lawrence replied, though he managed to keep a smile upon his face. "Thanks very much for the tea, Betty, but do you have any Guinness in?"

Doris pushed her seat back and stood up. "No, but give me a bit of time, and I'll get some in from the Victory." Finished, she made her way into the hall.

"Care for some company?" Walter asked over his shoulder.

"Always!" she replied, holding out her hand.

"Right, while you pair are getting in the drinks"— Lawrence clapped his hands together—"I'll go and get my attic spyhole sorted out."

"And Penny and I will get the stew on. Hurry back, you two!" Betty yelled as Doris and Walter shut the door behind them.

****

"Alone at last!" Doris whispered to Walter as she passed through the gate he graciously held open for her.

Walter scanned the riverbank before taking her arm as they began to walk along the now nearly pitch-black path.

"What're you looking for?"

"Do you think Duck's likely to attack us?" he asked nervously.

Doris let out a chuckle, shaking her head. "No, I doubt it. He's usually asleep by now," she said, feeling Walter relax a little at her words.

"Fair enough," he replied, drawing her in a little closer, the two falling naturally into step. "Come on, it's a chilly night, so the sooner we're back, the better."

Ten minutes later, carrying a wooden crate of the previously mentioned black liquid between them, they were comparing how their days had gone when they were brought to a sudden stop by what sounded like the crack of a stick being snapped. After looking at each other, they both shrugged their shoulders and carried on as before. They'd barely gone five yards before another crack broke the quiet, and this time, at virtually the same time, one of the bottles exploded.

"What the hell?" Doris yelled, as they both nearly dropped the case.

Another crack, and this time there could be no doubt. "Someone's shooting at us!" Walter yelled.

"Never!" Doris shouted, pulling Walter and their cargo behind a tree.

Only just in time, as no sooner had they'd hunkered down than two more shots struck the branches above their heads, showering them in twigs and pieces of bark. Covering their heads, the two huddled together, endeavoring to make themselves as small as possible. Another shot rang out, this time churning up the ground a foot or so to the left of Doris's outer foot.

"Bloody hell!" she quite rightly swore, tucking her foot farther under her body.

After this, the silence which followed seemed to stifle and surround them. Listening closely, neither could hear anything except the gurgle as the river flowed past.

When a minute had gone by and nothing further happened, Doris whispered, "I don't suppose you've a gun on you?"

"If I did," Walter replied, with a shake of his head, "I don't think I'd give it to you."

"Why not?" Doris exclaimed, snapping her head to frown at him. "I'll bet I'm a better shot than you!"

Another shot punctuated their argument, and this time the bullet slammed into the tree trunk itself.

"Let's have this argument later," Doris suggested.

The next bullet clipped the cap off another bottle, the liquid beginning to squirt in the air, soaking the rest of the crate.

Before she could stop herself, Doris shouted at the top of her voice, "Will you stop wasting my Guinness!"

When no further shots followed after five minutes, each edged a head cautiously around a side of the tree before jerking back. Another minute later, they looked again, and when no further fire came their way, they nodded at each other and, grabbing the crate once more, scrambled to their feet and took off as fast as their legs could carry them to The Old Lockkeepers Cottage, barely stopping to open the gate. Not troubling with the blackout, they burst through the door and promptly slid to the floor.

"What the hell?" Penny exclaimed, from where she was holding the telephone. Replacing the instrument, she knelt beside the pair, her mouth open to berate them for their disheveled and mucky state. However, before she could open her mouth, she noticed both were breathing heavily, and their eyes were wide and staring. She turned her head to shout, "Betty! Jane! Everyone! Get here, now!"

To the accompaniment of thundering feet and many different questions, all of which she endeavored to ignore, Penny gently prised the fingers of both from the crate they still held, noting with a deep frown the smashed bottles. "Someone get me some tea towels," she ordered. More gently, she took Doris's chin in hand and turned her so she could look her in the eyes. "What happened? Clearly you didn't break the bottles yourselves," she added, hoping a little levity would calm her friend down. "Take a deep breath. You're both safe."

After following Penny's advice, Doris said, "Someone tried to shoot us!"

Everyone, including Lawrence, who'd nearly fallen down the loft ladder in his haste to answer Penny's call for help, drew in a sharp breath. Acting on instinct,

Lawrence hurdled the pair, yanked open the door, and ran outside. Thirty seconds later, he was back in, shutting and locking the door behind him.

Mary immediately smacked him around the head. "That wasn't very smart, was it!"

Lawrence opened his mouth, but Ruth beat him to it, fixing him with a glare. "No, it flaming wasn't! What the hell did you think you were doing? Someone shot at this pair and you run outside, without knowing what's out there? Have you got a bloody death wish?"

Lawrence joined Penny in helping Doris to her feet and into the lounge. Jane and Betty did the same for Walter, and both were placed before the fire. "Stay there," Penny ordered. "I'll be back in a moment." Rushing into the kitchen, she came back with two mugs and a bottle of sherry. Pouring two generous measures, she pushed the glasses into Doris and Walter's unprotesting hands.

"You believe me?" Doris asked, before taking a sip.

Penny sat down beside her friend and flung an arm around her shoulders. "Of course I do! You're both mucky, there are smashed bottles—and I know you love your Guinness too much to allow that to happen by accident—and it's not the kind of thing anyone would make up. So, if you can, what happened?"

Doris and Walter shared a look before Doris told their story. When she'd finished, all their friends could do was sit there and shake their heads before Lawrence announced, somewhat understatedly, though echoing what everyone else was thinking, "This ramps things up. He's getting desperate." He strode to stand before the window where everyone could see him. "I wasn't expecting this. Doris, Walter, I can only say I'm sorry."

Both waved his apologies away. "I can't guarantee he won't try this again, but I doubt it. However, I want you all to not do what I just did when you go out. Be careful, and keep the front door locked for now. We won't find anything tonight, but I'll ring Terry and get him out here first thing tomorrow morning to see if he can find anything."

"Do you think they're watching us? Now?" Jane asked.

Lawrence shook his head. "All the same," he addressed Ruth and Walter, "I suggest when you go home tonight, you go out the back way and take Bobby's route home. I don't see how they'd know about that."

Ruth straightened up from where she'd been down beside her nephew. "I'm glad I left Bobby at home. How're you two doing?"

"Fine," Walter answered, holding out a hand to Doris, who gripped it tightly, not letting go. He looked up. "We'll be fine. Won't we?"

Doris's face took on a grim façade. "You just let him try something so cowardly again, and I'll show him the real meaning of hurt!"

Chapter Twenty-Four

Percy Croft propped his rifle against the table and went to fill up the kettle. Despite his heavy sweater and coat, he was shivering. It had been a cold evening. Though he'd deliberately missed, a part of him had enjoyed putting the wind up them with his near misses. He wiped the back of his free hand across his brow, popped the lid on the kettle, and lit the gas. Dropping a spoonful of tea into the teapot, he took his coat off and hung it behind the kitchen door. He'd just stepped back when the door flew open with such force it crashed back against the tallboy behind it, nearly hitting Verdon in the face.

"Well? Did you get them?" he demanded, pushing the door open a little more carefully.

Unwilling to face his boss yet, Croft kept his back to him whilst willing the kettle to boil. A cup of tea was just what he needed to thaw out his bones. "No," he replied, turning off the gas and taking the kettle to the table.

Verdon didn't wait for his servant to finish pouring the boiling water into the pot before he was in his face. "No? Is that all you've got to say?" Verdon turned and, throwing his hands into the air, proceeded to stride up and down, though no words left his mouth.

Surprised at how calm he felt, in spite of his boss's reaction, Croft stirred the teapot and asked, "Care for a cuppa?"

If Croft knew what color puce was, he'd have been amused at the shade his boss's face went at this innocent suggestion. However, he only just managed to snatch the teapot from the path of Verdon's sweeping arm.

"A cup of tea? Are you asking me if I want a cup of tea?" he demanded, spittle spraying from his lips, causing Croft to take a step back. This was misread by Moseley's man as an indication of supplication on the younger man's part, as Verdon took a step forward and took a handful of Croft's sweater. "I'm waiting for an explanation!"

Croft bunched his muscles before, with a supreme effort, he forced himself to look down into a pair of cold brown eyes. It helped his own temper that at least when Verdon had spoken he hadn't spat in his face. Croft was used to dealing with disrespectful people by using acts of extreme violence, but no matter the temptation, until he could see a way out, he'd stay his hand. However, this didn't mean he would put up with what he was increasingly coming to think of as an extremely obnoxious man trying to push him around. It wasn't like he was being paid. That thought prompted his hand to come up and prise Verdon's fingers off his jumper. This done, he turned to put the teapot back on the table.

"It's quite simple," Croft began whilst pouring himself a cup. "It's so dark out there, I could barely see a hand in front of my face."

"So? Why not just get closer?" Verdon demanded.

Croft picked up a spoon, poured a spot of milk, and stirred before replying, "Because I didn't want to give them a chance to see me, if I missed."

"And you did miss!" Verdon felt the need to shout.

Croft decided to remind him they were supposed to be in hiding, and the chip shop and its accommodation supposed to be empty. "Keep your voice down, sir," he said, casting a quick glance to make certain the blackout curtains were well in place so as not to give him any chance to argue. "We're supposed to be hiding, remember?"

Verdon opened and closed his mouth once, twice, a third time, knowing his servant was right but undecided as to how to react. He fell back on the age-old response of waving away what had been said as if it were of no consequence and told him nothing he didn't already know. "Never mind that," he began, though he had lowered the level of his voice. "I want you to have another go tomorrow night."

It didn't take Croft more than a few seconds to make up his mind. He shook his head.

"No?" Verdon said, shaking his head in disbelief. "I'm giving you an order!"

Croft took a seat and wrapped his hands around his cup to warm them up. "No. I won't do it."

Verdon pulled out a seat opposite Croft, paused, and then poured himself a cup before settling back, steepling his hands and asking, "Enlighten me. What's brought on this crisis of conscience?"

To give him some time to get his thoughts in order, Croft took a few sips of his drink, glad of the warmth it helped put back in his bones. It had been a chilly night, and the flat had no heat, not an ideal thing on a February night. "That was in the past."

"Which isn't very long ago, only a year or so," Verdon felt it necessary to point out.

Croft shook his head, as if trying to shake off the

memory of the deeds he'd done. "True, but these people are decent. They're not criminals. They're doing a good job of work, from what I can tell, so you tell me exactly what this Betty has done to you and let me think about what I'll do."

"You'll think about what you'll do?" Verdon repeated. Croft could see the effort it took not to shout. "You *don't* think what you'll do, you do what you're told," Verdon stated. "That's the way it's always been, and that's the way it will be…and don't you forget it."

Croft thought whilst Verdon sat and eyed him. Again he mused that if a way out presented itself, he'd take it. The only thing he could do was bide his time. "Perhaps," he said, whilst thinking the status quo could change before very much longer. He decided to ask, "Maybe you should tell me what this Betty's done to you?"

At first, it appeared Verdon would either shake his head or tell him to mind his own business. However, maybe the way Croft had stood up to him made him decide to tell him. He ran a hand through his thinning hair. "Betty Palmer had a twin sister, Eleanor. The bitch was a jewel thief known as Diamond Lil. Rubbish name, though I'll admit she was very good at what she did. She's dead now, so forget her, but her sister was her fence. Between the two, one cleaned out my safe, and this Betty fenced all the jewelry I kept there. I'll bet they got a tidy sum, too."

"So you want what they got from hawking that stuff?"

Verdon nodded, remembering his cup and taking a sip. "You bet. With my house gone and none of my old *friends*," he spat this out in distaste, "willing to help, it's the only way I'll get enough money to buy my way out of this country."

A thought struck Croft. "I take it you'll be getting two tickets?" He waggled his eyebrows suggestively.

Belatedly, Verdon nodded. Croft noticed the delay, though, and made a mental note not to forget this moment.

"Of course. Don't worry, I'll take good care of you," Verdon added, though his eyes never met Croft's. "Now, if you're not going to try and shoot them again…" He waited to see if Croft would change his mind. When he didn't, Verdon, with obvious reluctance, carried on. "…then at least go and put a letter through Palmer's letter box. Also, don't forget to give our *guest* something to eat." Without waiting for a reply, Verdon left the room, presumably, Croft thought, to write the missive to be delivered.

Knocking back the remainder of his tea, Croft decided two things. No way was he going to harm either this Betty or any of her friends, as none of them had done anything to deserve death, assuming what he'd just heard had been the truth. Even in the past, he doubted he'd have brought himself to do so. Helping them wouldn't do his cause any harm. And he definitely needed to find a way out of this mess. To hell with Verdon!

****

Jane threw a piece of chalk at Penny, which bounced off her head but still failed to garner her attention. Shoving away from the door where she'd been leaning, she took a few steps, bent over her friend's shoulder, and saw her friend had been doodling little Spitfires upon the report she was supposed to be writing. She bent down and said in her ear, "Earth to Penny!"

Glancing up, Penny put down her pen. "Sorry. I was miles away."

"I noticed." Jane smiled. She canted her head, the better to look at the report. "Nice doodles. If we need anyone to camouflage our planes, I'll keep you in mind."

Penny flipped the page over, a little embarrassed.

"Something on your mind?" Jane asked.

Penny got to her feet and went to switch on the kettle, only to find it empty and their water bottle also lacking. Seeing this, Jane swiftly returned to her office and grabbed her hat and jacket. "Come on. The next taxi isn't due back for a good half hour, so let's go and risk one of Mavis's."

Penny pulled her own hat and jacket on and followed her boss out of the hut. Neither said a word for the couple of minutes it took them to walk to the mess, and when they entered, they were the only occupants, barring the mess manager herself, who sat at a table reading a newspaper.

"That'd better be the *Hamble Gazette*," Jane said, taking a seat next to Mavis, "or Ruth may have a word or two to say to you."

As usual, Mavis didn't reply. Instead, she folded up the paper, which was the latest copy of the local newspaper, and got to her feet. "You two ran out of water again?"

"Uncanny," Jane said with a shake of her head.

Whilst Mavis busied herself, Jane turned to Penny. "Care to share? I know you don't like the job, but you don't usually lose focus like that."

It took a minute for Penny to gather herself. "I know." She sighed a bit before unbuttoning her jacket. "I'm...confused."

"About what?"

"About Tom. The walk we had, it felt like we didn't know each other. I'd made the decision not to even hold his hand, keep things as I'd suggested, you know, as if we were only starting out."

Jane frowned. "But isn't that exactly what you wanted?"

"It is!" Penny cried, her head slumping back.

"I'm confused," Jane muttered before saying, "And, how do you feel?"

"Rubbish! A fake!" Penny replied, letting out a bitter laugh.

"I'm going to say something silly," Jane ventured. "Have you asked yourself do you love him? Don't think about it."

"Yes. No! Yes, I think I do."

"And does he know this?"

Still with her head back, Penny laughed again. "I'm sure he's just as confused as me. Especially after the other night."

"Just talk to him," Mavis unexpectedly told them, depositing their cups and re-taking her seat. "Men are simple creatures. They need things spelled out to them. The shorter the words, the better."

Both Jane and Penny sipped from their cups before Penny said, "I can't deny that logic."

"Well?" Mavis asked.

Under Jane's and Mavis's scrutiny, Penny raised her cup to her lips again, though this time she didn't drink. Instead, she said, "I'll come to a conclusion and talk to him."

Mavis pulled her newspaper back toward her, opening it up once more and finding her page before saying, "Make sure you come to the right conclusion for you, that's all I'll say."

Jane turned to face her mess manager. "Mavis, you keep this up, I'll make you our station psychologist."

"Is there a raise in it?" Mavis enquired, not looking up from what she was reading.

"How does a new tea urn sound?"

Without looking up or batting an eyelid, she replied, "Let me think about it," causing Penny to cough up her last mouthful all over the table. Again without looking up, Mavis handed her a rag which, shaking her head, Penny used to clean up.

Jane flashed a raised eyebrow at her friend, which Penny answered with a nod and then, remembering what Doris had said about their enigmatic mess manager, asked, "Have you heard from your son lately, Mavis?"

This unexpected question caused Mavis to look up sharply. Contrary to the recent conversation, Mavis was usually a lady of few words, and she now reverted to form, though she did look happy to be asked. "Yes, I got a letter a week ago. He's been promoted to Lance Corporal."

Jane briefly squeezed one of Mavis's hands. "Oh, congratulations! You must be so proud."

Mavis took them by surprise by letting out a laugh which would more accurately be described as a cackle. "Oh, I am. Mind you, I pity his men. He'll be a holy terror!"

Any answer was cut off by the station alarm blaring out. Immediately, all three women shot to their feet, their chairs shooting backward and falling over.

"What's going on? Are we under attack?" Mavis cried as they all surged toward the door.

As Penny raced past them toward the flight line hut, Jane stopped long enough to grab hold of Mavis, stopping her from following Penny. Raising her voice to be heard above the wail, Jane told her, "Stay here. We're not under attack."

"But what does all this racket mean?" Mavis asked, cutting Jane's explanation off.

Grim-faced, Jane finished, "It means we've a plane coming in that's in trouble. Do me a favor, Mavis—get a big pot of strong tea ready. I've a feeling we're going to need it."

Chapter Twenty-Five

After the second time the Anson bounced back into the air, Doris swore loudly and gritted her teeth. Wishing she could wipe the sweat from her brow, she concentrated and set the taxi firmly down at the third time of asking and then focused on braking before she ran into the ditch at the end of the runway. She'd managed to avoid that ignoble honor so far and didn't intend to spoil her record today. Applying left rudder to counteract the lack of her right engine, she brought the Anson juddering to a halt a mere ten yards from the ditch. Now she had the chance, she wiped her forearm across her forehead and began to taxi toward the flight line hut.

"Everyone all right back there?" she hollered, jerking her head around to see her five passengers give her a nervous thumbs up.

Before the plane had come to a full stop, Penny was jerking the access door open, narrowly avoiding being dragged along the ground five yards for her trouble. Coming to a final stop, she held the door open as everyone hurried past her, all except Doris, who was performing the shut-down checks, and Mary and Betty.

"You okay?" Penny asked the two, and when they both nodded, asked, "What happened?"

Betty looked up from where she'd bent down with her hands upon her knees. "I hate bloody seagulls!"

Jane, who'd now caught up with the situation, was

shocked. Betty rarely used profanity, so she knew immediately something drastic had happened. "Er, explanation, please?"

Doris had joined them by now. "I'll tell you what happened. We ran into a flock of seagulls as we were on finals, and one lost a battle with my starboard engine. Had to feather the bloody prop," she ended, slapping the side of the fuselage in annoyance.

Penny pulled Doris into a tight hug. "Well done you!" She got what could have been a very muffled, "Thank you," but Penny proceeded to tell her, "Explain everything to the engineers, get changed, and then come over to the ops hut. I'm afraid there's some paperwork to fill out."

Whipping off her flying helmet, Doris placed it in the open door. "Certainly, Second Officer," she replied, though she threw in a jokey salute so her friend knew she wasn't serious. "I'll speak to them as soon as I've checked if there's any damage other than it needing a new prop or engine."

"Care for some company?" Mary asked, clapping her friend on the shoulder. When the American nodded, she was already ducking under the wing, and Mary turned and told everyone, "I'll stay here, and we'll see you all in a bit."

"Cup of tea?" Penny asked.

"Do you need to ask?" Mary replied.

"Any chance of a coffee?" Doris's voice asked from where she appeared to be trying to climb inside the engine nacelle.

"What do you think?" Jane quickly got in.

"Didn't think so," Doris muttered.

Jane bent down so her voice would carry better. "If

you will break one of my planes..."

"Ha, bloody ha!" Doris replied, emerging, hair all askew.

"Keep an eye on her," Jane whispered to Mary.

****

With all the required paperwork complete and the crippled Anson towed into the hangar for a thorough inspection and then repair, everyone was in the process of gathering their jackets and bags together when Penny's telephone rang.

"Second officer Penny Alsop," she answered. "What can I do for you? Uh-huh. Hold on! Mary!"

From where she waited leaning up against the doorway, Mary looked up and then went over to take the proffered receiver. "Hello, this is Mary Whitworth-Baines. Lieutenant Oxford? Ah, Lieutenant Oxford! Yes, I remember you now. What can I do for you?"

"Anyone know who this Oxford is?" Penny asked, going to stand beside Doris and Jane. Both shook their heads.

"Shh," Doris said. "Trying to listen," she added unashamedly and seemingly unaware her hair was standing on end, whilst she had oil marks streaking her face.

Meanwhile, Mary had perched on the edge of Penny's desk. "Hmm, yes, yes, I'm glad you decided to tell me. No, Captain Wood hasn't called. Yes, I think he should have too." Mary nodded increasingly vigorously whilst Lieutenant Oxford spoke at length until she said, "Leave it with me. I'll have a word with my boss, and I'll call you back as soon as I can. Do you have a number I can ring at any time? No, I'm not sure when that'll be, but I don't think it'll be long," she added, looking over at where Jane, who'd obviously heard this half of the conversation, had raised her eyebrows and was aiming a silent question Mary's way. Going slightly red, Mary then told him, "In fact, give me this number and I reckon I'll be five odd minutes, one way or another. Speak to you soon," she added after another few seconds.

Jane barely waited for Mary to replace the receiver, with both Penny and Betty watching with undisguised interest, before asking from across the room, "What's happened, and exactly what do you need to ask me?"

"Doris," Mary called, "perhaps you'd better come over. This may affect you too."

"Whatever it is, I didn't do it," Doris immediately joked as soon as she joined the other two.

"Mary…" Jane prompted.

"That was a Lieutenant Oxford, as you no doubt heard," Mary began. "He's a chap I ran into back home. He wanted to give me some, well, bad news."

Doris grabbed hold of one of Mary's hands. "What's happened?"

When Mary looked up, her face radiated fury from every pore. "My room's been wrecked! Someone even tried to set fire to it!"

Doris stumbled as Mary shot to her feet and ran over to Jane. Grabbing her hands, she implored Jane, "Please. I've got to go up there!"

Despite the desperation on Mary's face, Jane showed exactly why she was the boss. Instead of replying straight away, she kept her breathing steady, unhurried, not ignoring the way Mary was grasping her hands, merely not acknowledging it whilst she thought. After what probably felt like an eternity to her waiting friend, Jane blinked and said, "I understand how this must make you feel. You know that, don't you, Mary?" Mary nodded and went to speak, only for Jane to continue before she had a chance to interrupt. "However, I have to think of the deliveries. You know there's rarely a let-up, so my first thought is, can your parents go and look things over instead of you?"

Mary instantly let go of Jane's hands and turned her back. Betty went to move toward her. However, Jane shook her head. When she turned around, Mary's face didn't appear quite so anxious, though she did begin with a shake of her head. "I don't know."

"You know your father's telephone number?" Jane asked, and after Mary had nodded, said, "For me, give him a call, if you think he'll be available. We'll wait outside, give you some privacy."

"I think Father will be in. They're staying at the townhouse in Edinburgh for the duration," she added, picking up the telephone receiver whilst Jane ushered everyone outside.

As soon as she'd shut the door, Jane turned to Doris. "What do you think? Did anything happen whilst you were up there?"

"Just because things seem to happen to us…" Doris muttered.

Jane fixed her friend with a hard stare. "And…"

With a shrug of her shoulders, Doris replied, "Well, now you're asking about it."

"I knew it," Jane muttered, shaking her head. "Come on, out with it."

Doris sat down on the wooden steps before looking across to where Jane was waiting. "Neither of us mentioned it because, until now, I at least hadn't given it another thought. Mary thought one of her teddy bears—

don't laugh—was missing. In fact, we were about to begin a search when the officer from reception interrupted to say our transport was ready."

After a few moments, Jane said, shaking her head, "Is that it? Nothing else?"

Doris shook her head too. "I can't think of anything. Mary locked the door, pocketed the key, and we left. That's it, so far as I know."

They heard the door open behind them, and Mary came out, slamming the door behind her. "That's not all."

"What did your father say?" Betty asked.

Mary came and slumped down on the steps, resting her head against Betty's shoulder. "He said he'd be willing to go to the manor."

"Excellent!" Jane said, rubbing her hands together and beginning to button up her jacket once more.

Mary looked up at Jane and shook her head. "No, not excellent. He's broken his leg and can't go anywhere."

"What about your mother?" Penny suggested.

"She never goes anywhere without my father," she answered.

"Bugger," Jane swore, turning and going back into the hut.

The others exchanged glances before hurrying after her.

"What're you doing?" Betty asked, as Jane rummaged around on her desk.

"Checking the schedule for the next few days," she replied, as one piece of paper after another was looked at and discarded.

"Why?" Mary asked, poking her head around the

office door, though the others noted she'd crossed her fingers behind her back.

After scribbling on a fresh piece of paper for a minute, Jane then looked up and yelled, "Penny! Get in here!"

Nearly instantaneously, Penny appeared. "You called?"

Jane ran her hands through her hair before looking up. "I can't believe I'm saying this, so don't get your hopes up that this'll be a permanent thing, Penny." She looked over to where Mary was still poking her head around the door. "Mary, you're on leave tomorrow. Take a Magister and make your way up to Turnhouse. I'll have transport waiting to take you up to the manor. You'll have to make a couple of stops to refuel, but I'm sure you can work those out for yourself. Remember, this is only for tomorrow. I expect you back at work the day after. Go and work out your route whilst I chat with Penny."

"Are you sure?"

"Don't make me think twice," Jane replied. "This is obviously very important to you, and I'll always try and help one of my girls if I can."

"I hope you don't mind my asking," Mary ventured, "but how come you're able to arrange this transport? Doris and I were wondering if you've got something on…" Jane raised an eyebrow. "With someone," Mary finished, knowing it sounded a little lame.

"That's for me to know," Jane said after making Mary wait a minute. "Now, haven't you got something better you need to do, other than ask questions to which you won't get answers?"

Only pausing to nod, Mary turned back and made for the map storage.

Jane turned to address an obviously excited Penny. "I don't really need to say anything, do I?" Penny had the grace to at least appear contrite. "It's only for tomorrow. I'll take the blame if anything happens, so…" She looked up and smiled. "Make sure nothing does."

Penny held out her good arm, and Jane got to her feet to shake the hand. "I'll make certain it doesn't. Thanks for trusting me."

****

You were lucky last night. Take that as a warning. Time is running out, Aston. I want my money! You now have five days or I shall kill you.

"And you didn't see anyone?" Betty asked Lawrence again.

Lawrence shook his head, his frustration clear for anyone to see. "No. Whoever put this through the letterbox, they're as quiet as a cat."

At the mention of the word *cat*, Bobby, who'd been keeping Lawrence company by the expedient of sleeping on his lap, jarred awake. Looking around the lounge and not seeing any feline intruders, the cocker spaniel woofed once and then promptly went back to sleep.

"Neither did Bobby, it appears," Jane commented.

Doris turned the envelope over and pointed at the writing on the reverse. "What do you make of that? It's different writing to what's inside."

No one will die.

Chapter Twenty-Six

Taxiing her Spitfire toward the dispersal at RAF Church Fenton, Mary spotted a curious sight. An RAF Bedford truck had just pulled up a few yards from where she was being waved in to a halt. By itself, this wasn't anything out of the normal. However, what had just jumped down from the back was. Tapping the brakes, Mary brought the Spitfire to a stop, waited for the ground crewman to place chocks under her main wheels, and went through the shutdown procedure.

Sliding the cockpit hood back, she shucked off her harness and stood up on the seat. Glancing across, she was pleased to see that the man and his escort were both standing still, having watched the fighter roll up, and were waiting to see what would happen next. What she did next caused one to drop his flying helmet to the ground. Assessing the situation to be safe, she took off her own flying helmet and shook out her hair. Unhinging the door, she clambered onto the port wing before hopping off and walking over toward the two.

"I wouldn't go over there, miss," urged the same man who'd placed the chocks under her wheels.

Mary stopped and treated the man to a beaming smile, resting a hand upon his shoulder. "I'll be okay. Could you refuel her, please? I've got to be on my way in thirty minutes."

After initially scratching his head, the man shrugged

his shoulders and turned to the task, obviously feeling she must know what she was doing.

For her part, Mary left her Sidcot suit zipped up as she came to a stop before an RAF regiment corporal and his German officer prisoner. "Hello, Corporal, busy day?" she asked, nodding at the German.

Like many forces men, the corporal wasn't totally sure where he stood. He could see the wings on her suit which were not unlike Royal Air Force ones—you'd have to know what you were looking for to tell the difference from any distance. He decided to play safe and threw her a pretty good salute. "Pretty busy, ma'am. Just picked this bugger up."

"Spitfire...pilot?"

Turning her head a little so only the airman could see the right side of her face, Mary gave him a quick wink, then nodded at the German and said, "That's right, Fritz." She mimed machine guns, together with a "Dacka-dacka" noise. "Busy day." She finished by pointing up in the sky and then at the German airman.

As his prisoner promptly went white with shock, the airman caught on to what Mary was doing and added, "Many female fighter pilots"—and the German went even paler.

"That's enough of that."

Unseen by either of them, the corporal's sergeant had appeared behind them and, judging by the way he was struggling to keep a straight face, had heard every word.

"March our guest over to the guardroom, Ballcock, and lock him up."

The sergeant waited until the two, with much glancing back and scratching of his head on the part of the German, were out of earshot before turning his attention to Mary. "And who, may I ask, are you?"

Mary watched his right arm twitch, as if he was also unsure whether to salute or not, before quickly telling him, "Third Officer Mary Whitworth-Baines, Air Transport Auxiliary," and holding out her hand.

Shaking both it and his head, the sergeant replied, "Barry Nicols. Mind telling me what all that was about?" he asked, jerking his thumb over his shoulder.

Mary mulled over her answer for a few seconds before saying, "Call it a little psychological warfare." At his still bemused expression, Mary elaborated, "When he gets to a POW camp, he's not going to be able to stop himself. He'll have half of them wondering if they were shot down by a woman. Can you imagine how that'll affect the superior Nazi mind?"

She'd no sooner finished than Sergeant Nicols burst out laughing. "You cheeky bugger!" he told her. "I'll have to tell the bods who come to take him off our hands, make sure they use that to get some good intelligence out of him."

Pleased to see he'd seen the funny side, Mary relaxed a little.

The sergeant noticed the refueling operation going on. "I won't ask where you're off to, but do you have time for a cup of tea?"

Mary glanced both at her watch and then at the work going on behind her before turning back to the now friendly sergeant. "There's always time for a tea. Could you point me in the direction of the nearest toilet first, though?"

Smiling, Nicols offered her his arm. "Follow me."

****

Once again, though this time on her own, Mary settled into the back seat of the car which had picked her up from Turnhouse and squirmed around, willing some feeling to come back to her bottom. At least she wasn't frozen like she would be if she'd had to take a Magister as originally planned. Luckily, Jane had conjured out of nowhere the delivery of a Spitfire up to Scotland. One thing about the Spitfire—and most aircraft, if she thought about it—were the uncomfortable pilot's seats, which she'd never get used to. True, the last thing you need is to be so comfortable you'll fall asleep. Crashes tended to happen that way, but would it really be asking too much for someone to create something which met the two extremes half way?

The next thing she knew, the car was pulling up to the manor. Rubbing the sleep from her eyes, Mary looked at her watch. Two-ish in the afternoon. Not bad. Mind you, she was very aware she wouldn't be able to stay long, not if she was going to catch a train back home and still get any sleep that night.

Her door being opened snapped her back to the world. Hastily grabbing her bags and acutely aware she was still in her flying suit, Mary heaved herself out of the car, accepting the hand the driver gave her. "Thanks. Do you mind my asking? Will I be able to get a lift back to the train station?"

Before answering, the driver rummaged around in his top pocket, pulling out a note pad. Flipping it over, he came to a stop and read out, "I'm to be available to drive you into Aberdeen as soon as you're ready. That's what it says here, miss."

Suspecting she knew the answer, nevertheless Mary asked, "Who do your orders come from?"

"From my CO," he replied and, as Mary went past him, added, "though he did mutter something about cursing the day he met someone called Jane Howell. Does that name mean anything to you, miss?"

Stopping, Mary quickly decided she didn't want to know. Perhaps she and Doris were onto something after all? "Sorry, never heard of her. Meet me back here in an hour, please," she told him, before going up the steps and into the reception hall.

With only thoughts of seeing what had really happened to her room in the forefront of her mind, Mary was halfway up the stairs before she heard the voice of Captain Wood calling her name.

"Second Officer Baines! Is that you?"

Mary turned and waited until the army officer had reached the step below her. "It's Whitworth-Baines, to be exact. Good to see you, Captain Wood."

"What are you doing here?" he asked without preamble, staring up at her.

She couldn't help it. Something about this man set her senses on edge. It wasn't that he was particularly bad-looking—more ordinary, if anything. He had something to hide! The thought struck her out of nowhere and took her breath away. Exactly where or why it had come, she couldn't think. Maybe because she'd been hanging around her fellow mystery girls for what seemed like an age, she didn't dismiss the thought out of hand.

However, all this didn't mean she had any reason to be rude to him. Surmising, quite correctly as it turned out, that she should have seen him as soon as she came in, she put on a small smile. "Sorry about that, Captain. I suppose I should have…what, signed in first?"

This small sentence seemed to placate the man, and with a sweeping gesture, he motioned her to follow him back to his office. Once she'd signed in, he asked, "Would you be, if you brought anything, of course, more comfortable if you changed?"

Mary looked down at her rather disheveled state and shrugged. "That'd be a good idea."

"In that case," he said, getting to his feet, "I'll go out of my office, and you can get changed. Don't worry, I'll stand guard outside." Matching words to actions, he left the office, pulling the door shut behind him.

As Mary was pulling on her ATA jacket, she heard him say through the door, "Can I ask what brings you back up? I didn't know you were coming."

"I had a telephone call from a Lieutenant Oxford. He told me my old room had been ransacked, that someone had tried to set fire to it."

Only silence came from the other side of the door, and when still she heard nothing by the time she'd finished dressing, Mary flung the door open to find the man had gone.

"That's very rude," she muttered to herself, before shouldering her bag and making for the stairs once more.

As if she were once more a child, on her way to the one place in the building she'd felt safe in, she allowed her feet to take her up the stairs and through doors, until she stood before her bedroom door. Reaching out, she turned the handle, and her eyebrows rose in surprise to find it unlocked. Frowning, she took the key out of her pocket, pulled the door closed and tried the key. It gave her no problems, it locked, and the door wouldn't open until she unlocked it. With nothing else for it at that moment, she pushed the door open and went in.

Looking around, her eyes were immediately drawn to some scorch marks under one of the window panes. Well, if that was all the damage the supposed fire had done, she could live with it. Then she looked around more closely and found there were the same marks under each window. Why would someone try to set light to the windows? Surely there were easier things, much more inflammable things, which they could have chosen. Her eyes were drawn to her collection. Any of her teddy bears, for example. Or her books? Mary narrowed her eyes and scrutinized the shelves. Moving closer, she did another count, though it made no difference. Not only her favorite but another was also missing.

Pausing, she listened. At first all she could hear were the sounds of the hospital at work downstairs, nothing out of the unexpected. Closing her eyes, she turned slowly around on the spot, reaching out with her arms. That same feeling which had come to her before, just as Wood interrupted them, was back, and stronger than before. Something about her room felt…wrong, and it wasn't the minor fires, either.

Opening her eyes, she took in a deep breath. The closing eyes bit hadn't helped, not that she had any idea why she thought it would. From what she could see, if someone had ransacked the room, she couldn't see any sign of it now. Perhaps some of the books, toys and teddies were in the wrong place, but she could put those back easily enough. As her eyes passed the back wall, she stopped and canted her head to the side. Not really knowing why, she walked toward it, her fist raised, but before she could knock, the door opened.

Without looking, she asked, "Can I help you, Captain Wood?"

As she turned around, she saw she was right, and the man had stopped half in and half out of the room, his hand still on the door handle. "Sorry. I...I didn't realize you'd be here."

Mary shot him a quizzical look. "Strange thing to say, given what we talked about downstairs."

The officer appeared nonplussed and still hadn't let go of the door handle. "Yes. Sorry. Um, other things on my mind, you know. Is there anything I can do? To help?"

As he was there, Mary decided to ask, "I suppose you could tell me if you know who did this?" She went over to one of the windows, to make certain he could see what she was referring to. "Not to mention why. Plus, how come the door was unlocked? I've got the only key, but you obviously knew it *was* unlocked when you came in just now."

When Wood didn't say anything straight away, Mary decided she may as well go and investigate the wall, as she'd been about to before she'd been interrupted. Raising her fist, she brought it back and was about to hammer on the wall when there came a cry of, "No!"

Chapter Twenty-Seven

Mary stayed her fist and turned her head to look at where Wood was advancing toward her with his own hand raised. "No?"

The captain came to a halt only a few steps from where Mary stood before the wall. From the look on his face, he was as surprised as Mary to find himself where he was. His hand fell to his side, and he took a couple of steps back. "I'm sorry," he said, shuffling his feet. "I didn't mean that to come out as an order."

Turning around, though still not moving away from the wall, Mary told him, "That's okay. We don't take much notice of the military trying to order us around anyway."

From the way he didn't reply straight away, clearly Wood didn't know what to make of her statement.

Seeing this, Mary half turned back, began to raise her arm and then, without preamble, "What are you trying to hide?"

Instead of answering, Wood sprinted the few yards to the door and slammed it closed. Turning back, he walked more slowly until he came to a stop before her. His eyes appeared haunted. Mary put down the encyclopedia she'd picked up. If he'd attacked her, she'd been quite prepared to strike him around the head with it.

Desiring to keep things polite, she searched her

memory for Wood's first name. "Mark, why don't you tell me what's going on?" Mary laid a hand on the wall she had her suspicions about. "This wall." She rapped it, noting that it sounded hollow when it never had in the time she'd lived here, but she managed to keep her surprise from her face. "It's moved."

The lack of surprise at her statement on Wood's face only confirmed what she'd just heard. "How do you know?" he asked, though the question sounded more like he only asked it because he thought Mary was expecting it.

Wood pointed to the wall against the corridor. "The wallpaper is out of line, when it wasn't before. Plus..." She traced a faint line on the wood floor. "There's an arc here. As if some door swings out?" she ventured.

She was slightly annoyed when Wood slumped down on her bed, not that he noticed the frown upon her face. He glanced up at the wallpaper and then down at the marks and shook his head. "I thought we'd covered everything."

"We?"

Wood looked into Mary's eyes. "Can I trust you?"

Though her first impulse hadn't been to like this man, she hadn't given the matter of giving her trust to him any thought. In fact, after the earlier visit here with Doris, she hadn't expected to see him again, despite the feeling she'd had then of something being wrong. Taking her time, she studied his face, looked into his eyes. Nothing set off any alarms. Though he was obviously hiding something, she didn't get the impression he was likely to hurt her. She made up her mind.

She held out her hand. "You can trust me, Mark. Obviously, if you're up to anything which could hurt me, my friends, or anyone in this hospital, then any deals are off. But until then…"

"Fair enough."

"I have to ask, though, what's with the fire and some things being…not where they should be?" Mary asked.

"He was only looking at your things, and as for the fires? Well, that's my fault. Some matches slipped out of my pocket one time when I was up here, and he was playing around."

"He?"

Mark got up. "Watch," he simply said and walked past her to the wall. As Mary had done, he raised his fist and rapped quickly three times, followed by two slow ones and finally two quick raps.

A few seconds later, the wall beside the wallpaper she'd noticed as being wrong began to swing silently out. When it reached about forty-five degrees out, a slightly dirty hand appeared halfway up what was now obviously a door. Shortly after, an unshaven face followed it, the eyes nervously dancing around before settling upon Mary and bursting wide.

"John!" Wood hurried to grab hold of the door as it began to swing back. "Stop. It's all right. She's a friend, a friend."

For a few moments, despite Wood's hold of the door, it still continued to close. "Trust me!" he urged. "John, trust me, please."

This time, the door did stop and, a beat later, began to open once more. This time Wood helped. The head reappeared, its glance flicking between Mary and Wood's faces, settling upon that of Wood.

Sensing she should be quiet and let the two have some space, Mary slowly stepped backward, keeping her facial expression neutral, coming to a stop when she felt her backside bump against her old desk.

Taking the newcomer's hand in his, Wood led the man out of his hidey hole. Looking over at Mary, he asked, his voice low and slow, "Could you lock the door, please?"

Knowing she needed to keep her movements slow and deliberate, Mary went and did as he bid, then went back to sit down on the desk chair.

"Thank you," Wood said. Turning to the obviously nervous man next to him, he patted the back of the hand he held. "John, I'd like you to meet Mary Whitworth-Baines. She used to live here, and this was her room."

"Have I got to go?" John asked. His voice was clear, pleasant to the ear, but could only be described as slow, Mary thought.

Wanting to be honest and having to know if her first impression was correct, Mary said, "John, is it?" The man nodded at her, and though he let go of Wood's hand, he didn't move from his side. "Let's wait and see, shall we?"

John canted his head to one side whilst he mulled over what Mary had just said. Then he just nodded.

Deciding the newcomer wasn't any danger to her and making the effort to keep her voice level and calm, she asked Wood, "Mark, would you like to make the introductions?" Old habits of talking came to the fore. They were just the thing at these times.

"Do you mind if we sit on the bed?" Wood asked. By the sound of his question, he'd noticed the expression on Mary's face when he'd sat there before.

"Be my guest."

Once the two had sat, Wood looked over at Mary

and began his story. "I first came here after I'd been wounded in forty-one, and when I was allowed up, I took to walking the place in the night—sleeping was still too painful for long—and soon found this corridor. The whole place fascinated me! I love PG Wodehouse and used to imagine I was walking the grounds and the rooms and corridors like I was Wooster, pretending I had Jeeves to take care of me."

"You used to read Jeeves and Wooster to me, Mark!" John interrupted, closing his eyes as if he could see the two literary characters.

"Yes, I did. You enjoyed them, didn't you?" John nodded, his eyes still closed, allowing Wood to continue with his story. "Anyway, once I was released, I went back home and found John, my younger brother here, had been conscripted into the army. You may have noticed—in fact, I'm sure you have—that John is a little *simple*. He's not retarded, he just needs more time than normal people to understand what's said to him. The army should never have taken him!" Wood said, letting anger come forth, though he made certain to pat John's hand. "Apparently, nothing my mother or father could say would convince the conscription board. They even went so far as to say he was trying to pull one over on them."

"Is there nothing official—from a doctor, perhaps— to give them information about his condition?" Mary felt she had to ask.

Wood shook his head. "No, as soon as my parents realized what he was like, they home-schooled him as best they could. One thing about John, here, is that he's never been ill a day in his life, so no doctor's ever seen him." Mary nodded her understanding. "As you can imagine, I was furious, got myself into a lot of trouble with trying to track him down, not that it got me anywhere. The whole family was sick with worry, as we knew he wouldn't be able to complete basic training, and the thought of him going into combat?" He shuddered.

"How did he end up hidden here?" Mary asked.

"Through a wonderful coincidence," Wood told her. "I was called back here to be checked over and then released. On one of my night-time jaunts, I came across him in the next ward over! I got chatting to the nurse on duty, who told me he'd been concussed and wounded slightly when a grenade he'd been throwing had gone off prematurely, nothing serious, mild shrapnel, but enough to hospitalize him. As you can imagine, I was beside myself. I knew if he went back to his unit, it would only be a matter of time until something worse happened.

"So I called in a favor from a mate of mine—I won't tell you who—and got myself posted to the administrative department. Quickest posting in history, they tell me around here. Didn't even need to leave, once I'd been signed off as fit again.

"Well, like I said, I'd spent time looking around this place, and I knew no one ever went up to the attic anymore. So I smuggled John up to one of the rooms. John's always done what I say, without argument. He stayed in one of the rooms down the corridor, and I'd come up a few times a day to bring him food, empty his pot, get him washed, but I knew he couldn't stay like that without a big risk of being found."

"So you built him this hidey hole? How did you get in here, though? It's always been locked."

Wood shrugged. "I wasn't always a gentleman and an officer. I learned how to pick a lock a good while ago."

Thinking that Wood would get on well with Betty, Mary waved for him to go on. "And how did you build this without being discovered?"

"I got lucky. The day after I decided I needed to do something, the pioneers—you know, the construction battalion—came in to do some modifications. It's amazing what some people will do for a few cartons of cigarettes and a bottle of whiskey."

Mary got to her feet. "Do you mind if I have a look in your bedroom, John?"

John merely smiled at her before nodding his head and getting to his feet. He came and stood behind her as Mary bobbed her head inside.

Aware that what she was doing wouldn't be considered very smart by Miss Marple, she ducked her head around the side of the door. Inside was lit by a couple of candles set in a saucer upon a small wooden stool, which cast a very good light. The door obviously had a very good seal to it, as there hadn't been any sign of light showing from beneath the door before it had opened. Beside the stool was a single mattress, covered in blankets which were neatly made, with an upturned copy of *Right Ho, Jeeves*. Nodding her approval, Mary noted that apart from a newspaper-covered bucket, which she assumed was a makeshift toilet, little else was there except some clothes over the back of a chair. Trying not to think how long he'd been there, Mary backed out, nearly bumping into John himself.

"Sorry, John."

"No problem." He smiled back, going to sit next to his brother once more.

Once Mary had retaken her seat, Wood fixed her

with a worried yet determined look. "Now you know, what are you going to do?"

A very good question.

Chapter Twenty-Eight

For the second time, Terry Banks was poring through the mugshots books and cursing the war for taking his detective constable from him. What else was a constable good for, if not for dumping the menial and mind-numbing tasks on? Fumbling for his cup of tea, Terry winced as he took a sip. If anything was worse than wartime tea, it was stone-cold wartime tea; plus, he'd wasted precious sugar, as well! Still, it'd been his idea, so no point in moaning to anyone about it.

Since he'd heard about Doris and Walter getting shot at a couple of days ago, he'd thrown himself into the task of trying to identify Verdon's accomplice. Indeed, Lawrence had come in to find him already poring over the books, basing his search on the description and a crude drawing Lawrence had done after the one time he'd seen him. They'd both looked through the books before, but hadn't completed their search, as other duties had taken precedence. However, what with the shooting incident and the accompanying note and its threats, Lawrence had taken the decision to make the investigation official. Betty hadn't been too happy at first, when he'd told her this, but had soon understood, and from much experience with him, trusted the detective and his promise to keep things low-key.

Marking his spot, Terry stood up and stretched. He'd been at this task for a couple of hours, and both his eyes and mind needed a rest. After filling up the kettle, he knocked on the door frame of Lawrence's office. "Time for a cuppa?"

Pushing aside the file he'd been perusing, Lawrence looked up and smiled gratefully. "Always. Had any luck?"

Terry shook his head. "Thought I'd found the bugger a couple of times, but one turned out to be dead and the other was a rather ugly woman."

Lawrence laughed. "Thanks, I needed some light relief."

"I wasn't joking," Terry assured him. "I'd show you, only I wouldn't want you to lose your sight."

"That bad?" Lawrence shook his head. "Fair enough, my eyes thank you."

"They're welcome." Terry glanced at the in-tray on the desk. "Anything interesting?"

Lawrence shook his head. "I think there must be something in the water. All we seem to be getting at the moment are black market reports, cases of drunk and disorderly, petty theft, that type of thing."

"You want an outbreak of major crime? At this time?" Terry asked, incredulous.

"No, no," Lawrence assured him. "Believe me, I'm quite happy there's nothing else serious going on. I needed to check we hadn't missed anything, though."

"And?"

"Nothing that should take precedence," Lawrence told Terry.

Whilst Terry went and made the tea, Lawrence took the opportunity to go through the final file in his pile, which proved to be the most interesting by far. Some butcher had thought it'd be a good idea to rig his scales to shortchange his customers. One of those customers had also been a butcher before he'd retired and, unluckily for the butcher, was a veteran of the Great War. The man had accused the butcher of fiddling him, at which point most of the other people queueing up had joined in with their own accusations, and the butcher had immediately grabbed a cleaver and forced everyone out of his shop and locked up. Whilst most of the crowd stayed outside, a young lad being dispatched to fetch a policeman, the original accuser had returned wielding his Home Guard rifle. When the butcher had refused to open up, the man shot off the lock and forced his way in, disarming the butcher of his cleaver. At this point, the policeman had arrived. Fortunately, the two had been in the same regiment in the last war, and the policeman assured the veteran he'd make certain to investigate both his complaint and those of the crowd of people, who all came in to back him up with their own accusations. Lawrence found it very amusing when he came to the part in the report where the policeman stated that when he'd come to take possession of the rifle, it couldn't be found. Additionally, no one present—apart from the butcher, of course—knew anything about a rifle, and all told him the damage to the lock must have been caused by mice.

Lawrence slapped the folder shut at the same moment Terry put down a mug for him.

Noting the amused expression upon his superior's face, Terry asked, "Something funny?"

Pushing the file toward Terry, Lawrence took his mug. "Put it this way. I'd pay real money to be in court when that one goes before the judge!"

Terry raised an eyebrow and flicked it open, quickly

scanning the page before he closed it up with a shake of his head. "Thought I'd seen it all. Any news?"

Lawrence knew to what he was referring and shook his head, frustration clear on his face. "Nothing. It's been very quiet, which in one way is good, but I was hoping the shooting meant he was getting desperate and would make a mistake. I'm not sure if that's because the local Home Guard have taken to patrolling in front of Betty and Ruth's places so often I'm surprised they haven't pitched tents. They could be scaring him off."

"Thought about asking them to tone it down?" Terry asked.

Lawrence nodded. "Thought about it, and discounted it. Yes, if they weren't there, we'd have more a possibility he'd try something, only I'd much rather no harm came to them."

"I'm sure they'll appreciate the thought," Terry drily added, picking up the envelope the last note had been in and looking again at the cryptic words written there. "So what do you make of this?"

Taking the envelope back, Lawrence glanced at the words before taking another long sip from his mug. "Well, from what I've found out about Verdon, he comes across as an arrogant, upper-class twit who's used to getting his own way. I've read reports from when he was put in jail at the beginning of the war. If I tell you he barely managed to slop out for himself, would that tell you something about him?"

Terry thought things over for a minute or two. "With what you told me happened in the chip shop, I'd say he's been reliant upon someone to do his, ah, dirty work since he learned to walk. I doubt if he did the shooting, which leaves this lackey who did the flit I'm trying to find."

"Which makes it all the more important we find out who this man is. There has to be a firm connection, not family but perhaps a servant, between the two."

Terry got to his feet. "Which makes it all the more important I get back to the books. He's bound to have a record, so I'm sure it's only a matter of time."

Lawrence also got to his feet and, after taking a long, loud slurp of tea, reached for his hat and coat.

"Off somewhere?"

He nodded. "Whilst we were talking, something struck me. I can't see Verdon having the money to buy that shop. From what I've found, everything he owned disappeared, one way or another, whilst he was inside. So I'm thinking did he really buy the shop? And what happened to the previous owner? I'm going to drive over and speak with Ruth. If anyone in Hamble knows what's happened to him, she's going to be my best bet."

****

"Hello there, Bobby," Penny said, smiling as she reached down to give the cocker spaniel a fuss behind his ears. "Who let you in, then?"

"That would be me," said a familiar voice as a pair of hands suddenly swept down covering her eyes, causing her to shriek and knock her fork off the table.

"Alsop!" Mavis shouted, leaning over the serving hatch before saying, "Oh, I might have known it would be you causing trouble," though the smile upon her face together with her passing comment of, "Nice to see you," belied her words.

"Sorry, Mavis!" the voice said as the hands were removed.

Penny twisted her head up and around to be greeted by the sight of—"Shirley!"

Jumping to her feet, Penny sent her chair flying backward, whilst the plate with her bread and butter nearly shot off the table, spinning to a stop a mere inch from the edge. Flinging her arms around her erstwhile friend, Penny hugged her tightly before pounding her on the back and gripping her by the shoulders.

"Look at you! What are you doing here? Jane never mentioned anything about your coming back!"

Whipping off her ATA cap, Shirley tucked it into a pocket of her Sidcot suit and pulled up a seat. Making a great show of looking around, Shirley leant in close and stage-whispered, "Shh. I'm on a cross-country navigation exercise and thought I'd get a little...*lost.*"

Penny burst out laughing as she sat back down, retrieved her bread and butter, and took a good look at her friend. It'd been about three and a half months since Shirley had gone off to training to become an Air Transport Auxiliary pilot, after starting work originally as an engineer. Judging by the brightness in her eyes, the life suited her, and so Penny told her.

"You're looking so well! I can't believe you're here!"

Shirley reached out and nicked Penny's tea. "Me either," she said after knocking it back in one go. "I'm quite impressed with my navigation. Yesterday, I aimed for Oxford and ended up flying over Birmingham. Yeah, that wasn't so good."

"Shirley Tuttle! Well, I live and breathe!"

Looking over her shoulder, Shirley saw Jane standing framed in the open door, and immediately the girl was on her feet and running toward the station commander, her arms out wide. Before Jane had a chance to move, Shirley had engulfed her in a bigger hug than Penny had treated her to only moments before.

"Boss!" Shirley cried, jumping poor Jane up and down, much to the amusement of all and sundry. Momentarily, she pulled away and beamed at a rather shell-shocked Jane before deciding she hadn't finished and once more wrapped her arms around Jane and bounced her up and down a few more times before taking her by the hand and dragging her along to where Penny had nearly collapsed out of her seat in laughter.

As Jane gratefully took a seat, Mavis, as if by magic, appeared and placed a steaming cup of tea before her. "You look like you need this," she told her before disappearing as quickly as she'd appeared.

Before her brain could warn her, Jane automatically reached out for the cup and took what was supposed to be a nerve-settling sup. Unfortunately, her body suffered for her brain's lack of a reaction, and shuddering, she put the cup down and, with slightly shaking hands, pushed the cup as far away from her as possible.

"I see Mavis's tea is still up to its usual high standard," Shirley said, keeping her voice down in the hope the mess manager wouldn't hear her. She should have known better.

"I heard that, Shirley Tuttle!"

Shirley clamped her hands to her mouth to stave off a burst of her own laughter. "I see some things don't change."

Once everyone was satisfied Mavis had vanished from earshot, Jane had to ask, "So what are you doing here? I didn't think your training was due to finish for around another month."

"She's on a stopover during a navigational exercise," Penny provided.

Jane raised an eyebrow, but didn't say a word.

Shirley shrugged her shoulders. "Okay, so I'm a little off course. I couldn't resist popping in when I saw how near Hamble was to my course."

"How near?" Jane asked, a smile pursing her lips, pretty sure of what the answer would be.

"Well...not all that near," she admitted, before blurting out, "I couldn't resist it! I've missed you lot!"

Penny squeezed her friend's hands. "And we've missed you."

Jane nodded before suddenly lurching to her feet and muttering, "Back in a minute." She rushed to the door, jerked it open, and disappeared.

"Any idea what that's all about?" Shirley asked.

Penny was still staring at where the door banged shut. Turning back, she took a big bite of her bread and butter before replying, "Not got a clue. How long can you stay? The others are out on runs."

One corner of Shirley's lips curled up. "I thought so, when I looked at the time after I'd decided to make my detour, but I had to take the chance."

Looking grave, Penny asked, "I suppose you've heard about Thelma?"

Shirley, equally as grave, nodded her head once. "We all did. Well, we heard she'd been killed. Can you tell me what happened?"

Penny sighed, reluctant to go into the details once more, but as Shirley had known Thelma nearly as well as the rest of the group, she felt an obligation to tell her what little she knew. "Jane did all the ringing around, and from what she's been able to find, Thelma's Anson was jumped by a couple of Germans and shot down. She didn't stand a chance."

Once she'd finished her short explanation, Penny peered at her friend closely, watching as the pain she'd felt came to Shirley's eyes. Fighting back her own tears, Penny passed Shirley a handkerchief. Shirley quietly sobbed into it, and neither noticed Jane had come back into the mess until she pulled out a seat and sat back down.

"Is she all right? What's wrong?" Jane asked.

Fighting her own emotions, Penny managed to get out, "I've just filled her in about Thelma."

Jane nodded and reached out a hand to pat Shirley's heaving shoulders. "Take your time, take your time. Penny, get her some water, please?"

Whilst Penny went about her task, Jane placed a large brown envelope on the table, pushing it toward Shirley. As a way to distract her, it worked, as her eyes were drawn to the package. Sniffing and then blowing her nose and dabbing her eyes dry, she asked, "What's this?"

Jane smiled, indicating that whatever was contained, it wasn't bad news. "Letters from your husband."

"Ted? They're from my Ted?"

Penny, rejoining the pair, heard this brief conversation and was happy to see a smile slowly appearing upon her friend's face.

Gulping down half the glass of water, Shirley eagerly grabbed the package and after exchanging nods with Jane, happily tore the envelope open. Out tumbled a bunch of letters, all tied up with a neat red bow. Shirley chuckled. "The Ted I know could barely tie his own bootlaces."

"Oh, I did the bow," Jane admitted.

"Why so many?" Shirley asked, spreading the letters

around in wonder.

"I don't have an answer to that," Jane admitted. "Ruth has mentioned that sometimes the letters from her son arrive in bunches. Plus, Ruth wanted to give you a treat and hold on until there were a few, rather than have me forward a postcard or two. Was she right?"

The huge smile upon Shirley's face was all the answer Jane needed.

At their feet, Bobby twitched his legs and woofed slowly in his sleep, and for a short time, all seemed well with the world.

Chapter Twenty-Nine

Lawrence drummed his fingers on Walter's desk in frustration. "You're sure you've no idea where this"—he stopped to consult his notes again—"Fred Tanner could have gone to?"

Ruth stirred her tea and shook her head. "I'm afraid not. Even when he ran the chip shop, he tended to keep his own company. I don't recall seeing him in the Victory more than a couple of times, and if the place got busy, he always drank up and left."

"And there's no wife or children?"

Ruth again shook her head. "No one, so far as I can remember. He ran the place by himself, seemed to like it that way. Mind you…" She chuckled. "That didn't make him too popular with the local children, as he never had any part-time jobs for them. Didn't stop them eating his food, mind."

Lawrence dropped back against the back of the chair. He looked up. "Didn't anyone find it strange that one minute, here's old Fred, happily serving fish 'n' chips, keeping our Doris happy."

"Who's not happy now," Ruth added.

"No." He shook his head, chuckling. "She's not, is she? Then, the next minute, there's this Verdon chap and his mysterious helper taking over."

After a short pause, Ruth replied, "You know, I think most people have so much on their minds these days, who they get their chips from isn't the biggest problem on their minds."

"With your editor hat on, Aunt Ruth, have you heard anything from anyone?"

"I wish I could say yes," she admitted, "but I was in the same boat as everyone else. It wasn't until all this blew up that I gave him some thought. I'm not very happy to admit that."

"No one's posted a missing person report about him," Lawrence informed her. "I checked. So that leads me to believe he's still alive, possibly being held hostage by Verdon. That's pure guesswork, but it makes sense."

"What makes sense?" Walter asked as he was pulled through the door by a wet, mucky, and rather grumpy-looking Bobby.

Ruth's eyes went wide. "What the hell happened?"

Not able to prevent himself, Walter grinned as Bobby shook himself somewhat dry and curled up on Ruth's feet and proceeded to lick himself clean. "Blame Duck for that."

"Duck?" Lawrence asked. "Oh, I'd forgotten Doris's silly name for her aquatic friend."

"More like aquatic fiend," Ruth commented.

"Don't let her hear you say that," Walter said with a small laugh. "She loves the little bugger."

"Are you telling me," Lawrence put in, "that it attacks you? Even with Bobby by your side?"

"Excuse me," Walter said to Lawrence as he opened the bottom drawer in his desk and took out a small, rough towel. Kneeling down, he took hold of Bobby's front paws, dragged the reluctant cocker spaniel from his warming perch, and proceeded to give him a toweling down. From the way the dog struggled, he didn't enjoy the ministrations. Once he'd been released, he gave Walter a dirty look and took up residence once more beneath Ruth's desk, hogging the fire. Walter perched himself on the edge of his desk and told Lawrence, "Not a chance! Me and everyone else, including Ruth there, all believe Duck hates everyone and everything except Doris. Believe me, I think having Bobby by my side only acts like a red rag to a bull! Anyway, what were you two talking about?"

"Fred from the chippy," Ruth answered. "Lawrence—and I can't believe it didn't occur to me—was wondering what had happened to him."

Walter watched Bobby chew his toenails for a few minutes before saying, "We're not very good newspaper people, are we."

Ruth shook her head.

Lawrence got up, brushed a stray pencil shaving from his thigh, and retrieved his hat. "Well, I'm going to take a look around. I mentioned it to Ruth earlier, but I've a feeling this Fred is still around somewhere."

"You're certain you can't just bust into the shop?" Walter asked, taking his seat.

Lawrence shook his head. "Believe me, I wish I could. I need a reason to go in without permission."

"I could hide around the side and yell for help," Walter suggested.

Lawrence smiled as he opened the door. "I'll keep it in mind."

After saying his goodbyes, Lawrence strolled down the high street, passing a reasonably busy F. W. Woolworth's before coming once again to the chip shop replete with its prominent Closed sign. Stepping forward, he tried to see through the blinds but soon gave this up as a hopeless task. Verdon had done too good a job. Going back across the road until his back was against a wall, he leaned up and stared at the property, silently wishing he'd taken Walter up on his offer.

Shrugging his shoulders, he proceeded with his house-to-house visits, determined to at least see if anyone around knew anything further about Fred. He was so engrossed in speaking to one of Woolworth's delivery boys that he didn't spot a curtain twitch in the flat above the chip shop.

****

"Are they still there?"

Ruth twitched aside the blackout curtain for long enough to catch sight of the local Home Guard marching past her cottage. Turning back to Betty, she nodded. "Don't get me wrong. I'm very grateful to Matt for arranging this with his officer, but I'm with Lawrence here, and I really hope he's right. If this Verdon character did want to kill us, I don't think we'd be having this conversation."

Jane put down her empty bowl. "Well, I believe him. I'm certain he wouldn't have put a name to his suspicions without thoroughly checking his facts."

"Was there any reason he couldn't come over tonight?" Mary asked, finishing off her pea soup.

"He said he wanted to keep up the pretense we were all around Betty's," Doris informed them.

"And he learned nothing from knocking on every door in Hamble?" Jane asked.

Ruth shook her head. "All he gained were very sore feet."

"Speaking of investigations," Betty said, leaning forward, "what happened at your manor?"

To everyone's surprise, Mary squirmed in her seat, giving all indication of not wanting to answer.

"Come on," Jane prodded. "You've been very quiet all day, so something must be up."

Seeing she was the subject of intense scrutiny, Mary deliberately took her time over finishing up her own soup before answering. "It's…awkward."

"We'd figured out that much ourselves," Betty told her.

A knock on the door made everyone jump.

"I'll get it!" Mary declared, but found herself firmly pushed back into her seat by Ruth.

"Oh, no, you don't! You stay right there. I'll get it."

The girls heard some muffled conversation, and a moment after this ceased, Ruth came back into the room, closely followed by…

"Tom!" Penny exclaimed, stumbling to her feet. "What are you doing here? I wasn't expecting you."

Tucking his hat under his arm, Tom nodded his way around the room. "Ladies," he said first, before turning his full attention to his wife. "I know. I had the evening off, so took a gamble that you wouldn't be flying either. Do you mind if we go for a walk?"

"No!" everyone except for Penny instantly yelled. Tom nearly lost his footing as he staggered backward.

"Okay," he began, "I know I've hacked everyone off, but don't you think that reaction was a bit much?"

Not wishing to cause a scene, Penny grabbed her husband's hand and ushered him through to Ruth's kitchen. Taking a seat, she motioned him to take one beside her.

"Would you mind explaining just what that was all about?"

Penny ran her fingers through her hair. "That wasn't about you," she informed him, "though I wouldn't go outside with Doris. She's liable to set Duck on you."

"Duck?" Tom raised an eyebrow. "Is that a nickname for someone I wouldn't want to meet on a dark night?"

Penny chuckled. "Not quite. Yes, you wouldn't want to meet him on a dark night…or at any time, come to think of it, but it's actually her pet duck."

Tom couldn't help it. He laughed out loud.

"I'm not having you on. This is one vicious duck."

Doris chose that moment to stick her head around the door. "Everything all right, Penny?"

"We're all right," Penny assured her. "I've just told Tom about Duck."

"Do I need to go and get him?" Doris asked, a little too eagerly. "It shouldn't take me long to find him," she added, turning as if to go and fetch the fowl.

"I'll let you know," Penny said and waited a few seconds in case she heard the front door open and close.

When neither heard this, Tom admitted, "I've really upset her, haven't I."

Sensing this was a pivotal point in their relationship, Penny knew she had to be truthful. Only then would she know if they stood a chance of salvaging their relationship. "You have. I'm sure you know how protective Doris is of me…of us all, really. I wouldn't want to be the one who crossed her."

"And that's what I've done." Tom nodded. Rubbing the end of his nose, he looked up into his wife's eyes. "Penny, I'll tell you I'm sorry until the end of the world, if you want, and I'll mean it." He got up and began to pace up and down before her, pausing to close the door for privacy. "I am willing to do as you asked, to date, but I can't forget how we used to be, so I've got to ask you, do you think you could ever trust me again, as you once did? As I, perhaps, once deserved?"

To give her some thinking time, Penny too got up and filled the kettle. Not until the kettle boiled, during which waiting time Tom didn't utter a word, did she turn to face him.

"I've said it before and I'll say it again, Tom. You hurt me, really hurt me, far more than if you'd struck me, with your words and actions at the hospital." She paused as Tom unfalteringly nodded, keeping eye contact with his wife. "I don't ever want that feeling again."

"Certainly not my finest moment," Tom agreed. "I can only say I'll do my best. As you've found, I'm not perfect, and so I can't promise. I can only assure you I've learned my lesson. I was only thinking of myself then. If you'll take me back, I promise to take things as slowly as you wish. I want to get to know everything I never knew about you, and I'd like, if possible, for you to once again love me as much as I still love you."

Silence picked this moment to reign, only to be rudely broken by Doris's voice yelling, "Kiss him, you fool!"

****

Mary held the branches aside as Betty, Doris, and Jane made their way back to The Old Lockkeepers Cottage via Bobby's route around the back of the two cottages. "I don't mind saying that I, for one, shall be very glad for all this mess to come to an end, and we'll be able to use the front door at night once more."

"Believe me, so will I," Betty muttered as she passed through.

Hurrying to catch her up, Mary caught Betty by the elbow. "I'm sorry. I didn't mean to make it sound like you're to blame!"

Unlocking the door, Betty waited until everyone was inside before relocking it, arranging the blackout, and going into the kitchen, where Jane turned on the light. "It's all right, I know you didn't," Betty assured her. "Come on…" She grabbed Mary by the elbow this time and led her into the lounge. "We were interrupted before. It's time you told us what happened up in Scotland. We can fill Penny in later, once Tom's left."

Sighing, Mary allowed herself to be placed onto the sofa, where Doris immediately sat beside her and Betty put herself on the other side.

"Spill," their American friend ordered.

Mary looked around at her expectant audience, knowing she had to tell them something, only…how much? She knew they were a sympathetic audience. However, she had a proviso. "What I'm about to say, you cannot share with either Lawrence or his sergeant."

This raised more than one set of eyebrows. "Is it okay to tell Ruth and Walter?" Doris asked.

Nodding, Mary agreed, "So long as you get them to agree to the same proviso, if I don't get to speak to either first."

"Fair enough," Doris said.

"Thanks." Mary smiled. "Sorry, Doris, no ghost. However, something was going on which was centered on my old room. By the way, there wasn't much damage from the fire either. That was simply an accident. You remember Captain Wood, Doris?"

Doris nodded. "Bit of a nosy parker. The guy in charge of reception?"

"That's the one. Well, he's hiding his brother in my room."

"I didn't see anyone. Nor any sign of anyone," Doris stated.

"You wouldn't have," Mary assured her. "Wood put in a false wall, and his brother was hiding in a quite cozy room behind it. Only after I spotted a couple of signs did he show me the secret, all very clever."

"I wouldn't have had him down as *that* clever," Doris admitted.

"He's a lot more shrewd and clever than either of us gave him credit for," Mary told her.

"So why was he hiding his brother?" Betty asked.

Here goes, Mary thought. "He's a deserter."

As she expected, this got a round of comments, all along the lines of disbelief. Mary held up her hands to forestall any further comment.

"Hold on. Yes, he's a deserter, and my first reaction was much the same. It's not that clear-cut, though. The poor man's a bit...simple." At this, everyone's mouths dropped open a little, allowing Mary to continue. "Apparently, he's never been to a doctor, so there's nothing documented to back this up. But I've seen him, spoken to him, and I believe Wood. Despite all the protests of Wood's parents, the army still took him. He was wounded in training and ended up at the manor hospital, and that's where Wood ran into him. Well, not surprisingly, he didn't want him to go back, and that's when he decided to hide him, after arranging a posting to the hospital."

After Mary finished talking, everyone simply sat there, all a little dumbfounded at these revelations.

Finally, Betty said, "Wow! That was not what I was

expecting you to say. Any idea what you're going to do?"

Mary shook her head. "Not a clue. I'm hoping you lot will help."

Chapter Thirty

"You damned idiot! Do you have any idea how close that copper came to seeing him? I thought I'd told you to keep him locked up!"

Croft stood half to attention as Verdon berated him. His short time in the army had been good for one thing. Before, if his supposed superior had launched a verbal tirade at him, he'd have felt his knees quaking. Now, as he'd done before, he could let the words flow over him as water does over a rock, and they had no effect.

"If this happens again, we'll have to look at getting rid of him!"

Mentally shrugging, Croft thought that if he wanted to get rid of the chip shop owner, he could do it himself. If the police got hold of him, he didn't want to go down for murder. Tuning out, he went through an internal list of his options. Taking to his heels was the obvious one, only, like Verdon, he had little money, and without more, he'd have to rely on luck to find safety. Judging by how things had gone lately, the chances of that were slim. He'd checked if anything in the flat could bring in anything worthwhile and came up empty-handed. Any of his old friends from the Moseley days were either still in prison or on the run, so there could be no help there.

He'd toyed with the idea of taking over this venture for himself, only to come to the conclusion that it would be pointless. From his observations, this Betty woman didn't have any cash available worth the trouble of taking, plus he'd come to admire the work they did. He may have spent the vast majority of his life on the wrong side of the law, but that didn't mean he wasn't patriotic! The more he thought about it, the more he'd been coming to the conclusion that he only had one option left. The thought brought a scowl to his face, which Verdon misinterpreted.

"Don't you pull a face at me! You should know your place by now!"

Verdon, not being the smartest person to walk the earth, hadn't read his lackey's mood lately at all and then made the mistake of raising his arm to strike him around the head. Croft's hand shot up, grabbing his forearm before he could connect. "What the…"

"Don't," was all Croft muttered, not troubling to raise his voice. Without looking at his supposed employer, he started toward the door. "I'll go and have a word with him. Tell him to behave."

As he left the kitchen and made his way to the basement, Croft had the satisfaction of seeing Verdon's mouth hanging open like a wet fish. One thing he'd always known, yet never acted upon himself before, was that the criminal upper class didn't know how to react when their servants stood up to them. Taking the key down from the hook where it hung, he unlocked the cellar door, knocked, and announced, "I'm coming in. Sit on the bed, hands under your bum!"

When the door swung open, Croft was pleased to see that their captive had obeyed him. He also noticed the same belligerence in his eyes. He was silently pleased to see this still present after the near month he'd been held. Quite a few of the people he'd looked after had either never had this strength of character or had quickly lost it as the days crawled past. Glancing at the man's bed, he saw the book he'd given him a few days ago was open.

"How many times you read that, then, Fred?" Croft asked.

"Second time since you gave it to me," Fred replied. "Spoils the whodunit a bit when you already know the ending."

"I'll bring you a couple of replacements next time I'm down," Croft told him, leaning up against the open door. Though Fred's hands were where he'd been instructed, it didn't stop his eyes roaming toward the open door. "Don't even think of it," Croft told him with a smile. "I've no desire to hurt you, but I've a good ten years on you, and I've taken down much bigger men than you, and most have never got up again. Do I make myself clear?"

Reluctantly, whilst treating his captor to a master of a glower, Fred nodded. "How much longer are you going to keep me prisoner in my own house?"

Croft glanced upward but didn't answer.

Fred waited a few beats before asking, "And are you going to kill me? I've seen your face."

Though he already knew what his answer was, Croft made him wait a little while before replying. There was nothing wrong in keeping the man on edge; it made him less likely to try anything foolish. "So long as you don't make any more trouble, I don't think you should let that worry you."

"What do you mean, any more?" Fred asked. "And why should I believe you?"

Before answering, Croft took out a packet of Woodbines and offered Fred one.

"I don't normally," Fred replied. "Haven't smoked since the trenches, but why not," he finished, taking one and accepting the lit match he was offered. Though he hadn't been told he could, by taking the smoke, Fred took his other hand out and leant back against the wall to await the answers to his questions.

After he'd lit his own, Croft pulled up an old wooden chair, the only seat in the room which also doubled as a storeroom, and placed it in the still open doorway. He took a couple of long drags. "Firstly, the boss knows about your pulling the curtain aside in the toilet earlier. He could see you in the mirror from the bedroom. That's why the door's always open when you have to go. Don't do it again."

"Why isn't he giving me a rollicking? Or slapping me around?"

Croft let out a low laugh. "Not the type. Thinks that kind of thing is beneath him, and that's why he's got me."

"So why aren't you giving me a good slapping?" Fred asked before he could stop himself.

"You want me to hit you?" Croft couldn't help but ask.

Fred vigorously shook his head. "Don't trouble yourself on my behalf," he hastily said, hoping levity would defuse any tension.

"I won't," Croft replied, waving his free hand. "And because you haven't seen his face, there's your other reason why I don't see a good reason for knocking you off. I'm not bothered you've seen mine, as I've already told you."

Both men sat back and smoked in companionable silence, the peaceful scene only spoiled by the new lock on the cellar door and Croft blocking the exit.

"I have no choice but to accept your word on that," Fred said, "though I've received no such assurance," he hastened to add, to which Croft looked him in the eye and gave him a sharp nod. "Thank you," he added, unable to stop a sigh of relief from escaping. "If I may, how much longer am I to be kept here?"

Croft got to his feet, put the chair back, and then took hold of the door handle. He looked back. "One way or the other, not for much longer."

****

"Sergeant Banks, Terry, ma'am, at your service."

"Excellent timing, Sergeant, we were about to leave for work," Betty informed him, stepping aside so the policeman could enter the cottage. "Go and tell Lawrence his relief's here, please, Mary."

Nodding, Mary turned and hurried up the stairs toward the loft. "Hey, you," she said into the semi-darkness at the shadowy form sitting a short way back from the window, "your sergeant's here."

Getting up from his seat, the shadow yawned and stretched before reaching up and taking the blanket off his shoulders and laying it upon the vacated chair. "I won't say I'm not sorry," he muttered, before walking over to Mary and taking her in his arms. Leaning down, he whispered into her ear, "Knowing you were sleeping only next door was pure torture!"

Glad of the dark, as Lawrence couldn't see how red her cheeks were, nevertheless she reached up, dragged his face down to her level, and kissed him hard on the lips. In fact, if Betty hadn't shouted up the stairs, "Mary! We're going to be late!" she could have stayed like that all day long.

"Come on," she reluctantly said, taking him by the hand and leading him downstairs to the kitchen, where Betty was showing Terry how to make a cup of tea.

"He's a working copper," Lawrence informed Betty. "Believe me, he knows how to make a cup of tea. I can vouch for that."

Betty turned from the burners and noticed the amused expression upon Terry's face.

"I'm a modern married man, First Officer Palmer, and the detective is right. I make an excellent cup of tea," he confirmed.

"Perhaps you can teach our Doris sometime?" Betty said.

This got an immediate, "I heard that!" from the hall.

"You were meant to!" Betty retorted, before turning back to Terry. "Loft room's at the top of the stairs. We'll be back later."

"So did you tell your wife you'd be staying with five women, Terry?" Doris asked as he stepped back into the hall.

Terry shook his head. "No fear! She trusts me implicitly, but to tell her that…well, that may be pushing my luck a little."

"You don't talk in your sleep, do you?" Doris teased.

****

"Did anyone ever tell you, Doris, you've got an evil sense of humor?" Penny asked, as the two walked behind the others on the way to the station.

"Only pretty much everyone I've ever known," Doris admitted with a shrug, though she had a smile on her face as she spoke the words. "It was funny, though, wasn't it?"

Penny leaned in close so the others couldn't hear. "Very."

"No need to whisper," Jane said over her shoulder. "We all agree."

To change the subject, Penny asked, "So does a downgrade in rank mean the risk to us has lessened, Lawrence?"

The policeman turned around, and everyone stopped with him. Conveniently, they were still a hundred yards or so from the station guardroom, all quiet and secluded. "Possibly."

"Possibly?" Jane echoed. "I'm not sure if I like the sound of that. These are not only my staff, Detective," she told him, using his rank so he would know how serious her words were, "but my best friends. I don't like to think of them being in danger."

Lawrence fixed Jane with his full attention, so she'd know how serious *he* was. "Believe me, I know that," he said, briefly looking into Mary's eyes. "I would never put anyone here in danger knowingly."

Jane studied his face for a short while before nodding her head in satisfaction, "And the sergeant?"

"Terry has taken over because I believe it's prudent to keep a watch, though I don't believe there will be any more attacks. It's not this Verdon who's been making the direct attacks, so I don't think we should worry too much about him."

"Which begs the question," Betty said. "Who should we worry about?"

Instead of answering, Lawrence, perhaps a little unnecessarily, looked around to make sure no one was listening and then took a photograph out of his pocket and passed it to Jane, as the one most in need of reassurance, in his judgment. "This is Percival Croft. It took poor Terry a long time, but he finally tracked him down. This is the man who bolted as soon as I talked to him. Doris," he said as the American now had the photo in her hands, "is this the same chap you saw at the chippie?"

Doris handed the photo back to him, suppressing a shudder. "You don't forget a scar like that in a hurry. Yes."

"What's he to this Verdon chap?" Jane asked.

"He's what would have been called, a while ago, a vassal servant."

"A what?" Doris interrupted.

"Basically, his family has been serving Verdons for years and years. He's merely the latest in a long line of indentured muscle. If Verdon wants a dirty job done, then this bloke would be whom he'd call on to do it."

"Do you think this is the one who shot at Walter and me, then?" Doris asked.

Lawrence simply nodded. "Undoubtedly. Verdon typically wouldn't get his hands dirty, and I doubt if he knows how to handle a rifle. A shotgun, perhaps. A rifle, no. I checked up—he was declared unfit for military service in the Great War." He snorted. "Probably paid some friendly doctor to get him off."

"Do you think this Croft chap's the one who wrote on the back of the last envelope?" Mary enquired.

Shrugging his shoulders, Lawrence answered as best he could. "We tried to get a sample of his handwriting, but my Met contacts haven't been able to pull anything together yet."

"Best guess?" Betty said.

"If I were a gambling man, which I'm not," he added

for Mary's benefit, "I'd say so."

"I suppose the question is, then, if it is his writing, do we believe him? Do we, essentially, have someone on the inside?" Jane posed.

"Obviously I can't say yes," Lawrence replied, after thinking it over for a few seconds. "However, if I read him right, I'd say that at the very least he's having second thoughts."

"So he's not violent?" Penny asked.

"Oh, he's violent, all right," Lawrence told them without hesitation. "Believe me, you don't want to know what he's done."

"What could be different this time?" Jane wanted to know.

"This is educated deductions, you understand?" Lawrence began. "From what I can see, he's never hurt women, at least not seriously. Plus, for someone of his background, he's surprisingly patriotic. Fought in the last year of the last war, won a military medal for bravery."

"Let me get this right. You think we've a patriotic thug who's developing a conscience, possibly looking over us?"

"It'd match the words," Lawrence said.

When no one else could think of anything to say, Jane decided, "Come on, you lot, let's get to work before the guardroom chaps come over to find out what's wrong."

Chapter Thirty-One

After lowering the shoebox into the newly dug hole behind Riverview Cottage, Walter stood up straight again.

"Over to you, Ruth," he said, bowing his head.

Ruth nodded, bowed her head, and clasped her hands before her. "Dear Lord, whom we trust and worship, accept this, a symbolic foot, to your mercy. Look over my son in his time of need, all his friends, and the subjects of His Majesty, King George the Sixth. Amen."

"Amen," Walter echoed and handed Ruth a trowel.

Bending down, Ruth shoveled some dirt over the box before passing the tool back to Walter, who did the same. Turning around, Ruth called for Bobby and placed him on the leash once he came to a halt at her ankles. Walter now filled in the rest of the hole and patted it down with the back of the trowel.

Dusting some dirt off his knees, Walter got to his feet. "Ready for work?"

Ruth cast one glance down at the small mound of earth. "I suppose."

"There's the enthusiasm I love!" he joked, offering Ruth his arm.

Taking it, Ruth led him toward the side entrance with Bobby pulling on his leash, eager for an early morning walk. Squeezing Walter's hand, Ruth told him,

"At least I can put in my next letter to my son that we've held a funeral for his foot. I feel a little guilty, as it's a while now since I told him I'd do one."

"I'm sure he'll understand," Walter assured her, closing the gate. "You're sure you don't mind burying that old doll?"

Ruth shook her head. "No, I haven't played with it in a few years."

"Oh, ha-ha!" Walter laughed.

Halfway down the riverbank toward the village, Bobby began to bark like crazy, straining on his leash and nearly pulling it out of Ruth's hand.

"What the…?" she declared, as both the humans took to scanning the sky after checking for any unwary waterfowl or cats.

"I can't see anything," Walter shouted, turning around and around on the spot.

"Me either!" Ruth said, matching his movements, finding it more and more difficult to hold onto Bobby's leash.

"Can't hear anything, either!" Walter added looking over at Ruth who, after a short, silent conversation, nodded.

Bending down, Ruth unhooked Bobby's leash. With one glance and a quick *woof*, Bobby shot off in the direction of the airfield. Barely glancing at each other, Ruth and Walter took off after him as quickly as their feet could carry them. Faster than either would have believed possible, they reached the guardroom with Ruth only just behind Walter.

"If you're after Bobby," said the guard, "he jumped over the gate and kept on going. I didn't think he had it in him!" The man said this with his attention focused on the sky. "Do you think he's right?" he asked, briefly glancing at the pair.

"No idea," Ruth admitted. "Mind if we go and find him?" she asked.

"Be my guest," he said, opening the gate for them. "Be careful!"

"Same to you," Ruth shouted over her shoulder, noting the rest of the guardroom staff had come outside and were also searching the sky.

Coming to a stop outside the mess to listen, Bobby himself being nowhere in sight, they tried to track him by the noise he was making, only the echo around the airfield made this difficult. Mavis and her staff were all outside, all wearing their helmets and searching the sky from where they all stood beside the slit trenches around the hut.

"He went toward the ops hut!" Mavis yelled, without looking down.

"Thanks," Walter replied, and the pair headed off.

The nearer they got to the hut, the louder the barking got. Rounding a corner, they saw Penny had a grip of Bobby by the collar. Everywhere you looked, all you could see were people, some in helmets, scanning the sky, all work on the airfield having come to a halt. Walter and Ruth skidded to a stop next to Jane.

"I can't see anything!" Jane told them.

Walter was about to agree when the thrum of an aero-engine or two came to his ears. Quickly looking down, Walter saw that Bobby was turned inland, and if anything, his barking had increased in volume. He wasn't the only one to notice Bobby's behavior, as the other three were also now squinting in the same direction.

"Can you hear…" he began to say, but never completed the sentence as his companions all nodded their heads at the same time as the air raid siren went off.

All around, people disappeared into the slit trenches and air raid shelters, with Jane staying on her feet just long enough to satisfy herself everyone was as safe as possible before joining Penny, Ruth, Walter, and a still-barking Bobby in the slit trenches beside the ops hut. No sooner were they all under cover than the engine noise increased dramatically in volume, and before long, it seemed to be coming from every direction at once.

"Anyone see anything?" Jane yelled, her head jerking every which way.

No sooner had the words left her mouth than there came the sound of a high-performance engine backfiring in the direction Bobby was still barking at. Flashing over their heads at no more than fifty feet, a German twin-engine plane sped past, one of its engines belching black smoke and sparks. Close behind sped a pair of Spitfires, the port one spitting a burst of cannon shells in the enemy's direction as it cleared the airfield perimeter. No sooner had they appeared than they were gone, and thirty seconds later, the all-clear sounded.

Leaping out of the trench, Bobby let out a few barks as the specks faded from view, then sat down and looked up at his humans.

Ruth knelt down beside him and proceeded to rub his ears, sending the dog into squirms of delirium. "I'm so sorry about this, Jane," she said, looking up.

Jane looked down at Ruth as if she'd lost her mind, but finally found her voice. "Are you mad?"

"Pardon me?" Ruth replied, getting back to her feet. "The station didn't get bombed."

"Penny, will you go and pour us all something? You know the bottle I keep in my bottom drawer. Thanks. I need to have a word with our Ruth here."

Once Penny had gone back inside, a huge grin upon her face, Jane sat down on the steps and patted beside her for Ruth to join her. Uninvited, yet assuming, Walter took a seat next to Ruth. "Where was I? Oh, yes, you're mad! It doesn't matter we didn't get bombed—don't get me wrong, I'm very glad of that—the fact remains, Bobby was quite right. He knew something was wrong before we had an inkling! For all we knew, that Jerry could have dumped bombs on the station and we'd have had bare seconds of warning. My people could have been injured or killed. So never mind there wasn't an attack. Bobby wanted to protect us, and protect us he did! I'm sure you won't find a single person here who'll disagree with me."

Whilst Ruth was still trying to take this in, the hero in question had draped himself across Walter's knees and was looking around with a self-satisfied expression on his face, for a dog. All around, the station was getting back to work, and those who had to walk past the ops hut all waved or shouted out a cheery, "Thanks, Bobby!" on their way.

"See?" Jane smiled as Penny appeared at her other side, a bottle of gin and four glasses in her hands. "Thanks, Penny." She waited until everyone had a measure before raising her glass and toasting, "To Bobby! May your ears be ever on alert!"

Once everyone had downed their drink, Walter asked, "Shall I go and see if Mavis has a little treat for Bobby?"

The canine hero of the moment perked up and

271

barked his approval of this idea. "Woof!"

****

Doris came running up the steps of the ops hut, the door slamming open as she began to declare, "I've got it! I know…" and then the door rebounded, hitting her on the tip of her nose and knocking her back a step. "Oww!" And she fell onto her bottom.

Penny pushed out of her seat and rushed to her friend's aid, not that she was much help, as when she wrenched open the door to find Doris on the floor and holding her nose, she promptly burst into laughter.

"Don't just stand there," Doris said, glaring up at Penny and holding out one hand whilst the other was rubbing her nose. "Give me a hand up!"

Doing as she was asked, though she was still laughing, Penny heaved her friend to her feet and led her inside. Becoming aware of a commotion, Jane looked out of her office as Doris allowed herself to be led to a seat, punctuating each step with an "Ouch."

Penny knelt before her and reached up a hand with the intent of taking away her hand. "Come on, let me have a look."

"What do you see? Is it broken? Is there much blood?" Doris asked, her voice getting higher with each question. "Oh, I knew it! Walter's not going to want to marry someone who's disfigured!"

Obviously trying not to resume laughing, Penny got up, bent over Doris, kissed the end of the wounded nose in question, and then smacked her lightly around the top of her head. "You idiot! Look at my hands. Look at your fingers! There's no blood. It's not broken." She shook her head and took her own seat. "Darling, all you have is a slightly red tip to your nose, so stop worrying. You'll still be your normal gorgeous self for your wedding."

Doris spotted Jane watching this strange spectacle and, checking her fingers and looking at Penny's hands, asked, "Is she right, Jane? Do I look okay?"

With a sweet smile upon her face, Jane made her way over, studied Doris's face from every way she could, then also smacked her around the head.

"Hey!"

"You'll be fine," Jane agreed, perching on the edge of Penny's desk. "Now, what were you going to say? I mean, before that tremendous accident."

Rubbing the end of her nose a little gingerly, Doris looked for a few moments as if she would change her mind and keep whatever she'd been thinking to herself, only Penny sat there batting her eyelids at her like a maniac, and she couldn't help but smile. "All right, listen to this. You know Mary asked us for ideas to help Captain Wood's brother?"

"We remember," Jane answered.

"Well, I was wracking my mind on the way back from the maintenance unit just now. Anything to keep my mind off Mary's flying, to be honest…"

"What was that about my flying?" the pilot in question demanded from the open doorway.

Doris waved for Mary—and, hot on her heels, Betty—to come in. "Close the door, and don't let it worry you, Mary, it's not important."

"Not important, my aunt Fanny," Mary muttered. Nevertheless, she and Betty came in and leant against the wall, allowing Doris to carry on with her thought.

"Now, before I was so rudely interrupted…"

"Stop milking the moment," Mary told her, obviously still annoyed at her friend for besmirching her flying abilities.

Doris turned to face Mary. "Please, I may be about to solve your problem." After Mary had zipped her mouth closed, Doris seemed satisfied and continued, "Right, thank you. Here's my suggestion. For the moment, let's ignore the fact that Wood's brother…"

"John," Mary supplied.

"…John"—Doris nodded—"is a deserter. I propose paying a doctor, one in the right field, to do a complete examination of this man. If he comes to the conclusion that he's simple, as Mary has been told and believes, then he should be able to write up some documentation to that effect."

"Will that work?" Betty asked. "Won't the army still want to court-martial him for deserting?"

Doris shook her head. "I don't think so. So long as we do this right, I don't think it'll matter if this documentation is obtained long after it should have been. I think the army should have had a duty to utterly check out the health of those it conscripts, and when there is doubt of anything, then it should have been investigated. I don't think they'd be pleased if this story got to the newspapers. If it comes to it, I'm sure Ruth will be only too pleased to help get in contact with those on Fleet Street. They're always on the lookout for juicy stories."

"Do you think it would come to that?" Jane asked.

"I don't think it will," Doris answered. "For a start, he's only one man and hardly likely to be of much use to the army anyway. Faced with the possibility of bad publicity, I think they'll bite the bullet and give him a medical discharge. It's not going to make us very popular, but I'm prepared to do this on my own so no one else will be tarred with the same brush."

Everyone else's voices mingled into one before Jane banged her hand on a desk to get their attention. "Oh, no. We're all in this, as one. No arguments, Yank!"

"Hey! A little less of the 'Yank'!" Doris jokingly protested. "Oh, one more thing. Mary, how difficult do you think it'll be to smuggle John out of the manor? Is there a way of getting him out without anyone seeing him?"

Mary's grin would have made a shark proud. "Leave that to me. I can guarantee no one will see him leave the manor. Now, let's get home. I'm starving."

Silence prevailed whilst everyone took in Doris's plan, staring at their American friend.

"What goes on in that mind of yours?" Penny wondered. "Does Walter know what he's letting himself in for?"

Doris grinned. "Oh, he knows, he knows!"

Chapter Thirty-Two

"You're reading *The Moving Finger*?" Penny nearly squeaked, as she came into the mess for dinner. "Where've you been hiding that?"

Carefully putting a scrap of paper inside to mark her page, Betty laid the book aside and waited for Penny to sit down. "Hands off," she told her, as Penny's hands crawled toward the book. "If you're good, you can read it after me."

Waving Mavis and her cup of tea politely away, Penny eyed the latest Miss Marple enviously. "Does Doris know?"

Betty shook her head and leant back, letting out a deep sigh. "You're the only one that does. I suppose I'm more tired than I thought, or I wouldn't have brought this in to work."

Penny leaned forward and smiled the smile of a cobra hypnotizing a bird. "How did you hide it?"

Picking up the book, Betty revealed a dust jacket underneath, which she dangled in front of Penny's nose.

"What? You put another jacket over it?"

"You didn't think I was really taking so long to read *The Body in the Library*, did you?"

After a moment, Penny stood up and clapped and then sat back down. "I must be out of practice! Of course you weren't still reading the other one."

"Don't feel so bad," Betty told her. "You can read

the other when we get home, if you like. You haven't read it yet, have you?"

This brightened Penny's face. "Excellent! Can I have a look at it?" Penny nodded toward the cherished book.

Betty pretended to think about it and was about to pass over the book—in fact, she was holding out the book to Penny—when her hand stopped in midair, her eyes locked on something over Penny's shoulder.

Turning around, Penny saw immediately who had so riveted Betty's attention. By the time she turned back, Betty was out of her seat, pressing the book into Penny's hands and running toward the mess entrance. Standing in the open door, a big grin on his face, was Major Jim Fredericks of the USAAF. Cradling the book to her chest, Penny felt a surge of real joy for the first time in a while. Betty had met the American during the Clark Gable affair. He was the adjutant of the bomber squadron the film star had flown with, and the two had hit it off, though they'd kept it quiet, everyone becoming aware of it only just prior to last Christmas. She knew the two didn't get the chance to get together very often—in fact, she didn't know when the last time had been—though they did speak regularly on the telephone. That he'd turned up here was both a surprise and a source of obvious happiness to Betty.

Tucking the book carefully into her pocket, being very careful not to damage the cover, Penny got to her feet and finished off Betty's last slice of bread and jam. "I'll be in ops," she told Betty, plonking her hat on her head as she passed the two, who were now wrapped around each other. "Don't worry, I won't read the book. Sorry to tell you, but taxi take-off's in half an hour. Nice to see you, Major," she added.

Betty and Jim stood locked together for another few minutes before Betty leant her head back and suggested, "Let's go for a walk. I think..." She looked around. "We're in the way here."

They opened the door, and Betty ducked under his arm and then took it as he closed the door behind them. Ignoring the stares, Betty asked, "Don't get me wrong, I'm delighted to see you, but why didn't you tell me you were coming?"

"Believe me," Jim began, dipping down and whipping off Betty's hat, then kissing the top of her head, "I wish I could see you more often."

"I do too, you know I do," Betty assured him.

"As to why I'm here now? I didn't know I would be, myself, until a few hours ago." Walking slowly, Betty guided them back toward the ops hut. Leaning her head against his side, she waited for him to continue. "I've got both good and bad news, and it's good and bad news for us both."

"That sounds both ominous and...I don't know what," she finished with a slightly forced laugh. When Jim didn't join in, she added, "Probably slightly more ominous."

Neither said anything else until they found themselves at the foot of the steps leading up to the ops hut. Obviously they'd been observed, as Jane and Mary were waiting in the open door.

"Hey, Jim!" Jane said in greeting, as Mary stood beside her, adding a wave of hello.

"Jane, Mary," Jim said in reply. "I won't keep her long. I heard what Penny said about the taxi."

"She's plenty of time," Jane assured her, grabbing

hold of Mary's arm. "Come on, you. Let's give them a little privacy."

Jim stared as Jane shut the door behind her. "I like Jane."

"Me too," Betty replied, wondering how Jim was going to explain his cryptic words. Sitting on the steps, Jim gently pulled Betty down next to him. "I'm glad it's a sunny day," she said in an effort to lighten things up.

A frown appeared upon the American's face as he turned his head to the clear sky, then looked back into Betty's expectant eyes. "I'll never understand how you Brits can think this is a sunny day." Smiling, he shook his head.

Betty dug an elbow into his ribs. "Hey! We can't all come from California. This is England, that's the sun, and therefore, this is a sunny day."

Rubbing his side, Jim smiled down. "Fair enough. I won't make fun of the English weather again."

Betty waited a moment, decided enough was enough, and asked, "Just say whatever it is you've come to say, Jim. I don't know whether to be happy or…or prepare myself for a good cry."

In response, Jim wrapped his arms so tightly around Betty, she gasped for breath.

"Have I ever told you I love you, Betty?" His voice was so soft she had to ask him to repeat what he'd said.

Betty shook her head. "No, no, you haven't. And now, I'm more confused. If it comes to that, I love you too."

"I was hoping you'd say that." Jim smiled in response.

"Was that the good news?" Betty asked.

"It definitely is now," Jim answered.

Taking a deep breath, Betty said, "I suppose you'd better tell me the bad news, then."

Resting his head on top of Betty's, Jim told her, "I'm being posted back to the States."

"Ah," Betty said.

"Exactly."

"When?"

Jim took another deep breath. "The end of the month."

Betty couldn't help it. She broke away and looked at him askance. "That's not much notice."

"That's the Air Force for you." He shrugged.

"I don't know what to say," Betty admitted, before blurting out the first thing to come to her mind. "You'll still be here for Doris and Walter's wedding."

"That's…good news."

After a subjective eternity during which Betty had the time to think, she asked the only important question. "Where does this leave us?"

Though she hadn't expected Jim to have an answer, she still found it disappointing to hear him answer, "I'm not sure," though her heart was slightly warmed when he added, "All I do know is, I don't want to lose you."

Not knowing what else to do, Betty tipped her head upward, and Jim, taking the strong hint, leaned down to meet her waiting lips. Reaching around the back of his head, she grabbed hold of his hair as she put all the love she felt for this man from a strange land into the kiss. She felt herself losing all sense of time, as his lips ground against hers, both of them desperate to show the feelings they'd both kept hidden for too long, knowing the short time they had left. Stars sparkled at the edge of Betty's vision, finding the love she'd craved all her life about to be snatched away from her, but she didn't care and instead embraced the love they were sharing.

Who broke the moment, she didn't know, but she came to her senses with her head on Jim's shoulder and sniffing back tears she was determined not to show at this most precious of moments.

"God, you're quite a lady, Betty. If I had a plane right now, I'd go off and kill Hitler myself! End this goddamn war now, so we can be together."

Snuffling, Betty laughed. "You may not believe me, but that's the most romantic thing anyone's ever said to me!"

Jim swooped down for another quick kiss. "Then I'll have to do better, won't I!"

"I'm certainly not going to object if you try."

Both laughed at that, before the roar of an aircraft warming up, not far away, startled them.

"You're going to hate me, but I've got to get back."

"Already?"

"I know." Jim sighed. "I'm sorry. I knew this could only be a short trip. Is it okay to come down on Sunday?" he asked, getting to his feet and helping Betty up.

"More than okay," she replied.

"Good." Jim nodded. "I need to look into a few things, but I'm hoping to have something important to discuss with you by then." At her surprised face, he said, "Walk me back to my Jeep?"

In silence, the two walked back to where Jim had left his Jeep outside the mess. Sharing one more passionate kiss, something not helped by Mavis opening a window and wolf-whistling at the pair, Jim then fired up his Jeep, jammed his hat firmly onto his head, and said, "See you Sunday morning."

Not trusting her voice not to crack, Betty merely smiled and waved as he drove off. Once he was out of sight, she made her slow way back to the ops hut and once more sat down on the steps. How long she stared into the distance, not looking at anything in particular, she didn't know. However, she jumped clean off the boards as a hand landed upon her shoulder. Looking up, she saw the understanding face of Jane staring down at her. "Jim couldn't stay?"

"You could say that," Betty replied, not bothering to stop the tears from falling.

Chapter Thirty-Three

"Penny Alsop!" Doris shouted at the top of her voice as she slammed the door of The Old Lockkeepers Cottage behind her. She dumped her bag on the floor and ignored her hat bouncing off the hook and joining it. "Where are you?"

"What's up with you?" Penny's voice came from above her head.

Standing on the bottom step of the stairs, Doris looked up and saw the person she was searching for poking her head above the rails. "Why, pray tell, did you not wait for me?" Doris asked, mellowing her tone.

Not fooled for a second, Penny replied, "I wanted to get home as quickly as possible. Sorry about that," she added, her head slowly withdrawing.

"Oh, no, you don't!" Doris muttered, kicking off her shoes and bounding up the stairs until she came to Penny's room. The door was slightly open, so she knocked once and pushed it open. Penny was already on her bed, still in her uniform, stockinged legs crossed in the air, her toes bouncing around. As dramatically as any bad actor, Doris planted her feet half in and half out of the room and leveled a finger accusingly at her friend. "Ah-ha!"

Peering over the top of the book she was reading, Penny asked, "Ah-ha...what?"

Unable to continue the act, Doris relaxed her stance

and came to collapse upon Penny's bed beside her. "Shift up a little and turn back to page one, please."

Instead, Penny closed the book, shuffled over a little so she could lean on an elbow and regard her friend's strange behavior. "Would you care to explain exactly what you're playing at?"

Doris tapped the book Penny was clutching close to her chest. "That's what I'm playing at."

"You're playing at a book?"

Rolling her eyes, Doris allowed her head to slump back onto Penny's pillow. "Don't try to be cute, hon. You know exactly what I'm talking about."

Penny made a show of turning the book over to look at the cover before revealing it to her friend. "You mean this?"

Doris made a quick move to snatch the book out of Penny's hands, but she was too quick and tucked it out of her friend's way under the pillow on her side of the bed. "Oh, no, you don't!"

Unheard by either of them, Mary and Betty had come home and now ran upstairs and poked their heads around the door. "Is this a private party? Or can anyone join in?" Betty asked.

"What the heck's going on?" Mary added.

When Penny didn't provide an answer, Doris swiveled around so she could sit on the edge of the bed. "Did you tell Pens, here, she could read *The Body in the Library*?"

Betty came in and leant against the window sill. "I did. Why?"

"I was hoping to read it after you," Doris moaned. "I've been waiting long enough!"

"She saw me reading *The Moving Finger* in the mess

and asked," Betty merely said, before turning her back on the room to stare out the window.

Her friends, noticing this, forgot about the Miss Marple book and all gathered around their friend and landlady.

Doris put an arm around Betty's shoulders and asked, "What's wrong? You didn't say a word on the trip, nor whilst we were all getting changed over on the flight line."

Penny did the same from her other side. "Was it something Jim said? Jane mentioned you were crying when she found you on the steps of the ops hut."

"That's enough," Jane herself stated, coming into the room and placing both her hands on Betty's shoulders. "Everyone out."

Betty shook her head as she reached up and took a grip on one of Jane's hands. "No, it's all right. I'd like everyone to stay."

Not waiting any longer, Doris immediately asked, "What's Jim done? Do I need to have *words* with him?"

This typical question from their Yankee cousin got a slight chuckle from Betty. "No, you don't, but I'll keep you in mind if it comes to that."

"So what happened?" Doris was not the most patient of girls.

"Cup of tea first?" Jane suggested as Betty turned and everyone could see how red her eyes were.

"Always a good idea," Betty replied, sniffing.

As they led her out of Penny's room, Mary said, "I'll go and see how Terry is, and if he wants a cup."

Once they were all sitting around the kitchen table, except for Penny, who'd taken upon herself the task of making the tea, Betty told Doris, "Go and look in my bag. Jim brought you a little present."

Curious, Doris did as she was bid, and a few seconds later they all heard a whoop of joy, closely followed by thundering footsteps as Doris bounced back into the room. Clutched to her breast was a large tin container of coffee, the biggest smile upon her face.

"You found it, then?" Betty said, showing a weak smile.

Carefully keeping one hand upon the tin, Doris leant over Betty and gave her a hug. "I take it all back! I love Jim!"

"That makes two of us," Betty surprised everyone by replying.

After a short pause, Jane asked, "Is that what he came down to tell you? You didn't say why you were crying earlier."

Betty shook her head. "No. That would have been a great use of petrol, eh?"

Penny brought the now-boiled kettle to the table, poured the water into the teapot, and placed the kettle back on the burner. "Perhaps not," she agreed, but then added, "though it would have been incredibly romantic."

"It would, if that'd been the only thing he said."

Jane shuffled her seat along so she was right next to her friend, whereupon Betty immediately leant her head against Jane's shoulder.

Taking in the sight as she entered the room, Mary quickly said, "Terry would love a cup, thanks," before taking a seat.

They all heard Betty take a deep breath. "That was one of the things he came down to talk to me about, but then he told me he's being posted away at the end of the month."

"Oh, bugger!" Doris declared, which seemed to sum up the mood of the room.

Waiting until Penny had poured the tea, Betty dabbed her eyes on her handkerchief and added, "He's coming down on Sunday. Before he left, he told me he didn't want to lose me and was looking into something which he hoped he'd have sorted by then."

Nobody seemed to know what to say about this, nor how to interpret it. After taking a sip of her tea, Betty got to her feet, cleared her throat, and said, "Well, I'll leave you all to mull that over. I'm going to take Terry up his tea."

Once she'd left the kitchen and they'd heard her footsteps recede up the stairs, everyone began to speak at once. Eventually, by constantly tapping her spoon against her cup, Jane managed to wrest back some control.

"Thank you. Look, I'm sure we all have Betty's wellbeing in mind, but let's not jump to any wild conclusions."

"Do you think they'll be able to marry before he has to leave?" Doris immediately dived off the cliff face.

"Chop the potatoes," Jane told her, with a shake of her head.

****

Early Saturday morning, Penny had just put on the kettle when there came a sharp couple of raps at the front door. She was about to open it when she recalled, in time, they were supposed to be using caution. Admonishing herself, Penny stood against the wall to one side of the door and asked, "Who is it?"

"It's Grace, Penny!" was the reply, in what Penny knew was the nurse's voice.

Unlocking the door, she pulled it open. It still felt strange, as the door had rarely been locked since she'd come to reside at the cottage, unless they were all at work. "Lovely to see you, Grace," she said, giving her friend a quick hug before stepping back to allow the nurse to enter. "What brings you here?" she asked as she turned back toward the kitchen.

The answer of, "You," stayed Penny's hand from pushing the kitchen door open.

Turning, Penny echoed, "Me? Whatever for?"

Sitting herself at the table, Grace employed the smile which immediately put Penny on alert. "I think you know why."

Because she wasn't paying attention to what she was doing, Penny jerked slightly whilst in the process of cutting the bread to make toast, wrenching her shoulder. Grace didn't miss the wince of pain on Penny's face.

"And there's why," she said, frowning. "Are you flying again? A little bird, the station doctor I ran into at the hospital yesterday, may have let it slip."

Penny did her best to ignore the question, but when Grace asked it a second time, politeness decreed she should reply. "Not anymore. I did once, but only to cover Doris and Mary."

Now she'd hurt herself, Penny couldn't hide another wince as she finished up carving. One by one, the rest of the household marched into the room, with Jane bringing up the rear, though her loud complaints could be heard long before she'd come down the stairs.

"I said, has anyone seen my left glove?" she asked once again, as she entered the kitchen before doing a double-take upon noticing the nurse. "Grace! How are you?"

Grace smiled back. "I'm fine."

Jane then turned toward the lounge. "What brings you here?" she shouted, obviously still fixated upon finding her glove.

"Trying to decide whether I should tell you off or not."

"Well, I wasn't expecting that," Betty muttered, watching the toast to make certain it didn't burn. "Care to explain why?"

Instead of speaking, Grace got up and, unexpectedly, pressed her thumb directly where Penny had been shot.

"For Christ's sake!" Penny swore, jumping back and rubbing her sore arm. "What did you do that for?"

Grace at least looked contrite. "I'm sorry. I needed to see if you'd done any damage to it."

Jane reappeared, still gloveless. "And why, pray tell, were you thinking about telling me off?"

Not the least cowed, Grace moved her finger toward Penny's arm once more, prompting Penny to immediately back off. Grace arched an eyebrow toward Jane.

"Ah," Jane replied after a moment or two. "Yes, I see what you mean."

Penny immediately sprang to Jane's defense. "Don't blame Jane! I jumped at the chance to get back in the air, if only for one day."

Grace let the two stew for a minute, whilst accepting a piece of toast from Betty, before reaching down into the bag she carried. Taking out a bandage, she laid it upon the table. "Have you lost yours? Or do I have to tie you down, as well as back up?"

Penny shook her head in horror. "No fear! I've still

got one."

Grace dangled the bandage before Penny's face. "You have two minutes to go and get it and put it on. Go," she whispered, and Penny shot off as fast as she could.

Mary regarded the now grinning nurse. "You're going to make an imposing Sister, you know."

"Sister?" Grace queried, her eyes flitting toward the ceiling as multiple thumps and curses filtered through the ceiling. "Matron, thank you!"

"Remind me never to get injured if you're around," Doris put in, laughing.

****

Unseen by Terry on lookout upstairs and unbeknownst to the cottage's usual inhabitants, Verdon ducked back down from glancing in the kitchen window. Having come to the conclusion that he couldn't rely on his servant, he'd taken what courage he had in hand and staked out the cottage for himself. As he stood back, he heard something squelch beneath his foot and only just managed to stop himself from cursing at the top of his voice, as would normally have been his wont, especially as he'd heard nothing of interest from listening beneath the window.

Hugging the side of the cottage, he stayed as low as possible until he came to the path which led between the cottage and a hedge. For no reason other than he thought it would be a good idea, Verdon dragged his dark raincoat over his head and dived through the hedge. Landing in something soft and smelly rapidly convinced him it hadn't been his best idea. He had the presence of mind to check behind him, and when no one seemed about to pounce upon him, he stood up and surveyed his depressing appearance. Not only had he landed in a pile of smelly mud, but he was quite dismayed to find he'd stepped in a dog turd.

"Bloody country," he muttered, barely keeping his voice down.

Tearing up a large clump of grass, he did his best to wipe the worst of the mud from the front of his coat, but only succeeded in spreading it around. Giving this up as a bad idea, he began to scrape his shoe clean when a dog's nose appeared through the hedge, rapidly followed by the rest of the dog's head.

Reacting in anger, Verdon picked up the nearest stone and threw it with all his might, striking the poor dog above the left ear and sending the animal whimpering off back the way it had come.

Somewhat more satisfied than he'd been a few moments ago, Verdon made his way back to his hideout, not giving the dog he'd assaulted another moment's thought.

Chapter Thirty-Four

Betty was the last one left in the kitchen, placing the morning's breakfast cutlery and crockery in to soak, when she heard the dog-flap bumped. She waited, but when nothing happened, she placed the last cup in the sink. Turning to leave, she thought she heard the flap bump open once more and then…nothing. Something told her to go and take a closer look. Kneeling down, she pushed the flap up and was shocked at the sight before her.

Hurriedly, she unlocked the door, calling at the top of her voice, "Grace! I need you—now!"

To her credit, the nurse didn't hesitate and came at a run, only to literally skid to a halt at what confronted her.

Betty stood with Bobby in her arms. She'd stooped to pick him up from where she found him slumped against her back doorstep. Clearly shocked, she told them, "I heard a noise at the dog-flap, twice, and so opened the door. He…he didn't have the strength to push it open!"

"Christ! What happened?" Doris asked, nearly bumping into Grace's back before the nurse stepped toward the bloody pair.

"Is he alive?" Mary asked, holding onto Doris's shoulders.

Jane took one look, declared, "I'll go and get Ruth,"

292

and shot off through the back door.

"Grace?" Betty said, laying the dog on the kitchen table without a second thought.

"Someone get my bag, please! I dropped it in the hall," Grace asked, as she stepped forward. "Can I have a tea towel, Betty?" she asked as she laid a hand on Bobby's chest before looking up to assure the room, "He's alive. Wet it for me, Mary," she told her when presented with the requested item.

As Mary soaked the tea towel beneath the tap, Grace checked nothing was restricting the injured dog's airway before accepting the towel and proceeding to wash and wipe away the blood soaking the side of Bobby's face. When the cold towel touched his head, the dog's head perked up. "Betty, hold his head for me," Grace ordered.

That was how Ruth found the room when she ran in through the open back door. "What the hell? Bobby!" she cried, automatically springing toward her dog before being brought up short by Grace raising a hand to stop her.

Glancing up for a second, she told Ruth, "It's not as bad as it looks. Head wounds," she began, resuming her ministration, "be they in humans or animals, always tend to bleed a lot."

A few seconds later, both Jane and Walter followed Ruth into the kitchen.

"I had no idea you could run so..." Walter began to say, stopping when he saw what was happening on the table. Instead, he immediately went and gathered his landlady in a hug, turning her around so she could watch what Grace was doing.

The temporary quiet was broken by a noise on the stairs, shortly followed by Terry bursting into the room.

"What's all the noise about?" he managed to get out before noticing the injured dog. "What happened?" he asked, the policeman in him kicking into gear.

"Another wet tea towel!" Grace called out before answering everyone's question. "If I had to guess, I'd say he's been either hit with something, or someone threw something at him. Maybe a stone or brick."

Nobody could make out what Ruth mumbled into Walter's shoulder, not that anyone really needed to guess, as everyone shared her sentiments.

"Is he going to be all right?" Doris asked, looking slightly on the pale side, though she recovered a little of her color when Grace took a moment from her ministrations to look up and say, "I'd say he'll be fine. He'll probably feel a bit off color for a few days, but there shouldn't be any lasting harm. Though, Ruth, I'm not a vet, you know."

Ruth broke away from her nephew and announced, "I'd trust you more than any vet I know, my dear. You just do what you think needs to be done, and you won't find me ungrateful."

Muttering, "Don't be so silly," Grace bent to her work for a few minutes more before straightening up. "There, he looks a lot better now he's clean, doesn't he?"

Ruth let out a sob and made a move to engulf her beloved cocker spaniel, only for Grace to stop her from doing so. "Not yet, Ruth. I'd like to put a couple of stitches in."

"Stitches?" Ruth said, her hands flying to her mouth.

"Only a couple," Grace repeated, laying a reassuring hand upon Ruth's arm before taking her hand and pulling her a step closer. "Look down here. Betty, if you'd just hold him a bit harder, thanks. See, just above his ear?

That's the cut. It's not long, but it is a little deep. It'll only take me a minute, but I'd feel better if I stitched it up. It can't stay like that, as it'll only get dirty, and he's almost certain to pick up an infection then."

Ruth reached out her hand again, and this time Grace didn't stop her. Being very careful, she stroked the opposite side of his head, then asked, "Will it hurt?"

Slowly, Grace nodded. "I'm afraid so. I don't have any anesthetic on me." At Ruth's look of alarm, she hastened to say, "We can go and wake the vet up, if you'd prefer."

Everyone in the room could sense the internal conflict going on inside Ruth. She, of all people, wouldn't wish to hurt her dog, but trust in Grace's skills versus the uncertainty of causing Bobby any more stress and pain than necessary were warring away inside her. Bobby chose that moment to let out a whine, and Grace picked up the tea towel as his wound had begun to seep blood again. This made up her mind.

"Do it."

After taking a second to look up into Ruth's eyes, the nurse nodded and handed her the tea towel, guiding her hand. "Keep the pressure on. I'll just get ready," she told her, crossing to the sink and beginning to wash her hands, saying as she did, "Everyone, and I'm really sorry about this, Ruth, this is going to hurt Bobby. I'll be as quick as I can, but I'm going to need your help. We have to keep him as still as we can, so I'm going to need everyone, especially you, Walter, to hold Bobby down. I reckon it'll take two, possibly three stitches, and that's going to take me about a minute." Accepting a clean tea towel from Doris, she turned back to the room, drying her hands. "There's no sugar-coating it. This is going to hurt him, but you can't flinch, and you can't loosen your grip, no matter how much he'll howl—and he will. Ruth, I know that isn't what you want to hear, but I promise I'll be as quick as I possibly can."

Everyone turned to Ruth for her reaction. Without looking up, she put down the tea towel and took up position next to Betty where, grim-faced but determined, she took hold of Bobby, laying her arm firmly upon his neck, but without causing a restriction on his breathing. "Ready when you are," she said, though she didn't look up when she spoke. Everyone else took this as their cue and took up various positions as Ruth began to mutter as many soothing words into his ear as she could, her face down by his ear.

Without another word, Grace placed her bag on the table, quickly found a needle and some catgut, and without hesitation, began her work. True to her word, Bobby did howl, and though Ruth instantly had tears streaming down her face—not that she was the only one, by any means—to her credit, she followed Grace's orders to the letter and didn't let go her hold. Everyone else around the distressed animal did the same, taking their strength and determination from Ruth.

True to her hopes, around a minute later, Grace straightened up, gently wiped around Bobby's wound, and then threw the bloodied tea towel aside. Reaching down to stroke the panting dog, she told him, "Well done, you! You were so brave." She looked up. "Everyone, when I say so, let go and stand back a bit. Ruth, stay where you are but let go now and get ready to restrain him. He's going to want to jump down, and I don't want that just yet." Checking everyone had given her a nod, Grace said, "Now."

Immediately he felt the arms and hands loosen, Bobby did try to stand, only for Ruth to at once gently wrap her arms around his neck, being extra careful to avoid the stitches Grace had applied. His eyes were a little wide, and he was panting, but after an initial squirm, as Grace had predicted, he calmed and leant against his mistress's chest, his breathing gradually becoming normal.

"There you go," Ruth told him as he settled down into her familiar embrace, licking her tear-addled but smiling face.

Grace tentatively reached out a hand toward Bobby, as if half-expecting him to bite her. Instead, he turned his attention to the nurse and proceeded to baste her hand. Smiling at Ruth, Grace let out a deep sigh of relief. "He's a right little trooper, isn't he?"

"I'll say," Ruth agreed.

"The whole station's fallen in love with him again after yesterday," Jane piped up.

Grace looked up, her eyes wide as dishes. "Don't tell me! He didn't turn up on station when that Nazi plane went over, did he?"

Everyone in the room nodded their heads, beaming at the brave dog in undisguised pride.

Shaking her head, Grace told them, "Well, I never! We never got an air raid alarm, you know. Perhaps the hospital could hire him out, Ruth?"

"Not a chance!" Mary declared, laughing as the tension in the room began to ebb away.

It took Grace a while to make her exit after gathering her things together, as everyone in the house wanted to give her a thank-you hug and kiss, and Ruth kept coming back for more. Grace finally had to say, "You're going

297

to make me later than I already am," although she said it with a big smile.

"That goes for us too," Jane said.

Ruth gave her another unexpected hug. "I can't thank you enough. I really can't."

"There's no need, really. As for Bobby, he should be okay without anything for the pain. They're surprisingly sturdy. If he does appear in any discomfort, take him to the vet, but I doubt he'll need it, and if you see him scratching at his ear, which is entirely possible, then wind a bandage or rag around his head. It doesn't matter if he looks silly. Now, I really must go. I'll pop around tonight to see how he is."

"Don't forget to be careful," Betty told Grace as she went to leave. "Remember what Lawrence said."

"You beat me to it," Terry surprised everyone by saying from the top of the stairs. "Well done, Betty. How's the patient, nurse?"

"He's going to be fine!" Ruth answered, beaming, at the foot of the stairs, the patient clutched safely in her arms.

Chapter Thirty-Five

"Are you running off again, Alsop?" Doris shouted after Penny as her friend ran past the guardroom at the end of Saturday's shift.

"Can't stop! Got to get ready for my date!" she yelled back over her shoulder.

"Date?" Doris asked Betty as they waved to the guard as they left the station.

"Tom's coming over, and he's taking her for a walk around Lyndhurst and then a drink," Betty supplied.

"Aww," Mary said, "I'm so pleased they're getting back together."

Betty nodded with a smile. "Very true. It's a while since I've seen her so happy."

They were halfway toward the bend in the road which would take them toward home when they heard a shout from behind them. "Watch out!" Jane was running their way and waving her arms like a madwoman.

Looking around, nobody could see anything they should be worried about until Doris let out a cry of, "Duck!" whereupon everyone else turned their eyes upon the American and followed where she was looking. A loud and angry-sounding "Quack!" assaulted their ears, and amid a flurry of flapping wings and foaming water, everyone's feathery nemesis launched itself out of the river and flew into Doris's arms.

Only when they were certain Duck was securely

M. W. Arnold

locked in place did her friends creep back, though everyone kept a good few paces between themselves and the pair, just in case.

At last, Jane felt brave enough to walk next to Doris whilst everyone else contented themselves with trailing a few paces in their wake. "That's a new trick. When did Duck learn that?"

Doris shrugged her shoulders as she continued to stroke Duck's head, whilst Duck contentedly quacked in happiness. "Don't ask me. He just flew into my arms one evening, and he's been doing it ever since."

"Do you think he'd be interested in guarding the cottage?" Mary asked. "Perhaps Terry could use him as a kind of guard duck."

"Why've the tips of your ears gone red?" Penny asked, and when Doris brushed her fingers over said ears, Penny assured her, "Well, they have."

After Doris didn't answer after a few minutes, Mary clicked her fingers. "I've got it! You've already asked, haven't you?"

Jane turned her head. "I heard her and warned Terry against trying. For a second, after she'd told him about Duck, I thought he was seriously considering her suggestion, so I felt I had to jump in and tell him what a bad idea that would be."

"Honestly!" Doris shook her head, whilst everyone else rolled their eyes, knowing exactly what was coming. "If you lot would only try and make friends with Duck, I'm sure he wouldn't attack...or not so much, anyway."

"Whose turn is it?" Betty asked.

Penny put up her hand. "Mine! Doris, that's never going to happen. You know Duck hates us, and we're not very keen on him either."

Doris covered the duck's ears with a hand. "Don't listen to them, sweety!"

Unseen by the girls, Ruth, Walter, and Bobby were waiting for the group at the turn.

"Is Doris trying to convince you lot to be friends with Duck again?" Walter asked, when they were spotted. Walking tentatively up to his fiancée, he leant in to kiss her on the cheek and had to hastily jump back when Duck made a lunge for his nose. Things didn't go better for him when he tried to hold her hand. Visibly exasperated, he settled for standing by her side just out of range of Duck.

Jane put a hand on Ruth's shoulder before leaning down and gently patting Bobby on the back. "How's the wounded warrior?"

Ruth smiled down at Bobby, who was now enjoying everyone making a fuss of him. "As you can see, he's been trying to scratch his stitches, so I've had to tie a bandage around him. I know it makes him look a little silly…"

"Nonsense," Jane objected, standing straight again. "I think it makes him look the part of the wounded warrior! I'll tell you this—if he came onto station looking like that, he'd get fed so many tidbits he'd need to go on another diet!"

"Oh, no, you don't!" Ruth objected. "I've only just got him back to a decent weight, and that's during a blinking war."

"Steady, steady!"

"Doris? Have you got that thing under control?" Mary asked, backing off as Doris did a little duck juggling.

Said fowl was presently struggling against Doris's

grip, managing to get one wing free, which was currently flicking around her left ear. "Oww! Yes, all under control here."

Mary edged past Doris, who did her best not to get in everyone else's way by moving toward the river. Once her friends were safely out of range, she thrust her hands into the air, whereupon Duck took flight in a flurry of aquatic protests before alighting on the water, fluffing up his breast, and paddling away.

"I wonder what's gotten into him?" Doris mused, watching her feathered friend disappear from sight.

Honestly puzzled, Penny had to ask. Her eyes too had followed Duck until he'd disappeared. "How can you tell?"

****

"Take one duck..." Betty pretended to read from the newspaper cutting.

"Say that again?" Doris asked, sticking her head around the door to the kitchen. "Did I hear you right?"

Betty looked up. "You did," and went back to her reading.

"When you said you were going to make something special for tea tonight..." Doris said, craning her neck to look over Betty's shoulder. The landlady moved the mixing bowl over the recipe.

Doris had gone a little white. "But...duck?"

In the middle of tying an apron around her waist, Jane looked up. "We decided we could all do with something special, what with the wonderful time we've all been having lately."

"And, let me get this straight, you both decided duck would be a good idea?"

"Mock duck," Betty repeated, and as Doris had

moved toward Jane, she moved the bowl. "Take one duck. First, wring its neck, then chop off the head and throw away, or give to your dog, if you have one."

"No!" Doris yelled, spinning around wide-eyed before running out the front door without checking the coast was clear.

"I think we took it too far," Betty said, as she took to her heels and darted out the front door, closely followed by Jane.

"What the hell?" Mary declared, sticking her head out of the lounge as Jane sped by. In no time she also was taking after her friends.

Appearing at the top of the stairs, Terry, who had heard and then witnessed the mass exodus, slapped his forehead and rushed down the stairs. "Bloody madhouse," he muttered, pulling the door shut behind him. "Hey, you lot!" he shouted, though this proved unnecessary, as only Doris was the other side of the gate. Making his way to where Doris stood, her eyes dancing around and darting all over the place, he stood between her and the direction of the village and raised his voice to get everyone's attention. "Have you lot forgot what we agreed? We'd agreed not to use the front door after dark, at least not without checking first. We certainly don't all rush out without bothering to look!"

Everyone except Doris was now paying full attention to the words of the policeman. The American was now shouting, "Duck!" at the top of her voice.

Terry looked carefully around, satisfying himself nobody was around who shouldn't be. Then, his face as stern as any of them had ever seen it, he said, "Ladies, do you know what I found after you lot went to work this morning? I took a look around and found where Bobby was hurt and also where the person who threw the stone likely stood. So now do you understand why I'm angry?" Everyone looked sufficiently contrite except for Doris, who was still shouting. Turning his full attention to the American once more, he shouted, "What the hell do you think you're doing?"

Not looking at her friends, Doris wildly pointed behind at her friends. "Ask them! They're going to cook Duck for tea!"

"Duck?" Terry appeared confused. "Just who's Duck?"

Clearly struggling to keep a straight face, Mary supplied him the required information. "Duck's her name for her psychotic duck."

"Duck's a…duck?" he asked, clearly not believing his ears.

"That's right," Mary agreed, "and he's the most evil fowl fiend on the river."

Terry glanced around the group of friends. "Is this for real?"

Finally, Doris paid attention. "He's not evil. It's just that I'm the only one he likes."

"The rest of us he chases up trees," Betty helpfully supplied.

Terry's eyebrows shot up. "I think I'm with you, though I'm not certain I want to be. Okay, let's assume that's all true. Were you going to cook her duck?"

"Duck. His name is Duck," Doris insisted, still looking extremely agitated.

"And it's Mock Duck we're making," Betty said.

"Mock Duck?" Doris asked. "As in not real duck?"

"Exactly," agreed Jane. "But you hared out before we could make you hear that part."

These words got through to Doris as she slowly turned her head toward her friends, her eyes narrow and clearly as angry as any of them had ever seen. "Let me get this right. You're not cooking duck? You're not cooking *Duck*?"

Both Betty and Jane hung their heads as Betty answered for them both, "No. We…er…we were playing a joke…a nasty joke on you."

"And we're so very, very sorry," added Jane, holding out her hands to Doris.

"We really are," Betty said, looking close to tears. "Please, forgive us?"

Doris, though her eyes were still narrowed, at least softened her stance, though she did ask, "Is this because of how Duck behaves around you lot?"

Jane and Betty shared very contrite looks. "It seemed like a good idea at the time."

"And were you in on this?" Doris asked of Mary, who vigorously shook her head. Accepting this, Doris said, "Well, I suppose it's the kind of thing I'd do, and now I stop to think about it, I can't believe you'd ever cause anything harm, at least not deliberately."

"We wouldn't!" Jane implored. She then repeated what Betty had said, "Please, forgive us?"

Doris crossed her arms. "No more open cockpit flights for a month?"

"Two weeks," Jane offered.

"Three weeks, "Doris countered, then shook the hand Jane offered.

Terry opened his arms wide and did his best to herd the girls. "All very good. Now we're all friends again, can we please get back inside?"

"What is Mock Duck, anyway?" Doris asked as she

allowed Terry to show them back into the cottage.

"It's mainly sausage meat, onions, and apples," Betty supplied.

"So we could make a kind of topless pie instead?" Doris suggested.

"That's not a bad idea," Jane agreed. "We've got some carrots left."

"Great!" Doris clapped her hands together. "I'll get us a couple of Guinnesses from out back, and then come and watch you two make me a delicious tea!"

****

"Bread and bloody gooseberry jam? Is that all? This is what you've served me for tea for the last three nights!" Verdon spat out at Croft. "When I sit down to tea, I expect something much better."

Counting to ten in his head, Croft looked up, already halfway through his first sandwich. "You're the one who told me to turn the gas off. If you want something hot, turn it back on."

Croft finished his sandwich whilst he watched Verdon hold an internal argument. He knew exactly what he was thinking, the man was such a miser, he was too cheap to put a coin in the meter so he could have a hot meal. As for himself, he'd some cash he could spare, but he wasn't going to put himself out in any way for Verdon now. Having to wash the mud-ridden clothes the man had come back in that morning had been the straw to break the camel's back. Whilst Croft scrubbed away, the odious Verdon had boasted how he'd been able to sneak up, in daylight, no less, and listen at the kitchen window of the Betty woman's cottage. It had been so easy, he'd boasted, wondering aloud all the while why Croft had refused to perform any work against them in daylight.

Croft hadn't bothered to say he'd got lucky, as the man was so arrogant he wouldn't have believed him.

When he asked if Verdon had learned anything which could get him his money, he received a reluctant shake of the head.

"Notes and tactics designed to frighten them don't seem to be working."

No kidding, Croft had thought, but not said out loud.

"I don't think she's even trying to get any money together, you know," Verdon rambled on, glancing over Croft's shoulder and pointing out a spot of mud he'd missed. "I think more direct action will be required."

Croft's hands spasmed, tearing in half the shirt he was scrubbing.

Chapter Thirty-Six

"So how did you manage to get the morning off?"

Clutching her husband's arm a little tighter, a sensation she was finding both comforting and familiar once again, Penny glanced around the forest, suddenly very glad of the daylight. Though she had no memory of the last time she'd visited the New Forest, for which she was truly thankful, she was unable to suppress a shudder, which her husband felt through his fingers.

Stepping in front of her, he glanced up and down and, finding no obvious physical reason, not counting the arm in its sling, asked, "Penny for them? And sorry, I really couldn't think of any other way to ask."

"Be thankful my preferred fist is otherwise engaged at this time," she told him, hoping he'd let things drop. This was supposed to be the first of a proper set of dates, work allowing for both of them, and reliving a near-death experience wasn't top of her list. Taking his hand again in her free one, she led him off toward a glade she'd spotted a few minutes ago. If she was right, the sun should be shining through the gap in the trees, and if her luck was truly in, there'd be a fallen tree they could sit on and enjoy the sandwiches she'd made for them.

If he suspected she was avoiding the question, he merely allowed his suspicion to show with a raise of an eyebrow. Hopping over a puddle, he held out a hand to help Penny. "Careful, I can't swim very well," he told her with a smile as she took it and stepped gingerly around.

Penny stood on tiptoes and kissed Tom on the tip of the nose once she'd safely negotiated the hazard. "Now, there's the man I fell in love with."

Before she could object, Tom swept Penny off her feet, being very careful not to catch her bad arm, and kissed her passionately back. Losing herself in the moment, Penny wasn't sure if stars were flashing before her eyes or if Tom had always been this good a kisser. Deciding she was overthinking things, she relaxed into the moment and found herself more than a little disappointed when Tom pulled away.

"I, er, hope I didn't get ahead of myself?" he asked.

Looking up into his eyes, Penny could see the genuine concern there. Holding out her hand, she took his and waited until they were in the glade before replying, "You may have taken me a little by surprise, that's all."

With an expression of relief on his face, Tom took his cap off and swept a hand through his hair. "Would it be forward to ask if I may kiss you again?"

Her heart overwhelming her head, which was crying out for her to slow things down a little, Penny shook her head. "Yes, I think that would be all right."

The air crinkled with electricity as Penny spied exactly what she'd been hoping to find. Gripping his hand a little tighter, she took him toward a fallen tree which so very conveniently, she thought, lay in the middle of the glade, sunlight dancing off the lichen covering the bark. Sitting down, she patted the space beside her.

"Wow!" Tom exclaimed, glancing around. "This is

quite the sight!"

Penny joined him in examining their glade. "It is! There's something magical about it, I think."

"You knew it existed?"

"No, though it's nice when nature plays along."

"Great instincts!" he told her, leaning in to plant his lips upon her cheek.

After he'd taken them away, she could still feel their warmth. "I do try," she said.

"As do I," he told her. What he asked next spoiled the moment a little, though seeing as he had his own instincts which kept him alive each time he flew, she wasn't surprised. "So you never answered. What was the shiver for?"

Happily leaving her head against his chest, it being handy he couldn't see her face, she took a deep breath. "This is near where Jane crashed when we were…shot down."

Not unexpectedly, Tom jerked back. "In Lyndhurst?"

She shook her head as he gripped her free hand in a vise-like grip. "Ouch! Not so tight, please. Not in Lyndhurst, but not too far away. I meant this is the first time I've been back into the forest since then."

"You've not been able to visit anywhere in the forest since?" he asked.

"Just flying over was difficult," she admitted. Flapping her sling, Penny moaned, "When I was allowed to fly, that is."

Gently, Tom laid his other hand upon the hand within the sling. "How's it feeling? Any better?"

"I'm doing as my doctor and my nurse friend Grace advise," was all she answered.

"Medics are scary, eh."

"Speaking of, how's your head? I admit, I wasn't expecting you to be back on flying duties. Should you be?" she asked.

Tom didn't reply right away, until saying, "Possibly, possibly not, but it's where I should be. Plus, Stan's very happy to be flying with me again."

"How's Stan doing?" Penny asked. "Are his burns healed?"

Tom nodded. "As much as they're going to be, yes. He says they don't hurt anymore, but Sharon's told me that he's still in a bit of pain. I think he's better at hiding it from me than he is from his girlfriend! What kind of a friend does that make me?"

"A man," Penny said without hesitation. "Not the most observant of the species," she added with smile.

"Hey! I'll have you know I'm very observant!"

"Perhaps when you're flying," Penny allowed, "but not when it comes to fellow humans. However, if you pour me a cup of tea, I'll allow you that one."

As he passed her a cup, Tom asked, "Before I...flew off the handle, I never asked you about what happened, did I?"

Penny shook her head. "No, you didn't. Mind you, I don't know anything about what happened. I was unconscious from the moment I was shot until I woke up in the hospital. If you really need to know what happened, then Jane's who you should talk to. She did save my life, and ended up with a broken arm for her troubles. I haven't asked her for the full story."

Taking a sip of his tea, Tom admitted, "I guess we owe her a lot."

Penny could only smile. "Only my life."

"Do you want to know what happened?" Tom asked.

"Don't think I haven't thought about it, many a time."

"And…"

"And…I don't know," Penny admitted. "Perhaps it's best I don't know what happened." She rubbed her arm where she'd been shot. "I'm not certain I want to hear all the details."

****

"Are you all trying to tell me that I'm being rationed…again?"

"Doris!" Jane pleaded as she strolled alongside her on the way home that Saturday afternoon.

"Please don't say I'm being irrational, Jane. It's been a long morning."

Lengthening her stride, Jane caught up with her friend and hauled her to a stop. "You lot go ahead," she told everyone else as they came to a stop beside them. "We'll catch you up." Once they were alone, Jane said, "I'm not saying you're being irrational at all. All I'm saying is I know how much you like your coffee, especially as you haven't had so much for so long. All I am saying…asking, is that you pace yourself. Don't have more than one before flying, and try not to have more than that when you get back."

Doris put her head to one side. "Sounds suspiciously like rationing to me."

Jane put her hand through Doris's arm and steered her back toward home. "Call it what you will. I'm serious, my dear. If I may say, you tend to get a little overexcited when you have more than one cup, and I don't think that's a great thing when you should have a clear head whilst flying."

To Doris's credit, she didn't immediately reply, taking her time to think through what her friend had said. With a deep sigh, Doris came to a halt and, without looking at her, said, "You really are a good leader, Jane, you know that."

"I have my moments." Jane shrugged. "We've got a deal?"

Doris nodded. "We've got a deal."

Both were talking amicably away when they got to the door, only to find their way blocked by Penny and Tom engaged in making up for time.

"Cold out here!" Doris pointed out, tapping Penny on the shoulder.

Breaking apart, the two didn't look in the least embarrassed. In fact, Tom let out a huge cry of, "Jane!" and without warning, grabbed her around the middle. Hugging her tightly, he gave her a quick kiss on both cheeks before hastily stepping back next to where his wife looked as equally confused as everyone else.

It took Jane a few seconds to recover her wits. "What the hell was that?"

Now the act was over, Tom looked mightily embarrassed and indeed lowered his head as he answered, "I'm perfectly aware I've an awful lot to do before I can get your trust back, Jane—everyone's, come to that—but I couldn't help myself. Penny and I have been talking, and she made me realize I never thanked you for saving Penny's life!"

Now Jane took a turn at being embarrassed, though Tom noticed she was rubbing her arm where it had been broken.

He nodded his head toward the action. "And I'm so, so very sorry for what you went through as well. How's the arm now?"

Looking down, Jane became aware for the first time what she was doing. With one more quick rub, she crossed her arms. "Perhaps a little itchy, and I know Grace is annoyed I took off the cast early, but all's right, barring that."

Tentatively, Tom reached out a hand toward Jane, who took it without hesitation. "I've told Penny, and I'll say this before everyone here. I shall do everything I can to show I deserve Penny's love and trust, together with everyone here's too," he ended, raising his voice a little so Betty and Mary, who were in the kitchen, could hear.

"Closing the front door would be a bloody good way to start," Betty shouted.

"Just what I was about to say," Terry Banks commented from atop the stairs, "though without so much talk about love."

Now completely embarrassed, Tom hurriedly closed the door and rearranged the blackout. "Sorry, Terry," he told the policeman.

"Are you staying for tea?" Betty asked Tom as he followed Penny, Jane, and Doris through to the kitchen.

Tom shook his head. "I'd love to, Betty, but I'll have to start back soon. I will stay for a cup of tea, if there's one going, to warm up the bones before making a move."

"I'll do it," Doris volunteered.

"No!" pretty much everyone else immediately cried.

"Way to make someone feel wanted," Doris muttered, flopping down into a seat before getting back to her feet. "If that's how you all feel, I'm going to see if I can catch hold of Eddie Winters. If anyone's going to know a good doctor, and I mean an honestly good doctor, in case you were all wondering, one we can trust, it'll be him." As she got to the kitchen door, she turned and said, "I'm going to close the door for some privacy."

"Who's this Eddie Winters?" Tom asked.

Mary looked at the other members of the Mystery Club before replying, "Officially, he's a member of the US Embassy press pool."

"Unofficially?" Tom asked.

"Probably best not to ask," Penny replied, flashing her husband a sly smile. "Suffice to say, Doris reckons if there's anything or anyone you'd need, he's the one she'd go to."

"And she trusts him?"

Mary nodded. "Implicitly. If I remember right, they grew up near each other and think the same way."

Five minutes later, Doris came back into the room, her face a picture of smiles. "Got one!"

"Just like that?" Tom couldn't help but say, earning himself a dirty look from Doris.

"Yes, just like that," she told him without elaborating.

"And what exactly is this all about?" Tom asked the question everyone in the room had been waiting for.

Penny looked directly into Tom's eyes. "You trust me?"

"Completely," he replied without hesitation.

"Good," she nodded. "In that case, you'll have to believe me when I tell you that we can't tell you." Tom went to open his mouth in protest, but Penny laid her good hand upon his on the table. "This is for your own good, Tom. What you don't know, you can't tell."

Looking around the room, it didn't take very long for Tom to say, "Everyone here knows what this is about, though, don't you." When no one denied this, Tom nodded once and then went silent. Everyone gave him the time to come to his own decision. Getting to his feet, Tom bent down and kissed the top of Penny's head. "Well, I guess I'd better be on my way. Ladies," he made sure to catch everyone's eye as he spoke, "keep well and keep safe."

After making sure they were safe from prying eyes, Penny gave her husband a reassuring hug. "I promise you, we're not in any physical danger. Once this is all over, I'll tell you everything, I promise."

After kissing her once more, Tom replied, "And I believe you."

Switching the hall light off, Penny twitched the blackout aside and followed Tom down the path to the gate. In the second he bent down to open the gate, a shot rang out, Tom dropped to the ground, and Penny screamed!

Chapter Thirty-Seven

To his credit, Terry made it to the front door at the same time as Doris, who was heading up the rest of the household, though there then entailed a brief tussle before he managed to wedge himself between the now wide open door and the girls.

"Stay here!" Terry tried to order the American, who was trying to duck under his arm. Gripping her by the shoulders, he had to use all his strength to stop her from forcing her way past him. "Look, if you want to help, telephone for the police and an ambulance. Now!" he added, when she still looked like arguing.

Turning her back on the group, Betty had already picked up the telephone to do his bidding, while Terry caused consternation by pulling his revolver out of his pocket. Without hesitation, he darted through the door, pulling it shut behind him, not noticing Doris attempting to follow and being restrained by Mary and Jane for her trouble. Keeping the revolver out before him at the ready, he hurried, bent as low as possible, toward the gate where Tom was sitting up holding his head, with his wife's arms, the sling flapping uselessly by her side, tightly around him.

Kneeling down and still peering around into the darkness, Terry asked without glancing down, "Can you move?"

"I'll help," Penny replied for her husband.

M. W. Arnold

Still with the revolver leveled into the darkness, Terry hooked his free hand under Tom's armpit as Penny used both of hers under his other. Together, they managed to lift Tom back to his feet, where he swayed a little before regaining his balance a little. "Come on, let's move," Terry urged, and the two half dragged, half carried Tom back to the cottage, where they were met by Doris and Mary.

"We'll take him from here," Mary said as she went to help Penny, whilst Jane and Doris took over from Terry.

"I've telephoned for help," Betty announced, opening the lounge door.

Terry nodded, then told them, "I'm going to take a quick look outside. I'll only be a minute, though I doubt anyone's still around. Do not open the door for anyone but me! I'll knock twice and then announce myself by my full name."

"Don't you think that's being a little over-cautious?" Betty asked.

Looking into the lounge only long enough to satisfy himself Tom was breathing, he turned to say, "With Mary being my boss's girlfriend and Penny's husband getting shot on my watch, I don't want to leave any stone unturned."

"Wise move!" Mary shouted from the lounge.

As soon as the door slammed, Betty turned and shouted, "How's Tom?" then told Doris, "Stay here!" before rushing into the lounge, where she was surprised to find Tom sitting up on the sofa, albeit with his head in his bloody hands. "Thank Christ for that!" she exclaimed and without another word, rushed toward the kitchen where the sound of rushing water was shortly heard.

Whilst Mary stayed with the pair, Jane hurried to give her friend a hand, and very shortly afterwards, Jane came back into the room bearing a basin of water and with a towel over her arm. "Betty's just boiling a kettle," she said, kneeling before Tom.

"Good. I could do with a cuppa," he unexpectedly said, looking up for a moment.

Penny didn't seem able to find her voice, so Jane spoke for her. Quickly catching hold of his chin before he could put it back down into his hands, she picked up the now wet towel and told him, "Let me look at you," and before he could say anything else, Jane was turning his head this way and that, telling him, after a quick examination, "From what I can see, you've been a lucky man. The bullet scraped along your skull, a little above the left ear. Which would explain why it's bleeding so much. Penny..." She took a grip of Penny's left hand. "I've cleaned up as best I can, but it's still bleeding. Press this here, hard. I'm going to get another towel."

"Don't forget the tea!" Tom muttered, his voice slightly muffled as part of the towel had slipped down over his mouth.

"Sorry about that, love," Penny said, tucking the offending part out of the way. "How d'you feel?"

"Stonking headache," he replied.

"Did you see anything?" Mary couldn't help but ask. "Either of you?"

Tom went to shake his head but appeared to rethink that idea, instead merely saying, "No," whilst Penny shook her head.

"Too dark, I expect. Is there anything I can do?" Mary then asked, at a bit of a loss.

"I don't think there's much to do until the police and

ambulance arrive," Jane said, re-entering the room with another towel. "Tea's on its way," she announced, knowing this would keep Tom's spirits up.

Two sharp raps at the front door interrupted them, and everyone's head, except for Tom, who let out a small moan of pain, jerked up. Immediately, Doris's voice shouted, "Who is it?"

"Detective Sergeant Terry Banks!" came the reply.

Jane quickly poked her head around the lounge door to find Doris glancing back toward her as if she'd been expecting this. "Go ahead," she told the American, though Jane didn't withdraw her head until Doris had opened the door, admitting a rather cold-looking Terry, and then closed and locked it behind him.

"Anything?" Doris asked as he passed her, though her tone implied she didn't expect any good news.

"Nothing. It's too dark out there to see a thing. How's Tom?" he asked, popping his head into the lounge.

"I'll live," the patient replied.

"He was lucky," Jane began, then explained what she'd found from her examination.

Terry stood there, shook his head, and put his revolver away. "You certainly seem to have your share of luck, Tom. Long may it continue," he added. "Penny," he said, going to stand beside her, "how are you doing? You weren't hit?"

Her voice a little shaky, Penny informed him, "No. I think I only heard one shot."

Noting her voice, Terry called out, "Betty! If you've anything stronger than tea, could you put a spot in both Tom and Penny's cups, please?"

"Will do!" Betty shouted in reply from the doorway

where she'd appeared holding a steaming basin of water.

Jane dipped the fresh towel into the hot water, wrung it, and handed it to Penny, taking the cold bloody one from her. "Here, take this."

The sound of an ambulance bell made itself heard as the vehicle pulled up outside the cottage. Terry twitched the blackout aside quickly enough to check before placing his hand upon his holstered revolver and making his way toward the front door. Waiting until there came a knock on the door, he noticed Doris's eyes were fixed upon where his hand was. "I'm not taking any chances," he told her before opening the door to show one man bearing a red cross-marked bag upon his hip.

Close behind him, though, was a rather flustered-looking nurse. "Grace! What are you doing here?" Doris exclaimed, reaching past the other man and grabbing hold of her friend's arm.

"I was around when the call came in, and I heard the address. No way were they going without me!"

"Too bloody true," the man said, looking rather put out, his eyes shooting daggers Grace's way. "She pushed my usual partner out and told me to get moving. I won't repeat what she threatened to do to me if I argued!"

"Never mind that codswallop, Jeff." Grace waved away his protests. "What's happened, Doris? Who's hurt this time?"

"This time?" Jeff couldn't stop himself from saying.

"In here!" Jane's voice shouted from the lounge.

Pushing past her colleague, Grace ran into the lounge, stopping before the sight of a still quite bloody Tom, with Penny pressing a wet and now quite red towel to the side of her husband's head.

"Bloody hell!"

"Not quite," the patient managed to say, before being shushed into silence.

Opening her first-aid kit, Grace sat down on Tom's other side, gently pushing Penny's hand aside. "Let's see what damage you've done," she muttered.

"Someone took a pop…"

"Hold on," Betty interrupted Penny. "Terry! Could you do…something…with Jeff here?" She threw a wink at the policeman.

Nodding his head, Terry stepped forward and took the confused medic under the elbow. "It looks like Grace has everything in hand, Jeff. As you can see, the gentleman's a Wing Commander, and I can't risk you hearing something he may blurt out. So if you'd accompany me outside, I'm sure you understand. State secrets, sir!" he added when Jeff looked like he would object. This did the job, and with one last look into the lounge, he went with Terry, his face looking like he was half expecting Winston Churchill himself to appear.

"Sorry," Penny said, "I wasn't thinking.

As Grace was still examining and cleaning up Tom, Terry came back into the room, closely followed by a white-faced Lawrence. Taking in the scene, he rushed toward Tom, only to be firmly pushed away by the force of Grace's glare. "Sorry," he muttered.

"What brought you here?" Mary asked, appearing by his side and grabbing his hand. "Not that I'm not pleased to see you, of course."

Quickly kissing his girlfriend on the cheek, Lawrence unbuttoned his coat. "I wanted to come and get an update from the horse's mouth rather than over the telephone, but I ran into a local copper on my way here and ran the rest of the way. Told him I'd take care of things. It looks like I'm about to get more than I bargained for."

"Someone took a shot at Tom, or Penny—we're not sure who the target was," Terry supplied.

"Fortunately," Grace looked up to tell them, "whoever the shooter was, he wasn't that good a shot."

"Tell my head that," Tom put in.

None too gently, Grace pushed his head back. "Stop talking and let me patch you up. You've been lucky once. Don't try me on for size." The grin she delivered was feral and had the desired effect.

"The shooter's also stupid. It's pitch black out there. I don't think a sniper could hit anyone if they were more than ten yards away out there."

Lawrence looked around. "Nobody else is hurt? Penny?"

"Just a little shaken up," she replied with a weak smile.

Looking around the room, Lawrence took in his friends, the determination on their faces and the looks of expectation they were all giving him. He closed his eyes.

"Penny for them?" Mary asked.

He opened them and looked at the concern in her face and came to a decision. Turning his head, he addressed Terry, "Care for some exercise?"

****

"Can you make anything out?" Lawrence asked, his hand over his mouth as he crept up to where Terry was hidden in the shadows.

"Nothing," he replied. "We've been watching this place for the past thirty minutes, and I haven't seen any sign of movement."

Lawrence glanced at his watch before coming to a

decision. "Come on, let's go and check the lock on that shop over there. I've a feeling it's not locked up right."

Quickly slipping across the street, the pair made their way to the chip shop door. At Lawrence's nod, Terry tried the door, and when he found it locked, he put the full force of his shoulder to it, and it popped open with barely any noise.

"You were right, boss, it wasn't locked."

"Revolvers out, Terry, and be on your guard," Lawrence said, going into the shop first. Finding nothing in the actual serving part of the shop, Lawrence led the way toward the basement. The first curious thing they found was a lock on the outside of the basement, lying on the floor but, nevertheless, a lock where it wouldn't normally be. Pushing the door open with his foot, he switched on the light and found the next curiosity.

"Who puts a bed in a basement?" he asked, walking toward the bed. On it were a few books and, by the bed, a half full glass of water.

"Come on," he told Terry, closing the door behind him and leading his sergeant up the stairs.

Leaving the lights off, they made their way up the stairs as silently as possible, but could hear nothing, not even the tick of a clock. The kitchen door was wide open, whilst the kitchen itself was empty, though there were two cups on the table with a teapot in between them, steam issuing from the spout.

Without needing any words to be said out loud, both tightened their grips on their revolvers and crept out of the kitchen. Passing the lounge, they both looked in, but that room too was empty. That left one room to be investigated, the bedroom at the end of the hall, its door closed. Terry went to move before Lawrence, but he stopped him with a shake of his head. Reaching out a hand, he placed it on the doorknob but didn't turn it yet. When nothing happened, he took a deep breath, turned the knob as quietly as possible to its full extent, then pushed it open with all his strength. He launched himself into the room, prepared to shout out he was the police, whilst hoping not to feel the impact of a bullet to his chest—he was disappointed to find this final room too was empty.

After the two had checked the wardrobe and under the bed, to ascertain this was indeed the case, he told Terry, "Holster it, they've gone, but we didn't miss them by much, I'd say."

Chapter Thirty-Eight

"Any idea where we're going?" Croft asked, not troubling to keep his voice down. The barrel of a rifle jabbed him in the back, causing him to stumble and nearly fall. "I mean, you must have a plan, other than taking pot shots in the pitch darkness and then turfing us all out of the flat!"

"Shut up, Croft! If you'd done your job as ordered, we wouldn't be in this mess!"

"And if you had half the brains of your old pet dog, Verdon, you'd have simply robbed a bank."

Immediately the words were out of his mouth, Croft felt something hard smack against the space between his shoulder blades with enough force to drive him to his knees and bring stars before his eyes.

"Leave him!" Verdon snapped, causing Croft, despite the pain, to look around as best he could. Somewhat surprisingly, as his eyes began to focus, he found Fred kneeling down beside him. Exactly what he hoped to do was up for debate, since his hands were tied together with cord. In the man's eyes, though, he saw only concern, and as he heaved himself back to his feet, Croft made certain the man saw his nod of thanks.

Turning around, Croft wasn't entirely surprised to find Verdon had the rifle leveled at him. Making sure he was in front of Fred, doing his best to provide a shield, he tried to gauge the man's mood, only the little light provided by the moon wasn't enough to allow him to see his face. Still, a rifle levelled at you is hard to misinterpret. "I would ask where we're going, but there's only one place it could be. Just what do you hope to accomplish?"

Verdon took a step nearer Croft, only stopping when the rifle's barrel came to a stop against Croft's belly once more. "Accomplish? Accomplish?" he spat out the words, and Croft had to force himself not to wipe his face, not trusting the way he could see Verdon's trigger finger twitch. He may not have managed to hit anyone earlier that night, but even he couldn't miss at zero range.

He tried to change the subject. "Why don't we let Fred here go? He won't tell anyone where we're going, will you?"

The problem with this was, nobody had asked Fred.

"If you're going to harm our Betty," he said, standing tall and proud despite the precarious situation he found himself in, "then you're going to have to kill me."

Croft rolled his eyes and held his breath. It's all very well saying this kind of thing in a film. It's quite another in real life when the one you're speaking to is, in Croft's opinion, about to go off the deep end. Allowing this thought, what happened next still shocked Croft, as he'd come to quite like the amiable chip shop owner.

Without warning, Verdon took a step or two toward Fred and swung the butt of the rifle up with all the force he could muster, catching the man square on the chin and knocking him flat upon his back.

Flinging himself down beside him and cracking a knee on a stone for his trouble, Croft was relieved to see the man was still breathing, though blood was trickling out of his mouth. If he was a betting man, he'd say he had at least a broken jaw. He looked up at where Verdon was standing over the pair and left what he was about to say unspoken. However, a groan from the prostrate man brought him to his senses. "Help me! We need to get him to a doctor!"

"Get up!" Verdon snapped, waving the rifle before Croft's face. "Leave him and move!"

Torn between the inbuilt urge to obey and the way he'd now come to think, Croft hesitated a moment too long.

"That's how it's going to be, eh? Well, who needs you anyway? If Palmer won't give me my money, then I'll take her life!"

As strong as his instincts were, Croft barely moved in time to save his own life as Verdon cocked the rifle, loaded another round, and drew a bead on his erstwhile servant before pulling the trigger. Only because Croft changed his stance slightly did the bullet crash into his right shoulder instead of his chest, though the impact still sent him flying backward to end up sprawled over Fred.

Not wishing to get his trousers dirty, Verdon kicked Croft in the ribs and, getting no reaction, a smug expression graced his face. Chambering another round, he spat on the fallen man. "There'll be no running off to the police from you!" and then turned on his heel and strode off down the riverbank, not giving either man a single thought more, nor heeding if he might run into anyone on the trail. There would be no more hiding in the shadows for Harold Verdon!

These thoughts of bravado were challenged as he turned a slight bend and caught sight of a couple of men in uniform suddenly appearing out of the gloom. Quickly looking around, he ducked behind the only cover available, a large tree beside the dark river. Cursing, he watched as they stopped at the gate to what he knew to be Palmer's cottage. They went through and stopped before the front door to knock. He was about to follow, hoping his nerve would hold a while longer, when there came a bark from out of the gloom. Not far behind this pair came a woman with a dog he suspected was the one he'd thrown a stone at. So the bloody thing had survived! He'd have to amend that mistake, he decided. Taking a deep breath, he stepped out and ran toward the cottage, timing his arrival at the same moment the front door opened to admit the woman together with the cursed animal.

Sticking the rifle into the gap, he forced the door open and then gave it a kick with his shoe. "Hands up!" he shouted to the hall, causing the woman and the two men who'd entered just before her to spin around in shock.

"What the hell?" cried the younger of the men, both of whom were in what he could now see to be Home Guard uniform.

"Not another bloody word!" Verdon told them, quickly scanning to see if they were armed. Seeing nothing obvious, he then shouted, "Everyone into the kitchen!"

From upstairs, this commotion had the natural effect of bringing Doris onto the landing.

He quickly levelled the rifle toward her. "Downstairs, hands where I can see them," he ordered.

Doris did as she was ordered, though if looks could kill, her glare would have had Verdon dead in a second. Kicking the front door closed behind him, he backed up against it so Doris could get past him with plenty of room.

Ushering the four before him in the hall, he ducked his head around the lounge door and was most annoyed to find a man lying on the sofa being tended to by a woman.

"Didn't you hear me? Both of you, into the kitchen, now!"

"My husband's been shot," the woman simply said, not bothering to look over at Verdon.

Now angry, Verdon pulled the trigger, sending a bullet through a front window. "So I did hit someone!" he crowed.

This made the woman turn her head, her eyes ablaze, she said, "More from luck than anything else, I'd say."

Verdon hurriedly chambered another round. "I don't have time to argue," he told her. "You lot," he shouted into the kitchen, "get in here!" He stepped back to allow them to enter, and once the room was full, stepped in and closed the door behind him. "Right. Which one of you lot's Betty Palmer? I won't miss at this range!"

****

Croft's eyes snapped open, and the pain in his shoulder hit him like a hammer.

Gritting his teeth, he realized he was draped half over the poor chip shop owner, and despite the pain, he rolled off him, ending up on his side, barely able to stop himself from ending up on his front.

"You look worse than me," Fred surprised him by saying, though the pain it caused him to speak was obvious even to Croft's pain-addled mind.

Struggling into a sitting position, he waited for his swimming head to settle down a little. "I'd argue with you about that," he replied, "but I don't think either of us is in a state for that."

Seeing Fred trying to sit up, Croft shuffled toward him and, with one hand pressed to his shoulder, he helped the other injured man up.

"Thanks," Fred told him, immediately wincing.

Seeing this, Croft advised him through his own gritted teeth, "Try not to speak. I think your jaw's broken. Just nod, or shake your head." A nod was received in reply. "Do you think you can make it to the Victory? Get someone to telephone the police." Another nod, just as firm, but Croft could see the amount of pain he was in. "Tell them Harold Verdon's trying to kill Betty Palmer, if you can."

"And you?" Fred managed to ask.

Croft got himself onto his knees. "I'm going after him," and when Fred looked obviously quizzical, in spite of the lack of light, Croft ducked his head before looking into Fred's face. "You don't have to believe me, and after all I've done to you I wouldn't blame you, but I have to try and stop him. I've done a lot I'm not proud of, so perhaps I should try and do one thing I *can* take pride in. I've watched those women, and they've done nothing to deserve this. From what I can see, they're doing a hard job for the war effort and deserve a medal, not some nutter trying to kill them."

In the ensuing silence, Fred got to his feet, held out a hand to help Croft to his, and then took a handkerchief from his pocket. "It's not clean, but…" he shrugged and, before Croft could protest, stuffed it under Croft's jacket and into his wound, causing Croft to roar in agony and jerk his head back. Taking advantage of this, Fred looked behind the man, placed a hand first behind Croft's back, and then held it under the moonlight. When he held it up so Croft could see, he said, "No exit wound."

Croft nodded once, not trusting his voice, and then turned toward the riverbank. He stumbled once before finding his feet, and with a more determined gait, disappeared into the dark. Also ignoring the possibility of being seen, Croft made his way as quickly as he could down the riverbank. In spite of the well-meaning handkerchief, he could feel the blood soaking through and beginning to run down his chest once more. Ignoring this, his one thought was to do something right before he died. He was under no illusions as to the severity of his wound. Left untreated for much longer, he'd likely bleed to death. Still, this wasn't important. All that mattered was stopping Verdon from carrying out his mad scheme.

Much sooner than he expected, he found himself outside the gate of The Old Lockkeepers Cottage. Briefly leaning his free hand upon the gate, he caught his breath, shoved it open, and lurched forward, not hearing a distant pounding of feet behind him.

****

"Where do you think they've gone?" Terry asked Lawrence as they turned the corner and onto the riverbank.

Frustrated, Lawrence kicked a couple of stones, which landed with a plop in the river. With a shrug of his shoulders, he replied, "I wish I knew."

"But why leave now? Surely they know we've suspected that's where they've been hiding out for a while."

Lawrence looked at his sergeant, and despite the poor light, he could make out the same frustration upon his face. "If I had to guess, I'd say one or the other of them took things too far tonight and decided we'd find an excuse to search the shop. Which," he sighed, "doesn't mean I've the slightest idea where they've gone."

As they came to the last bend before Betty's cottage, they were startled to hear a shot ring out.

"What the hell…" Terry exclaimed.

Taking to his heels, Lawrence shouted, "Come on!" and ran as fast as he could toward the source of the report, Terry close behind. Unfortunately, their goal appeared to be the cottage they'd left just shortly before.

****

Creeping up to the window through which the shot had come, Croft saw the force had blown the blackout slightly askew. Carefully, he peeked through the gap and saw Verdon wildly waving the rifle around before settling upon a woman who stood beside the one he knew to be the American, Doris something-or-other.

"So we meet at last, Betty Palmer," Verdon was saying, as if he were in some second-class melodrama. "I suppose it's too much to expect you've got my money?"

"If I had that amount of money, I wouldn't give it to the likes of you, Verdon," she added, and Croft saw her head tilt back as she jutted her chin out in defiance.

From where he hid, Croft could see Verdon's eye twitch and made a decision. If he didn't act now, the lounge could easily become a bloodbath. Turning too quickly, he felt his wound stab his senses, forcing him to take a few deep breaths before he felt steady enough on his feet to move again. Removing his hand from against his wound, the act of which caused the blood to flow more freely, he hurried as best he could toward the front door, hoping his luck would be in and it would be unlocked.

His hand sticky with blood, Croft reached for the door handle and moved it slowly, pushing. It opened! Nearly tripping over a pair of shoes and an Air Transport Auxiliary cap on the floor, he made his way down the hall until he stood outside the door to the lounge. Inside he could hear Verdon spouting how life had been cruel to him and he deserved that money. To his surprise, Betty, the object of his vehemence, simply told him, "Do your worst, but let my friends go. They've never done you any harm."

The woman had such courage, he thought, taking a grip of the lounge door's handle. Such a person deserved to live! Taking a deep breath and shoving the pain of his wound to the back of his head, he shoved his shoulder against the door and burst into the room. As he'd hoped when he'd looked through the window, he'd got his distances right, and he cannoned right into Verdon's back, sending the loathsome man flying, the rifle soaring out of his grip toward the Doris woman.

As the two fell into a heap, with Croft unfortunately at the bottom, he became vaguely aware of footsteps and shouts of "Mary!" and "Betty!" as two men hared up the path and into the house.

Using what little strength he had left, Croft struggled to push Verdon off him, but instead, Verdon pushed himself off his old servant. Whether by accident or design, he placed his hands on Croft's wound, causing him to yell out in agony. Feebly, Croft clutched at Verdon's coat, but his weak grip was torn away by the man as he scrambled to his feet.

"I'll kill the bloody lot of you!" he screamed, foam

flecking the edges of his lips. In his fury, his eyes flicked around the room, searching for the rifle. As he turned around, he came face to face with a grim-faced and very obviously angry Doris.

"Looking for something?" she asked, levelling the weapon at Verdon.

Suddenly on the receiving end, Verdon's knees gave out, he flopped to the ground, and his lip began to quiver. All the fight went out of him as suddenly as it had come to him a few short hours ago. "Don't hurt me! I...I never meant to cause you any harm!"

Lawrence and Terry appeared in the lounge doorway just then, quite out of breath, and were stunned by the scene before them.

"Don't make any sudden moves, Verdon," Doris announced, rattling the rifle's bolt.

"Could someone explain to me exactly what's just hap..."

A single gunshot interrupted Lawrence as Verdon screamed and fell to the floor, clutching his groin.

Quickly crossing the room, Terry took a grip of the rifle and gently prised it out of Doris's unprotesting hands, as Jane knelt down next to the screaming villain and helped to put pressure on the wound.

"I'll get some towels," Mary announced, dashing out of the room.

"I'll call for an ambulance," Betty added, doing the same.

Tom got up, with a little help from Penny, and held out a hand to Terry. "Shall I take care of that for you?"

"You're okay with that?" Terry asked, glancing at the bandage Grace had put around his head.

Tom gingerly tapped the side of his head. "A bit of

a headache, but I can manage this for you."

Meanwhile, Lawrence took Doris out into the hall. For someone who'd just shot someone, she seemed remarkably calm.

"Tell me," he began without preamble, "did you mean to do that?"

Doris turned her sweetest smile upon the policeman. "I've no idea what you mean."

Chapter Thirty-Nine

True to his word, Major Jim Fredericks was on the doorstep of The Old Lockkeepers Cottage, looking spick and span in his Class A uniform.

"My, don't you look good enough to eat," Doris greeted him at the door with a grin.

"Nice to see you too, Doris," he said, not falling for her wind-up attempt. "Is the lady of the house in?"

"How very English of you," Doris tried again. This, too, was ignored by the officer as he stepped past her and into the hall.

Dancing down the stairs, Betty hopped off the last step and gave Doris a swat on her bottom for her cheekiness. "Ignore her, she's being Doris."

"What else am I supposed to be?" the girl in question asked, though she didn't hang around to find out, instead skipping past the two toward the kitchen. "Sorry, can't stop, my morning coffee's getting cold." However, as she crossed the threshold, she looked back at Jim and told him, "I'm going to miss the coffee…and you," before going to finally retrieve her coffee.

"Come into the lounge," Betty said, taking Jim's hand and pushing open the door, only to stand stock still.

Wondering why they weren't moving, Jim glanced over Betty's head and immediately let out a laugh. "Why, how do you do, Penny, Tom," he said, deliberately affecting another caricature of an English accent.

Much to her embarrassment, Betty allowed herself to be led into the lounge where Penny and Tom had been in the middle of testing how his headache was this morning.

After shaking hands, Jim pointed to the bandage around Tom's head. "What's the story? Enemy action?"

Though he didn't know what it meant, Jim spotted the exchange of looks which went on between the other three, but didn't comment on it. "You could put it that way." Tom laughed.

"I assume you're feeling better this morning, Tom?" Betty asked, leaning into Jim's side and threading her arm through his.

Letting out a small cough, Tom got to his feet, smoothed down his uniform jacket, and held out a hand to his wife. "Much, thank you. Grace did a great job patching me—" he started, only to stop himself before he inadvertently revealed something to someone who didn't need to know what was going on. "I'm very sorry, but I'll have to be making a move. Things to do tonight which can't wait. You understand what I mean."

Nobody failed to notice Penny's face drop at hearing this, including most importantly her husband. "I really am sorry, Penny. I wish I could stay longer. If it's all right, I'll call you when I next know I'm free?"

If Jim considered this a strange thing to say to your wife, no more than a raised eyebrow showed this.

"Call me," Penny simply replied.

"Betty, thank you for everything. Would you do me a favor and thank Grace for me, when you next see her?" Betty, of course, nodded. "And give the rest of the house my best wishes, please. I'd like to take off a bit quieter than I arrived," he added, with a smile only Jim didn't understand. Finally, he held out a hand to the American officer. "Jim. A pleasure to see you once more, though I hope not for the last time. Take care of yourself," he added before leaving the room, closely followed by Penny.

After a few seconds' awkward silence at being left alone, Betty cleared her throat. "Would you like a cup of tea? Or I can see if Doris can be persuaded to share a cup of coffee."

Jim shook his head. "No, thanks. I've got a good idea of how protective Doris is about her coffee. Oh, don't let me forget I've another tin in the Jeep for her, together with a few other items, mainly some booze you can keep for her wedding."

Crossing to the sofa, Betty sat and patted beside her, and Jim instantly sat there, taking her hands in his. Looking deep into her eyes, he raised her hand to his lips, not losing eye contact with her for one second. His voice was tender, warm, seductive, and despite there not being a fire in the grate, Betty's cheeks began to take on a rosy glow.

"Now I have your attention," Jim teased, settling back into the sofa, Betty snuggling happily into his side, "let me say what I came here to say."

Mary chose that moment to open the door but never got to set foot in the room as Doris shouted at the top of her voice, "Out!"

"You were about to say?" Betty said, batting her eyelids as a startled Mary shut the door.

"I've been looking into it, and there're no rules preventing an American marrying a Brit." Jim couldn't miss how Betty suddenly tensed. Nevertheless he continued, "There's a lot of paperwork to do, and it'll take time, especially with my going back Stateside, but," Jim didn't miss a beat, "will you marry me, Betty Palmer?"

Betty didn't hesitate. "Yes!" she nearly screamed, launching herself at Jim's lips.

"Yes!" came from outside the door. Obviously Mary hadn't gone far. Indeed, ignoring Doris's order of a few moments ago, she burst through the door, closely followed by Jane, and both were wearing identical ear-to-ear grins.

"So many congratulations!" Jane cried, trying and failing to pry Betty's arms from around her new fiancée. "Doris will be back in a bit. She's gone next door to get Ruth and Walter."

Finally releasing her grip, Betty told Jim, "We'd better get some of that booze in. I think we're going to need it."

****

"Doris!" Jane stuck her head out of the ops hut window on Monday morning, and when her American friend kept walking, yelled a little louder, "Doris!" this time with success.

A moment later, Doris trotted over, her parachute pack bumping awkwardly against the back of her thigh. "You haven't changed your mind, have you?"

"What?" Jane said, momentarily flummoxed before she realized what Doris meant. "No, of course not."

"Then what's up?"

"I've just had the padre on the telephone. He wanted to check you're still getting married on the twenty-seventh?"

"Of course," she replied after a moment. "What

makes him think otherwise?"

Jane shrugged. "Nothing. He said he was merely checking."

"But I'd have told him if we'd changed anything."

Before replying, Jane checked no one else was within earshot. Waving her friend a little closer, Jane leaned out the window and said, "I shouldn't be telling you this, as it's supposed to be a surprise. A lot of people have been chipping in their eggs, sugar, and other things for your wedding cake, and the padre's the one who's been keeping them safe."

Doris almost let out a squeal of surprise and delight, however Jane managed to shush her into silence just in time. "Quiet, you! Try to forget I've just told you that, and if you can't, remember to act surprised at your wedding."

"Deal!" Doris said, standing on her tiptoes and kissing Jane on the cheek.

"Good girl. Now, you and Mary had better get going, and the best of British to the both of you."

"Jane!" Penny stuck her head around her boss's door. "Has Doris left yet?"

Stepping back, Jane waved Penny forward so she could take her place at the window. "Good, I'm glad I caught you. Sorry to be the bearer of well, possibly, bad news."

Penny had both her friends' full attention now.

"I've just had Walter on the telephone. He's going to be away for the next couple of days. Matt Green came around with the offer of a last-minute place on a grenade course."

"Grenade course?" both Doris and Jane exclaimed at the same time.

M. W. Arnold

Penny flushed. "He did want me to apologize to you for not being able to tell you in person, but if he didn't leave"—she paused to look at her watch—"five minutes ago, he'd miss his transport."

Both Jane and Penny waited to see Doris's reaction, which was interesting—she began laughing. "Oh, I'd pay good money to watch that! I wouldn't think Walter could throw a wet newspaper, let alone a hand grenade!"

"So you're not angry?" Penny asked.

Doris immediately stopped laughing. "Oh, I'm angry to end all hell! You wait until I get hold of him! Going on a silly hand grenade course less than a week before our wedding? Right now, I'd better get to Mary before she takes off without me. It's a long way to Scotland, and I can't tell you how glad I am Jane managed to wrangle a Harvard for us. I wasn't looking forward to flying all that way in a Magister."

Jane had the last word. "If I let that happen, I don't think you'd ever let me hear the end of it!"

****

"So who's this doctor you've got lined up, and why couldn't we use Grace's pet one?" Mary asked, as they entered a pub a few miles outside Aberdeen where Doris had arranged to meet the doctor and the Woods brothers.

Leading the way to the bar, Doris ordered, waited, and paid for two bottles of stout before making her way to a booth along the side of the pub from where she could see the entrance. "I'm sure Grace's doctor is very nice and honest, but he's down on the south coast and the *problem* is up here in the wilds of Scotland. Plus, I'd rather not have to rely on someone I may end up seeing again. You know my luck with getting injured."

"Did you, er, have to pay this doctor to come up

342

here?"

Doris took a long swig from her glass before replying, "Not as such." She hastily elaborated. "I asked Eddie if he knew anyone who'd be prepared to travel with no questions asked."

Mary raised an eyebrow in surprise. "And this chap's trustworthy? And a licensed doctor?"

"With a bad gambling habit," Doris added, at which Mary nodded her understanding. "My turn now. How's Mark going to get his brother out of the manor without being seen?"

"You're going to love this!" Mary declared.

"Oh?"

"Oh, yes," Mary replied, looking like the cat that got the cream. "Did you know there are secret passages in the manor?"

Doris promptly spat out the mouthful of stout she'd been drinking. "And you're only telling me this now?"

"Be nice, and I'll tell you how to find a few more for your honeymoon," Mary teased her friend. "Anyway, I told Mark how to find the nearest one to my room. It leads to a passage which leads under the garden for a short way before coming out next to the stables."

Doris simply sat and shook her head in silent wonder. "I'm going to be so nice to you, you'll be sick of me!"

Mary let out a short laugh. "No chance." She looked at her watch. "Nearly two. Mark and John should be here soon. No, he didn't tell me how they were going to get here, and I didn't ask."

"Mary, what if he isn't simple?" Doris suddenly blurted out as the door swung open to admit Mark Wood and, presumably, his brother John, who was in army uniform.

"I don't know." She shook her head, getting to her feet to wave the two over. There wasn't time to say anything, as the door had no sooner closed than it swung open again to admit a man in a herringbone-tweed overcoat and flat cap and carrying a doctor's bag. Nothing about him stood out, except a rather red nose, but that could have been caused by the cold weather.

"That's our man," Doris said. "Eddie said he'd be wearing that pattern overcoat and cap." Without another word, she made her way over to the bar and motioned for the barman to follow her toward the far end, away from everyone else.

Mary kept half an eye on what her friend was up to. She couldn't be certain, but it looked like Doris had jabbed a thumb at the ceiling and then what looked like a wad of banknotes appeared in the American's hand.

"Come over!" Doris called to her, and with some shooing, Mary herded everyone over to her friend. "If you'll follow Angus upstairs, he'll show you to a private room where you can do your examination, Doctor."

Just before following the doctor and the barman, Mark clasped the hands of both women. "Thank you. No matter the outcome, thank you both for caring."

"Now what?" Doris suddenly found herself asking.

Mary took up a glass and shrugged. "Now, we wait."

Chapter Forty

"He was a bundle of fun," Mary declared with a shake of her head.

"I wouldn't be too hard on him, Mary," Doris said, placing a hand on her shoulder as they both watched the doctor hastily leave the pub an hour later, clutching a fat brown envelope in his hand. "I doubt if he enjoyed coming all this way for only a few hours."

"Even if you did pay him a lot of money?"

Doris nodded. "Even if I did pay him a lot of money."

"Do you think it's been worth it?" Mary asked, turning her attention back to the door leading upstairs.

As the door swung open once more, Doris held up both her hands and crossed her fingers. "I guess we're about to find out."

Though there wasn't a huge smile on Captain Wood's face as he followed his brother through the door, he did appear a little more relaxed than when he arrived. Indeed, as they joined the two waiting ATA girls, he was holding out his hand. "Whatever happens, I can't thank the two of you enough."

Mary's face fell. "You mean it's been a waste of time?"

Mark Wood shook his head. "I don't think so."

"What happened?" Doris asked. "What did the doctor say?"

"Well," Wood replied, taking a seat and accepting the bottle of stout Doris pushed into his hands, "you know doctors. Amongst a lot of muttering, some poking and prodding, he asked John a load of questions. I'll be honest. I really don't know what he expected to find out, but he seemed satisfied. He seemed to nod a lot to himself as he was making his notes, too."

"And...?" Mary asked impatiently.

"And," Wood added after taking another mouthful of drink, "though he doesn't think John's condition is enough to exclude him from serving, he believes the report he's going to submit will be enough to see him transferred to a non-combat role."

"That's...good news?" Doris offered.

"Probably the best, if that's how things turn out. No messy court-martial for him. Of course, this will all take a good while to sort out. You know how slow the military bureaucracy is."

Mary asked John, "How do you feel, John?"

This man put down his glass of water and looked squarely into Mary's eyes. Slowly, but very clearly, he told her, "I trust our Mark. If he thinks this is for the best, then that's fine by me. I'm a good cook! Just ask him," he added with a smile.

Mark beamed and clapped his brother on the shoulder. "That he is. Cooks the best fried breakfast you'll ever taste!"

"And where does this leave you? What next? I mean," Doris managed to get out, "do you have a plan for getting out of this mess?"

"Ah," Mark said, slumping back in his seat a little. "That's where it's likely to get tricky and a little messy. You see, John could easily be charged with going Absent

Without Leave, or desertion." Both girls nodded gravely. "We've talked about it, and we're going to try convincing his unit he simply got confused when he was at the hospital and wandered out, and that he eventually remembered where he was supposed to be and persuaded someone to telephone the hospital. I must say, the barman's done well out of us tonight! Most expensive phone call I've ever made," he added with a shake of his head. "Still, I think he'll stick to the story."

"That's something!" Mary suddenly said. "Weren't they looking for John? Back at the hospital, I mean."

Mark looked a little sheepish as he replied, "They were. Fortunately, they weren't looking inside the manor. Now," he said, sitting forward, "I need to take John outside and muck up his face and clothes a little, make him look like he's been living off the land for a while. You pair should make yourselves scarce. The barman's making the call as we speak."

Mary and Doris exchanged worried looks. "Do you think they'll believe your story?"

Mark shrugged. "It's the best we've got. I can see it getting a bit sticky for me, but I think it'll work. Of course, a lot will depend on the doctor's report. Do you think he'll keep to the deal?"

Doris's eyes glinted. "Oh, believe me, he'd better."

"Your friend's a little scary at times," he promptly told Mary.

"Quite true," she agreed. "But most of the time she's a real sweety, so long as you can get past her Americanisms."

"Hey!" Doris jokingly objected.

"What about you?" Mary asked. "How are you going to explain your presence here?"

Mark's jaw dropped open. "I hadn't thought of that."

John held up a hand. "I've an idea."

"Go on, please," Mary said with a smile.

"Why doesn't Mark drive you two away, and I'll wait for the hospital people here?"

The girls and Mark exchanged glances before Mark started to chuckle. Reaching out, he ruffled his brother's hair. "Don't you start getting too smart on me, or this isn't going to work! However..." he quickly added as John's face fell, "that is a wonderful idea. Come on, let's go and get John looking a bit rough, and then I'll drive you to the airfield."

"Before we go," John said, "I've got something for you, Mary." Reaching into his jacket, he pulled out a rather battered-looking teddy bear and held it out to her.

"Mr. Bunsen!" Mary exclaimed, an expression of sheer delight upon her face.

Looking a little sheepish, John told her, "I know you didn't lend him to me, but thank you. He's good company."

Mary reached out for the offered bear, but then hesitated and, with a deep breath, pushed him gently back into John's hands. "I'd like you to keep him safe for me, John, for good luck. Let us know how things work out, please, Mark."

****

"Exactly how much trouble do you think we'll be in?" Mary asked as she tucked her feet beneath her.

Doris unscrewed the lid of her flask and poured them each a cup of lukewarm tea before doing the same. "It depends," she said.

"On what?" Mary asked, accepting her cup.

"On how fond of that Harvard Jane is."

Mary sipped and thought before replying, "She didn't sound very happy when we called yesterday."

Shaking her head, Doris smiled ruefully. "No, she didn't, did she. For a second, I thought she was going to say I arranged for the tire to burst."

"It's not our fault they weren't able to get a replacement in until this morning," Mary added.

Doris looked around Mary. "How long did they say it's going to take?"

"By the looks of that chap waving at us, I'd say it's ready about now," Mary declared, getting to her feet and holding out her hand to her friend.

"You get our things together, and I'll go and do a check and sign off on the work," Doris told Mary.

"Did that fitter really say that?" Mary asked over the radio once they'd taken off and set course southward.

"Told me he'd never met such a demanding woman," Doris replied. "I told him he hadn't seen nothin' yet!"

"What happened then?"

"Little bugger scooted off to moan to his sergeant. I don't think it got him anywhere. Last I saw, he'd just been clipped around the ear!"

"Serves him right." Mary laughed.

****

"There you two are!" Jane stated, as both Doris and Mary climbed very stiffly out of the Harvard back at Hamble much later that day.

With a loud groan, Doris slid down off the wing and only just kept her feet as she landed on the ground. "Please, boss, can I get a cup of coffee inside me first? Then you can chew me out as much as you want."

349

"Same here," Mary agreed, leaning heavily on the American's shoulder, "apart from the coffee. Devil's brew!"

"If I had the energy, I'd smack you around the head," Doris remarked.

"You can owe me?" Mary amiably suggested, to which Doris shook her hand.

"When you've both quite finished…" Jane said. Her voice was annoyed, but her face told a different picture. "Doris, you need to get yourself to the hospital."

Instantly on the alert, Doris fixed upon Jane and asked, "What's happened?"

"It's Walter," Jane began gravely. "He's been in an accident."

The blood drained from Doris's face, and she had to hold onto Mary or her legs would have folded beneath her. "Is he okay?"

Jane helped the shocked girl to regain her feet. "He will be. From what Matt Green's told me, he saved a man who fumbled a grenade from being killed."

"He'd better be all right," Doris mumbled, "because when I get hold of him, I'm going to kill him!"

Chapter Forty-One

"Good morning, Patrick," Ruth greeted the postman as the door of the *Hamble Gazette* opened. "Got anything interesting for me today?"

"Yes," he replied, tipping his cap back on his head, "I think I do. I've a postcard from a POW camp for you."

Ruth's eyes popped at hearing this, and she missed what he asked and had to get him to repeat.

"I asked, how's Walter? Word around's that he was playing silly buggers with a grenade and now's in hospital."

Barely had the words left his mouth than Ruth had rushed around to the other side of the desk and had grabbed hold of the postman by his jacket lapels. If he'd have been able to, the poor man would have stepped back in alarm, only the newspaperwoman's grip was so tight he couldn't move an inch.

"Now look here, Patrick Roach. I don't know who told you that load of codswallop, but you can stick it in your pipe and smoke it! Not only is Walter a very good friend of mine, but that couldn't be further from the truth! Do you want to know what really happened?"

Too terrified to speak, Patrick nodded vigorously.

"Good. In that case, listen closely. I shall say this only once. The soldier next to Walter panicked at his turn to throw a grenade and dropped it in the trench the two of them were in. Walter grabbed it and managed to throw it, only he was a bit late. He's now in hospital after having shrapnel taken out of his right hand, arm, and skull. He's in a bad way, and the other chap? Got off without a scratch on the stupid bugger. Did you get that?" she asked, letting him go and brushing his lapels.

It took the postman a few seconds to find his voice, but when he did, he hung his head as he replied, "Yes, yes, Ruth, I got all that." Deeply sighing, he finally met Ruth's eyes. "Please, will you accept the apology of this silly old man who should know better than to listen to gossip. I've known Walter long enough that I should never have believed her."

"Believed who?" Ruth pounced.

Patrick shook his head. "Sorry, I won't tell you her name, but please believe me, I'm going to go and speak to her right now and put her right."

Ruth stood tall and took a few deep, steadying breaths. "All right, I'll trust you. I'm sorry for how I reacted…a little."

"Mind if I take the weight off my feet for a minute?" Patrick asked, and perched on the edge of Walter's desk upon getting a nod. "Can I ask? Do you know if he's going to be all right?"

Before replying, Ruth went and put the kettle on. She waited until it had boiled and made a couple of cups of tea before speaking. Placing a cup next to the postman, Ruth went and picked up Bobby from beneath her desk and sat with him on her lap, "I don't know. I mean, the doctors don't think he'll have any lasting physical problems. The trouble is, and this is my main worry, he's always had a bit of a problem with self-confidence, and I'm worried this will set him back to his old ways."

"Has Doris seen him yet?"

Ruth nodded. "Hasn't left his bedside since he was settled at the local hospital. In confidence, my friend Grace, who's a nurse that works there, has telephoned me twice—and Jane Howell on station three times—begging us to come and take Doris away. The last time, she swore she'd sedate Doris if she annoyed her one more time."

Patrick had a small chuckle and a sip of tea. "Well, it sounds like Doris is behaving like…well…Doris."

Ruth raised her mug. "Touché."

"And are you going to this nurse's aid?"

Ruth shook her head and tapped her typewriter. "Can't. Too busy. I'm in the middle of a story, and I'm trying not to let it go to Bobby's head."

"I was going to ask. Why the bandage?" Patrick asked, pointing at the dirty white bandage around the cocker spaniel's head.

"That's all part of the story. You'll have to wait and read it, the same as everyone else."

"Come on, Ruth, I know I've just mucked up, but we've known each other long enough. You can trust me not to breathe a word to anyone."

Ruth straightened Bobby's bandage, kissed her beloved dog on the head, and put him back on the floor where he immediately settled down next to the fire, letting out a deep, doggy sigh of contentment. "Sorry, all I can tell you is there's kidnapping, shooting, and blackmail involved."

"And, er, Bobby?"

Ruth's face became deadly serious. "We believe the person behind all this threw a stone at poor Bobby."

"I'm sorry, Ruth. How's he doing?"

Stroking Bobby with her feet, Ruth managed a small

smile. "No lasting damage, thank God. Anyway, I can't tell you more, as I'm not sure how much I'm going to be allowed to tell in my article anyway. I'm waiting on the police to let me know."

"I take it that's Lawrence. I heard he's the new Inspector around here."

"That's right," Ruth said, more than a hint of pride in her voice.

Patrick finished his tea, put his cup down, and got up and stretched. "Well, must be getting on, things to do, people to see." He gave a wink. "Say hello to Walter for me and wish him all my best. Don't forget the postcard," he said as he opened the door to leave.

No sooner had the postman left than Ruth pounced upon the postcard. Relief flooded through her when she recognized her son's handwriting.

Hi mum. Sorry I didn't tell you before. Had to have another operation as I had an infection, but all better now. Leg's a bit shorter now. I think the Germans believe I'm trying to escape a piece at a time! Ha ha! Please don't worry about me, not going to be stupid anymore. Love Joe.

Ruth had to read it through twice before she allowed herself to flop back into her seat, relief flooding through her bones, which rapidly led to a flood of tears. Ignoring her typewriter and the story she'd begun, Ruth grabbed a piece of paper and started to write.

My dear Joe. Lawrence and I buried your 'foot' in the garden. The ceremony was spoiled by Bobby watering the grave, however…

****

Sister Henry sat at her desk and fumed. For once, Doris didn't notice, though Nurse Grace did, and for who knew how many times that morning. She hurried over to where Doris was berating Walter again.

"Doris!" she hissed, catching hold of her friend's arm to get her attention. "Doris! Will you please keep it down, or Sister will throw you out. If it comes to that, I will too!"

Though he didn't speak, Walter gave Grace a quick smile when Doris turned her head to glare at Grace.

"You wouldn't!"

"I would," Grace assured her, exuding all the authority she had. "You know how much I care for you, and for Walter. You're very good friends, but this is my place of work, and I can't play favorites. Of course you're worried about Walter." She smiled. "But try not to be. He's going to be fine. However, if you want to stay, then keep your voice down. You're disturbing the rest of the patients. I can appreciate you're a little over-excited to see him this morning, but please, try to hold it in."

Having listened to her friend's lecture, Doris hung her head and nodded. Finally, looking into the nurse's kindly face, she told her, "Your hearing's still fine then."

Going a little red, Grace glanced around to make certain no one had heard what Doris had said, but her friend had made certain to keep her voice low enough so only Grace would hear. Absently, she rubbed an ear. "Yes, it's really made things much easier."

Doris took her seat and looked up at Grace. "Look, I'm sorry I've been a nuisance. I'll keep my voice down," she said, though she was unable to resist looking around Grace to where Sister Henry was watching them.

"Thank you," Grace said, adding before moving off, "Ten minutes of visiting time left."

"That was a bit much," Doris moaned to Walter once they were alone.

Walter raised the one eyebrow to be seen under the bandage wrapped around his head. "Really? You were a little loud, love."

It took a little while before Doris replied, "I know, I know. I'm sorry. It's just that I'm worried about you and," she added as Walter opened his mouth, "also very proud of you. Though if you ever do something so stupid again, I'll kill you myself!"

For the first time since she'd been there, Doris heard Walter laugh. "I'll tell Matt to get behind you, then. That's roughly what he told me whilst he was patching me up."

"Good for him," Doris agreed. "Remind me to buy him a drink, next time I see him. Now, onto a more serious subject, our wedding."

Walter held up a right arm completely encased in white bandages with the odd spot of blood here and there.

Doris waved away any protests he may have been about to make. "You can walk, can't you? Can you still talk?"

"When I'm given the chance," Walter made the mistake of muttering.

Doris leaned in close to his face to whisper, "It's a good thing I love you, or you'd be getting fitted for a wire jaw for that remark," and then kissed him like she hadn't seen him in a year. She only broke off when Sister Henry appeared at her shoulder.

"That is it! Second Officer Winter, you've caused more than enough disruption for today. Out!"

"But…" Doris began to protest, only she failed,

possibly for the first time since she came to Hamble, to get anywhere.

Presenting her with her hat and bag, Sister Henry thrust the items into the American's arms and pointed in the direction of the exit. "But, nothing! This is not a bordello. Out! You may come back tomorrow, but you must be on your best behavior, or I'll make certain you are never allowed to visit again."

Despite the ignobility of her exit, Doris couldn't resist getting in the last word. "Five days! In five days, Walter Johnson, you're marrying me! So don't think you're getting out of it that easy!"

****

"Yes, I'm sorry you couldn't make it down for the funeral too. Of course we can lay some flowers when you're next here. I'm sure Thelma would appreciate it. All right, I've got to go now. I'll speak to you soon. Love you, sis!"

"How're studies going?" Jane shouted from her office.

Penny trotted over toward her. "Well, I think the best thing we can say is, she hasn't been called to the head's office again. Though reading between the lines, she's apparently doing rather well and enjoying school once more."

"Are you looking forward to having her come to live with you?" Jane wanted to know.

Penny had to think about this. "I suppose so. Mind you, she hasn't had anything to do with Tom since that day at the hospital, and I don't know how she'll react when she finds out we're giving things a go."

"Hmm," Jane mused. "I do remember she was upset."

Penny laughed. "Upset? I think she was all for joining Doris and hunting him down."

"Did I hear my name?" came an American drawl from the ops hut doorway.

Penny looked up and waved her friend over. "As always, you have great timing. Yes, you did."

Doris frowned. "Am I in trouble here too?"

Jane looked at her watch. "You're back early. You didn't break my Jeep, did you?" she asked, rushing past her to look outside.

Waiting until Jane came back inside, Doris treated her to a big grin. "She's all in one piece. Thanks for lending her to me."

"So why are you back early?" Penny asked. "We weren't expecting you for another hour."

When Doris didn't reply straight away, Jane and Penny shared a look before Jane finally asked, "Okay, what did you do?"

"I may have got myself chucked out of the hospital by the Sister."

"You didn't!" both Jane and Penny exclaimed at the same time.

"Perhaps I was a little…loud?" Doris suggested.

As if they were a comic double act, her friends once more exchanged looks before saying, "You? Loud?"

"Oh, very funny." Doris folded her arms and pouted at her friends. "All I was doing was making certain my Walter was fine."

"And…" Penny prompted.

"And, I may have been a little bit…loud," she admitted.

"What's Doris been up to now?"

Turning around, Doris found Betty and Mary behind

her, both with grins to match those of Jane and Penny.

"Oh, don't you start as well!" Doris pleaded.

"It depends," Mary replied. "What did you do?"

"Got herself kicked out of the hospital," Penny said before Doris could get her side in.

Betty engulfed the American in a hug before stepping back. "I'm sure you were only being yourself."

"Of course I was…hey!"

Chapter Forty-Two

"Have you considered where you and Walter are going to live?" Mary asked as she fed some brandy to the fruit cake she was nursing for Doris's wedding.

"Good point," Betty remarked, looking up from her newspaper that Wednesday evening. "I love having you here, but you've got to admit, it is a little crowded, and if you add a man to the equation…"

"I know, I know," Doris replied, slumping down onto the sofa before looking up to say, "That's why I've asked Ruth over tonight."

"I was wondering why the extra Guinness was outside the kitchen door," Betty replied.

"Well, I have to butter her up somehow, and I know she's partial."

"That's probably your fault," Betty said from behind the paper. "The Ruth I knew always preferred sherry, but since meeting you…well, I can't deny she loves the stuff."

"I've always said she was a lady of refined taste," Doris declared, raising an imaginary glass in toast.

The lounge door opened to admit Jane and the lady in question. "Did I hear my name being taken in vain?" Ruth said, though the smile upon her face clearly showed she wasn't being serious.

"Oh, absolutely you did," Mary decided. "Doris is up to something."

"I am not!"

Ruth looked around at the room's occupants before joining her American friend on the sofa. "Of course you are, but in the best possible taste."

"Would anyone like to join me in a Guinness?" Doris asked, getting to her feet.

Ruth stared for a second before saying, "Okay, I believe you all. She's up to something."

"I am not"—Doris stamped her foot in emphasis—"up to something!" But she didn't help her cause by stopping in the doorway and saying to Ruth, "I may have something to run by you, though."

"Told you." Mary shrugged.

"So how're you?" Jane asked, coming into the room in her dressing gown, having just finished her bath. "And what's our Doris up to now?"

"Does everyone think I'm always up to mischief?" Doris shouted from the kitchen, where the sound of bottle tops being removed could be heard.

Penny conducted the response. "Yes!" everyone cried.

Kicking the door wider, Doris reentered the room bearing a tray of bottles and glasses. "Honestly, I don't know why I put up with you lot," she grumbled.

Quickly going to her aid, Penny lifted some bottles and distributed them around the room, whilst Doris placed the tray on a side table before handing out the rest. To everyone's surprise, Doris had a mug in her hands, instead, and a very satisfied expression upon her face.

Jane's nose began to twitch and, suspicion upon her face, she took a deep sniff as Doris wafted past her to perch upon the windowsill. "Is that what I suspect it is?"

Before she replied, Doris lowered her head and

inhaled deeply. "Mmm, coffee. The only drink better than Guinness! Bless Jim, a saint amongst men."

"I thought we'd rationed you," Penny said.

"I'm in shock, after what happened to my poor fiancé," she countered.

"Isn't Walter the one who should be in shock?" Mary pointed out.

Just in case anyone decided to try taking it from her, Doris took a deep and evidently satisfying sip from her mug. "I'm sure he is. I'm simply coming out in sympathy."

Ruth blew a raspberry, before bursting out laughing. She then shared some news of her own. "From what Matt's told me, he may be getting some kind of award for what he did."

This brought more than one whistle of appreciation and a sharp intake of breath from Doris. "He never told me!"

Shaking her head, Ruth quickly placated her. "I don't think he knows yet. Matt's only just left, and he's only just told me."

Doris immediately raised her cup. "To Walter!"

Once everyone had toasted him, Ruth asked, "What were you going to run by me?"

"Well," Doris began, "I've been thinking if there's a way for Walter and me to live together after we're married."

"And…" Ruth prompted when Doris didn't immediately elaborate.

Obviously in need of the caffeine courage, Doris drank down the rest of her mug of coffee.

"I swear that girl's got an asbestos throat!" Mary said with a shake of her head.

"And I was wondering how you'd feel if I moved in with you?"

"With me?" Ruth asked, slightly puzzled.

"To be more precise, into Walter's room."

"You do know he lives in the attic? And that there's no window up there?" Ruth needed to check.

Doris nodded enthusiastically. "I do. We do, I should say, as we have talked about this. That's to say, it isn't only my idea."

"Very glad to hear that," Ruth told her.

"I'm sorry to spring this upon you, Ruth. We only discussed it the other week, and we were going to talk with you a few days ago, only, well, with what happened to Walter, it's only just come back to me. What do you think?" she asked, unable to keep a slight tremor from her voice.

Ruth was silent for a minute or two, taking the odd sip from her glass, before she finally asked, "I don't see a problem with that, but how do you feel about this, Betty?"

"I can't deny it'll be quieter around here without her," Betty announced, to general amusement. "Girls?"

"At least you're only going to be next door," Penny said, though everyone saw her wipe the side of her eye.

Doris went and wrapped her friend in a hug. "You don't get rid of me that easily, Alsop," she told her.

"Does that mean I can move into Doris's old room?" Jane asked.

"Hey! Wait until I've moved out, at least!" the American replied, before breaking out into a smile.

Jane waved away her jocular protest. "That's settled, then. Ruth, I don't envy you young Doris's singing in the bath."

"Oh, my God! What is this? Pick-on-Doris day?"

"No different to any other, then," Mary added, to which, after a very short period of thinking, Doris could only nod.

****

Penny was tucked up on the sofa after Ruth had gone home later that night, happily lost in *The Body in the Library* and lost to the world, when Doris tapped her on the knee.

"What's up?" she asked, without looking up.

"Not what I was going to ask, but haven't you finished yet?"

"No," Penny replied. "I'm savoring it. The best Miss Marple I've read yet!"

Doris frowned. "Can't you savor it a little faster?"

Penny peered at her friend over the top of the book. "Just for that…no. Now, what did you want to ask me?"

Tearing her gaze from the treasured novel, Doris asked, "Do you think Celia will be able to make it for my wedding?"

The book flopped down onto Penny's lap, and she only just prevented it falling onto the floor.

"Hey! Careful with that book, or I'll take it off you!" Betty told her from across the room where she was just as engrossed in *The Moving Finger*, the newest Miss Marple story.

"Doris made me do it," Penny pouted, carefully closing the book and placing it beside her. She looked back at where Doris was waiting. "Let's find out. Luckily it's on a weekend. Hang on. I've got her school's telephone number upstairs. I'll go and make a call."

"Thank you!" Doris shouted after her, immediately sitting down where Penny had been and taking up the book.

"She won't thank you for that," Betty remarked.

With the book already open, Doris didn't look up as she replied, "Just a little taster. I'm getting withdrawal symptoms."

Five minutes later, Penny stuck her head around the door. "Celia asks if she can be a bridesmaid."

Quickly hiding the book and adopting an innocent expression, Doris told her, "I'd love that! Tell her yes."

"Great!" Penny said, following up with, "Put my book down, madam," before closing the door and going back to the phone.

"Told you," Betty mumbled, turning the page on her own book, whilst Jane and Mary, who were playing a game of chess, both chuckled to themselves.

Penny was back in the lounge when a rap came on the front door. "I'll get it!" she announced and reappeared a half minute later with Grace in tow.

"Hello! What brings you here this late at night?" Betty asked, putting her bookmark in place before carefully putting her novel aside.

Without preamble, Grace sat down beside Doris, who promptly turned white as all the blood drained from her face.

"Oh, hell. What's happened? Is Walter d…"

Grace quickly and vigorously shook her head. "No! God, no!"

Doris fell back and began to fan her face. She turned her best glare upon the nurse. "Don't do that to me!"

Mary felt she had to say, "To be fair, she hasn't actually said anything."

Doris, who looked on the cusp of speaking again, instead took a couple of gulps of air before, looking a little contrite, she told Grace, "I'm sorry. I guess I must be more on edge than I thought. He is all right, though, isn't he?"

Grace nodded and kept nodding until Doris had to place a hand on the girl's thigh to stop her. Then the nurse told her, "Yes, he's fine. The only thing is, and I knew you'd want to know as soon as possible, and it's only been decided tonight…"

"Out with it…please," Doris snapped, and then immediately apologized. "Sorry, I didn't mean to snap."

"That's okay. I was carrying on a bit. He's fine, but the doctors want to keep him in for a week. He had another x-ray today, and they found another grenade fragment in his skull." Doris drew in a deep breath of shock, and Grace quickly took hold of her hands and squeezed them tightly. "He's already had the operation. They've removed it, and he's recovering now."

"Bloody hell!" Doris said into the silence. After a few moments, she grabbed Grace before she could object and did her best to squeeze the air out of her lungs before holding her startled friend at arm's length, "Thank you for coming to tell me. You're sure he's going to be okay?"

Grace nodded. "Very sure. I didn't want to leave until he'd come around and I could talk to him."

The emotion of the moment and the news suddenly hit home, and Doris burst into tears.

Chapter Forty-Three

Doris slumped back into Penny's seat and let out a sigh of relief.

"If you've quite finished, Doris Winter, any chance of having my seat back?" Penny asked, standing over her with her arms crossed.

"Hmm? Oh, sorry," she muttered, getting to her feet.

Jane poked her head around the corner of her office. "Any reason you're not over at the flight line getting ready, Doris?"

Shaking her head, Doris held out the seat for Penny to sit down before asking, "Sorry about that, boss." Picking up her bag, Doris strode to the door before turning back. "It's something I was thinking about after last night."

Jane appeared at a scramble by her side. "You do know Walter's going to be all right? We were all there when you all but threw Penny off the telephone to call the hospital, and the doctor told you he would be."

Doris managed a smile. "I know, and I'm sorry about last night, Penny."

"Considering the circumstances, I'll forgive you," Penny told her.

"What were you thinking about, then?" Jane asked.

"That with my history of being in the wrong place at the wrong time, together with the fact that now Walter's not going to be out of the hospital in time for the wedding, and all that's gone on this past couple of weeks, we should bring it forward. I'm not going to postpone it again!"

"Well, it's certainly been a hectic, trying time, I can't deny that," Jane agreed.

Penny asked, "And does this have anything to do with who you were just phoning?"

Doris nodded. "That was the padre. He's agreed to marry us at the hospital on Saturday afternoon. That's if—and I suppose I should have checked with you first, Jane, sorry—we've got that afternoon off?"

Jane frowned and turned back to her office, coming back a few seconds later bearing her diary. "Yes, I wanted to double-check before saying anything. Our refueling system's down for maintenance that day, so there's no flying. Saturday will be fine. Any idea what time?"

Doris looked sheepish. There was no other way to put it.

"You haven't agreed the time yet, have you," Jane stated.

"Not quite."

"Not quite?"

"That's why I was speaking to the padre. He's on better terms with the staff at the hospital than I am, so he agreed to go and speak to them while we're out on deliveries today."

Jane sighed and shook her head, though by the time she looked up she was smiling. "You don't believe in doing things the easy way, do you."

"Sorry." Doris shrugged.

"All right," Jane decided, shutting her diary. "Get yourself over to the flight line hut and get changed. I'm sure the taxi's almost ready to go by now. Penny and I've got some things to sort out."

"I'll just nip into the mess and tell Mavis of the date change first," Doris said, before throwing a quick salute at the pair. She took off at a run, and Penny turned to where Jane was watching the departing American. "I didn't think the maintenance was due for another week."

Jane shook her head before turning back and closing the door against the chill morning air. "It isn't—or rather, it wasn't." Penny looked confused.

Disappearing back into her office for a few seconds, Jane reappeared with a bottle of American bourbon, turning the bottle around to stare at the label. When she looked back at Penny, it was with a sad smile. "Frank gave this to me. I was going to keep it to celebrate the end of the war, but I can put it to better use today. Wish me luck!" She glanced up. "I've got an engineering staff to bribe!"

****

"There's your tea, Croft," Terry said, placing a steaming cup before their prisoner. Turning the statement which had just been signed, he asked, "Anything else you want to say?"

Croft shook his head, wincing as he inadvertently moved his right shoulder. Rubbing his arm through the sling he wore, he picked up the mug in his left hand, blew on it, and took a quick sip. "No, that's exactly as I remember things."

Lawrence looked over from his desk, regarding the strange scene before him. Only rarely had he conducted a major interview anywhere but in an interview room. To be truthful, he'd never done so, but something had told him that going against correct protocol would bring them the best results this time. Hiding a smile behind his cup, he was very pleased to have been proved right.

"How's the shoulder?" he asked.

Stopping himself from shrugging barely in time, Croft replied, "I've had worse. Doctors told me the bullet wasn't a problem to take out, and it didn't break a bone."

"Lucky man," Lawrence commented, before prodding the rifle before him. "Rather strange, though. This is a Lee-Enfield. A three-oh-three round, at the range you told me you were shot at, I'm surprised it didn't blow your shoulder off."

Croft gave a small smile, telling the policemen, "That's probably because the ammunition was some my old dad brought back from the Great War. It wasn't exactly stored in the best place, so I'm not surprised it's lost a lot of its power."

"I suppose that's also the reason you missed Third Officer Winter and Mr. Johnson that night?" Lawrence asked, watching Croft carefully for any sign of hesitation, or a change to what he'd put in the statement.

"A bit," Croft replied, "but I was also aiming to deliberately miss."

"Not by much," Terry commented.

"What can I say? I'm a good shot," Croft replied.

"Perhaps too good," Lawrence agreed, only getting a small smile in reply.

Taking his cue from his Inspector, Terry waited until he got the nod. "Constable!" he called, sticking his head around the office door and then stepping back to admit a uniformed officer. Addressing Croft, he told him, "To your feet, Croft. We're sending you to the hospital for another check-up, and then it's off to prison with you."

Obediently getting to his feet, Croft quickly finished

his tea and didn't object when the constable took him by the left elbow. However, once he got to the door, he turned his head. "Do we have a deal?"

Without nodding his head in any way, Lawrence looked up and told him, "So long as what's in your statement checks out, I'll speak to the judge." He picked up another piece of paper. "You also seem to have made a bit of a friend in Fred, the fish 'n' chip shop owner. He's put in a good word, so you've got that going for you too."

Croft seemed to breathe a sigh of relief, then allowed himself to be led out of the room.

Once he'd gone, Terry went over and closed the door. "What do you think?"

Lawrence picked up the statement before quickly putting it down again. "Well, from what we've seen at the incident sites, everything tallies with what this says," he stated, tapping the statement sheet.

"I know I shouldn't, but I've my fingers crossed," Terry uttered, picking up his own mug. "If we can get that scumbag Verdon back into the nick, I'll consider it a very good week. Do you mind my asking, boss, how's Doris?"

What could only be called an evil grin spread over Lawrence's face. "Still sticking to her story."

"You know, old rifles, they do have a tendency to misfire," Terry replied, hiding his mouth behind his mug.

Lawrence tried to hide a laugh. "That they do. Still, he'll live."

"Bit of a shame he won't be able to have children, though," Terry mentioned, at which point he had to put his mug down on the table and take a seat. "Misfire or not, it was a hell of a good shot."

"I'm very glad that door's closed, or I'd have to give you a rollocking for that remark, Terry."

"Sorry, boss," Terry said, not sounding in the least bit sorry.

"Not sure I've ever seen anyone press their knee to someone's groin to stop bleeding before, either," Lawrence said, not helping matters as his shoulders began to shake in unmistakable laughter too.

"Do you think Walter knows what he's letting himself in for?"

Lawrence stopped laughing to think the question through, and said, "You know, I think he does."

"Well, it's going to be an interesting talk with Verdon, once he's up to it, anyway," Terry mused. "Do you think he's going to try to blame this whole hare-brained scheme onto Croft?"

"Without a doubt," Lawrence quickly replied. "However, what with the chippy's statement, and what we've already gathered, and undoubtedly we'll add to that over the coming days too, I don't think a jury will be taken in. Don't forget, the girls are witnesses to him barging in and threatening to kill Betty, too."

"I doubt we'll see trouble from him again, then," Terry said. "How about Croft? He's not the nicest of villains, and one good turn can't defend a lifetime of crime."

"No, it doesn't," Lawrence agreed. "However, a promise is a promise, and he did risk his life. Not only to save Betty, but also for his actions with Fred. I believe the judge and jury will take that into account. I may ask the judge if he'll be willing to let me speak to his regiment, see if they'd take him back. I don't know where it's come from, but he seems to have become quite the patriot! Perhaps after a spell inside a military prison, he'll turn into a good soldier."

****

Not having bothered to get changed, Doris came racing up to the ops hut still in her Sidcot suit. "How did it go? Have you heard from him?"

"I assume you mean the padre?" Penny said, putting the receiver back onto its cradle. "Good timing. That was him."

"And?" Doris asked, when Penny didn't carry on, instead finishing off a biscuit.

"And he's squared everything with the hospital. He's also got Walter moved into a side ward on his own, so you'll have some privacy."

"Woo-hoo!" Doris rejoiced, punching the air.

"Not that much privacy," Jane teased, causing Doris to go cherry red with embarrassment.

"Eleven in the morning, before I forget," Penny added.

"Eleven! Oh, God, that's in…" She staggered back against a desk and tried to count on her fingers.

"Somewhere less than two days," Jane helpfully supplied.

Doris nearly fainted.

"Oh, no, you don't!" Jane told her, darting forward and grabbing her before she slid to the floor. Slapping her lightly on the cheek, Jane quickly brought her back to her senses and led her to a seat.

"Sorry," Doris mumbled once her eyes regained their focus. "I think it's just hitting me. I'm getting married in less than two days!"

"Breathe, just breathe," Jane urged.

"There you are!" Mary's voice said, closely

followed by Mary herself.

Betty came in behind her and, quickly taking in what was happening, made her way to Doris's side. "Is she okay?" She looked up at Jane from where she'd knelt down.

"She's fine," Doris assured. "I'm just abusing the privilege of the bride being fussed over."

"In that case," Penny said, coming to joining the others, "you'll be pleased to know that Celia's coming down on the late train tomorrow night. You're under orders, by the way, not to get married until she arrives. That's in case there's any trouble with the train."

"Great!" Doris replied, and then made the mistake of trying to stand up—and had to sit back down.

"Whilst you're still our captive audience," Jane joined in, "I'm sure you'll be pleased to hear that Shirley's also flying down tomorrow afternoon."

"Brilliant!" Betty was the first to speak up. "I can't wait to see her. She can't have long left on her course."

"Just over a month, I think," Jane replied.

Apparently recovered, Doris stood up, gripped the edge of the table whilst her friends watched her carefully, and clapped her hands together. "Right, girls! Time to get home. We've got to finish off the cake, make sure everything else is in tip-top shape for Saturday, and... What was it? Oh, I'd better go to the hospital and make sure Walter's all right with this."

"I thought you said you'd talked this over with him," Mary said.

"We have," Doris said, swaying a little as she bent to pick up her bag. "I just really need to see him after, well...you know, the other operation. I need to make sure he's still okay with this."

"Betty, you go with Doris, please. We'll get things home for you both," Jane decided.

After the two had left, with Betty fussing around Doris like a mother hen, Mary went to get changed, and Penny asked the one question left she needed an answer to. "How did things go with the mechs?"

Jane let out a small laugh. "Let's put it this way…it's fortunate Doris is popular with them."

****

"Doris!"

Looking over her shoulder, Doris turned to find one of her favorite people in the village waving and walking toward her. "Fred!" she shouted and grabbed hold of Betty's hand, waiting for her chip shop friend to meet them. She firmly shook his hand. "It's very good to see you again. How're you feeling?"

A reasonably large man, Fred nevertheless came across as one of the most gentle souls she knew, and it hurt her to see pain cross his face as he rubbed his jaw.

"It could have been much worse. My jaw's got a slight crack to it, the doctor tells me, but it'll be all right."

Doris leaned in and kissed him on the cheek. "I'm very pleased to hear that. Look, if you're not doing anything on Saturday, come to my wedding! Eleven in the morning, at the hospital."

Fred mustered a smile. "That's very kind of you," he said. "That brings me to what I wanted to talk to you about. Have you got a meal for the party afterwards? I'm assuming there's going to be a party?"

"Of course," Betty answered for Doris. "I'm not sure how many are going to be there, but everyone's coming to my place after the ceremony. We've some cakes and sandwiches laid on."

"In that case, can I offer a fish-and-chip dinner for everyone…on the house?"

Betty thought Doris was going to faint.

"That…that's unbelievable, and so generous! Are you sure, Fred?" the American managed to say.

Fred nodded. "It's the least I can do for my best customer. You, and your friends," he turned as wide a smile as he could onto her, "are unbelievable! I'll never be able to thank you enough, so allow me to do this one thing for you. Agreed?"

Doris grabbed his hand and energetically pumped it up and down. "Are you kidding? Fish 'n' chips, with a Guinness chaser! Never mind the wedding, that's my idea of heaven!"

Chapter Forty-Four

"Has anyone seen my veil?" Doris wailed, sticking her head out of her bedroom.

Mary and Jane glanced out of their room, as did Betty and Penny from theirs. Celia, who'd slept for the night with her sister, asked what was on everyone's lips. "A veil? You're going to wear a veil? With your ATA hat? Isn't that going to look a little...funny?"

Perhaps the events of the last few weeks had clouded her memory, but at hearing this conversation, Betty suddenly asked, "What happened to the dress I made you? Don't tell me you've changed your mind!"

Doris shuffled her stockinged feet before looking up. "I guess this is me being silly again."

"What happened?" Betty asked kindly.

"The dress you made? Well, that seems to have gone missing too."

"What?" more than one girl asked at once.

"When did this happen?" Jane wanted to know.

Doris shrugged. "I've no idea. Oh, Betty!" She reached for and gripped her friend's hands. "Can you forgive me? I didn't know how to tell you. It was so beautiful, and I'd teased Walter how lovely I intended to look for him at our wedding..."

Betty didn't have to give it a thought. "Don't fret. He's a man, and I doubt he'll notice what you're wearing."

"So you forgive me?" Doris asked once more. "I only found out last night, honest!"

"I forgive you," Betty assured her. "Don't give it one more thought."

"But a veil with an ATA hat?" Celia persisted.

Doris opened her mouth to protest, but then closed it. Her friends could almost see her mind ticking over, and gradually, likely with a picture forming in her mind as to what she'd look like, she shook her head. Still in her slip and stockinged feet, she padded over to Celia and kissed her on her forehead. "You're quite right. Of course you are. I mean, it's only something I'd made up from some old net curtain, but I'd still like to know where it's got to."

"You know," Betty mused, "one of these days, we're going to have to look into the biggest mystery we've never solved."

"Which is?" Jane asked. "Though a big part of me fears to ask."

"The whereabouts of our missing clothes, of course," Betty announced.

"I do miss my lucky bra," Penny absently uttered.

"I beg your pardon?" Celia cried out in wonder. "You've a lucky bra?"

Going a little red, Penny nodded her bead. "It's a superstition…" she waved her hands around, searching for the right word, "thing."

"Oh, I've really got to become a pilot, if this is what you can get away with!" Celia declared.

"Oh, God, not two of you, please," Jane muttered almost to herself, before turning and going back into her bedroom.

"It does make you wonder, though," Mary said,

"about what happened to our clothes. We know we didn't *borrow* each other's clothes, so where did they go?"

No one knew how to answer, so by unspoken agreement, they all turned and went back into their rooms to finish getting ready.

Ten minutes later, Betty knocked on Doris's door. "Are you decent?"

"Come in!" Doris called.

Unexpectedly, Betty was followed by everyone in the cottage.

"It's just as well I'm not in my knickers!" Doris commented, getting up from her bed.

"We don't have much time before we've got to make a move," Betty began. "Have you heard of the rhyme?

"Something old,

"Something new,

"Something borrowed,

"Something blue,

"And a silver sixpence in her shoe."

"I don't think so." Doris shook her head.

"Beginning with me and something old," said Penny. "My mother used to tatt lace, and this doily is the first thing she ever made me. I didn't know what to get the girl who's got or could get everything, so I want you to have this."

Mary stepped forward. "This is a new uniform I had made for you by my family's tailor on Savile Row. I wasn't sure it'd arrive in time for your wedding. However, obviously it did," Mary said, holding out a beautiful deep, deep dark blue uniform.

Doris held the uniform against her body and then hung it up before beginning to strip out of the uniform she was wearing. "Walter's going to love this! Thank you so much, Mary! Oh, and I must remember to thank your Lawrence for getting my fish 'n' chip shop back!" she added with a smile.

"Here's something borrowed from me." Betty brought her hands from behind her back and held out a crucifix on a chain. "This belonged to my sister. I'm sure Eleanor would have loved you, and I know you'll take good care of it." Stepping forward, Betty fastened it around her friend's neck.

Doris swallowed, barely able to speak, so overwhelmed was she. "I'll let you have it back straight afterward, I promise." She looked over at Jane, who appeared to be hanging back. Was that an embarrassed hue upon her cheeks? "Jane?"

"You're never going to let me live this down," Jane said as she finally stepped forward. From behind her back, she brought forth a small brown paper bag. "Here, something blue."

Taking the bag, Doris raised her eyebrows. "I'm intrigued."

"So are we," Betty said. "She wouldn't tell us what she'd got you."

At this, everyone crowded around as Doris pulled out a handful of fabric. "Blue silk cami-knickers! Why, Jane, you dark horse!"

Celia reached forward and pointed out, "Look, they've got little blue bows, too!"

If it were possible, Jane went even redder. She was saved by the sound of the back door opening and closing, quickly followed by a loud, "Woof!"

"Up here, Ruth!" Jane yelled, taking the opportunity to leave the group, and as she was fully dressed, she hurried downstairs.

"Your turn." Penny tapped her sister on the shoulder.

"Um, this is from both me and my sister. Open your hand," she asked and when Doris did so, she dropped a small silver coin into her hand. "It's a silver sixpence. You put it in your left shoe," Celia explained.

As this, the last of the rhyme's gifts, was presented to her, Doris lost her fragile grasp on composure and burst into tears.

"Oh, no, you don't," Betty said, darting forward and wielding a handkerchief. "None of that! Your makeup's perfect, and we don't have time to do it again."

Tackling the other side of Doris's face, Penny agreed. "Betty's right. We only have ten minutes before we must leave, so chin up, sniff those tears back in, and let's get you married!"

****

Having picked up Grace and Shirley from Riverview Cottage, it having been decided on Friday night that it would have been too crowded for everyone to get ready at Betty's, everyone enjoyed some good-natured banter as they walked through a joyous spring morning toward the hospital. With the Air Transport Auxiliary girls resplendent in their dark blue uniforms, Ruth in a rather fetching gingham-patterned dress, and Celia looking years older than she was in a buttercup-yellow dress she'd borrowed from a school friend, the group were a picture of happiness and camaraderie. To everyone's surprise, Duck merely quacked loudly at the group as he swam past. Doris admitted to being slightly disappointed he couldn't be part of the ceremony. Needless to say, she was the only one who felt like that, especially Bobby, who pretended he hadn't been hiding behind his owner's legs.

As they arrived at the hospital, Doris hesitated at the sight which greeted them. Lined up on both sides of the entryway to the main entrance seemed to be every nurse and doctor who wasn't on duty, with Fred standing proud and tall next to them. Catching sight of her nemesis, Sister Henry, the bride-to-be suddenly lost her nerve. Seeing this, Nurse Grace hurried over and, hooking one of Doris's arms through hers, led her between the honor guard, all of whom broke into a round of spontaneous applause as the girls in blue passed between them. If anything, this further unnerved the American, though what nearly caused her to turn around was when Sister Henry hurried forward to kiss her on the cheek as she passed.

"Told you she wasn't all bad," Grace whispered as they entered and began the walk toward Walter's room.

Doris shook her head. "No, you bloody well did not!" though her shoulders were shaking with laughter as she said the words.

As they came within view of Walter's room, there was a loud scratching noise before Bing Crosby began to croon "Moonlight Becomes You."

"No tears," Grace whispered before relinquishing her place to Betty, who had the honor of giving Doris away.

Before taking the walk, her posse hurried past to take their places along the other side of Walter's bed. Grace looked delighted to be reunited with Marcus, who was a picture in his RAF uniform, with his newfound sister, Betty, by his other side. Shirley and Celia were both already dabbing at their eyes, whilst Mary had already jabbed Lawrence, in his position as best man, in the ribs and was nodding her head at the proceedings in a none-too-subtle hint. Terry chuckled at his boss's obvious discomfort, while Jane appeared sad, not a surprise after losing her boyfriend last year. However, Penny noticed this and took her by the hand. With Tom on duty, the pair would look after each other. With everyone in place who should be there, Doris and Betty started their slow way into the room.

Fate decided to break the last remaining tension, for as Doris took her first step into the room, the elastic on her new knickers snapped, and down they fell to gather around her ankles. Barely breaking her stride, she stooped down, scooped them up, and stuffed them into a pocket. As everyone in the room broke into a mixture of laughter and applause, Doris led Betty once more toward her fiancé, a mere tinge of red on her cheeks the only allowance she showed to the incident.

Walter, looking rather dapper in a pair of blue-striped pajamas, was sitting up in bed, a grin splitting his face. He looked like he was the happiest man in the world. Holding out his uninjured arm, he took his American's hand in his. Raising it to his lips, he looked up into her eyes. "I've never seen you look so beautiful," he told Doris as she took her place by his side.

The padre turned Bing down a little before looking around at the happy, expectant gathering, smiling, and announced, "As we're ready, let us proceed."

****

The Guinness was flowing like…Guinness, when there was a loud rap on the front door. From where he was ensconced on the sofa, Walter looked up as his new wife shouted, "I'll get it!" and leapt up from beside him to run toward the door.

"You know," he said to Lawrence, "I'm quite glad I'm only allowed out for this evening. I don't think I could do Doris justice. If you know what I mean?" he ended with a waggle of eyebrows barely visible under the bandage skirting his head.

From her place perched on the sofa's arm, Mary told him, "I think we all know what you mean. By the way, what's it worth not to tell your lady wife what you just said?"

"What did he just say?" Doris asked, appearing as if from nowhere.

"Nothing, darling," Walter quickly answered, before either of his friends could say anything. "Who was at the front door?"

Clearly having decided whether to believe him or not, Doris retook her place next to Walter, gathering his uninjured hand in hers. "That was Mavis. She's brought some rock cakes she made. Thought we would like some as dessert."

Jane looked up from where she'd been in conversation with Shirley, "Rock cakes. And Mavis made them?" When Doris nodded, Jane shuddered and, after making certain the cook in question wasn't able to hear, suggested, "Maybe we could save them in case we get bombed again? We could use them to fill in the bomb craters."

A voice from the kitchen boomed out, "I heard that, Jane Howell!"

As Jane went crimson with embarrassment, Walter said to Doris, "You deserted me quickly enough just then. Had enough of me already? You know I've only a few hours until the hospital comes to pick me up?"

Doris immediately kissed him hard on the lips before surfacing to tell him, "I thought it was Fred with the wedding tea."

"Ah. Well," he said, "how about we cut the cake before that arrives?"

"Great idea!" she agreed, bouncing to her feet.

With the aid of Lawrence and Marcus, Walter was gently heaved to his feet, where Doris took his hand and, with Walter a little unsteady on his feet, led him to where a magnificent three-tiered, iced wedding cake sat on a small table before the window. With the afternoon's sunshine flooding through the panes, Doris accepted Betty's best kitchen knife, the lady having torn herself away from catching up with Marcus.

"Are you ready to take the photo, Ruth?" she asked.

"Place your hand over Doris's, Walter," Ruth instructed him and waited whilst Doris guided Walter's hand into position. "Ready? Say cheese!"

Once a few more photographs had been taken, the newly married couple laid the knife aside and stepped to one side to allow Betty and Penny to stand either side of the cake. Each dug the tips of their fingers under the edges, looked across at the other and lifted the edges of the cake up. With one swift movement, the cardboard façade was taken away to reveal the small fruit cake Mary had been lovingly feeding with brandy and for which so many people had generously donated their eggs and fruit.

At another loud rap upon the front door, Doris once more took off to answer it. Taking her chance, Mary came up to where Walter had been led back to the sofa, took a seat next to him, and gave him a kiss on the cheek. "For the groom," she told him, smiling. "Now, I thought

I'd clear this up. Obviously you're in no shape to go on a honeymoon at the moment. However, I'm certain that whenever both Jane and Ruth can spare the pair of you, Captain Wood will be able to make certain my family's apartment is free for you."

Walter held open his arms, and Mary cautiously slid into them for a quick hug. "You're the best," he told her, as Doris made the entrance to end all entrances.

With her arms full of newspaper-wrapped packages, Doris joyfully declared, "Fish 'n' chips for everyone!"

A word about the author…

Mick is a hopeless romantic who was born in England but spent fifteen years roaming around the world in the pay of HM Queen Elizabeth II in the Royal Air Force before putting down roots…and realizing how much he missed the travel. This he's replaced somewhat with his writing, including reviewing books and supporting fellow saga and romance authors in promoting their novels.

He's the proud keeper of two cats bent on world domination, is mad on the music of the Beach Boys, and enjoys the theater and humoring his Manchester-United-supporting wife.

Finally, and most importantly, Mick is a full member of the Romantic Novelists Association. *In The Mood* is his fifth published novel, the fourth in the Broken Wings series.

CPSIA information can be obtained
at www.ICGtesting.com
Printed in the USA
LVHW080838150922
728284LV00013B/303